Patricia Thayer was born in Muncie, Indiana, the ~~~ eight children. She attended Ball State University before heading to California. A longtime member of RWA, Patricia has authored fifty books. She's been nominated for the Prestige RITA® award and winner of the RT Reviewer's Choice award. She loves travelling with her husband, Steve, calling it research. When she wants some time with her guy, they escape to their mountain cabin and sit on the deck and let the world race by.

Born and raised just outside of Toronto, Ontario, **Amy Ruttan** fled the big city to settle down with the country boy of her dreams. After the birth of her second child, Amy was lucky enough to realise her life long dream of becoming a romance author. When she's not furiously typing away at her computer, she's a mum to three wonderful children who use her as a personal taxi and chef.

Three-times Golden Heart® finalist **Tina Beckett** learned to pack her suitcases almost before she learned to read. Born to a military family, she has lived in the United States, Puerto Rico, Portugal and Brazil. In addition to travelling, Tina loves to cuddle with her pug, Alex, spend time with her family, and hit the trails on her horse. Learn more about Tina from her website, or 'friend' her on Facebook.

Flirting with the Boss

PATRICIA THAYER
AMY RUTTAN
TINA BECKETT

MILLS & BOON

First Published in Great Britain 2019
by Mills & Boon, an imprint of HarperCollins*Publishers*
1 London Bridge Street, London, SE1 9GF

FLIRTING WITH THE BOSS © 2019 Harlequin Books S. A.

Single Dad's Holiday Wedding © 2012 Patricia Wright
Melting the Ice Queen's Heart © 2014 Amy Ruttan
Her Playboy's Secret © 2015 Harlequin Books S.A.

Special thanks and acknowledgement are given to Tina Beckett for her contribution to the *Midwives On-Call* series

ISBN: 978-0-263-27948-1

1119

MIX
Paper from
responsible sources
FSC
www.fsc.org
FSC® C007454

This book is produced from independently certified FSC™ paper to ensure responsible forest management.

For more information visit: www.harpercollins.co.uk/green

Printed and bound in Spain
by CPI, Barcelona

SINGLE DAD'S HOLIDAY WEDDING

PATRICIA THAYER

CHAPTER ONE

SHE still wasn't sure if coming here was a good idea.

Lorelei Hutchinson drove along First Street to the downtown area of the small community of Destiny, Colorado. She reached the historic square and parked her rental car in an angled spot by a huge three-tiered fountain. The centerpiece of the brick-lined plaza was trimmed with a hedge and benches for visitors. A pathway led to a park where children were playing.

She got out, wrapped her coat sweater tighter against the cold autumn temperature and walked closer to watch the water cascade over the marble structure. After nearly twenty years many of her memories had faded, but some were just as vivid as if they'd happened yesterday.

One Christmas she remembered the fountain water was red, the giant tree decorated with multicolored lights and ornaments and everyone singing carols. She had a family then.

A rush of emotions hit her when she recalled being in this exact spot, holding her father's hand as he took her to the park swings. One of the rare occasions she'd spent time with the man. He'd always been too busy building his empire. Too busy for his wife and daughter. So many times she had wanted just a little of his attention, his love. She never got it.

Now it was too late. Lyle Hutchinson was gone.

With a cleansing breath, she turned toward the rows of storefront buildings. She smiled. Not many towns had this step-back-into-the-nineteen-thirties look, but it seemed that Destiny was thriving.

The wind blew dried leaves as she crossed the two-lane street and strolled past Clark's Hardware Store and Save More Pharmacy, where her mother took her for candy and ice cream cones as a child. A good memory. She sure could use some of those right now.

There was a new addition to the block, a bridal shop called Rocky Mountain Bridal Shop. She kept walking, past an antiques store toward a law office with the name Paige Keenan Larkin, Attorney at Law, stenciled on the glass.

She paused at the door to the office. This was her father's town, not hers. Lyle Hutchinson had made sure of that. That was why she needed someone on her side. She pushed the door open and a bell tinkled as she walked into the reception area.

The light coming through the windows of the storefront office illuminated the high ceilings and hardwood floors that smelled of polish and age, but also gave off a homey feeling.

She heard the sound of high heels against the bare floors as a petite woman came down the long hall. She had dark brown hair worn in a blunt cut that brushed her shoulders. A white tailored blouse tucked into a black shirt gave her a professional look.

A bright smile appeared. "Lorelei Hutchinson? I'm Paige Larkin. Welcome home."

* * *

After exchanging pleasantries, Lori was ushered into a small conference room to find a middle-aged man seated at the head of the table, going through a folder. No doubt, her father's attorney.

He saw her and stood. "Lorelei Hutchinson, I'm Dennis Bradley."

She shook his offered hand. "Mr. Bradley."

When the lawyer phoned her last week, and told her of her father's sudden death and that she'd been mentioned in his will, she was shocked about both. She hadn't seen or talked with her father since she'd been seven years old.

All Lori was hoping for now was that she could come into town today, sign any papers for Lyle's will and leave tomorrow.

The middle-aged attorney began, "First of all, Lorelei, I want to express my condolences for your loss. Lyle wasn't only my business associate, but my friend, too." He glanced at Paige and back at her. "I agreed to see you today knowing your reluctance. Your father wanted the formal reading of his will at Hutchinson House tomorrow."

Great. Not the plans she had. "Mr. Bradley, as you know, I haven't seen my father in years. I'm not sure why you insisted I come here." He'd sent her the airline ticket and reserved a rental car. "If Lyle Hutchinson left me anything, couldn't you have sent it to me?"

The man frowned. "As I explained on the phone, Ms. Hutchinson, you're Lyle's sole heir." He shook his head. "And that's all I'm at liberty to say until tomorrow at the reading of the will. Please just stay until then. Believe me, it will benefit not only you, but this town."

Before she could comprehend or react to the news,

the door opened and another man walked into the room. He looked her over and said, "So the prodigal daughter finally made it to town."

The big man had a rough edge to him, his dark hair a little on the shaggy side. He was dressed in charcoal trousers and a collared shirt, minus the tie. His hooded blue-eyed gaze fringed by spiky black lashes didn't waver from her.

Paige stood. "Jace, you shouldn't be here. This is a private meeting between me and my client."

He didn't retreat. "I just wanted to make sure she doesn't take the money and run. Lyle had obligations he needed to fulfill before that happens."

Lori wasn't sure how to handle this—Jace's attack. But having heard of her father's shrewd business deals, she wasn't surprised by the man's anger.

"I'm Lorelei Hutchinson, Mr...."

He stepped closer. "Yeager. Jace Yeager. Your father and I were partners on a construction project until I realized Lyle pulled one over on me."

"Jace," Bradley warned. "Work stopped because of Lyle's death."

The man made a snorting sound. "It wouldn't have if Lyle had put his share of money into the business account in the first place." He glared at Lori. "Sorry if my impatience bothers you, but I've been waiting nearly three weeks and so have my men."

"Be patient a little while longer," Bradley told him. "Everything should be resolved tomorrow."

That didn't appease Mr. Yeager. "You don't understand. I can't keep the project site shut down indefinitely, or I go broke." He turned that heated look on her and she oddly felt a stirring. "It seems tomorrow you're coming into all the money. I want you to know that a chunk of that belongs to me."

Lori fought a gasp. "Look, Mr. Yeager, I don't know anything about your partnership with Lyle, but I'll have Paige look into it."

Jace Yeager had to work hard to keep himself under control. Okay, so he wasn't doing a very good job. When he'd heard that Lorelei Hutchinson was coming today, he only saw red. Was she going to stroll in here, grab her daddy's money and take off? He wasn't going to be on the losing end with a woman again.

Not when his business was on the chopping block, along with his and Cassie's future. Just about every dime he had was wrapped up in this project. And it was already coming to the end of October as it was, with only bad weather on the horizon. It needed to be completed without any more delays.

Jace looked over Lyle's daughter. The pretty blonde with big brown eyes stared back at him. She had a clean-scrubbed look with a dusting of freckles across her nose, and very little makeup.

Okay, she wasn't what he expected, but he'd been wrong about women before. And the last thing he wanted to do was work for her. After his ex-wife, he wasn't going to let another woman have all the control.

He looked at Bradley. "What does Lyle's will say?"

"It won't be read until tomorrow."

Lori saw Jace Yeager's frustration, and felt obligated to say, "Maybe then we'll have some news about the project."

He glared. "There's no doubt I will. I might not have your father's money, Ms. Hutchinson, but I'll fight to keep what's mine."

Jace Yeager turned and stormed out right past a tall redheaded woman who was rushing in. "Oh, dear," she said, "I was hoping I could get here in time." Her green eyes lit up when she saw Lori. "Hi, I'm Morgan Keenan Hilliard."

"Lori Hutchinson," Lori said as she went to shake Morgan's hand.

"It's nice to meet you. As mayor, I wanted to be here to welcome you back to town, and to try and slow down Jace. Not an easy job."

Since Paige and Bradley had their heads together going over papers, they walked out into the hall. "I'm not sure if you remember me."

"I remember a lot about Destiny. Like you and your sisters. You were a little older than I was in school, but everyone knew about the Keenan girls."

Morgan smiled. "And of course being Lyle's daughter, everyone knew of you, too. I hope you have good memories of our town."

Except for her parents' marriage falling apart, along with her childhood. "Mostly, especially the decorated Christmas tree in the square. Do you still do that?"

Morgan smiled. "Oh, yes and it's grown bigger and better every year." She paused. "Our mom said you have a reservation at the inn for tonight."

She nodded. "I don't feel right about staying at the house."

The redhead gripped her hand. "You don't have to explain. I only want your visit here to be as pleasant as possible. If there is anything else, any details about your father's funeral."

Lori quickly shook her head. "Not now."

Morgan quickly changed the subject. "Look, I know

Jace isn't giving you a very good impression at the moment, but he's having some trouble with the Mountain Heritage complex."

"I take it my father was involved in it, too."

Morgan waved her hand. "We can save that discussion for another time. You need to rest after your trip. Be warned, Mom will ask you to dinner…with the family."

Lori wasn't really up to it. She wanted a room and a bed, and to make a quick call back home to her sister.

Morgan must have sensed it. "It's only the family and no business, or probing questions. We'll probably bore you to death talking about kids."

Lori relaxed. She truly didn't want to think about what would happen tomorrow.

"You're right. That's what I need tonight."

That evening as Jace was driving to the Keenan Inn, he came to the conclusion that he'd blown his chance earlier today. He tapped his fist against the steering wheel, angry about the entire mess.

"Daaad, you're not listening."

Jace looked in the rearview mirror to the backseat. "What, sweetie?"

"Do I look all right?"

He glanced over his shoulder. His daughter, Cassandra Marie Yeager, was a pretty girl. She had on stretchy jean pants that covered coltish long legs and a pink sweater that had ruffles around the hem. Her long blond hair had curled around her face with a few tiny braids. Something she'd talked him into helping with.

"You look nice. But you always do."

"We're going to Ellie's grandmother's house. Ellie Larkin is my best friend."

"I think she'll like your outfit."

"What about my hair?"

"Honey, I've always loved your blond curls. The braids are a nice touch."

That brought a big smile to her face and a tightening in his throat. All he ever wanted was for her to be happy.

When they'd moved here six months ago, it hadn't been easy for her. He still only had temporary custody of his daughter. It was supposed to be only during the time when her mother remarried a guy from England. Jace had different plans. He wanted to make Cassie's life here with him permanent. Optimistic that could happen, he went out and bought a run-down house with horse property. Although it needed a lot of work, it felt like the perfect home for them. A couple horses helped coax his seven-year-old daughter into adjusting a little faster to their new life.

A life away from a mother who'd planned to take his Cassie off to Europe. He was so afraid that his little girl would end up in boarding school and he'd only get to see her on holidays.

No, he wouldn't let that happen. A product of the foster care system himself, he'd always longed for a home and family. It hadn't worked out with ex-wife Shelly, and that mistake cost him dearly—a big divorce settlement that had nearly wiped him out. Jace hadn't cared about the money, not if he got his daughter. He only hoped they weren't going to be homeless anytime soon.

His thoughts turned to Lorelei Hutchinson. He didn't like how he reacted to her. Why had she angered him so much? He knew why. She had nothing to do with Lyle's business dealings. But she was due to inherit a lot of money tomorrow, and he could be handed the shaft at the same time. It could cost him everything that mattered. His daughter. No, he wouldn't let that happen.

He pulled up in front of the beautiful three-story Victorian home painted dove-gray with white shutters and trim. The Keenan Inn was a historical landmark, a bed-and-breakfast that was also the home of Tim and Claire Keenan. Jace had heard the story about how three tiny girls had been left with them to raise as their own. That would be Morgan, Paige and Leah. After college all three returned to Destiny to marry and raise their own families.

Right now there was someone else staying in the inn—Lorelei Hutchinson. Somehow he had to convince her that this downtown project needed to move forward. Not only for him, but also for Destiny.

Just then Tim Keenan came out the front door, followed closely by some of their grandkids, Corey, Ellie and Kate.

His daughter grabbed her overnight bag and was out of the car before he could say anything. He climbed out, too.

Tim Keenan waved from the porch. "Hello, Jace."

"Hi, Tim." He walked toward him. "Thank you for inviting Cassie to the sleepover. I think she's getting tired of her father's bad company."

"You have a lot on your mind."

Tim was in his early sixties, but he looked a lot younger. His wife was also attractive, and one of the best cooks in town. He knew that because the Keenans had been the first to stop by when he and Cassie moved into their house. They'd brought enough food for a week.

"Hey, why don't you stay for supper, too?"

He wasn't surprised by the invitation. "Probably not a good idea. I don't think I made much of an impression on Ms. Hutchinson."

The big Irishman grinned. "Have faith, son, and use a little charm. Give Paige a chance to help resolve this." They started toward the door, as Tim continued, "I'm concerned about Lorelei. She wasn't very old, maybe seven, when her parents divorced. Lyle wrote them off, both his ex-wife and his daughter. As far as I know, he never visited her. Now, she has to deal with her estranged father's mess."

Jace felt his chest tighten because this woman's scenario hit too close to home. "That's the trouble with divorce, it's the kids who lose."

They stepped through a wide front door with an etched glass oval that read Keenan Inn and into the lobby. The walls were an ecru color that highlighted the heavy oak wainscoting. A staircase with a hand-carved banister was open all the way to the second floor. All the wood, including the hardwood floors, were polished to a high gloss. He suspected he wasn't the only one who was an expert at restoration.

"This house still amazes me," he said.

"Thanks," Tim acknowledged. "It's been a lot of work over the years, but so worth it. The bed-and-breakfast has allowed me to spend more time with Claire and my girls."

Jace shook his head. "I can't imagine having three daughters."

Keenan's smile brightened. "You have one who gives you joy. I'm a lucky man, I tripled that joy." Tim sobered. "Too bad Lyle didn't feel the same about his child. Maybe we wouldn't be having this conversation tonight."

The sound of laughter drifted in from the back of the house. "That sounds encouraging," Tim said. "Come on, son. Let's go enjoy the evening."

They walked through a large dining room with several small tables covered in white tablecloths for the inn's guests. They continued through a pantry and into a huge kitchen.

Okay, Jace was impressed. There was a large working area with an eight-burner cooktop and industrial-sized oven and refrigerator, and all stainless steel counters, including the prep station. On one side a bank of windows showed the vast lawn and wooded area out back and, of course, a view of the San Juan Mountains. A group of women were gathered at the large round table. He recognized all of them. Morgan because she was married to his good friend Justin Hilliard, another business owner in town. Paige he'd met briefly before today. The petite blonde was Leah Keenan Rawlins. She lived outside of town with her rancher husband, Holt.

And Lorelei.

Tonight, she seemed different, more approachable. She was dressed in nice-fitting jeans, a light blue sweater and a pair of sneakers on her feet. Her hair was pulled back into a ponytail and it brushed her shoulders when she turned her head. She looked about eighteen, which meant whatever he was feeling about her was totally inappropriate.

Those rich, chocolate-brown eyes turned toward him and her smile faded. "Mr. Yeager?"

He went to the group. "It's Jace."

"And I go by Lori," she told him.

He didn't want to like her. He couldn't afford to, not with his future in the balance. "Okay."

"Oh, Jace." Claire Keenan came up to them. "Good, you're able to stay for dinner. We don't get to see enough of you." She smiled. "I get to see your daughter when I volunteer at school."

He nodded. "And I'm happy Ellie and Cassie are friends. Thank you for including her in the kids' sleepovers." He glanced out the window to see his daughter running around with the other children. Happy. "Your granddaughter Ellie helped Cassie adjust to the move here."

Claire's smile was warm. "We all want to make sure you both got settled in and are happy."

That all depended on so many things, he thought. "You've certainly done that."

The older woman turned to Lori. "I wish I could talk you into staying longer. One day isn't much time." Claire looked back at Jace. "Lori is a second grade teacher in Colorado Springs."

Lori didn't want to correct Claire Keenan. She *had* been a second grade teacher before she'd been laid off last month. So she didn't mind that her dear father had decided to leave her a little something. It would be greatly appreciated.

But, no, she couldn't stay. Only long enough to finish up Lyle's unfinished business. She hoped that would be concluded by tomorrow.

Claire excused herself. Tim arrived, handed them both glasses of wine and wandered off, too, leaving them alone.

Lori took a sip of wine, trying not to be too obvious

as she glanced at the large-built man with the broad shoulders and narrow waist. No flab there. He definitely did physical work for a living.

"How long have you lived in Destiny, Mr.… Jace?"

"About six months, and I'm hoping to make it permanent."

She didn't look away. "I'm sure things will be straightened out tomorrow."

"I'm glad someone is optimistic."

She sighed. "Look, can't we put this away for the evening? I've had a long day."

He studied her with those deep blue eyes. "If you'd rather I leave, I will. I was only planning to drop my daughter off."

In the past few hours Lori had learned more about Jace Yeager. She knew that Lyle probably had the upper hand with the partnership. "As long as you don't try to pin me down on something I know nothing about. It isn't going to get us anywhere except frustrated."

He raised his glass in salute. "And I'm way beyond that."

CHAPTER TWO

Two hours later, after a delicious pot roast dinner, Lori stood on the back deck at the Keenan Inn. She'd said her goodbyes to everyone at the front door, but wasn't ready to go upstairs to bed yet.

She looked up at the full moon over the mountain peak and wondered what she was doing here. Couldn't she have had a lawyer back in Colorado Springs handle this? First of all, she didn't have the extra money to spend on an attorney when she didn't have a job and very little savings. She needed every penny.

So this was the last place she needed to be, especially with someone like Jace Yeager. She didn't want to deal with him. She only planned to come here, sign any papers to her father's estate and leave.

Now there was another complication, the Mountain Heritage complex. She had to make sure the project moved forward before she left town. She didn't need to be told again that the project would mean employment for several dozen people in Destiny.

"Why, Dad? Why are you doing this?" He hadn't wanted her all those years, now suddenly his daughter needed to return to his town. How many years had she ached for him to come and visit her, or to send for her.

Even a phone call would have been nice. The scars he'd caused made it hard for his daughter to trust. Anyone.

She felt a warm tear on her cold cheek and brushed it away. No. She refused to cry over a man who couldn't give her his time.

"Are you sad?"

Hearing the child's voice, Lori turned around to find Jace Yeager's daughter, Cassie.

Lori put on a smile. "A little. It's been a long time since I've been here. A lot of memories."

The young girl stood under the porch light. "I cried, too, when my daddy made me come here."

"It's hard to move to a new place."

"At first I didn't like it 'cause our house was ugly. When it rained, the ceiling had holes in it." She giggled. "Daddy had to put pans out to catch all the water. My bedroom needed the walls fixed, too. So I had to sleep downstairs by the fireplace while some men put on a new roof."

"So your dad fixed everything?"

She nodded. "He painted my room pink and made me a princess bed like he promised. And I have a horse named Dixie, and Ellie is my best friend."

Her opinion of Jace Yeager just went up several notches. "Sounds like you're a very lucky girl."

The smile disappeared. "But my mommy might come and make me go away."

Jace Yeager didn't have custody of his daughter? "Does your mom live close?"

The child shook her head. "No, she's gonna live in England, but I don't want to live there. I miss her, but I like it here with Daddy, too."

It sounded familiar. "I'm sure they'll work it out."

The girl studied her with the same piercing blue eyes as her father. "Are you going to live here and teach second grade? My school already has Mrs. Miller."

"And I bet you like her, too. No, I'm not going to teach in town, I'm only here for a visit. My dad died not too long ago, and I have to take care of some things."

"Is that why you were crying, because you're sad?"

"Cassie…"

They both turned around and saw Jace.

"Oh, Daddy," Cassie said.

Jace Yeager didn't look happy as he came up the steps. "Ellie's been looking for you." He studied Lori. "The rest of the girls took the party upstairs."

"Oh, I gotta go." She reached up as her father leaned over and kissed her. "'Bye, Daddy, 'bye, Miss Lori." The child took off.

Jace looked at Lori Hutchinson as his gaze locked on her dark eyes.

Finally Lori broke the connection. "I thought you'd left."

"I'd planned to, but I got caught up at the front porch with the Keenans."

He had wanted to speak to Paige, hoping she could give him some encouragement. She'd said she'd work to find a solution to help everyone. Then she rounded up her husband, Sheriff Reed Larkin, leaving her daughters Ellie and Rachel for Grandma Claire's sleepover.

The other sisters, Morgan and Leah, kissed their parents and thanked them for keeping the kids. He caught the look exchanged between the couples, knowing they had a rare night alone. The shared intimacy had him envious, and he turned away. He, too, planned to leave when he spotted his daughter on the back deck with Lori.

"And I was finishing my coffee." He'd had two glasses of wine at dinner. He had to be extra careful, not wanting to give his ex-wife any ammunition. "Well, I should head home."

She nodded. "Your daughter is adorable."

"Thank you. I think so." Jace had to cool it with Lori Hutchinson. "I just wanted to say something before tomorrow...."

She raised a hand. "I told you, I'll do everything I can to get your project operational again."

He just looked at her.

"Whether you believe it or not, I don't plan to cause any more delays than necessary."

"I wish I could believe that."

"After the meeting, how about I come by the building site and tell you what happened?"

He shook his head. "The site's been shut down. Until this matter is settled, I can't afford to pay the subcontractors. So you see there's a lot at stake for me."

"And I understand that. But I still have no idea what's going to happen tomorrow, or what Lyle Hutchinson's plans are. It's not a secret that I haven't seen the man in years." She blinked several times, fighting tears. "He's dead now." Her voice was hoarse. "And I feel nothing."

Jace was learning quickly that Lyle Hutchinson was a piece of work. "Okay, we can both agree your father was a bastard."

She turned toward the railing. "The worst thing is, you probably knew the man better than I did." She glanced over her shoulder. "So you tell me, Jace Yeager, what is my father planning for me? For his town?"

* * *

Tim Keenan stood at the big picture window at the inn as he waved at the last of dinner guests left.

He was a lucky man. He loved his wife and his family. He'd been blessed with a great life running the inn for the past thirty-plus years. Mostly he enjoyed people and prided himself on being able to read body language.

For example, Jace and Lori had been dancing around each other all night. Not too close, but never out of eye sight. And the looks shared between them…oh, my.

Claire came down the steps and toward him, slipping into his arms. "I got the girls settled down for now, but I have a feeling they're plotting against me."

He kissed her cheek. "Not those little angels."

She smiled. "Seems you thought the same about your daughters, too."

"They are angels." He thought about the years raising his girls. And the grandchildren. "And we're truly blessed." He glanced out to see the lonely-looking woman on the porch. Not everyone was as lucky.

Lori watched from the inn's porch as Jace walked to his truck. He was strong and a little cocky. She had to like that about him. She also liked the way he interacted with his daughter. Clearly they loved each other. What about his ex-wife? She seemed to have moved on, in Europe. Who broke it off? She couldn't help but wonder what woman in her right mind would leave a man like Jace Yeager. She straightened. There could be a lot of reasons. Reasons she didn't need to think about. Even though she'd seen his intensity over the project, she'd also seen the gentleness in those work-roughened hands when he touched his daughter.

She shivered. One thing was, he wasn't going to be

put off about the project. And she couldn't wait for this mess to be settled. Then she could put her past behind her and move on.

She walked inside and up to the second floor. Overhead she heard the muffled voices of the kids. Her room was at the front of the house. A large canopy bed had an overstuffed print comforter opposite a brick fireplace. She took out her cell phone and checked her messages. Two missed calls.

Fear hit her as she listened to the message from Gina. She could hear the panic in her half sister's voice, but it had been like that since childhood.

Lori's mother had remarried shortly after moving to Colorado Springs. Not her best idea, losing Lyle's alimony, but Jocelyn was the type of woman who needed a man. She just hadn't been good at picking the right ones. Her short union with Dave Williams had produced a daughter, Regina. Lori had been the one who raised her, until big sister had gone off to college.

Without Lori around, and given the neglect of their mother, Gina had run wild and ended up pregnant and married to her boyfriend, Eric Lowell, at barely eighteen. Except for Gina's son, Zack, her life had been a mess ever since. It became worse when her husband became abusive, though the marriage ended with the man going to jail. Now Lori was tangled up in this mess, too.

She punched in the number. "Gina, what happened?"

"Oh, Lori, I think Eric found us."

Over a year ago, Lori had moved her sister into her apartment while Eric served a jail sentence for drug possession and spousal abuse. This hadn't been the first time he'd smacked Gina around, but the first conviction. That was the reason they'd planned to move out of state when Lori had been notified about Lyle's death.

"No, Gina, he doesn't get out until the first of the month."

"Maybe he got an early release."

"Detective Rogers would have called you. You still have a few weeks."

"What about you? Are you flying home soon?"

She knew this delay would worry Gina more. "I can't yet. I still need to meet with the lawyer tomorrow."

She heard a sigh. "I'm sorry, Lori. You've done so much for us. You have a life of your own."

"No, Gina. You're my sister. Zack is my nephew. I told you, I won't let Eric hurt you again. But I still need a day or so to get things straightened out. Then hopefully we'll have some money to start over and get away from Eric." She prayed that her father had left her something. Since their mother had died a few years ago, there wasn't anything holding them in Colorado Springs. They could go anywhere. "Think about where you and Zack want to move to." Preferably somewhere they needed a second grade teacher.

"No, you decide, Lori. We'll go anywhere you want. We just can't stay here. I won't survive it."

Lori could hear the fear in her voice. "I promise I'll do whatever it takes to keep you safe. Now go get some sleep and give my special guy a kiss from me."

Lori hung up the phone and hoped everything she said was true. Unlike Lyle Hutchinson, she didn't walk away from family.

The next morning, Lori was up early. She was used to being at school ahead of her students to plan the day.

Not anymore. Not since she'd gotten her pink slip at the start of the school year. She'd been told it was because of cutbacks and low enrollment, but she wondered if it was due to the trouble Eric had caused her at the upscale private school where she taught.

No, she couldn't think about that now. She needed to have a clear head for the meeting. Was Lyle Hutchinson as wealthy as people said? Normally she wouldn't care, but it could help both her and Gina relocate to another part of the country. Somewhere Gina could raise Zack without the fear of her ex-husband coming after her again. Enough money so Lori had time to find a job.

She drove her car to the end of First Street. A sixfoot, wrought-iron fence circled the property that had belonged to the Hutchinsons for over the past hundred years. Her heart raced as she raised her eyes and saw the majestic, three-story white house perched on the hilltop surrounded by trees. Memories bombarded her as she eased past the stone pillars at the gate entrance. The gold plaque read Hutchinson House.

She drove along the hedge-lined circular drive toward the house. She looked over the vast manicured lawn and remembered running through the thick grass, and a swing hanging from a tree out back. She parked in front of the house behind a familiar truck of Jace Yeager. Oh, no. Was the man following her?

Then she saw him standing on the porch leaning against the ornate wrought-iron railing. He was dressed in jeans and a denim shirt and heavy work boots. Without any effort, this man managed to conjure up all sorts of fantasies that had nothing to do with business.

She pulled herself out of her daydream. What was he doing here?

He came down the steps to meet her.

She got out of her car. "Jace, is there a problem?"

He raised a hand in defense. "Mr. Bradley called me this morning. Said he needed me here for after the reading."

Lori was confused. "Why?"

"I hope it's to tell me it's a go-ahead on the Mountain Heritage project."

They started up the steps when she saw a man in a khaki work uniform come around the side porch. He looked to be in his late sixties, maybe seventies. When he got closer she saw something familiar.

"Uncle Charlie?"

The man's weathered face brightened as he smiled. "You remember me, Miss Lorelei?"

"Of course I do. You built me my tree swing." She felt tears sting her eyes. "You let me help plant flowers, too."

He nodded and gripped her hands in his. "That was a lot of years ago, missy. You were a tiny bit of a thing." His tired eyes locked on hers. "You've turned into a beautiful young lady." His grip tightened. "I'm so sorry about your father."

Before Lori could say anything more, another car pulled up. Paige Larkin stepped out of her SUV. Briefcase in hand, she walked up the steps toward them.

They shook hands and Paige spoke briefly to Charlie before the man walked off. Paige turned to Jace. "So you've been summoned, too."

"I got a call from Bradley first thing this morning."

Paige frowned. "Dennis must have a reason for wanting you here." She turned back to her client. "Let's not speculate until we hear what's in Lyle's will."

Lori nodded and together they walked up to the large porch, where greenery filled the pots on either side of the wide door with the leaded glass panels.

She knew that her great-great-grandfather had built this house during the height of the mining era. It was said that Raymond Hutchinson never trusted banks. That was why he didn't lose much during the Great Depression.

They went inside the huge entry with high-gloss hardwood floors. A crystal chandelier hung from the high ceiling and underneath was a round table adorned with a large vase of fresh-cut flowers. The winding staircase circled up to the second story, the banister of hand-carved oak. Cream and deep maroon brocade wallpaper added a formality to the space.

Lori released a breath. "Oh, my."

She was reminded of Jace's presence when he let out a low whistle. "Nice."

"Do you remember this house?" Paige asked.

"Not much. I spent most of my time in the sunroom off the kitchen."

Paige shook her head. "Well, I wouldn't be surprised if this becomes yours. And then you can go anywhere in it you want."

Lori started to tell her she didn't want any part of this house when a thin woman came rushing into the room. Her gray hair was pulled back into a bun. She looked familiar as she smiled and her hazel eyes sparkled. Lori suddenly recognized her.

"Maggie?" she managed to say.

The woman nodded with watery eyes. "Miss Lorelei."

"I can't believe it." Lori didn't hesitate, and went

and hugged the woman. It felt good to be wrapped in the housekeeper's arms again. Years ago, Maggie had been her nanny.

"It's good to have you home." The older woman stepped back and her gaze searched Lori's face. "How pretty you are."

Lori felt herself blush. She wasn't used to all this attention. "Thank you, Maggie."

The housekeeper turned sad. "I'm so sorry about your father." Then squeezed her hands tighter. "I want you to know he went in his sleep. They said a heart attack. Maybe if we would have been there…"

Lori could only nod. "No. He couldn't be helped." She had no idea this would be so hard.

Dennis Bradley walked down the hall. "Good. You made it." He turned and nodded toward Jace. "Mr. Yeager, would you mind waiting a few minutes until I've gone over the will with Ms. Hutchinson?"

"Not a problem." He looked at Maggie and smiled. "I wonder if you could find a cup of coffee for me."

"I'll bring some out."

Once she left, the lawyer said, "We should get started."

He motioned them down the hall and into an office. Lori paused at the doorway. The walls were a deep green with dark stained wainscoting. The plush carpet was slate-gray. Bradley sat down behind the huge desk that already had a folder open.

After they were seated, the lawyer began, "I'll read through Lyle's requests. His first was that the will be read here at the family home." He handed Paige and her copies. "We can go over any details later."

The lawyer slipped on his glasses. "I don't know if

you knew that Lyle had remarried for a short time about ten years ago."

Nothing about her father surprised her. She shook her head.

"There was a prenuptial agreement, then two years later a divorce." He glanced down at the paper. "Lyle did have one other relative, a distant cousin who lives back in Ohio." He read off the generous sum left to Adam Johnson. Also he read the amount given to the household staff, which included Maggie and Charlie.

"I'm glad my father remembered them," Lori said.

Bradley smiled. "They were loyal to him for a lot of years." He sighed. "Now, let's move on to the main part of the will.

"Lyle Hutchinson has bequeathed to his only living child, Lorelei Marie Hutchinson, all his holdings in Hutchinson Corp." He read off the businesses, including Destiny Community Bank, two silver mines, Sunny Hill and Lucky Day. There were six buildings on First Street, and this house at 100 North Street along with all its contents, the furnishings and artwork.

Lori was stunned. "Are you sure this is right?" She looked down at Paige's copy to see the monetary amount stated. "My father was worth this much?"

Bradley nodded. "Lyle was a shrewd businessman. Maybe it was because your grandfather Billy lost nearly everything with his bad investments and eccentric living. Lyle spent years rebuilding the family name and recouping the money. And he also invested a lot into this town."

Bradley looked at her, then at Paige. "Are there any questions?"

Lori gave a sideways glance to her lawyer.

"I probably will once we go over everything."

Bradley nodded. "Call me whenever you need to. Now, for the rest I think Mr. Yeager should hear this. Do you have any objections, Lorelei?" With her agreement, he went to the door and had Jace come in.

He sat down in the chair next to Lori.

Bradley looked at Jace. "Whatever you thought, Mr. Yeager, Lyle went into the Heritage project honestly. The business complex was to promote more jobs and revenue for the town. He wasn't trying to swindle you. As we all know, his death was sudden and unexpected."

Jace nodded. "Of course I understand, but you have to see my side, too. I need to finish this job, get tenants in and paying rent."

Bradley nodded and looked at Lori. "And that will happen if Lorelei will agree to the terms."

"Of course I'll agree to finish this project."

"There is a stipulation in the will." Bradley paused. "You are the last living heir in the Hutchinson line, Lorelei. And this town was founded by your great-great-grandfather, Raymond William Hutchinson, after he struck it rich mining gold and silver. But other business has been coming to Destiny and your father invested wisely. He wants you to continue the tradition."

"And I will," she promised. "I plan to release money right away so the work on Mountain Heritage complex can resume."

Bradley exchanged a look with Paige, then continued on to say, "Everything your father left you is only yours if you take over as CEO of Hutchinson Corporation… and stay in Destiny for the next year."

CHAPTER THREE

LORI had trouble catching her breath. Why? Why would her father want her to stay here to run his company?

"Are you all right?" Jace asked.

She nodded, but it was a lie. "Excuse me." She got up and hurried from the room. Instead of going out the front door, she headed in the other direction.

She ended up in the large kitchen with rows of white cabinets and marble countertops. Of course it was different than she remembered. The old stove was gone, replaced with a huge stainless steel one with black grates.

Suddenly the smell of coffee assaulted her nose and she nearly gagged.

"Miss Lorelei, are you all right?"

She turned around to see a concerned Maggie. She managed a nod. "I just need some air." She fought to walk slowly to the back door and stepped out onto the porch. She drew in a long breath of the brisk air and released it, trying to slow her rapidly beating heart.

Two weeks ago, she couldn't say she even remembered her life here, or the father who hadn't had any time for her. Then the call came about Lyle's death, and she'd been swept up into a whirlwind of emotions and confusion. She couldn't even get herself to visit his grave site.

"Are you sure you're okay?"

She turned around and found Jace standing in the doorway. A shiver ran through her and she pulled her sweater coat tighter around her. "You were there. Would you be okay?"

He came to the railing. "Hell, with that kind of money, I could solve a lot of problems."

She caught a hint of his familiar scent, soap and just his own clean manly smell. She shifted away. She didn't need him distracting her, or his opinion.

"Easy for you to say, your life is here, and you wouldn't have to pull up and move." Lori stole a glance at him. "Or have Lyle Hutchinson running that life."

Jace didn't know the exact amount of money Lyle had left his daughter, but knew it had to be sizable from the investigation Jace had done before he'd entered into the Mountain Heritage project. And he needed that project to move ahead, no matter what he had to do. "It's only a year out of your life."

She glared at him. "That I have no control of."

He studied her face. She was pretty with her small straight nose and big brown eyes. His attention went to her mouth and her perfectly formed lips. He glanced away from the distraction.

Yet, how could he not worry about Lorelei Hutchinson when her decision could put his own livelihood in jeopardy? His other concern was having any more delays, especially when the weather could be a problem. This was business. Only.

"Look, I get it that you and your father had problems,

but you can't change that now. He put you in charge of his company. Surely you can't walk away."

She sent him another piercing look. "My father didn't have a problem walking away from his daughter."

He tried to tell himself she wasn't his problem. Then he remembered if she didn't take over the company, then that was exactly what he'd have to do. Walk away from Cassie. "Then don't walk away like he did. This town needs Hutchinson Corporation to exist."

"Don't you think I know that?"

He sat on the porch railing facing her. "I know it's a three-hundred-mile move from Colorado Springs, but you'll have a great income and a place to live." He nodded toward the house. Then he remembered. "I know you'll have to give up your teaching job."

She glanced out at the lawn. "That I don't have to worry about. I was laid off when the school year started. I have my résumé out in several places."

Jace felt bad for her, but at the same time was hopeful. "It's a bad time for teachers. So maybe it's time for a change. Why can't you take over your father's company?"

"There's so many reasons I can't even count them. First of all, I'm not qualified. I have limited business experience. I could lose everything by managing things badly."

He felt a twinge of hope. "You can learn. Besides, Lyle has lawyers and accountants for a lot of it. I'll be the person at the construction site. You can check out my credentials. I'm damn good at what I do."

This time she studied him.

"I can give you references in Denver," he offered.

Lori couldn't help but be curious. Her life had been

exposed, yet she knew nothing about him. "Why did you leave there? Denver."

"Divorce. I had to sell the business to divide the joint assets. Moving here was my best chance to make a good home for my daughter. Best chance at getting full custody."

She might not like the man's bad attitude toward her, but wanting to be a good father gave him a lot of points.

"Once I finish Mountain Heritage and the spaces are leased, I'll have some revenue coming in. It'll allow me to control my work hours. I can pick and choose construction jobs so I can spend more time with Cassie." His gaze met hers. "Best of all, Destiny is a great place to raise children."

She smiled. "That I remember about this town, and how they decorated at Christmas."

She watched conflict play across his face. "That's what I want Cassie to experience, too. I don't want her in some boarding school in Europe because her mother doesn't have time for her." He stood, and quickly changed the subject. "I also have several men that are depending on this job."

"I need to talk to my lawyer before I can make any decision." And she needed to speak to Gina. Her sister weighed heavily in this decision. She turned toward Jace. "I know you were hoping for more."

He nodded. "Of course I was, but I can't wait much longer. Just so you know, I'll be contacting my own lawyer. I have to protect my investment."

Lori tried not to act surprised as she nodded. Jace Yeager finally said his goodbye as he stepped off the porch and walked around the house to the driveway.

She heard his truck start up. Just one more problem to deal with.

"Thanks, Dad." She glanced skyward. "You couldn't give me the time of day when you were alive, but now that you're gone, you turn my life upside down."

She walked back inside the house and back into her father's office. Paige and Mr. Bradley had their heads together. They spent the next twenty minutes going over all the details. She could contest the will, but if she lost, she'd lose everything and so would this town.

Mr. Bradley checked his watch, gathered up his papers and put them in his briefcase. "Lorelei, if you need anything else from me, just call." He handed her a business card. "There's one other thing I didn't get a chance to tell you. You only have seventy-two hours to make your decision," he said then walked out the door.

Lori looked at Paige. "How can I make a life-changing decision in three days?"

"I know it's difficult, Lori, but there isn't a choice. What can I say? Lyle liked being in control." The brunette smiled. "Sorry, I hate to speak ill of the dead."

"No need to apologize. Over the years, my mother never had anything nice to say about the man. It doesn't seem as if he ever changed."

She thought about what Lyle had done to Jace Yeager. The man would lose everything he'd invested in this project if he couldn't complete it. She closed her eyes. "What should I do?"

"Are you asking me as your lawyer or as a citizen of Destiny?"

"Both."

"As your lawyer, if you turn down Lyle's bequest, the corporation and the partnerships would be dissolved and all moneys would be given to charity. You'd get nothing, Lori." Paige went on to add, "As a citizen of a town I love, I hope you accept. Hutchinson Corporation employs many of the people in this community."

She groaned. "Lyle really did own this town."

Paige shrugged. "A fair share of it. But remember, the Hutchinsons built this town with the money they got from mining." She smiled. "Times are changing, though. My brother-in-law Justin is moving at a pretty good pace to take that status. He has an extreme skiing business. And don't count out Jace Yeager. He's got some other projects in the works."

"And now he's tied up in this mess," Lori said. "Dear Lord, you all must have hated my father."

"Like I said there's always been a Hutchinson here to deal with. Your grandfather Billy was a piece of work, too. He'd done a few shady deals in his time. The family has done a lot of good for Destiny." She tried not to smile. "Maybe Lyle was a little arrogant about it."

"And now it looks like you all have me to continue the tradition."

Paige raised an eyebrow. "Does that mean you're staying?"

"Do I have a choice?" She knew it was all about Lyle protecting the Hutchinsons' legacy. Not about his daughter's needs or wants. He had never cared about that.

Well, she had to think about what was best for her family. She and Gina had planned to move away from Colorado, and her sister's ex-husband. Most important they had to be safe. Could Eric find them here in Destiny? Would he try? Of course he would if he had any idea where to look.

If Lori decided to stay, at least she could afford to hire a bodyguard. "I need to talk to my sister. She would have to move here, too."

Paige nodded. "I understand. So when you make your decision give me a call anytime. I need to get back to the office." Her lawyer walked out, leaving her alone.

Lori went to the desk, sat down and opened the file. She stared once again at the exorbitant amount of money her father was worth. Although she was far from comfortable taking anything from Lyle, how could she walk away from this? The money would help her sister and nephew so much. Not to mention the other people in Destiny.

But she'd have to be able to work with Jace Yeager, too. The man had his own anger issues when it came to a Hutchinson. Could she handle that, or him? No, she doubted any woman could, but if she stayed out of his way, they might be able to be partners.

She took her cell phone from her purse and punched in the familiar number. When Gina answered, she said, "How would you feel about moving into a big house in Destiny?"

The next morning, Jace took his daughter to school then drove to the site. He needed to do everything he could to save this project. That meant convince Lori Hutchinson to stay. And that was what he planned to do.

He unlocked the chain-link fence that surrounded the deserted construction site. After opening the gate, he climbed back into his truck, pulled inside and parked in front of the two-story structure. The outside was nearly completed, except for some facade work.

Yet, inside was a different story. The loft apartments

upstairs were still only framed in and the same with the retail stores/office spaces on the bottom floor. He got out as the cool wind caused him to shove his cowboy hat down on his head. Checking the sky overhead, he could feel the moisture in the air. They were predicting rain for later today. How soon before it turned to snow? He'd seen it snow in October, in Colorado.

He heard a car and looked toward the dirt road to see Lori pull in next to his truck and get out. Though tall and slender, she still didn't reach his chin. He glanced down at her booted feet, then did a slow gaze over those long legs encased in a pair of worn jeans. Even in the cold air, his body took notice.

Calm down, boy. She was off-limits.

His gaze shot to her face. "Good morning. Welcome to Mountain Heritage."

"Morning," Lori returned as she burrowed deeper in her coat. "I hope this tour is going to be on the inside," she said. "It's really cold."

He nodded. "Come on."

He led her along the makeshift path through the maze of building materials to the entry. He'd been surprised when he'd gotten the call last night from her, saying she wanted to see Mountain Heritage.

"As you can see, the outside is nearly completed, just a little work left on the trim." He unlocked the door, and let her inside.

"We're ready to blow in insulation and hang Sheetrock. The electricians have completed the rough wiring." He glanced at her, but couldn't read anything from her expression. "This is going to be a green building, totally energy efficient, from the solar panels on the roof, to the tankless water heaters. Best of all, the outside of the structure blends in with the surrounding buildings. But this complex will offer so much more."

He pushed open the double doors and allowed her to go in first. He followed as she walked into the main lobby. This was where it all looked so different. The open concept was what he loved the most about the business complex. He'd done most of the design himself and was proud of how well it was turning out.

The framework of a winding staircase to the second-story balcony still needed the wooden banister. He motioned for her to follow him across the subfloor to the back hall, finding the elevators. He explained about the hardwood floors and the large stone fireplace.

"It's so large."

"We need the space to entice our clients. These back elevators lead to the ten loft apartments upstairs. Both Lyle and I figured they'd rent pretty well to the winter skiers. Of course our ideal renter would be long-term. We were hoping to make it a great place to live, shop and dine all without leaving the premises.

"We have a tentative agreement to lease office spaces for a ski rental company from Justin Hilliard. He's planning on doing a line of custom skis and snowboards."

"How soon were you supposed to have this all completed?"

Was she going to stay? "We'd been on schedule for the end of November." Now he was hoping he still had a full crew. Some of the subcontractors he'd been working with had come up from Durango.

Lori felt ignorant. She'd never been to a construction site. Doubts filled her again as she wondered for the hundredth time if she'd be any good taking over for

Lyle. So many people were depending on her. "How are you at teaching, Jace?"

He looked confused, then said, "I guess that depends on the student and how willing they are to learn."

"She's very serious." She released a sigh. "It looks like we're going to be partners."

Damn. Jace had a woman for his partner, a woman who didn't know squat about construction. And he was even taking her to lunch. He'd do whatever it took to provide for his daughter.

He escorted Lori into a booth at the local coffee shop, the Silver Spoon. He hadn't expected her to accept his lunch invitation, but they'd spent the past two hours at the site, going over everything that would need to happen in the next seven weeks to meet completion. She took notes, a lot of notes.

He'd made a call to his project manager, Toby Edwards, and had asked him to get together a crew. Within an hour, his foreman had called back to tell him they got most of the people on board to start first thing in the morning.

So it seemed natural that he would take her to lunch to celebrate. He glanced across the table. She still looked a little shell-shocked from all the information she'd consumed this morning, but she hadn't complained once.

"This place is nice, homey," she said. "Reminds me of the café I worked in during college."

Okay, that surprised him. "It's your typical family-run restaurant that serves good home cooking, a hearty breakfast in the morning and steak for supper. Outside of a steak house, there isn't any fine dining in Destiny, and Durango is forty-eight miles away. We're hoping a restaurant will be added to our complex. Not only more revenue for us, but more choice when you want to go out."

He smiled and Lori felt a sudden rush go through her. No. No. No. She didn't want to think about Jace Yeager being a man. Well, he was a man, just not the man she needed to be interested in. He was far too handsome, too distracting, and they would be working together. Correction, he was doing the work, she would be watching…and learning.

"I hear from your daughter that you've been remodeling your house."

"Restoration," he corrected. "And yes, it's a lot of work, but I enjoy it. So many people just want to tear out and put in new. There is so much you can save. I'm refinishing the hardwood floors, and stripping the crown moldings and the built-in cabinet in the dining room. What I've replaced is an outdated furnace and water heater."

She smiled. "And the roof?"

He raised an eyebrow.

She went on to say, "Cassie told me that you had to put out pans when it rained."

She caught a hint of his smile, making him even more handsome. "Yeah, we had a few adventurous nights. We stayed dry, though."

She couldn't help but be curious about him, but no more personal questions. Focus on his profession. "I bet my father's house could use some updating, too."

"I wouldn't know. Yesterday was the first time I'd been there. I conducted all my business with Lyle in his office at the bank."

She didn't get the chance to comment as the middle-aged waitress came to the table carrying two mugs and a coffeepot. With their nods, she filled the cups.

"Hi, Jace. How's that little one of yours?"

"She keeps me on my toes." He smiled. "Helen, this is Lorelei Hutchinson. Lori, this is Helen Turner. She and her husband, Alan, are the owners of the Silver Spoon."

The woman smiled. "It's nice to meet you, Ms. Hutchinson. I'm sorry about your father."

"Thank you. And please, call me Lori."

"Will you be staying in town long?" the woman asked.

Lori glanced at Jace. "It looks that way."

She couldn't tell if Helen was happy about that or not. They placed their order and the woman walked away.

"I guess she hasn't decided if she's happy about me staying."

Jace leaned forward. "Everyone is curious about what you're going to do. Whether you'll change things at Hutchinson Corp." He shrugged. "These days everyone worries about their jobs."

"I don't want that to happen. That's one of the main reasons I'm staying in town."

Jace leaned back in the booth. "Of course it has nothing to do with the millions your father left you."

Lori felt the shock. "Money doesn't solve every problem."

"My ex-wife thought it did."

Before she could react to Jace's bitter words, Helen brought their food to the table. Their focus turned to their meal until a middle-aged man approached their booth.

"Excuse me, ma'am, sir," he began hesitantly. "Helen told me that you're Mr. Hutchinson's daughter."

Lori smiled. "I am Lori Hutchinson and you are…?"

"Mac Burleson."

She had a feeling that he wasn't just here to be neighborly. Had her father done something to him? "It's nice to meet you, Mr. Burleson."

Mr. Burleson looked to be in his early thirties. Dressed in faded jeans, a denim shirt and warm winter jacket, he held his battered cowboy hat in his hands. "I hope you'll pardon the intrusion, ma'am, but your father and I had business before his death. First, I'm sorry for your loss."

She nodded. "Thank you."

"I was also wondering if you'll be taking over his position at the bank."

She was startled by the question. "To be honest with you, Mr. Burleson, I haven't had much chance to decide what my involvement would be. Is there a problem?"

The man was nervous. "It's just that, Mr. Neal, in the loan department, is going to foreclose on my house next week." The man glanced at Jace, then back at her.

"I know I've been late on my payments, but I haven't been able to find work in a while. No one is hiring…." He stopped and gathered his emotions. "I have three kids, Miss Hutchinson. If I can have a little more time, I swear I'll catch up. Just don't make my family leave their home."

Lori was caught off guard. Her father planned to evict a family?

"Mac," Jace said, drawing the man's attention, "do you have any experience working construction?"

Hope lit up the man's tired eyes. "I've worked on a

few crews. I can hang drywall and do rough framing. Heck, I'll even clean up trash." He swallowed hard. "I'm not too proud to do anything to feed my family."

Lori felt an ache building in her stomach as Jace talked. "If you can report to the Mountain Heritage site tomorrow morning at seven, I'll give you a chance to prove yourself."

"I'll be there," Mac promised. "Thank you."

Jace nodded. "Report to the foreman, Toby."

Mac shook Jace's hand. "I won't let you down, Mr. Yeager." He turned back to Lori. "Could you tell Mr. Neal that I have a job now? And maybe give me a few months to catch up on my payments."

Lori's heart ached. She didn't even know her loan officer, but it seemed she needed to meet him right away. "Mac, I can't make any promises, but give me a few days and I'll get back to you."

He shook her hand. "That's all I can ask. Thank you, Ms. Hutchinson." He walked away.

Lori released a sigh. "I guess I have a lot more to do now than worry about one building."

"Your job as Hutchinson CEO covers a lot of areas."

Helen came over to the table, this time wearing a grin.

"I hoped you've enjoyed your lunch."

"Great as usual," Jace said.

The waitress started to turn away, then stopped and said, "By the way, it's on the house." She picked up the bill from the table. "Thank you both for what you did for Mac."

"I haven't done anything yet," Lori clarified, now afraid she'd spoken too soon.

"You both gave him hope. He's had a rough time of

late." Helen blinked. "A few years ago, he left the army and came back home a decorated war hero. At the very least, he deserves our respect, and a chance. So thank you for taking the time to listen to him." The woman turned and walked back toward the kitchen.

She looked at Jace, remembering what he said about her inheritance. She also wasn't sure she liked being compared to his ex. "I better go and stop by the bank." She pushed her plate away. "Who knows, maybe all those 'millions' just might do some good."

CHAPTER FOUR

LORI couldn't decide if she was hurt or angry over Jace's assumption about the inheritance. She'd lost her appetite and excused herself immediately after lunch.

She was glad when he didn't try to stop her, because she had a lot of thinking to do without the opinion of a man she'd be working with. And who seemed to have a lot of issues about women.

Was he like her father? What she'd learned from her mother about Lyle over the years had been his need to control, whether in business or his personal life. When Jocelyn Hutchinson couldn't take any more she'd gotten out of the marriage, but their child had still been trapped in the middle of her parents' feud. The scars they'd caused made it hard for Lori to trust.

But was coming back to Destiny worth putting her smack-dab into dealing with the past? All the childhood hurt and pain? It also put her in charge of Lyle's domain, and his business dealings, including the Mountain Heritage complex. And a lot more time with the handsome but irritating Jace Yeager.

The man had been right about something. She had a lot of money and it could do a lot of good. She recalled the look of hope on Mac Burleson's face and knew she needed to find an answer for the man.

She crossed the street to Destiny Community Bank. The two-story brick structure was probably from her grandfather's era. With renewed confidence she walked inside to a large open space with four teller windows. Along the wall were portraits of generations of the Hutchinson men—Raymond, William, Billy and Lyle. They were all strangers to her. She studied her handsome father's picture. This man especially.

She turned around and found several of the bank customers watching her. She put on a smile and they greeted her the same way as if they knew who she was.

She went to the reception desk and spoke to the young brunette woman seated there. "Is it possible to see Mr. Neal? Tell him Lorelei Hutchinson is here."

"Yes, Miss Hutchinson." The woman picked up the phone, and when she hung up said, "Mr. Neal said to have a seat and he'll be out…shortly."

Lori wasn't in the mood to wait. "Is he in a meeting?"

The girl shook her head.

"Then I'll just head to his office. Where is it?"

The receptionist stood and together they went toward a row of offices. "Actually, he's in Mr. Hutchinson's office."

Lori smiled. "Oh, is he? Excuse me, I didn't get your name."

"It's Erin Peters."

"Well, Erin, it's very nice to meet you. I'm Lori." She stuck out her hand. "Have you worked at the bank for long?"

"Three years. I've been taking college classes for my business degree."

"That's nice to know. I'm sure my father appreciated his employees continuing their education."

Erin only nodded as they walked toward the office at the end of the hall. Lori knocked right under the nameplate on the last door that read Lyle W. Hutchinson. She paused as she gathered courage, then turned the knob and walked in.

There was a balding man of about fifty seated behind her father's desk. He seemed busy trying to stack folders. When he saw her he froze, then quickly put on a smile.

"Well, you must be Lorelei Hutchinson." He rounded the desk. "I'm Gary Neal. It's a pleasure to finally meet you. Lyle talked about you often."

She shook his hand, seriously doubting Lyle said much about her. Her father hadn't taken the time to know her. Now, did she have to prove herself worthy of being his daughter?

"Hello, Mr. Neal."

"First off, I want to express my deepest sympathies for your loss. Lyle and I were not only colleagues, but friends. So if there is anything you need…"

"Thank you, I'm fine." She nodded. "I've only been in town a few days, but I wanted to stop by the bank. I'm sure you've already heard that I'm going to be staying in Destiny."

He nodded. "Dennis Bradley explained as much."

She hesitated. "Good. Do you have a few minutes to talk with me?"

"Of course."

Still feeling brave, she walked behind the desk and took the seat in her father's chair as if she belonged.

She didn't miss the surprise on the loan officer's face. "Where's your office, Mr. Neal?"

He blinked, then finally said, "It's two doors down the hall. Since your father's death, I've had to access some files from here. Lyle was hands-on when it came to bank business. I'm his assistant manager."

"Good. Then you're who I need to speak with." She motioned for him to sit down, but she was feeling a little shaky trying to pull this off. This man could be perfectly wonderful at his job, but she needed to trust him. "I take it you handle the mortgage loans." With his nod, she asked, "What do you know about the Mac Burleson mortgage?"

The man frowned. "Funny you should ask, I was just working on the Burleson file."

"Could I have a look?"

He hesitated, then relented. "It's a shame we're going to have to start foreclosure proceedings in a few days."

Neal dug through the stack, located the file and handed it to her. She looked over pages of delinquent notices, the huge late fees. And an interest rate that was nearly three points higher than the norm. No wonder the man was six months behind. "Has Mr. Burleson paid anything during all this time?"

"Yes, but it could barely cover the interest."

"Why didn't you help him by dropping the interest rate and lowering the payments?"

"It's not the bank's policy. Your father—"

"Well, my father is gone now, and he wanted me to take over in his place."

"I'm *sure* he did, but with your limited experience…"

"That may be, but I feel that given the state of the economy we need to help people, too. It's a rough time."

She knew firsthand. "I want to stop the foreclosure, or at least delay it."

"But Mr. Burleson isn't even employed."

"As of an hour ago, he's gotten a job offer." She looked at the remaining eight files. "Are these other homes to be foreclosed on, too?"

The loan officer looked reluctant to answer, but nodded. "Would you please halt all proceedings until I have a look at each case? I want to try everything to keep these families in their homes." She stood. "Maybe if we can set up a meeting next week and see what we can come up with."

Mr. Neal stood. "This isn't bank policy. If people aren't held accountable for their debts, we'd be out of business. I'm sure your father wouldn't agree with this, either."

For the first time in days, Lori felt as if she were doing the right thing. "As I said before, my father left me in charge. Do you have a problem with that, Mr. Neal?"

With the shaking of his head, she tossed out one more request. "Good. I also need money transferred into the escrow account for the Mountain Heritage project as soon as possible. Mr. Yeager will have his crew back to work first thing in the morning. And if you have any questions about my position here, talk to Mr. Bradley."

She walked out to the reception desk and found Jace standing there, talking with Erin. He was smiling at the pretty brunette woman. Why not? He was handsome and single. And why did she even care?

He finally saw her and walked over. "Hi, Lori."

"What are you doing here? I told you that I'd get the money for the project."

"I know you did, but that's not why I'm here—"

"I'm really busy now, Jace. Could we do this later?" She cut him off and turned to the receptionist. "Erin, would you schedule a meeting for all employees for nine o'clock tomorrow in the conference room?"

With Erin's agreement, Lori walked out of the bank, feeling Jace's gaze on her. She couldn't deal with him. She had more pressing things to do, like moving out of the inn and into her father's house, where she had to face more ghosts.

Jace was angry that he let Lori get to him. He'd wasted his afternoon chasing after a woman who didn't want to be found. At least not by him.

He hadn't blamed Lori for walking out on him at lunch. Okay, maybe he had no right to say what he did to her. Damn. He'd let his past dictate his feelings about women. Like it or not, Lori Hutchinson was his partner. More importantly, she had the money to keep the project going. If he wanted any chance of keeping Cassie he had to complete his job.

An apology was due to Lori. And he needed to deliver it in person. If only she'd give him a minute to listen to him. He also needed her to sign some papers that needed her authorization.

Jace left the bank to meet up with his foreman to finalize the crew for tomorrow. Then the search for Lori continued as he'd gone around town and ended up at the inn, where he finally got an answer as to her whereabouts.

He had to pick up Cassie from school, but went straight to the Hutchinson house after. He drove through the gates, hoping he could come up with something to say to her. The last thing he wanted was to start off on the wrong foot.

"Wow! Daddy, this is pretty. Does Ms. Lori really live here?"

He parked in the driveway and saw the rental car there. "Yes, she does. It was her father's, now it's hers."

He climbed out and helped Cassie from the backseat. They went up the steps as the front door opened and Maggie appeared. "This is a wonderful day. First, Ms. Lorelei comes home and now, Mr. Yeager and this beautiful child come to visit."

"Hi, Maggie," Jace said. "This is my daughter, Cassie. Cassie, this is Maggie."

They exchanged greetings then the housekeeper opened the door wider.

"I'd like to see Lori if she isn't too busy."

"Of course." Maggie motioned them inside the entry. "She's in her father's upstairs office." The housekeeper looked at Cassie. "Why don't I take you into the kitchen and see if there are some fresh baked cookies on my cooling rack? They're so good along with some milk." The housekeeper looked concerned. "Coming back here is hard for her."

"I expect it is. Are you sure it's okay?"

Maggie smiled. "I think that would be good. The office is the first door on the left."

Still he hesitated.

"You should go up," the woman said. "She could use a friend right about now."

Jace glanced up the curved staircase and murmured, "I'm not sure she'd call me 'friend' right now."

* * *

Lori had trouble deciding where to put her things. There were six bedrooms and a master suite. One had been turned into an office, and the one next to it was non-descript, with only a queen-size bed covered by a soft floral comforter. It had a connecting bath, so that was where she put her one bag.

She unpacked the few items she had, but went into her father's office. She couldn't get into his computer because she didn't have access.

"Okay, need to make a call to Dennis Bradley first thing tomorrow."

What she knew for sure was she needed to have someone to work with. Someone she trusted. As far as she knew her father had worked out of his office at the bank and from home. Did Lyle handle everything himself? Had he not trusted anyone? She rubbed her hands over her face. She didn't know the man. She stood up and walked out.

In the hall curiosity got the best of her and she began to look around. She peeked into the next room, then the next until she came to the master suite. She opened the door but didn't go inside.

The dark room had a big four-poster bed that dominated the space. The windows were covered with heavy brocade drapes and the bedspread was the same fabric. The furniture was also stained dark. Bits and pieces of childhood memories hit her. She pushed them aside and journeyed on to the next room. She paused at the door, feeling a little shaky, then she turned the knob and pushed it open.

She gasped, seeing the familiar pale pink walls. The double bed with the sheer white canopy and matching sheer curtains. There was a miniature table with stuffed animals seated in the matching chairs as if waiting for a tea party.

Oh, my God.

Nothing had been changed since she'd lived here. Lori crossed the room to the bed where a brown teddy bear was propped against the pillow.

"Buddy?" She picked up the furry toy, feeling a rush of emotions, along with the memory of her father bringing the stuffed animal home one night.

She hugged the bear close and fought tears. No, she didn't want to feel like this. She didn't want to care about the man who didn't want her. Yet, she couldn't stop the flood of tears. A sob tore from her throat as she sank down onto the mattress and cried.

"Lori?"

She heard Jace's voice and stiffened. She quickly walked to the window, wiping her eyes. She fought to compose herself before she had to face him.

He followed her, refusing to be ignored.

"It's okay to be sad," he said, his voice husky and soft.

She finally swung around. "Don't talk about what you know nothing about."

Jace was taken aback by her anger. "It seems that everything I've said to you today has been wrong. I won't bother you again."

She stopped him. "No, please, don't go."

She wiped the last of the tears off her face. "It's me who should apologize for my rudeness. You caught me at a bad moment. Why are you here?"

"Maggie sent me up to Lyle's office. I have some papers for you to sign, but they can wait. Believe it or not, Lori, I came to apologize for what I said to you at lunch. I had no right to judge your motivation."

Jace glanced around the bedroom and hated what he was feeling. What Lyle must have felt when his daughter left. Would this happen to him if his ex got Cassie back? "I take it you were about six or seven when you left here?"

She nodded. "It was so long ago, I feel silly for letting it upset me now."

"You were old enough to have memories. Your childhood affects you all your life. It was your father who chose not to spend time with you." It seemed odd, he thought, because Lyle had kept her room like a shrine.

Lori suddenly brightened as if all the pain went away. "Well, as you can see, I'll need to do some painting. My sister, Gina, is coming soon along with my nephew, Zack." She put on a smile. "I don't think he'd like a pink bedroom."

Before Jace could say anything, he heard his daughter calling for him. "I'm in here, Cassie. I picked her up from school, and I wanted to see you before work tomorrow. To make sure everything is okay…between us."

The expression on his seven-year-old's face was priceless as she stopped at the door. "Oh, it's so pretty." She looked at Lori. "Do you have a little girl, too?"

An hour later, with Cassie busy doing homework at the kitchen table, Jace and Lori went to do their work in Lyle's office.

"I hate that you have to keep going over everything again and again," Lori told him.

"It's not a problem. Better now, when I'm around to answer your questions. There aren't too many decisions to make right now. If you'd like to put in some input on finishes, like tile and countertops, you're more than welcome. A woman's touch." He held up a hand. "I didn't mean anything about that. A second opinion would be nice."

"I'd like that."

She smiled and he felt a tightening in his gut. Damn. He looked back at the work sheet.

"Well, the crew is showing up tomorrow to start the finish work on the outside. If we're lucky the weather will hold and we can complete everything before the snow comes."

"Will it affect the work inside?"

"Only if we can't get the materials to the site because the roads aren't passable."

She nodded, chewing her bottom lip. He found it hard to look away.

"What about Mac Burleson? Do you really have a job for him?"

Jace nodded. "If he can do the work."

"I wonder if Mac can paint," Lori said.

Jace looked at her to see a mischievous grin on her pretty face. She wasn't beautiful as much as striking. Those sparkling brown eyes and full mouth… "That was probably going to be one of his jobs—priming the walls once they're up. What were you thinking?"

"I doubt my father has done much work on this house in years." She shrugged. "I don't mind so much for myself, but Gina and Zack. I want this place…" She glanced around the dark room. "A little more homey. I want to talk to Charlie and see what he has to say about repairs."

"How soon are you expecting your family?"

"Next week. Gina is packing and putting most of the furniture in storage." She sighed. "I should go back to help her, but I want to make sure there won't be any holdup on the project."

Jace needed to remember that her entire life had been turned upside down by Lyle's death. "It's a shame you have to leave everything behind, like your friends. A boyfriend...?"

She looked surprised at his question. Not as much as he was. He stood and went to the window. "I only meant, Lyle had you make a tough choice."

"No, I don't have a boyfriend at the moment, and my sister is my best friend. So sometimes a fresh start is good." She turned the tables on him. "Isn't that why you came to Destiny?"

He didn't look at her, but that didn't mean he couldn't catch her scent, or wasn't aware of her closeness. He took a step back. "I came here to make a life for my daughter. She's everything to me."

Lori smiled at him and again his body took notice. "From what I've seen, Cassie feels the same way about you. You're a good father."

"Thank you. I'm not perfect. But I do try and want to make the job permanent."

His gaze went back to her. Darn. What was it about her that drew him? Suddenly he thought about his ex-wife, and the caution flag came out. He needed to stay focused on two things—business and his daughter.

A happy Cassie skipped into the room and rushed to him. "Maggie said to tell you that dinner is ready."

"Oh, honey. We should head home." He glanced at his watch. "Maybe another time."

"No, Daddy. We can't go. I helped Maggie make the biscuits, so we have to stay and eat them."

He was caught as he looked down at his daughter, then at Lori.

"I can't believe you're passing up a home-cooked meal, Jace Yeager," Lori said. "Maggie's biscuits are the best around, and probably even better with Cassie helping."

"Please, Daddy. I'll go to bed right on time. I won't argue or anything."

Jace looked back at Lori. It was her first night here, and would probably be a rough one.

Lori smiled. "Now that's a hard offer to turn down."

"You're no help," he told Lori.

"Sorry, us girls have to stick together."

That was what he was afraid of. He was losing more than just this round. He hated that he didn't mind one bit.

"Okay, but we can't stay long. We have a bedtime schedule."

"I promise, I'll go to bed right on time," Cassie said, then took off toward the kitchen.

He looked at a smiling Lori. "Okay, I'm a pushover."

"Buck up, Dad. It's only going to get worse before it gets better."

Suddenly their eyes locked and the amused look disappeared. Lori was the first to speak. "Please, I want you to stay for dinner. I think we both agree that eating alone isn't fun."

"Yes, we can agree on that."

He followed Lori into the kitchen, knowing this

woman could easily fill those lonely times. He just couldn't let that happen. No more women for a while, at least not over the age of seven.

CHAPTER FIVE

AT EIGHT-THIRTY the next morning, Lori was up and dressed, and grabbed a travel mug of coffee from Maggie, then she was out the door to the construction site. Not that she didn't think Jace could do his job, but she wanted to meet the crew and assure them that there wouldn't be any more delays with the project.

When she pulled through the gate and saw the buzz of activity, she was suddenly concerned about disturbing everyone.

She had every right to be here, she thought as she climbed out of her car and watched the men working on the trim work of the two-story structure. Jace hadn't wasted any time.

She walked carefully on the soggy ground. Okay, she needed more protection than her loafers. A good pair of sturdy boots was on her list. She headed up the plywood-covered path when a young man dressed in jeans, a denim work shirt and lace-up steel-toed boots came toward her.

He gave her a big smile and tipped back his hard hat. "Can I help you, ma'am?"

"I'm looking for Jace Yeager."

The man's smile grew bigger. "Aren't they all? I'm Mike Parker, maybe I can help you."

All? Lori couldn't help but wonder what that meant. She started to speak when she heard a familiar voice call out. They both turned to see Jace. He was dressed pretty much like the others, but he had on a leather vest over a black Henley shirt even though the temperature was in the low fifties.

Lori froze as he gave her a once-over. He didn't look happy to see her as he made his way toward them.

Jace ignored her as he looked at Mike. "Don't you have anything to do?"

"I was headed to my truck for some tools." He nodded to her. "And I ran across this nice lady. Sorry, I didn't catch your name."

"Lori Hutchinson."

Mike let out a low whistle. "So you're the big boss? I can't tell you how good it is to meet you, Ms. Hutchinson."

She tried not to cringe at the description. "It's Lori. I'm not anyone's boss. Jace is in charge of this project."

That was when Jace spoke up. "Mike, they've finished spraying the insulation up in the lofts, so I need you to get started hanging drywall."

"Right, I'll get on it." He tipped his hat to Lori. "Nice to meet you, ma'am."

"Nice to meet you, too, Mike."

She watched him hurry off, then turned back to Jace. "Good morning. Seems you've been busy. What time did you start?"

"I had a partial crew in at five."

"What about Cassie?"

He seemed surprised at her question. "I wasn't here,

but my foreman was. My daughter comes first, Lori. She always will."

"I didn't mean… I apologize."

That didn't ease the scowl on his face. "Were we supposed to meet this morning?"

She shook her head. "No."

"Did you come to work?" He looked over her attire. "You're not exactly dressed for a construction site."

She glanced down at her dark trousers and soft blue sweater under her coat. "I have an appointment at the bank later this morning. I wanted to stop here first to see if everything got off okay. Do you need anything?"

"No, it's fine. I know it looks a little chaotic, but things are running pretty smoothly for the first day back to work. It's most of the same crew so they know what I expect from them."

Lori had no doubt that Jace Yeager was good at his job. "So everything is on schedule?"

"If the weather holds." The wind picked up and brushed her hair back. "Come inside where it's a little warmer," he said. "I'll introduce you to the foreman."

"I don't want to disturb him."

"As you can see, it's a little late for that." He nodded toward the men who were watching.

She could feel a blush rising over her face as she followed Jace inside the building to a worktable that had blueprints spread out on top. A middle-aged man was talking with another workman.

"Hey, Toby," Jace called as he reached into a bin and pulled out a hard hat. He came to her and placed it on her head. "You need to wear this if you come here. Safety rules."

Their eyes met. "Thank you."

Toby walked up to them. "What, Jace?"

"This is Lori Hutchinson. Lori, this is my foreman, Toby Edwards."

The man smiled at her and tiny lines crinkled around his eyes. "So you're the one who saved this guy's as… sets."

Lori felt Jace tense. "I'd say I was just lucky to inherit some money," she told Toby. "Speaking of money…" She turned to Jace. "Were the funds transferred into the Mountain Heritage account?"

He nodded. "Yes. We're expecting materials to be delivered later today."

"Good." She glanced around, feeling a little excited about being a part of this. "It's nice to see all the work going on." It was a little noisy with the saws and nail guns.

Jace watched Lori. He wasn't expecting her here. Not that she didn't have a right, but she was a big distraction. He caught the guys watching her, too. Okay, they were curious about their attractive new boss. He hoped that was all it was. There could be a problem if she stopped by every day. And not only for his men, either. He eyed her pretty face and those big brown eyes that a man could get lost in.

No way. One woman had already cost him his career and future, and maybe his daughter. He wasn't going to get involved with another, especially in his workplace. Or any other place. He thought about the cozy dinner last night in the Hutchinson kitchen.

It was a little too cozy.

Enough reminiscing, he thought, and stuck his fingers in his mouth, letting go with a piercing whistle. "Let's get this over with so we can all get on with our day." All work stopped and the men came to the center of the main room.

"Everyone, this is Lorelei Hutchinson. Since Lyle Hutchinson's death, Lori will be taking over in her father's place. It's thanks to her we're all back to work on this project." The men let go with cheers and whistles. Jace forced a smile, knowing this was a means to get this project completed. But damn, being beholden to a woman stuck in his craw. "Okay, now back to work."

"Thank you," Lori said. "So many people in town have been looking at me like I have two heads."

"Has someone said anything to you?" he asked.

"No, but they're wondering what I'm going to do." She shrugged. "Maybe I should just make a big announcement in the town square. 'Hey, everyone, I'm not here to cause trouble.'"

A strange protective feeling came over him. "Now that the project has started up again, maybe they'll stop worrying."

"I hope so. I'm bringing my sister and nephew here to live. I want to be part of this community."

"What you did for Mac Burleson yesterday was a pretty good start."

"Oh, Mac. Is he here?"

Jace nodded. "Yeah, he was here waiting when Toby opened the gates."

She glanced around the area. "How is he doing?"

"Good so far."

She looked up at Jace. "There he is. Would you mind if I talked to him for a moment?"

"No, not a problem."

She walked across the large entry to the wall. Jace watched her acknowledge a lot of the workers before she got to Mac. She smiled and the man returned it. In fact he was smiling the whole time Lori was talking. Then he shook her hand and Lori walked back. "I just hired Mac to paint a couple of bedrooms at the house."

"Hey, are you stealing my help?"

"No. He's agreed to come over this weekend with his brother and paint the upstairs. I don't think my nephew wants to sleep in a pink room."

Jace nodded, knowing she would be erasing the last of her own memories of her childhood. "There are other bedrooms for him to sleep in."

"I know, but it should have been changed years ago."

"Maybe there was a reason why it hadn't been."

She looked at him. He saw pain, but also hope. "Lyle Hutchinson knew where I was since I left here twenty-two years ago. My father could have invited me back anytime. He chose not to."

Lori turned to walk out and he hurried to catch up with her. "Look, Lori. I don't know the situation."

She stopped abruptly. "That's right, you don't." She closed her eyes. "Look, it was a long time ago. My father is gone, and I'll never know why he never came to see me. And now, why in heaven's name does he want me to run his company?"

"I can't answer that, either."

"I've dealt with it. So now I move on and start my new life with Gina and Zack. I want them to have a fresh start here, in a new place, a new house and especially a new bedroom for my seven-year-old nephew."

Jace frowned. "I take it Zack is without his father."

Lori straightened. "His parents are divorced." She glanced around. "I should be going."

"I need to get back, too."

They started walking toward the door. "If there's anything you need," she offered, "just give me a call. You have my cell phone number. I'll be at the bank most of today."

He walked her out. "I can handle things here." Then he felt bad. "Maybe in a few days if you're available we could go over some samples of tiles and flooring."

She looked surprised at his request. "I'd like that. I want to be a part of this project."

Her steps slowed as she made her way over the uneven boards. He took Lori's arm, helping her along the path.

"What about the bank?"

"I doubt Mr. Neal will enjoy having me around." She stopped suddenly and nearly lost her balance. "Oh," she gasped.

"I got you." He caught her in his arms. Suddenly her trim body was plastered up against him. Even with her coat he wasn't immune to her soft curves. And he liked it. Too much. He finally got her back on her feet. "You need practical boots if you come to a construction site. Go to Travers's Outfitters and get some that are waterproof. You don't want to be caught in bad weather without protection."

She stopped next to her compact car. "I need a lot of things since I'll be living here awhile."

"Like a car that will get through the snow. This thing will put you in a ditch on the first bad day. Get something with bulk to it. You'll be driving your family around."

She nodded. "I guess I need to head down to Durango and visit a dealership next week when my sister flies in."

Before he could stop himself, he offered, "If you need any help, let me know."

She gave him a surprised look, mirroring his own feelings.

Two hours later, Lori glanced across the conference table at the Destiny Community Bank's loan officers, Gary Neal, Harold Brownlee and Larry McClain. The gentlemen's club. "I disagree. In this day and age, we need to work with people and help adjust their loans."

"In my experience," Neal said, "if we start giving handouts, people will take advantage. And no one will pay us."

She tried to remain calm, but she was so far out of her element it wasn't funny.

"I never said this is a handout, more like a hand up. All I suggested is we lower the interest rates on these loans." She pointed to the eight mortgages. "Two points. Waive the late fees and penalties. Just give these families a fighting chance to keep their homes. We'll get the money we loaned back." She paused to see their stunned looks and wondered if she were crazy, too.

She hurried on to say, "Mac Burleson has a job now, but he can't catch up on his mortgage if we don't help him."

"We've always done things this way," Larry McClain said. "Your father would never—"

Lori stiffened. "Well, I'm not my father, but he did put me in charge. In fact, I'm going to become more involved in day-to-day working here at the bank. I can see that there aren't any women in management positions. That needs to change, too."

The threesome gave each other panicked looks. "That's not true. Mary O'Brien manages the tellers."

Were these men from the Dark Ages? "I mean women in decision-making positions. It's a changing world out there and we need to keep up. I've seen the profit sheet for this bank. Over the years, it's done very well."

Neal spoke up again. "You can't come in here and just change everything. You're a schoolteacher."

Lori held her temper. "I became an expert when my father put me in charge of his company. Just so you know, not only am I a good teacher, but I also minored in business. So, gentlemen, whether you like it or not, I'm here."

She was feeling a little shaky. What if she was making a mistake? She glanced at her watch. "I think we've said about everything that needs to be said for now. Good morning." She took her purse and walked out.

She needed someone here on her side. She walked to Erin's desk.

The girl smiled when she approached. "Hello, Ms. Hutchinson. How was your meeting?"

"Not as productive as I would have liked." She sat down in the chair next to the desk. "Erin, could you help me?"

The girl nodded. "If I can."

"I'm looking for someone, a woman who is qualified for a managerial position. Could you give me some candidates?"

The pretty brunette looked surprised, but then answered. "That would be Mary O'Brien and Lisa Kramer. They've both worked for the bank for over five years.

I know Lisa has a college degree. I'm not sure Mary does, but she practically runs this bank."

"That's good to know, because I need someone to help me." She was going to need a lot of help. Since her father had never promoted a woman that was one of the things she needed to change. Immediately.

"Could you call a meeting with all the employees?" She looked at her watch. "And call the Silver Spoon and have them send over sandwiches and drinks."

Erin smiled. "This is going to be fun."

"We're going to need our strength to get this bank into the twenty-first century."

Two mornings later, Lori had been awakened by a call from a sick Claire Keenan, asking her for a favor. Would Lori like to take her place as a volunteer in the second grade classroom this afternoon?

There might have been several other things to do, but Lori found she wanted to check out the school. After her trip to the paint store and picking her colors for the bedroom, she had her purchase sent to the house.

She grabbed a quick lunch at the Silver Spoon, and after a friendly chat with Helen, she arrived at Destiny Elementary with time to spare. She went through the office then was taken down the hall to the second grade classroom.

Outside, she was greeted by the teacher. "It's good to meet you, I'm Julie Miller."

"Lori Hutchinson. I'm substituting for Claire Keenan. She's sick."

The young strawberry blonde smiled eagerly. "I'm glad you could make it. I've heard a lot about you."

"Well, I guess Lyle's long-lost daughter would be news in a small town."

Julie smiled. "No, I heard it all from Cassie Yeager. Seems you live in a castle and have a princess bedroom like hers."

That brought a smile to Lori's lips, too. "If only."

"I also heard you teach second grade."

"I did. I was laid off this year."

"I'm sorry to hear that, but you're welcome to come and help out in my class anytime. But it sounds like you've been pretty busy with other projects around town."

Lori blinked. "You must have a good source."

"My sister, Erin, works at the bank. You've really impressed her."

"Oh, Erin. She's been a big help showing me around. There do need to be some changes."

Julie smiled brightly. "I can't tell you how happy I am that you came to Destiny and I hope you stay."

"I'll be here for this year anyway. In fact, my sister and her son will be coming in next week. Zack will be in second grade."

"That's wonderful. Then you'll want to see how I run my class."

Julie Miller opened the door to a room that was buzzing with about twenty-five seven-year-olds. The room was divided in sections, half with desks, the other half with tables and a circle of chairs for reading time.

Suddenly two little blonde girls came up to her—Ellie Larkin and Cassie Yeager.

"Miss Lori, what are you doing here?" Cassie asked.

"Hi, girls. Ellie, your grandmother isn't feeling well today."

Both girls looked worried. "Really?" Ellie said.

"It's nothing serious, don't worry. But she asked if I'd come in her place."

They got excited again. "We're going to try out for our Christmas program today."

"That's wonderful," Lori said. This was what she missed about teaching, the children's enthusiasm.

"It's called Destiny's First Christmas," Cassie said as she clasped her hands together. "And everyone gets to be in it."

"But we want to be the angels," Ellie added.

Just then Mrs. Miller got their attention. "Okay, class, you need to return to your desks. We have a special guest today and we need to show her how well-behaved we are so she'll want to come back." A bright smile. "Maybe Miss Hutchinson will help us with our Christmas play."

CHAPTER SIX

LATER that evening, Jace finally headed home. He was beat to say the least. A twelve-hour day was usually nothing for him, but he'd been off for three weeks. He needed to oversee everything today to make sure that the schedule for tomorrow went off without a hitch. The one thing he knew, he didn't like to be away from Cassie that long. Luckily, he had good childcare.

He came up the road and the welcoming two-story clapboard house came into view. Although the sun had set an hour ago, he had installed plenty of lighting to illuminate the grounds, including the small barn. He had a lot of work yet to do on the place, but a new roof and paint job made the house livable for now.

The barn had been redone, plus he'd added stalls for his two horses, Rocky and Dixie. Maybe it was a luxury he couldn't afford right now, but it was something that had helped Cassie adjust to her move. Luckily he'd been able to hire the neighbor's teenage son to do the feeding and cleaning.

Jace frowned at the sight of a new SUV parked by the back door. Had Heather, the babysitter, gotten a new car? Then dread washed over him. Was it his ex-wife?

Panic surged through him as he got out of his truck

and hurried up the back steps into the mudroom. After shucking his boots, he walked into the kitchen. He froze, then almost with relief, he sagged against the counter when he saw his daughter at the kitchen table with Lori Hutchinson.

He took a moment and watched the interaction of the two. Their blond heads together, working on the math paper. Then Lori reached out and stroked Cassie's hair and it looked as natural as if they were mother and daughter. His throat suddenly went dry. His business partner had a whole new side to her, a very appealing side.

Too appealing. Lorelei Hutchinson was beginning to be more than a business partner and a pretty face. She had him thinking about the things he'd always wanted in his life. In his daughter's life.

Cassie finally turned to him. "Daddy." She got up and rushed over to him. "You're home."

He hugged her, but his gaze was on Lori. "Yes, sorry I'm so late."

"It's okay," she said. "Miss Lori drove me home." His daughter gave him a bright smile. "She's helping me with my homework."

"I thought Mrs. Keenan was going to do that." He'd made the arrangements with her yesterday.

Lori stood. "Claire would have, but she got sick. I took over for her this afternoon in Cassie's classroom, and I offered to bring her home. I knew you would be busy at the site."

Jace tensed. "My daughter is a priority. I'm never too busy to be here for her. At the very least I should have been called." He glanced around for the teenager who he depended on. "Where's Heather?"

"She had a 'mergency at her house," Cassie told him.

He turned to the jean-clad Lori. She didn't look much older than the high school babysitter.

"We tried to call you but I got your voice mail," Lori said. "It wasn't a problem for me to stay with Cassie until you got home."

Jace felt the air go out of him, remembering he hadn't had his phone on him. He wasn't sure where it was at the site. He looked at Lori. "Thank you. I guess I got wrapped up in getting things back on target at the job site."

"It's okay, Daddy." His daughter looked up at him. "'Cause we made supper."

Great. All he needed was for this woman to get involved in his personal life. "You didn't need to do that."

Lori caught on pretty quickly that Jace didn't want her here. She'd gotten rejection before, so why had his bothered her so much?

"Look, it's just some potato soup and corn bread." She checked her watch. "Oh, my, it's late, I should go."

"No!" Cassie said. "You have to stay. You said you'd help me practice my part in the play." She turned back to her father. "Daddy, Miss Lori has to stay."

Lori hated to put Jace on the spot. Whatever the issues he had about women, she didn't want to know. She had enough to deal with. "It's okay, Cassie, we'll work on it another time."

"But Miss Lori, you wanted to show Daddy your new car, too."

Lori picked up her coat and was slipping it on when Jace came after her.

"Cassie's right, Lori. Please stay."

His husky voice stopped her, but those blue eyes convinced her to change her mind about leaving.

His voice lowered when he continued. "I was rude. I should thank you for spending time with my daughter." He smiled. "Please, stay for supper and let me make it up to you."

Lori glanced away, knowing this man was trouble. She wasn't his type. Men like Jace Yeager didn't give her much notice. *Keep it light.* "We're getting an early start on the Christmas pageant. How are you at playing the part of an angel?"

Cassie giggled.

He smiled, too. "Maybe I'd do better playing a devil."

She had no doubt. "I guess I could write in that part."

She knew coming here would be crossing the line. They worked together, but it needed to stay business. Instead she was in Jace Yeager's home. And even with all the unfinished projects he had going on, it already felt like a real home. It set off a different kind of yearning inside her. That elusive traditional family she'd always wanted. Something all the money from her inheritance couldn't buy her.

Two hours later, Jace finished up the supper dishes, recalling the laughter he heard from his daughter and their guest.

It let him know how much Cassie missed having another female around. A mother. He tensed. Shelly Yeager—soon-to-be Layfield—had never been the typical mother. She'd only cared about money and her social status and her daughter ranked a poor second. More than anything he wanted to give Cassie a home and a life where she'd grow up happy and well-adjusted. He could only do that if she was with him. He'd do whatever it took to keep it that way.

In the past, money, mostly his, had pacified Shelly. Now, she'd landed another prospective husband, a rich one. So she had even more power to keep turning the screws on him, threatening to take Cassie back.

He climbed the steps to his daughter's bedroom and found her already dressed in pajamas. Lori was sitting with her on the canopy bed reading her a story.

His chest tightened at the domestic scene. They looked so much alike they could be mother and daughter. He quickly shook away the thought and walked in.

"The end," Lori said as she closed the book and Cassie yawned.

"I see a very sleepy little girl."

"No, Daddy." She yawned again. "I want another story."

He shook his head and looked at Lori. "The rule is only one bedtime story on a school night." He checked his watch. "Besides, we've taken up enough of Lori's time tonight."

Cassie looked at her. "I'm sorry."

"No, don't be sorry, Cassie." She hugged the girl. "I enjoyed every minute. I told you I read to my nephew."

Cassie's eyes brightened. "Daddy, Lori's nephew, Zack, is coming here to live. He's going to be in my class."

"That'll be nice. How about we talk about it tomorrow? Now, you go to sleep."

Jace watched Lori and his daughter exchange another hug, then she got up and left the room. After he kissed his daughter, he turned off the light and headed downstairs. He found Lori putting on her coat and heading for the back door.

"Trying to make your escape?"

She turned around. "I'm sure you're tired, too."

He walked to her. "I think you might win that contest. Spending four hours with my daughter, not counting the time at school, had to be exhausting."

She smiled. "Remember, I'm a trained professional."

His gut tightened at the teasing glint in her incredible eyes. "And I know my daughter. She can try anyone's patience, but she's the love of my life."

He saw Lori's expression turn a little sad. "She's a lucky little girl." She turned away. "I should get home."

Something made him go after her. Before she could make it to the back door, he reached for her and turned her around. "I wish things could have been different for you, Lori. I'm sorry that you had to suffer as a child."

She shook her head. "It was a long time ago and I've dealt with it."

"Hey, you can't fool a foster kid. I was in the system most of my life. We're experts on rejection."

Her gaze went to his, those brown eyes compelling. "What happened to your family?"

"My parents were in a car accident when I was eight. What relatives I had didn't want me, so I went into foster care."

"Oh, Jace," she whispered.

Her little breathless gasp caused a different kind of reaction from him. Then he saw the tears in her eyes.

His chest tightened. "Hey, don't. I survived. Look at me. A success story."

Jace reached out and touched her cheek. The next thing he knew he pulled her toward him, then wrapped her in his arms. He silenced a groan as he felt her sweet body tucked against his. It had been so long since he'd held a woman. So long since he'd felt the warmth, the glorious softness.

He pulled back trying to put some space between them, but couldn't seem to let her go. His gaze went to her face; her dark eyes mirrored the same desire. He was in big trouble.

He lowered his head and whispered, "This is probably a really bad idea." His mouth brushed over hers, once, then again. Each time she made a little breathy sound that ripped at his gut until he couldn't resist any longer and he captured her tempting mouth.

She wrapped her arms around his neck and leaned into him as her fingers played with the hair at his nape. He pushed his tongue into her mouth and found heaven. She was the sweetest woman he'd ever tasted, and the last thing he ever wanted to do was stop. He wanted so much more, but also knew he couldn't have it.

He tore his mouth away and took a step back. "Damn, woman. You pack a punch. I just can't…"

"It's okay." She pulled her coat tighter. "It would be crazy to start something."

He couldn't believe how badly he wanted to. "Right. Bad idea. We're business partners. Besides, I have room for only one female in my life. Cassie."

Her gaze wouldn't meet his. "I should go."

"Let me walk you out."

"No, you don't need to do that. It's too cold."

He tried to make light of the situation. "Right now, I could use a blast of cold air." He followed her out. Grabbing his coat off the hook, he slipped it on as they went through the mudroom. The frigid air hit him hard as they hurried out to the well-lit driveway and around to her side of the car.

"Nice ride." He glanced over the four-wheel-drive SUV. "You're ready for the snow." He held on to the door so she couldn't rush off. "Are you coming by the site tomorrow?"

"No." She paused. "Unless you need me for something."

He found he wanted to see her again. "I guess not."

"Okay then, good night, Jace."

"Thank you, Lori. Thank you for being there for Cassie."

"You're welcome. Goodbye." She shut her door and started the engine and was backing out of the drive before Jace could stop her. That was the last thing he needed to do. He didn't need to be involved with this woman.

Any woman.

It would be a long time before he could trust again. But if he let her, Lori Hutchinson could come close to melting his cold, cold heart.

Lori had spent the past two days at the bank where she'd been trying to familiarize herself with her father's business dealings. How many people expected her to fail at this?

She'd stayed far away from Jace Yeager, although that didn't change the fact that she'd been thinking about him.

Had he been thinking about her? No. If he had been, wouldn't he have called? Or maybe he'd resisted, knowing getting involved could create more problems.

Lori looked up from the desk as Erin walked into

the office. The receptionist had been such a big help to her, going through files and being the liaison between Lori and Dennis Bradley's office.

Erin sat down in the chair across from the desk. "I found this in an old personnel file, and it's kind of interesting. Kaley Sims did used to work for Mr. Hutchinson. It states that she managed his properties up until two years ago."

Lori had found this woman's notes on several contracts. "Why isn't she working for him now?"

Erin gave her a funny look and glanced away.

"You know something?"

"It's just some bank gossip, but there might have been something between Kaley and Mr. Hutchinson, beyond professional."

So her father had someone after his divorce. "I take it they were discreet."

"They went to business and social functions together, but no one saw any signs of affection between them."

Lori shrugged. "Maybe that's the reason Kaley left here. She wanted more from Lyle."

"If you want to talk to her, I could call her mother and see if she's available to come back to work here."

Lori needed the help. "I guess it wouldn't hurt to call. I sure could use the help, especially someone who already knows the business. I don't want to put in twelve-hour days."

Had Lyle Hutchinson become that much of a recluse that all he did was work? She was curious. Had her father driven off Kaley?

"Okay, I'll make the call tomorrow," Erin said as she stood. "Is there anything more you need today?"

Lori checked her watch. It was after five o'clock. "I'm sorry. You need to get home."

"Normally I'd stay, but I have a date tonight."

Lori smiled, feeling a little twinge of envy, and immediately thought about Jace. Since the kiss she hadn't heard a word from him in two days. *Stop.* She couldn't let one kiss affect her. She wasn't a teenager. "Well, you're great, Erin. I'm grateful to have all your help." She paused. "How would you like to be my assistant?"

"Really?"

"Really. But you have to promise to stay in college. We can schedule hours around your classes, and you'll get a pay raise."

"Oh, wow. Thank you. I'd love to be your assistant." Erin reached out and shook her hand. "And everyone thought you coming to town would be a bad thing."

"Oh, they did, huh?"

This time, Erin hesitated. "I think they thought that a lot of jobs might be lost." The pretty brunette beamed. "Instead, you've come here and come up with ideas so people can save their homes, and you're helping women advance, too."

Lori was happy she could do something. "So it's a good thing?"

"Very good." The girl turned and left the office.

Lori sank back into her father's overstuffed leather chair. "Lyle Hutchinson, you must have really been some kind of tyrant. What made you so unhappy?"

She thought about the sizable amount of money Lyle had acquired over the years. When the waiting period was over next year, she'd never be able to spend it all. She could give the money away. Right now, she received a large income just from his properties.

Sadness hit her hard. Seeing how her father lived, she realized he'd died a lonely man. Outside his few male friends, he didn't go out with anyone. "I was always there, Dad. Just a call away. Your daughter. I would have loved to spend time with you."

It might be too late for a family with her father, but there was a second chance, because she had a sister and nephew. Gina and Zack would always be her family.

A few days had passed and Jace hadn't been able to get Lori, or the kiss, out of his head. Even working nonstop at the site couldn't keep his mind from wandering back to Lori Hutchinson. Until work came to a sudden halt when problems with the staircase came up and didn't meet code. They had to make some changes in the design.

He needed Lori's okay to move ahead with the architect's revisions. He went by the bank, but discovered she was at home. So that was where he was headed when he realized he was looking forward to seeing her. Glad for the excuse.

He pulled up out front, sat there a moment to pull it together. Then he jerked open the door and got out of his truck. The early November day was cold. He looked up at the gray sky, glad that they'd finished the outside of the building. At the very least they would get some rain.

He walked up to the porch, but slowed his steps at the door, feeling his heart rate accelerate.

He hadn't seen Lori since the night at his house. When she had been in his arms. He released a breath. Even time away didn't change the fact that he was eager to see her.

Maggie opened the door with her usual smile. "Mr. Yeager. It's nice to see you again."

He stepped inside. "Hi, Maggie. Is Lori here?" He held up his folder. "I have more papers for her to sign," he said, suddenly hearing the noises coming from upstairs.

"Oh, she's here." Maggie grinned. "Been working all day trying to get things finished before her sister and nephew's arrival tomorrow. Charlie's helping." There was a big thud and Maggie looked concerned. "But maybe you should have a look."

Jace nodded. He headed for the stairs and took them two at a time to shorten the trip. He walked down the hall and was surprised when he found the source of the noise. It was coming from the room across from Lori's childhood bedroom.

He looked in the slightly open door and found Charlie and Lori kneeling on the floor with sections of wood spread out. The two were engrossed in reading a sheet of directions.

Lori brushed back a strand of hair, revealing her pretty face. Then his heart went soaring and his body heated up as she reached for something and her jeans pulled taut over her cute, rounded bottom.

"It says right here that *A* goes into *B*. Okay we got that, but I can't find the next piece." She held up the sheet of paper. "Do you see this one?"

Hiding his amusement, Jace stepped into the room. "Could you two use some help?"

They both swung around. "Mr. Yeager," Charlie said and got to his feet. "Oh, yes, we could use your expertise. And since you're here to help, I'll go do my work." The older man left, looking relieved.

Jace turned back at Lori. "What are you building?"

"Bunk beds," she offered.

Jace pulled off his jacket as he glanced over the stacks of boxes. "Why not buy it assembled?"

Lori stood. "I didn't have time to go to Durango, so I got them online. I didn't realize it would come in boxes."

"You should have called me. I would have sent Mac over." He took the paper from her. Their hands brushed, and he quickly busied himself by looking over the directions. "Okay, let's lay out the rails and the end pieces."

Lori took one end and he took the other. He set the bolts, then went to her end. He was close and could breathe in her scent, which distracted the hell out of him. He finally got the bolt tightened. He got up and went to the other side, away from temptation, but she followed him.

Over the next hour, they'd become engrossed in building the elaborate bunk-bed set. They stood back and looked over their accomplishment.

"Not bad work." He glanced at the woman beside him and saw her blink. "What's wrong?"

She shook her head. "Zack is going to love it. He's had to share a room with his mother the past few months. Thank you for this."

"Not a problem," he told her. "You helped me out with Cassie. I know how much you want to make a home for your sister and your nephew."

"They've had a rough time of it lately." She put on a smile. "It's going to be great for them to be here."

Jace looked around the freshly painted blue room. "I thought you were going to put Zack in your old bedroom."

She shrugged. "I tried, but I couldn't bring myself

to touch it." She looked at him and he saw the pain in her eyes. "I guess I'm still trying to figure out why my father kept it the same all these years. Crazy, huh?"

Unable to help himself, he draped his arm across her shoulders. "It's okay, Lori. You have a lot to work through. You've pulled up your roots and come back here. There's a lot to deal with."

She looked up. "But I have the funds now to take care of my family."

That was the one thing that kind of bothered him. He'd been pretty well-off financially before his divorce, but to have a woman with so much money when he was trying to scrape by hit him in his pride. But he truly thought it bothered her more.

"So how does it feel to have that kind of money?"

She scrunched up her nose. "Oddly strange," she admitted. "It's far too much. I'm the kind of girl who's had to work all my life, and when I lost my job a few months ago, I was really worried about what was going to happen, especially for Gina and Zack."

"They have you now."

She looked up at him, her eyes bright and rich in color. "And I have them. I wouldn't stay here in Destiny, money or no money, if they couldn't be with me. Their safety and well-being is the most important thing to me."

He frowned. "Why wouldn't they be safe here?"

She glanced away. "It's just a worry I have."

He touched her chin to get her to look at him. "Lori, what aren't you telling me? Is someone threatening you or your family?"

She finally looked at him. "It's Gina's ex-husband. He'll be getting out of jail soon."

"Why did he go to jail?"

"Look, Jace, I'm not sure Gina wants anyone to know her private business."

"I'm not a gossip. If your family needs protection then I want to help."

Lori was surprised at his offer. She wasn't used to anyone helping them. "Eric is in for drug possession and spousal abuse. He swore when he got out he'd make Gina pay for having him arrested."

She felt Jace tense. "So that's why you were headed out of state?"

She nodded.

"Does this Eric guy know where Gina is moving to?"

"No one knows. We haven't even told Zack. I want so badly for Gina to make a life here. She has full custody of her son, but we're still afraid of what the man might do."

"This house has a security system. I hope you're using it."

She nodded.

"And I think you should have protection for yourself, also. You're worth a lot of money and you could be a target for threats from this guy. Maybe a security guard isn't out of the question."

"I can't let my life be dictated by a coward."

Jace clenched his fists. "I don't care for a creep who gets his jollies by beating women, either, but you still need to take precautions. Not an armed guard, but maybe a security man disguised as a gardener or handyman."

She hesitated. "If Gina will agree."

"What about you? I'm sure you've had some run-ins with your brother-in-law."

Lori shivered, recalling Eric's threats.

Jace's eyes narrowed. "Did he hurt you, too?"

"Just a few shoves here and there, but I couldn't let him hurt Gina."

He cursed and walked away, then came back to her. He reached out and cupped her face. "He put his hands on you, Lori. No man ever has the right to do that unless the woman wants it."

She stared into his eyes. That was the problem. She wanted Jace's hands on her. Badly.

CHAPTER SEVEN

JACE had trouble letting go of Lori. He knew the minute he touched her again this would happen.

He cursed under his breath. "This isn't a good idea." His gaze searched her pretty face, those bedroom eyes, then he stopped at her perfect rosy mouth. He suddenly felt like a man dying of thirst. Especially when her tongue darted out over her lips. With a groan, he leaned down and brushed his mouth across hers, hearing her quick intake of breath.

"I swore I'd stay away from you. We shouldn't start something…." His mouth brushed over hers again and then again. "My life doesn't need to get any more complicated."

"Mine, either," she whispered.

He fought the smile, but it didn't stop the hunger, or the anticipation of the kiss he so desperately wanted more than his next breath.

Then Lori took the decision out of his hands as she rose up on her toes and pressed her mouth against his. That was all it took. His arms circled her waist and he pulled her against him, unable to tolerate the space between them any longer. Their bodies meshed so easily it was as if they were meant to be together. All he knew was he didn't want to let her go anytime soon.

His mouth slanted over hers, wanting to taste her, but all too quickly they were getting carried away.

He tore his mouth from hers, and trailed kisses along her jaw to her ear. "I could get drunk on you." Then he let his tongue trace her earlobe, feeling her shiver. He found her mouth again for another hungry kiss.

Then suddenly the sound of his cell phone brought him back to reality. He stepped back, and his gaze was drawn to Lori's thoroughly kissed mouth. Desire shot through him and he had to turn away.

"Yeager," he growled into the phone.

"Hey, Jace," Toby said. "What happened? I thought you were coming right back."

He glanced over his shoulder at Lori. "Sorry, something came up. I'm heading back now." He shut his phone. "I'm needed at the site."

"Of course," Lori said, wrapping honey-blond strands behind her ear. "I can't thank you enough for your help. I couldn't have done this on my own."

Unable to resist, he went back to her and stole another kiss. They were both breathless by the time he released her. "Your sister and nephew arrive tomorrow, right?"

She nodded.

"Okay, I'll have a security guy in place here before you get back from the airport." When Lori started to disagree, he put his finger over those very inviting lips. "He'll work with Charlie so Gina doesn't have to know. I want you and your family safe."

Lori smiled. "I wasn't going to disagree. I think it's a good idea."

He blinked. "You're agreeing with me? That's a first."

"Don't get used to it, Yeager."

The next afternoon, Lori had agreed to let Charlie drive her father's town car the 47 miles to the Durango airport to pick up Gina and Zack.

She couldn't hide her excitement as she watched her sister and nephew come out of the terminal. She gave them a big hug, then herded them into the backseat of the car while Charlie stowed the few belongings in the trunk.

They talked all the way to Destiny. It was as if they'd been apart for months instead of only two weeks.

Lori kept hugging her seven-year-old nephew beside her in the backseat. She'd missed him. "Zack. I was able to work in the second grade classroom last week and met your teacher, Mrs. Miller. I think you're going to like her."

The little dark-haired child didn't look happy. "But I don't know any kids."

"The class knows you're coming. And there's Ellie and Cassie, who will help you learn your way around the school."

"Girls?"

That brought a smile as Lori looked at her sister. Although beautiful, with her rich, dark brown hair and wide green eyes, Regina Williams Lowell looked a little pale and far too thin. Lori hoped she could erase her sister's fear once she knew she was safe living in Destiny. And her son would blossom here, too.

"It might take a little time, Zack, but I know you'll make lots of friends."

They drove through town, past the square and fountain, then down the row of storefronts. "Just wait. Soon they'll be putting up a big Christmas tree with colorful lights. The whole town will be decorated."

"Can we have a Christmas tree at your house?"

Suddenly Lori got excited. This was going to be a special holiday. And a new year that meant a fresh beginning for all of them. "You bet we can. And you can pick out a really big one."

Zack grinned as they pulled through the gate. "Wow!" The boy's eyes lit up. "Mom, are we really going to live here?"

"We sure are." Gina looked like a kid herself. "Although, I can hardly believe it myself."

Lori glanced at her sister's face. "That was my first reaction, too. Welcome to Hutchinson House."

Charlie drove up the long drive and stopped in front of the house. He opened the back door and helped them out, then sent them up the porch steps.

Maggie swung open the front door and opened her arms. "Welcome, welcome," the older woman said as she swept them inside the warm house. First, the older woman embraced Zack, then Gina.

"We're so happy you're here. Oh, my, and to have a child in this big house again is wonderful."

"It's so big," Zack said. "What if I get lost?"

"Don't worry. Charlie will show you around. The important thing to remember is there are two sets of stairs. One leads down here." Maggie pointed to the circular staircase. "Most important, the other one leads to the kitchen and I'm usually there."

Zack looked a little more comfortable after the quick explanation.

Maggie turned to Gina and smiled. "Goodness, my, you look so much like Lorelei and your mother. Your coloring might be different, but there's no doubt you're sisters. And both beautiful."

Her sister seemed embarrassed. "Thank you."

"How was your flight?"

"Not too bad, especially sitting in first class." Gina glanced at Lori. "It was a big treat for Zack and me."

"Well, we're planning on a lot of treats for Master Zack." The older woman placed her hands on the boy's shoulders. "After you go and see your new bedroom, come down to the kitchen so you can tell me all your favorite foods. And if it's okay with your mother you can sample some of my cookies." Maggie raised a hand and glanced at Gina. "I promise not to spoil his appetite for our special dinner tonight."

"The way my son eats, I doubt anything can." Gina smiled, which made Lori hopeful that her sister would start relaxing.

"We're also having a couple of guests for dinner," Maggie announced. "Mr. Yeager and his daughter, Cassie. And before you frown, Zack, the girl has a horse. That's a good friend to have."

Lori was surprised by the news, and a little too happy, feeling a stir of excitement. Maybe he was bringing the security guard they'd talked about.

Maggie gave her the answer. "Jace has something to discuss with you. So I invited them both to dinner."

Her nephew called to her. "Can I go see my new bedroom, Aunt Lori?"

"Sure. How about we all head up and see it?"

The child ran ahead of them, following Charlie up the steps with the bags.

Lori hung back with Gina. "Lori, you never said the place was a—" she looked around the huge entry, her eyes wide "—mansion."

"Okay, so the Hutchinson family liked things on the large size. Now that you and Zack are here, it's already starting to feel more like a home." She hugged her sister again. "I want you and Zack to think of this place as home. More important, I want you to feel safe here."

Gina looked a little panicked. "Just so long as Eric never finds us."

Another precaution had been for Gina to take back her maiden name, Williams.

"If he shows up in Destiny, you can believe he'll be arrested." Jace had convinced her to let Sheriff Reed Larkin in on the situation.

"Does everyone in town know?"

Lori shook her head. "No, only the people who work here at the house. And Jace Yeager, my business partner. He suggested that I hire some security." Lori raised a hand. "Only just as a precaution."

"That has to cost a lot of money."

Lori smiled. "Look at this place, Gina. Lyle Hutchinson might have been a lousy father, but he knew how to make money. And taking care of you and Zack is worth whatever it costs."

Tears filled her sister's eyes. "Thank you."

Before Lori started crying, too, she said, "Come on, I hope you like your bedroom. It's got a connecting bath with Zack's room."

They started up the steps arm in arm. "I can't imagine I wouldn't love it."

"If you don't like it, you can redo it. You're the one

with experience. In fact, I'd be happy if you would redo the entire place."

Gina turned to Lori. "Decorating a boutique window doesn't make me a professional." She looked around. "It's so grand as it is."

Lori knew what her sister had been thinking. There had been a lot of times when their living quarters hadn't been that great, especially when Gina was married. Being a school dropout, Eric hadn't been able to do much, and he spent his paycheck on alcohol instead of diapers.

"This is our fresh start, Gina. You don't have to worry about Eric anymore. I'm not going to let anything happen to either you or Zack."

Lori prayed that was a promise she could keep.

Three hours later, Jace walked up the steps to the Hutchinson home, carrying a bottle of wine and flowers. He normally didn't take Cassie out on a school night, but this was a special occasion and he knew how it was to be the new kid in town.

Okay, the truth was he wanted to see Lori. He'd tried to keep focused on work, but she was messing with his head. Last night he couldn't sleep, recalling their kisses, but he knew from now on that he had to keep his hands to himself. If Shelly got wind of any of this, she would make his life miserable just for the hell of it.

He had to focus on Cassie and getting the project completed on time. That was all. Once he had custody settled, he could think about a life for himself.

The front door opened and a little boy stuck his head out. "Hi," he said shyly.

His daughter answered back. "Hi. You're Zack. I'm Cassie Yeager. You're going to be in my class at school."

The boy looked up at Jace as if asking for help. His daughter never had a problem with being shy.

"I'm Jace. I think your aunt is expecting us."

Zack nodded. "You want to come in?"

"Sounds good. It's a little cold out here."

The door opened wider as another woman appeared. She smiled, showing off the resemblance to Lori.

"Hello, you must be Gina. I'm Jace Yeager. I'm Lori's business partner."

She took his hand. "It's nice to meet you."

"This is my daughter, Cassie."

His daughter beamed as she came up to Gina. "Hi, Miss Gina. My dad brought you flowers and for Miss Lori, wine. And I bought Zack a school sweatshirt." She held up the burgundy-colored shirt with Destiny Elementary School printed on it.

"Hello, Cassie. That's very nice."

Cassie turned to Zack. "My dad said you have a new bedroom."

"Yeah, it's cool."

"Can I see it?"

Zack looked at his mother for permission. With Gina's nod the two seven-year-olds took off upstairs.

"My son's a little shy," Gina admitted.

"Well, that won't last long if Cassie has anything to say about it."

He finally got a smile out of the pretty dark-haired woman with green eyes. There was definitely a strong resemblance between the two sisters, except for their coloring. Both women were lovely.

"Here, these are for you. Welcome to Destiny."

He watched her blush as she took the bouquet. "Thank you."

"It's rough having to pick up and move everything. I had to do it about six months ago, but it was worth it. Destiny is a wonderful place to raise kids. Cassie loves it here."

"I'm glad." Gina hesitated. "Lori said she told you about my…situation."

He watched her hesitation, maybe more embarrassment. "I assure you, Gina, no one else will know about your past. It's no one's business. Your sister only wants you safe. I agreed to help her take some precautions."

"I appreciate it, really. I'm sure Eric wouldn't think to look for us here. He knows nothing about Lori's father." She sighed. "But I wouldn't put anything past him. So I thank you for the extra security."

Jace was about to speak when Lori came down the steps. She was wearing a black turtleneck sweater and gray slacks. He was caught up in her grace as she descended the winding stairs. She smiled at him, and his insides went all haywire.

Lori felt Jace's gaze on her and it made her nervous, also a little warm. She'd missed seeing him. The last time had only been a little over twenty-four hours ago when he'd helped her with the bed, and they almost fell into it. A warm shiver moved up her spine. How did he feel about it?

She walked across the tiled floor, seeing her sister holding flowers. That was so nice of him. "Hi, Jace."

"Lori."

She went to him. "Sorry, I wasn't here when you arrived. I just saw Cassie upstairs."

"Has she reorganized Zack's bedroom yet?"

Lori couldn't help but laugh. "I think he's safe for the moment."

Gina spoke up. "Excuse me. I'll go put these in water, then go up and have the kids wash up for dinner." She turned and walked to the kitchen.

Jace looked at Lori. "I don't want to barge in on your family dinner."

"You're not at all. You're always welcome here," she told him, knowing that was probably admitting too much. "Maggie loves to have company. She hasn't been able to cook this much in a long time."

"Anytime she wants company tell her I'll be here." He held up the bottle. "I brought wine."

Lori smiled. "Why don't we open it?"

"Lead the way," he said and they started toward the dining room. Lori watched as he stared at the dark burgundy wallpaper, dark-stained wainscoting and long, long table with the upholstered chairs, also dark.

"It's pretty bad. This room is like a mausoleum. It's going to be my first redecorating project. In fact, I'll put Gina in charge. I hope you don't mind eating in the kitchen."

"I prefer the kitchen." He glanced down at his jeans and sweater pulled over a collared shirt. He followed Lori to the sideboard. In actuality, he preferred her over it all, but he tried to stay focused on the conversation. "As you can see, I'm not dressed for anything fancy."

Lori thought he was dressed perfectly. The man would look good in…nothing. Oh, no. *Don't think about that.* She busied herself by opening a drawer and searching for a corkscrew. Once she found it, she handed it to him, then crossed to the glass-front hutch and took out two crystal wineglasses.

"Gina won't drink, so we'll have to toast my sister and nephew's arrival on our own."

"I think I can handle that." He managed to uncork the bottle and when she brought over the glasses, he filled them with the rosy liquid.

He held out the stemmed glass to her. She brushed his hand and tried to remain calm. It was only a drink, she told herself.

Jace picked up his. "To yours, Gina's and Zack's new home," he said.

Lori took a slow sip, allowing herself to enjoy the sweet taste. She took another, and soon the alcohol went to her head, making her feel a little more relaxed. Then her eyes connected with Jace, and suddenly her heart was racing once again.

"This tastes nice," she said, unable to get her mouth to work. "I mean, I'm not much of a drinker, but I like this."

His deep sapphire gaze never left hers as he set his glass down on the sideboard. "Let me see." Then he leaned forward and touched his mouth to hers.

She froze, unable to do anything but feel as his firm mouth caressed her lips, coaxing her to open for him with a stroke of his tongue.

She whimpered as her hand rested against his chest, feeling his pounding heart. She only ached for more.

He pulled back a little. "You're right. Sweet." He took her glass from her and set it down beside his. "But I need another taste to be sure."

He bent down and took her mouth again. She went willingly as her arms circled his neck, and she wanted to close out the rest of the world. Just the two of them. She refused to think about how stupid it was to let this happen with Jace. When his tongue stroked against hers, and he drew her against his body, she lost all common sense.

Then it quickly returned when the sound of footsteps overhead alerted them to the fact that the kids were coming.

He broke off, and pressed his head against hers. "Damn, Lorelei Hutchinson, if you don't make me forget my own name."

She could only manage a nod. Then he leaned forward again. "Not that you don't look beautiful thoroughly kissed, but you might have to answer too many questions."

She smoothed her hair. "Tell everyone I'll be in shortly." She took off, knowing she was a fool when it came to this man. It had to stop before someone got hurt.

Jace had trouble concentrating on his pot roast dinner. Why couldn't he keep his hands off Lori? She wasn't even his type. Not that he had a type. He'd sworn off women for the time being. So why had he been trying to play tonsil hockey with her just thirty minutes ago?

"Daddy?"

He turned to his daughter. "What, Cassie?"

"Can Zack go riding with me tomorrow?"

Jace glanced at Gina and saw her concerned look. "Maybe it's a little cold right now, sweetheart. Let Zack and his mother get settled in first. Besides, you both have school all day."

Those pretty blue eyes blinked up at him. "I know, Daddy," she said. "I'm gonna help Zack get used to the class."

Jace fought a smile and stole a glance at Lori, then at the poor boy who'd become his daughter's newest project. "I'm sure Zack appreciates all your help, sweetheart, but remember, Miss Lori is a teacher. She can help, too."

The child looked deflated. "Oh."

"I can sure use your help," Lori said. "And we're all going to be working on the Christmas play together. I'm sure Zack would like to do that."

"I guess," he said. "Are there other boys in the play?"

Cassie nodded. "Everyone is in the play. Cody Peters and Owen Hansen and Willie Burns." She smiled. "And now, you."

Jace wasn't sure he liked how his daughter was smiling at Zack. *Oh, no, not her first crush.*

Maggie came in with dessert and after everyone enjoyed the chocolate cake, the kids were excused and went up to Zack's bedroom.

"Seems like they've become fast friends," Gina said. "I thank you, Jace. Your daughter is helping my son a lot." She glanced at her sister. "I hated that Zack had to go through all the pain of the last few years."

"You need to put that in the past. This is a new start."

Lori reached over and covered her sister's hand. "It's a new beginning, Gina. We're going to keep you safe."

"Lori's right," Jace told her. "The security guard is on duty as we speak. Wyatt McCray will be touring the grounds during the night. He's moved into the room behind the garage. His cover will be he's working with Charlie. No one is going to hurt you or your son again."

Tears formed in Gina's eyes. "Thank you."

Lori spoke up. "Has Eric been released yet?"

"Detective Rogers said he is scheduled to get out this Friday."

"Good." Jace nodded. "You and Zack were gone before he had a chance to know what your plans were. The fewer people who know the better. So we three, Maggie, Charlie, Wyatt and Sheriff Larkin are the only people who know about your situation. You're divorced, and your past life is private."

"I'm grateful, Jace. Thank you." Gina stood. "I think I'll go check on the kids."

Lori watched her sister leave. "She's still scared to death."

"I know," Jace said, hating that he couldn't do more. "And I almost wish the creep would show up here so I could get my hands on him."

"No, I don't want that man anywhere near them ever again. Zack still has nightmares." She put on a smile. "Thank you for all your help."

His gaze held hers for longer than necessary. "Hey, we're partners."

Problem was, he wanted to be so much more.

CHAPTER EIGHT

BY THE end of the week Gina and Zack had settled in and were getting into a routine. Her nephew had started school and was making new friends. Of course, Cassie was still taking charge of Zack's social schedule.

Life was great, Lori thought, as she arrived at the bank that cold, gray November morning. Thank goodness her car had seat warmers to ward off the near-freezing temperatures. She thought about the upcoming holidays and couldn't help but smile. Her family would all be together.

She also thought of Jace. She wanted to invite him and Cassie to Thanksgiving at the house. Would he come? The memory of the kisses they'd shared caused a shiver down her spine. She was crazy to think about a future with the man, especially when he'd been telling her all along he didn't want to get involved.

As she entered her office, she decided not to go to the construction site unless absolutely necessary. Besides, she had plenty to do at the bank to keep her busy for a long time. She looked down at the several stacks of files and paperwork covering the desktop. The last thing she wanted to do was spend all her time managing the number of properties, and the rest of the time at the bank. If only she could hire someone to oversee it all. And she didn't trust the "three amigos" loan officers to handle things on their own. They'd already thought she was in over her head. Maybe she was, but she wasn't going to let them see it.

She'd been working nearly two hours when there was a knock on the door. "Come in," Lori called.

Erin walked in. She wore a simple black A-line skirt and a pin-striped red-and-white blouse. She was carrying a coffee mug and a white paper sack. "Break time?"

"Thank you, I could use it. Everything is getting a little blurry."

"You should have more than coffee. Helen sent over some scones from the Silver Spoon. A thank-you for putting a six-month moratorium on foreclosures."

Lori thought of her own childhood after her mother remarried. They'd had some rough times over the years. "I refuse to let this bank play Scrooge especially with Christmas coming soon. The first thing on the agenda for the first of next year is reworking these loans."

Erin smiled. "You know, the other bank officers aren't happy with your decision."

Lori took a sip of her drink. "Yes. Mr. Neal has already decided to retire." She thought about the generous retirement package her father had given him. He wouldn't be giving up his lifestyle.

"Oh, I almost forgot," Erin said. "I located Kaley Sims. She's working for a management company in Durango. I have the phone number."

"Good. Would you put in a call to her and see if she's willing to talk with me?"

"Of course. Anything else?"

Erin was so efficient at her job, Lori wasn't sure what she would have done without her.

"There is one thing. In looking over my father's properties, I found a place called—" she searched through the list "—Hidden Hills Lodge. I'm not sure if it's a rental property, or what. It doesn't show any reported income."

"Maybe it was a place Mr. Hutchinson had for his personal use. Do you want me to find out more about it?"

Lori shook her head. "No, you have more than enough to do now." Maybe she would look into this herself. She had a great GPS in her new car. Surely she could find her way. She stood. "I'm going to be gone the rest of the afternoon. If you need me, call me on my cell phone."

Maybe it was time she delved a little further into her father's past and the opportunity was right in front of her.

Later that afternoon, Jace got out of his truck as snow flurries floated in the air, clinging to his coat and hat. He took a breath as he walked to the bank. Okay, he'd been avoiding going anywhere he might see Lori Hutchinson. He couldn't seem to keep his hands off the woman, but since he needed her signature on some changes in the project, he didn't have a choice.

He walked through the doors and Erin greeted him. "Is Miss Hutchinson in?"

"No, she's not. She left about noon."

"She go home?"

"No, I've tried to reach her there. I also tried her cell

phone, but it goes to voice mail." Erin frowned. "I'm worried about her, especially with this weather."

Suddenly Jace was concerned, too. "And she didn't say where she was going? A property? Out to the site?"

"That's what I'm worried about. I think she might have gone to the Hidden Hills Lodge."

"Where is this place?"

Erin sat down at her desk and printed out directions from the computer. Jace looked them over. He wasn't sure about this area, only that it was pretty rural.

He wrote down his number and handed it to Erin. "Give me a call if Lori gets in touch with you."

He left as he pulled out his cell phone and gave Claire Keenan a call, asking if she'd watch Cassie a little later, then he hung up and glanced up at the sky. An odd feeling came over him, and not a good one. "Where are you, Lori?"

An hour later, Lori had turned off the highway to a private road, just as her GPS had instructed her to do. She shifted her car into four-wheel drive and began to move slowly along the narrowing path.

It wasn't long before she realized coming today wasn't a good idea. Deciding to go back, she shifted her SUV into Reverse and pushed on the gas pedal, and all that happened was the tires began to spin.

"Great. Please, I don't need this." She glanced out her windshield as her wipers pushed away the blowing snow, which didn't look like it was going to stop anytime soon.

She took out her cell phone. No signal. The one thing that was working was her GPS and it showed her destination was a quarter mile up the road. What should she do? Stay in the car, or walk to Hidden Hills Lodge?

She buttoned her coat, wrapped her scarf around her neck and grabbed a flashlight. She turned on her emergency blinkers and climbed out as the blowing snow hit her. She started her trek up the dirt road and her fear rose. What if she got lost and froze to death? Her thoughts turned to Gina and Zack. And Jace. She cared more about the man than she even wanted to admit. And she wanted to see him again. She quickened her pace, keeping to the center of the dirt road.

Ten minutes later, cold and tired, she finally saw the structure through the blowing snow. It was almost like a mirage in the middle of the trees. She hurried up the steps to the porch and tried the door. Locked.

"Key, where are you?" she murmured, hating to break a window. It took a few minutes, but she found a metal box behind the log bench. After unlocking the dead bolt with nearly frozen fingers, she hurried into the dark structure and closed the door. She reached for the switch on the wall and light illuminated the huge main room. With a gasp, she glanced around. The walls were made out of rough logs and the open-beam ceiling showed off the loft area overhead. Below the upstairs were two doorways leading to bedrooms. The floors were high-gloss pine with large area rugs and overstuffed furniture was arranged in front of a massive fireplace. She found a thermostat on the wall and flipped it, immediately hearing the heater come on.

Shivering, Lori walked to the fireplace and added some logs. With the aid of the gas starter, flames shot over the wood. She sat on the hearth, feeling warmth begin to seep through her chilled body.

Once warmed, she got up and looked around. The kitchen was tucked in the back side of the structure, revealing granite counters and dark cabinets.

She checked out the two bedrooms and a bath on the main floor. Then she climbed up to the loft and found another bedroom. One of the walls was all windows with a view of the forest. She walked into the connecting bathroom. This one had a soaker tub and a huge walk-in shower.

"I guess if you have to be stranded in a snowstorm, a mountain retreat isn't a bad place to be." At least she'd stay warm until someone found her. When? Next spring?

She came back downstairs trying to think of a plan to get her back to town, when a sudden noise drew her attention. She froze as the door opened and Jace Yeager walked in.

"Jace!" she cried and leaped into his arms.

He held her close and whispered, "I take it you're happy to see me."

Jace didn't want to let Lori go. Thank God, she was safe. When he found her deserted car, he wasn't sure if she would find cover.

He pulled back. "Are you crazy, woman? Why did you go out in this weather?"

She blinked back the obvious tears in her eyes. "It wasn't this bad when I started out. Besides, I didn't think it was that far. I tried to go back when the weather turned, but my car got stuck. How did you know where I went?"

"I stopped by the bank. Erin was worried because she couldn't get ahold of you."

"No cell service."

Jace pulled out his phone and examined it. "I have a few bars." He walked toward the front door, where the signal seemed to be a little stronger. "I'll call the Keenans." He punched in the number and prayed he could get a message out. Tim answered.

"Tim. It's Jace." He went on to explain what had happened and that Lori was with him. Most importantly they were safe. He asked Tim to keep Cassie, then to call Lori's sister and let her know they wouldn't be back tonight. "Tell Cassie I love her and not to worry."

He flipped the phone closed and looked around the large room, then he turned back to Lori. "Tim will call Gina and let her know you're okay."

Lori's eyes widened. "We're not going back now?"

He shook his head. "Can't risk it. The storm is too bad so we're safer staying put." That was only partly true. He glanced around, knowing being alone with Lori wasn't safe anywhere. "I'd say this isn't a bad place to be stranded in." He looked at her. "This is one of your properties?"

She nodded. "I think my father came here…to get away."

Jace grinned. "So this was Lyle's secret hideaway?"

Lori frowned. "Please, I don't want that picture in my mind."

Jace looked around at the structure. "Well, whatever he used it for, it's well built. And it seems to have all the modern conveniences."

He went on a search, and found two bedrooms, then a utility room off the kitchen. There was a large generator and tankless water system. "Bingo," he called to Lori. "All the conveniences of home. In fact, it's better than back home." He nodded to the fire. "Propane gas for the kitchen stove and most importantly there's heat."

Lori looked at him. "You really think my father used this place for his own personal use?"

Jace shrugged. "Or he let clients use it. Come on, Lori, did you think your father lived like a monk?"

She shrugged. "Truthfully, I hadn't thought much about my father's personal business in a long time. So what if he came here." She walked to the kitchen. "Maybe we should look for something to eat." Opening the cabinets, she found some canned goods, soup, beans and tuna.

Jace opened the refrigerator. Empty, but the freezer was filled with different cuts of meat, steaks, chicken. "I'll say one thing about Lyle. He believed in being prepared." He pulled out two steaks. "Hungry?"

She arched an eyebrow. "Are you cooking?"

"Hey, I can cook." He took the meat from the package, put it on a plate and into the microwave to defrost. "I've been on my own for a long time."

Lori had wondered about his childhood since he'd mentioned that he'd been in foster care. "How old were you?"

"At eighteen they release you. So you're on your own," he told her as he found a can of green beans in another cabinet. "I got a job working construction and signed up for college classes."

Jace didn't have it much better than she did, Lori thought. "That had to be hard for you."

"Not too bad," Jace said. "I found out later, I had a small inheritance from my parents. It was in trust until I turned twenty-five." He turned on the broiler in the oven then washed his hands. "I used it to start my company. Yeager Construction."

Lori found she liked listening to Jace talk. He was a confident man, in his words and movements. Okay, so she more than liked him.

The microwave dinged and he took out the meat. "How about a little seasoning for your steak?" He held up a small jar.

"Sure."

He added the rub to the meat. She watched as he worked efficiently to prepare the meal. She couldn't help but wonder about how those broad hands and tapered fingers would feel against her skin.

She suddenly heard her name and looked at him. "What?"

He gave her an odd look. "How do you like your steak?"

"Any way you fix it is fine," she said, not really caring at all. Then he smiled and she couldn't find enough air to draw into her lungs.

He winked. "Medium rare it is," he said and slid the tray into the broiler.

Pull it together, girl, she told herself then went to the cupboard. She got out two plates and some flatware from the drawer, then set the table by the fire. No need for candles. She glanced around the room. It looked so intimate.

She went and found a can of pineapple and opened it, then heated the green beans just as the steaks came off the broiler.

Jace added another log to the fire, then they sat down to dinner. "Man, this looks good. Too bad we can't do a salad and some garlic bread."

"I find it amazing that there's so much food here."

"Your father struck me as well prepared. Hold on a minute." He got up, went into the utility room and came out with a bottle of wine. "In every way."

He opened the bottle and poured two glasses. He took them to the table, sat in his chair and began to cut his steak. "If he used this place, he wanted all the comforts money could buy," Jace said, nodding to the wine.

"I'm wondering who he shared all this with."

Jace took a drink. "You might never know. One thing for sure, Lyle had good taste."

She took a sip from her glass, too, and had to agree. Then she began to eat, discovering she was hungry. "I guess I'm still the daughter who wonders why he was such a loner, not even finding time for his only child."

"We can spend hours on that subject." Jace continued to eat. "Some people aren't cut out for the job of parenting."

She hated that her father's rejection still bothered her after all these years. She wanted to think she'd moved on. Maybe not.

She turned her attention back to the conversation. "Shelly hated anything to do with being a mother," Jace said. "That's why I can't let her have Cassie."

"Does Cassie want to live with her mother?"

"Cassie wants to be *loved* by her mother, but my ex is too selfish. She's been jealous of her daughter since her birth. And I'll do anything to prevent Cassie from taking a backseat to that. I know how it feels."

"Cassie's lucky she has you."

He smiled. "It's easy to love that little girl. I know I spoil her, but she's been so happy since she moved here. I have to make it permanent."

Lori put on a smile. "You're a good father, Jace Yeager." She placed her hand on his arm. "I'll help you in any way I can."

He stopped eating. "What do you mean? Help. I can afford to handle this custody battle on my own."

She shook her head. "I know that. I only meant that I know what it's like to not have a father in my life. I was offering moral support, nothing else. But don't be too bullheaded to take any and everything you can to keep your daughter. She needs you in her life, more than you know." Lori stood and carried her plate to the sink. Her appetite was gone.

He came to her. "I'm sorry, Lori."

She could feel his heat behind her. Good Lord, the man made his presence known. She wanted desperately to lean back into him. "For years Lyle Hutchinson never even acknowledged that I existed. I can't tell you how much that hurt."

She hated feeling needy. When Jace turned her around and touched her cheek, she couldn't deny she wanted his comfort.

"I can't imagine doing that to my child. I don't want to think about Cassie not being in my life. I know from experience that adults do dumb things, and in the end it's the kids that get hurt the most."

Lori felt a tear drop and he wiped it away. "It's not fair."

Jace leaned forward. "I wish I could change it." He brushed his mouth across hers. "I wish I could make you feel better."

She released a shaky breath. "What you're doing is nice."

His blue-eyed gaze searched her face. "Damn, Lori.

What I'm thinking about doing with you isn't nice."
Then he pulled her close and captured her mouth. Desire
burst within her, if possible more intense than ever before, pooling deep in her center. She could feel his heat
even through their clothes as she arched into his body.
She whimpered her need as his tongue danced against
hers.

"You make me want so many things," he breathed
as his tongue tormented her skin. He found his way to
her collarbone. "I want you, Lorelei Hutchinson." His
mouth closed over hers once again, giving her a hint of
the pleasure this man offered her.

She arched against him, her fingers threading
through his hair, holding him close. Mouths slanted,
their tongues mated as his hands moved over her back
and down to her bottom, pulling her closer to feel his
desire.

Jace was on the edge. On hearing her soft moan, he
drew back with his last ounce of sanity. Then he made
the mistake of looking into her eyes and all good inten-
tions flew out the window. "Tell me to stop now, Lori."

She swallowed. "I can't, Jace. I don't want you to
stop."

His heart skipped a beat as he swung her up into his
arms. With a quick glance around, he headed to one of
the rooms under the loft, only caring there was a bed
past the door.

The daylight was fading, but there was enough light
from the main room. He set her down next to a four-
poster bed. He captured her mouth in a long kiss, then
reached behind her and threw back the thick comforter.

He returned to her. "I've dreamed of being with you

like this." He drew her into his arms. "So be sure you want the same."

She nodded.

He let out a frustrated breath. "You have to do better than that, Lori."

"I'm very sure, Jace."

Those big brown eyes looked up at him. He inhaled her soft scent and was lost, so lost that he couldn't think about anything except sharing this intimacy with this special woman.

His mouth descended to hers and the rest of the snowstorm and the world disappeared. There was only the two of them caught up in their own storm.

CHAPTER NINE

SOMETIME around dawn, Jace woke suddenly, aware he wasn't alone in bed. And it wasn't his bed. He blinked and raised his head from the pillow to find Lori beside him. He bit back a groan as images of last night came flooding into his mind.

He'd come looking for her, afraid she'd been stranded in the freak storm. He found her all right, and had given in to temptation. They'd made love last night. Right now her sweet body pressed against his had him aching again.

He lay his head back on the pillow. Why did she have to come into his life now? He didn't have anything to offer her. Not a future anyway. He couldn't let anyone distract him from getting custody of Cassie.

Lori stirred, then rolled over and peered at him through the dim light. Her soft yellow hair was mussed, but definitely added to her sex appeal.

"Hi," she said in a husky voice that had him thinking about forgetting everything and getting lost in her once again.

"Hi, yourself."

She pulled the sheet up to cover her breasts. "I guess

this is what they call the awkward morning-after moment."

He knew Lori well enough to know that she wasn't the type to jump into bed with just any man. That wasn't the type he needed right now. "The last thing I want to do is make you feel uncomfortable," he said, and leaned toward her. "It's just us, Lori."

She glanced away shyly. "I haven't had a relationship since college."

He found that made him happy. "That's hard to believe." He touched her face. "You're a very beautiful woman, Lorelei Hutchinson."

"Thank you." She glanced away. "I didn't have time for a personal life. Gina and Zack needed me."

"I take it Gina's ex has caused her and you a lot of trouble."

She nodded. "Sober Eric had a mean streak, but when drunk he was really scary. Even with his obvious abuse, it took a lot to convince Gina that the man would never change. Then one day he went after Zack and she finally realized how dangerous he was. That's what it took for her to go to court and testify against him. After that Eric threatened to come after her." Lori's large eyes met his. "That's why it was so hard for me to come to Destiny. When my father made the stipulation in the will about staying a year, I wasn't sure if I could."

"I'm glad you did," he told her, unable to stop touching her. His hand moved over her bare arm, her skin so soft.

She looked surprised. "Is that because I rescued your project?"

"No, it's because you're beautiful and generous." He decided not to fight whatever was going on between them any longer. He leaned down and brushed his mouth over hers, enjoying that she eagerly opened for him. He drew back and added, "You've also taken time with Cassie. Before we moved here she didn't have much female attention."

Lori wasn't sure what she'd expected this morning, but not this. "It's easy to be nice to her. Cassie's a sweet girl."

"Hey, what about me?"

She wrinkled her nose. "I wouldn't call you sweet. Not your disposition anyway."

"Maybe I can change your mind." He caressed her mouth again. "Is that any better?"

"Fishing for a compliment?"

He shifted against her. "How about we continue this without conversation?"

Though Lori wanted the same thing, they needed to get home. "Shouldn't we think about heading back?"

"It's barely dawn." He started working his magic as his mouth moved upward along her jawline. "What's your hurry?" His tongue circled her ear. "Are you trying to get rid of me?"

She gasped, unable to fight the sensation. "No, it's just that it's…" She forgot what she wanted to say as his lips continued along her neck. "Don't we need to leave?"

He raised his head and she could see the desire in his eyes. "I want to do one thing right and it only involves the two of us." He arched an eyebrow. "But if you'd rather go out in that cold weather and start digging out, I'll do it. Your choice."

Lori knew what she wanted, all right. This man. But the fear was that she could never really have him. Last night and these few early hours might be all she would ever have. She wrapped her arms around his neck and pulled his mouth down to hers. "I choose you."

Two hours later, Jace stood at the railing on the cabin porch, drinking coffee. The sun was bright, reflecting off the ten inches of snow covering the ground. The highways would be plowed by now, but not the private road that led to the cabin. He had four-wheel drive on his truck, so they could probably get out and make it to the main road. It better be sooner than later before he got in any deeper.

He had no regrets being with Lori. Making love with her had been incredible. He'd never felt anything like it in his life. Even the best times during his marriage hadn't come close to what he'd shared with Lori.

In just the past three weeks, he'd come to care about this woman more than he had any business doing. But he had strong feelings for Lori and that scared the hell out of him.

Worse, there was no guarantee and he couldn't even offer her a future. He had no extra money. Hell, he needed to rebuild his business. He had to get things settled with the custody issue before he could have a personal life. The question was, would he be able to walk away from Lori? Did he want to?

The front door opened and she stepped out. "I wondered where you went."

"Sorry." He pulled up the collar on her coat and kissed her. "I was just figuring out if we can make it back to town."

"I wouldn't mind getting stuck here a few more days," she admitted. "It's beautiful."

He wouldn't mind pushing reality away for a little

time with this woman. "That would be nice, but we both have jobs to do. Family to take care of."

"Oh, gosh. Gina. I bet she's going crazy with worry."

"Tim called her last night."

"She'll still worry, and be afraid."

Jace wondered who worried about Lori. Seemed she took care of everyone else. "Gina and Zack have Wyatt McCray, Lori. He'll protect them."

"I know," she said with a smile.

His heart began pounding in his chest. The effect she had on him could be a big distraction.

"Thank you for giving us that peace of mind. You've been so kind."

He wondered if she'd always think that. "I didn't do that much."

Those dark eyes locked with his. "You seem to be there whenever I need you."

He found he might not mind being that man. He leaned down to kiss her when he heard something and looked toward the road. "Looks like we're getting rescued."

Jace pointed to a large truck with a plow attached to the front. It stopped a few yards from the door and Toby and Joe climbed out.

Smiling brightly, his foreman called, "I hear someone here might need a ride back to town."

"Toby," Lori cried and hurried down the steps Jace had cleared earlier.

He watched as she ran through the snow to get to Toby. She hugged the big foreman. Jace felt a stab of jealousy stir inside him, but he didn't have any right to claim her. Not yet, maybe never.

* * *

After stopping to get Jace's truck, the ride back to town took about thirty minutes. He followed behind the plow truck until they reached the highway. After Lori gave Toby her car keys, she got into Jace's truck and drove to the Keenan Inn.

She knew she should probably go straight to the house but asked Toby to tow her car to the inn. Besides, she wasn't ready to leave Jace yet.

When they got to the porch, the door opened and they were immediately greeted by Claire and Tim.

"Well, you had yourself quite an adventure," Tim said.

Lori felt a blush rising up her neck as they crossed the threshold. "I guess I should pay better attention to the weather forecast before heading out into the countryside. I did discover my father has a lovely cabin. Thank goodness there was heat."

"Where's Cassie?" Jace asked, looking around.

Claire looked worried. "She's in the kitchen. She's with one of our new guests."

Lori caught Jace's frown. Then he took off and Lori followed him through the dining area and into the large kitchen.

She found Cassie at the counter with a tall, statuesque woman. Her hair was a glossy black in a blunt shoulder-length cut. Her face was flawless, her eyes an azure-blue. She was a beautiful woman until she flashed a hard look at Jace.

The child ran to him. "Daddy. Daddy, you're back."

"Yes, baby." He hugged his daughter. "I told you we got stuck in the snow."

Cassie looked at Lori. "Miss Lori, did you get stuck, too?"

"Yes, your daddy found me."

The child turned back to her father and whispered, "Daddy, don't let Mommy take me away."

Shelly Yeager stood and walked toward them. "Hello, Jace." She gave Lori a once-over. "It's nice to see that you could make it back to take care of our daughter."

"Shelly. What are you doing here?"

"I came to take my little girl home, of course."

An hour later, Lori's car had arrived and she got in and drove home to find a relieved Gina. She'd taken a long shower and gotten dressed in clean clothes, but couldn't push aside the memories from last night. The incredible night she'd shared with Jace, then reality hit them in the face with Shelly Yeager.

She couldn't stop thinking about Cassie and what her mother had said. Was she going to take the child back to Denver? No, Jace couldn't lose his daughter. She wished she could help him, like he'd helped her.

Lori came downstairs to find her sister in the dining room working with Wyatt. The security guard was a retired army man in his forties with buzz-cut hair. She smiled. He didn't look out of place pulling down twenty-year-old brocade drapes. No doubt this wasn't in the man's job description.

Standing back, Maggie was smiling at what was going on. "It's about time someone got rid of those awful things, don't you think?"

"The room does look brighter." Lori had put her sister in charge of making changes to the house. Gina had told her a few days ago about the plans for the dining room. This was good since it had taken her sister's mind off her ex-husband and any trouble he could cause.

Gina finally turned around. "Oh, yes, you look better now. Still a little tired, but better." She walked over as Maggie left the room. "You okay?"

Lori wasn't sure what she was. "I'm fine. We'll talk later." She sighed, not ready to share what had happened with Jace. "So what are you doing in here?"

Her sister smiled. "I hope you don't mind. I decided to take you up on your suggestion and redo the room. I'm going to order some sheer curtains and light-colored linen drapes. Then I'll plan to strip the wallpaper and paint." She went to the sideboard to find the paint chips. "I've narrowed it down to either shaker beige, or winter sunshine."

Lori tried to focus on her sister's selection and push Jace out of her head. It wasn't working. "You're the decorator, you decide."

"Well, since I'm going to keep the woodwork dark, I'm thinking shaker beige." She glanced at Wyatt. "What do you like?"

Lori found herself smiling. At least something was going well today.

"I can do anything I damn well please," Shelly told Jace as she paced her suite upstairs at the inn. Cassie stayed downstairs with the Keenans while her parents talked.

Jace knew better than to get into a fight with this woman. "I thought you wanted me to have Cassie until the first of next year. You were going to be on an extended honeymoon."

Shelly glanced away. "Plans change."

She was hiding something. "So you're going to just rip Cassie out of school and drag her back to Denver? Well, that's as far as you're going, Shelly. You can't take her out of state, and forget about out of the country." He glanced around the large room and into the connecting bedroom. "Where is your so-called duke?"

Shelly glared at him. "His name is Edmund. And he's not a duke." She raised her head as if she was better than everyone. That was always what Shelly wanted to be, but she had come from the same background he had. "He might not be a duke, but he's got money and a bloodline linked to the royal family. And he can take care of me."

That always got to him. He could never make enough money to satisfy her. "I'm happy for you, Shelly. So why are you here and not with…Edmund?"

"There's been a delay in our wedding plans. I might be having second thoughts. So I decided I'd come to see Cassie. And you. You were always good at calming me down."

Something was up with her, and Jace was going to find out what it was. First stop was to visit his lawyer, Paige Keenan Larkin. No one was taking Cassie away from him.

That afternoon, Lori went into her office at the bank. She had to do something to keep her mind off what had happened at the cabin. She also had to think realistically. She couldn't hold out hope about having a future with Jace. His ex-wife showing up in Destiny proved that.

The most important thing she had to remember was that a child was in the middle of this mess. That meant Cassie's welfare had to come first. She had to stay away from Jace Yeager.

A sudden knock brought her back to the present. "Come in."

Jace walked into her office and her breath caught in her throat. Would she ever stop reacting to this man? Her gaze roamed over Jace's six-foot-two frame, recalling how she'd clung to those broad shoulders.

"Lori."

"Jace. What are you doing here?"

"I needed to see you."

Once again she got caught up in his clean-shaven face. Suddenly the memory of his beard stubble moving against her skin caused her to shiver. The sensation had nearly driven her out of her mind.

He closed the door and went to her desk. "I thought we should talk."

She managed a smile, hoping she was covering her insecurities. "There's no need to. Cassie's mother is in town and you need to take care of them. I understand."

"There's nothing to understand except I don't want you caught up in this mess. I have no idea what Shelly is even doing in Destiny. She was supposed to be in England, married and heading off on her honeymoon."

Lori stood. "Did she give you any explanation?"

"Only that plans change," he told her as he crossed the room toward her.

Lori wanted to back away, to tell Jace to leave, that being together now could be dangerous. Instead, she rounded the desk and met him in the middle of the room.

It wasn't planned, but she didn't turn away when his head descended and his mouth captured hers. She surrendered to his eager assault and returned the kiss, hungry for this man. Finally she came to her senses and broke away. "We shouldn't be doing this."

"Are we breaking any laws?"

"But I don't think Shelly was happy when I walked into the inn with you today."

"It's none of her business."

"Jace, you need to get along with her. At least for Cassie's sake."

He pressed his head against hers. "It's funny. Shelly thinks I'm not worthy of her, but she has this need to interfere in my life."

Lori sighed. "I'm so sorry, Jace."

He drew back. "That's the reason I don't want you involved in this fight, Lori. Maybe it would be best if we cool it for a while. I have to think about Cassie."

Lori knew in her head this was the way it had to be, but her heart still ached. She was losing someone she truly cared about. She managed to nod. "Of course. Besides, we both have too much going on to think that far in the future, or at least to make any promises."

This time he looked surprised.

She moved away from him, or he might see how she truly felt. "Come on, Jace. We work together. Last night we gave in to an attraction. It might not have been the wisest thing to do, but it happened."

He studied her a moment. "Are you saying you regret it?"

"That's not the point."

Jace glared at her. The hell it wasn't. He wanted to reach for her, wanted her to admit more than she was. To tell him how incredible their night was. The worst of it was she couldn't do it any more than he could. "You're right."

She nodded. "Goodbye, Jace."

That was the last thing he wanted to hear, but he would only hurt her more if he stayed. He nodded and walked toward the door. It was a lot harder than he ever dreamed it would be, but he couldn't drag Lori into his fight.

CHAPTER TEN

OVER the next three days, Lori felt like she was walking around in a fog. After the incredible night with Jace, then his quick, easy dismissal of it, how could she not? It would be so easy to pull the covers over her head and just stay in bed. If she were living alone she might do just that. Instead she'd stayed home and gotten involved in Gina's redecorating projects. She tried to fill her time with other things, rather than thinking about a tall, dark and handsome contractor.

Then she'd gotten a call from Erin, telling her that Kaley Sims was in town and had agreed to see her. Anxious for the meeting, Lori arrived right at one o'clock and found an attractive woman with short, honey-blond hair and striking gray eyes waiting in her office.

"Ms. Sims. I'm Lori Hutchinson."

Kaley Sims stood up and they shook hands. "It's nice to meet you. And please call me Kaley." The woman studied her and smiled. "I see some resemblance. You have Lyle's eyes." The woman sobered. "I am sorry to hear of his passing."

"Thank you." Lori motioned for Kaley to sit in the chair across from the desk. "I can't tell you how happy

I am that you agreed to meet with me. I see in my files that you worked for my father a few years back."

Kaley nodded. "I was selling real estate in Destiny before he offered me a job as his property manager. I worked for Lyle about three years."

"You managed all his properties?

"I did."

"I'm impressed," Lori said with a smile. "He has a big operation. I can't handle it all, nor do I have the experience to deal with the properties."

Kaley seemed to relax. "I was a single mother, so I needed the money. And the market was different then. Now, property values are a lot lower. You'd lose a fortune selling in this market."

"See, that's something I don't know. You've probably heard that my father left me in charge of all this."

Kaley's eyes widened, then she smiled. "Lyle would be proud. He talked about you a few times."

Lori froze. "He did?" Why did she still want Lyle's approval?

Kaley looked thoughtful. "One day I came in and found him looking at pictures of you. I think you were about eight or nine in the photo. And of course, Destiny being a small town, everyone knew about your parents' divorce. I mentioned to Lyle how cute you were and he should have you come back for a visit. He said he blew his chance."

Lori felt her chest tighten as she fought tears. This wasn't the time to relive the past. She blinked rapidly at the flooding emotions.

Kaley looked panicked. "I'm sorry, I didn't mean to make you sad."

Lori put on a smile, finding she liked this woman.

"You didn't. I never heard anything from my father since the day I left Destiny."

Kaley sighed. "That was Lyle. The only family he had was his father. Poor Billy had lived to be ninety-two and ended up in the nursing home outside of town until his death a few years ago." Kaley studied her. "Do you remember your grandfather?

Lori shook her head. "No, he wasn't around that I recall."

"You were probably lucky. Old Billy boy was what my mother called a hell-raiser. He was one of the last of the miners. Spent his gold as fast as he dug it out. Story has it that he loved gambling and women." Kaley raised an eyebrow. "His exploits were well-known around town. He was nearly broke when he suffered a stroke. It was Lyle who took over running what was left of the family fortune."

"Looks like he did a pretty good job," Lori said.

Kaley nodded in agreement. "I worked for the man, so I know how driven he was." She paused. "I also went with him to visit his father. Old Billy Hutchinson never had a good word to say to his son."

Lori didn't want to get her hopes up that there was something redeeming about Lyle Hutchinson.

Nor did she want to know about any personal relationship her father might have had with Kaley.

She quickly brought herself back to the present. "Well, I didn't ask you to come in to reminisce about my childhood. I was wondering if you'd be interested in coming back here and being my property manager." When Kaley started to speak, Lori stopped her. "I'll double whatever my father paid you."

The woman looked shocked to say the least. "You want me to work for you?"

Lori shook her head. "No, I want you to work *with* me. You have a good business sense, or my father wouldn't have trusted you. The one thing my father didn't offer, I will. There's a place in this company for advancement. Seems the women employees have been overlooked."

Kaley laughed. "I'm sure your father is somewhere cursing your words."

For the first time in two days, Lori laughed. It felt good. "So what do you say, Kaley?"

"I hear around town that you have to stay a year before you get your inheritance. Will you leave after that?"

Lori thought about her sister and nephew. How easily they had adapted to their new life. How Lori herself had, but could she be around Jace knowing she'd never have a life with the man?

She looked at Kaley. "News does travel fast, but no, I want to stay. I care about the residents of Destiny and I want to see the town prosper. Maybe it's my Hutchinson blood, but I can't let the town die away. That's why I need your help. I want to bring more businesses here and create more jobs."

The pretty woman studied her. "I'd like that, too, but there's one thing you need to know about your father and me—"

Lori raised her hand to stop her. "No, I don't need to know anything about your personal life. Makes no difference to me. I only care that you want to work for Hutchinson Corporation." Lori mentioned a yearly salary and benefits.

"Looks like you've got me on your team."

Lori smiled. "How soon can you start?"

"Give me a week to get moved back and get my daughter, Heather, settled in school."

"Let me know if there's anything I can do to help." The phone began to ring. She said goodbye to Kaley then answered.

"Lori Hutchinson."

"Hello, Lori. It's Claire Keenan. I hope I'm not interrupting you."

"Of course not, Claire. What can I do for you?"

"I need a big favor."

Tim Keenan eyed his wife of nearly forty years as she hung up the phone. He knew when she was planning something.

"Okay, what's going on, Claire?"

She turned those gorgeous green eyes toward him. She was also trying to distract him. "Whatever do you mean?"

"I thought you were looking forward to your afternoon volunteering in Ellie's class."

"I was," she admitted. "But I think Lori might need it more. She has to miss teaching. Besides, they're starting the Christmas pageant practice. She's volunteered to help."

Tim arched an eyebrow. "I'd say she has plenty to do taking over for Lyle. What's the real reason?"

"Did you happen to notice Lori and Jace when they were here the other day?"

"You mean after they'd been stranded at the cabin overnight? It was hard not to."

She nodded. "There were several looks exchanged between them." She sighed. "That only proves what

I've known from the moment I saw them together. They would be so perfect for each other, if only they got the chance."

He drew his wife into his arms. Besides her big emerald-green eyes, her loving heart was what drew him to her. The feel of her close still stirred him. "Playing matchmaker again?"

"It's just a little nudge. I'm hoping maybe they'll catch a glimpse of each other when Jace picks up Cassie."

"Sounds good in theory, but what about Shelly Yeager?" He raised his eyes toward the ceiling. The suite on the second floor was still occupied by the ex-wife. "She's been all but shadowing Jace's every move."

A mischievous smile appeared on his bride's lovely face. "I have plans for her."

About four-thirty that afternoon, Jace pulled up at the school and parked his truck. He was tired. More like exhausted ever since Shelly had arrived in town. And she showed no sign of leaving anytime soon. Something was up with her, but he couldn't figure out what it was.

He climbed out of his truck and started toward the auditorium. The last thing he wanted to do was anger his ex so much she'd walk away with Cassie. That was the only reason he'd put up with her dogging him everywhere, including several trips to the construction site. She even showed up at his house most evenings.

He hoped that Paige Larkin would get things in order, and fast, so he could finally go to the judge and stop Shelly's daily threats to take their daughter back to Denver. He liked the fact that Cassie got to spend time with her mother, but only if Shelly didn't end up hurting her.

No, he didn't trust Shelly one bit.

He opened the large door and walked into the theater-style room. Up on stage were several kids along with some teachers giving directions. That was when he caught sight of the petite blonde that haunted his dreams.

He froze as he took in Lori. She had on dark slacks and a gray sweater that revealed her curves and small waist. He closed his eyes and could see her lying naked on the big bed, her hair spread out on the pillow, her arms open wide to him.

He released a long breath. As much as he'd tried to forget Lori, she wouldn't leave his head, or his heart. All right, he'd come to care about her, but that didn't mean he could do anything about it.

The rehearsal ended and his daughter came running toward him. "Daddy! Daddy!" She ran into his arms and hugged him. "Did you see me practice?"

He loved seeing her enthusiasm. "I sure did."

Jace glanced up to see Lori coming toward them. His heart thudded in his chest as his gaze ate her up. Those dark eyes, her bright smile. His attention went to her mouth as he recalled how sweet she tasted. He quickly pulled himself back to the present, realizing the direction of his thoughts.

"Hello, Lori."

Her gaze avoided his. "Hi, Jace."

"Looks like you've got your hands full here."

"I don't mind at all. I love working with the kids. I gladly volunteered."

Why couldn't he have met this woman years ago?

Cassie drew his attention back to her. "Daddy, did you know that our play is called *Destiny's First Christmas*? It's about Lori's great-great grandfather Raymond Hutchinson. On Christmas Eve, he was working in his mine, 'The Lucky Strike,' and found gold. That night he made a promise to his wife to build a town."

Jace looked at Lori. "Not exactly the traditional Christmas story."

She shrugged. "Not my choice, but the kids voted to do this one. Probably because of my father's passing."

"No, I'd say because of you. You've made a lot of positive changes in the last month."

She shook her head. "Just trying to bring Lyle Hutchinson's business practices into the new century."

Jace found he didn't want to leave, but he couldn't keep staring at her and remembering how it was to hold her in his arms and make love to her.

Cassie tugged on his coat sleeve. "Daddy, I forgot to tell you, Miss Lori invited us to her house for Thanksgiving."

That surprised Jace.

"She's invited a whole bunch of people. It's going to be a big party. Can we go?"

The last thing he wanted to do was disappoint his daughter. "We'll talk about it. Why don't you go get your books." After he sent Cassie off, he turned back to Lori. "Please, don't feel you have to invite us."

"I don't. I wanted to invite you and Cassie, Jace. Besides, practically everyone else in town is coming. The Keenans and Erin and her family. A lot of the bank employees." She glanced away, not meeting his eyes. "And I plan to extend the invitation to Toby and the construction crew. There's going to be a lot of people at the house. I did it mainly for Gina and Zack so they could meet everyone. So you and Cassie are welcome."

Jace wanted so badly to reach out and touch her. He told himself that would be enough, but that was a lie. He wanted her like he'd never wanted a woman ever. "If you're sure."

She frowned. "Of course. We're business partners."

And that was all they could be, he thought. "Speaking of that, you need to come by the site. We're down to doing the finish trim work and adding fixtures. I'd like your opinion on how things are turning out."

She nodded. "How soon to completion?"

"Toby estimates two weeks."

"That's great. Then we can concentrate on getting the spaces rented. I can help with that since I've hired a property manager, Kaley Sims. If it's okay with you, I'd like her to come by and talk with you about listing the loft apartments."

Jace smiled. "So she's handling the rest of your properties?"

Lori nodded. "Yes, she worked for my father years ago, so she knows what she's doing. I convinced her to come back to work with me."

"Good, I'm ready to get this done."

She stiffened. "And you don't have to deal with a rookie partner."

He cursed. "Ah, Lori, I didn't mean it that way. It's just with all the delays we've had, I'm ready to be finished. You're a great partner. I'd work with you again."

She looked surprised. "You would?"

"In a heartbeat." He took a step toward her. There was so much he wanted to say, but he had no right to make promises when he wasn't sure what was in store for him and Cassie. He was in the middle of a messy custody battle. "Just come by the site tomorrow."

Lori started to speak when he heard his name called. He turned around to find Shelly coming toward him. Great. He didn't need this.

He turned back around but Lori had walked off. He wanted to go after her, but he couldn't, not until he got things settled. He'd better do it quickly, or he might lose one of the best things that ever happened to him.

The next week, Lori did what Jace asked and came by the site. She'd purposely stayed away from the project to avoid the man, so she was amazed at the difference.

The chain-link fence had been removed. They'd already started to do some stone landscape. Planters and retaining walls had been built, and a parking area.

"I'm impressed," Kaley said as she got out of the car and looked at the two-story wood-and-stone structure.

So was Lori. "Wait until you see the inside."

They headed up the path to the double-door entry. The door swung open and Toby greeted them with a big smile.

"Well, it's about time you showed up again."

Lori returned the smile. "Well, I knew you were in charge so I didn't worry about things getting done. Hello, Toby."

After a greeting, the foreman turned to Kaley and grinned. "Well, well, who's your friend, Lori?"

Lori made the introductions. "Kaley Sims, Hutchinson Corp's property manager, Toby Edwards."

"So you're not just a pretty face," Toby said.

"And you'd be wise to remember that, Mr. Edwards."

She took a step toward him, grinning. "Now, let's go see if this place looks as good as Lori says it does."

"Well, damn. You're making my day brighter and brighter."

Lori was surprised to see these two throw off sparks. "Go on ahead and don't mind me," she called as the two took off, not paying any attention to her.

She stepped through the entry and gasped as she looked around. The dark hardwood floors had been laid and the massive fireplace completed. She eyed the golden tones of the stacked stones that ran all the way from the hearth to the open-beam ceiling.

Then her attention went to the main attraction of the huge room. The arching staircase. The new design was an improvement from the old as the natural wood banister wrapped around the edge of the first floor, showing off the mezzanine. A front desk had been built for a receptionist for the tenants.

"So how do you like it so far?"

Lori swung around to see Jace. "It looks wonderful."

Then she took in the man. In his usual uniform of faded jeans and a dark Henley shirt, Jace also wore a carpenter's tool belt around his waist. Somehow that even looked sexy.

"Am I disturbing your work?"

He grinned. "Darlin', you've been disturbing a lot more than my work since the minute I met you."

Jace was in a good mood today. Although Shelly had no plans to leave town, he had talked to Paige first thing that morning. He now had a court date and also a preliminary injunction so Shelly couldn't run off with Cassie. At least not until after the custody hearing back in Denver.

"We butted heads a lot, too," she said.

He leaned forward and breathed, "And there were times when we couldn't keep our hands off each other." Before she could do more than gasp, he took her hand. "Come on, I want to show you around."

"I need to go with Toby and Kaley."

He led her up the staircase. "I think Toby can handle the job." He took her into the first loft apartment, showing off ebony-colored hardwood floors. The open kitchen had dark-colored cabinets, but the counters weren't installed yet. "Here are some granite samples for the countertops and tile for the backsplash."

He watched her study the light-colored granite, with the earth-toned contrasting tile. The other was a glossy black, with white subway tile. "I like the earth tone," she told him.

He smiled. "My choice, too. The next stop is the bathroom." He led her across the main living space, where the floor-to-ceiling windows stopped her.

"Oh, Jace. This is a wonderful view."

He stood behind her, careful not to touch her as they glanced out the window at the San Juan Mountains. He worked hard to concentrate on the snow-filled creases in the rock formations and evergreen trees dotting the landscape. "It's almost as beautiful as the view from the cabin."

She glanced up at him and he saw the longing in her dark eyes. "It was lovely there, wasn't it?"

"You were even more beautiful, Lori."

She shook her head. "Don't, Jace. We decided that we shouldn't be involved."

"What if I can't stay away from you?"

Lori closed her eyes. She didn't want to hope and be

hurt in the end. Then his mouth closed over hers and she lost all reasonable thoughts. With a whimper of need she moved her hands up his chest and around his neck and gave in to the feelings.

He broke off the kiss. "I've missed you, Lori. I missed holding you, touching you, kissing you."

"Jace…"

His mouth found hers again and again.

Finally the sound of voices broke them apart. His gaze searched her face. "Lucky for you we're not alone. I'm pretty close to losing control." He sighed. "And with you, Lorelei Hutchinson, that happens every time I get close." He pulled her against him so there was no doubt. "Please, say you'll come by the house tonight. There are so many things I want to tell you."

Lori wanted to hope that everything would work out with Jace. Yet, still Shelly Yeager lingered in town. The last thing Lori wanted was to jeopardize Jace getting custody of his daughter.

Yet, she wanted them both—Jace and Cassie—in her life. Question was, was she ready to fight for what she wanted? Yes. "What time?"

CHAPTER ELEVEN

AT THE site, Jace kept checking his watch, but it was only two o'clock. He had three more hours before he could call it a day and see Lori again.

He was crazy to add any more complications to his life, but he hadn't been able to get her out of his head. For weeks, he'd tried to deny his feelings, tried to convince himself that he didn't care about Lori, but he did care. A lot.

He hadn't been able to forget her or what happened between them. The night at the cabin, what they'd shared, made him think it was possible to have a relationship again. Tonight, when she came by the house, he planned to tell her. He only hoped she could be patient and hang in there a little while longer, until this custody mess was finally straightened out.

"Hey, are you listening?"

Jace turned toward his friend Justin Hilliard. "Sorry, what did you say?"

Justin smiled. "Seems you have something or someone else on your mind."

"Yeah, I do. But I can't do anything about it right now so I'd rather not talk about it."

"I understand. If you need a friend to talk later, I'm your guy. I'll even buy the beer."

Justin was the one who'd brought him to Destiny after Yeager Construction tanked following his divorce. He'd always be grateful. "I appreciate that."

His friend nodded. "Now, tell me when can I move in?" He motioned around the office space on the main floor at the Mountain Heritage complex.

"Is next week soon enough?"

"Great. I'll have Morgan go shopping for office furniture. And I'll need a loft apartment upstairs for out-of-town clients. Is there someone handling the loft rentals?"

Jace nodded. "Kaley Sims. I'll have her get in touch with you to negotiate the lease."

"Good. I'm available all this week." Justin studied Jace. "So what are your plans for your next project?"

"Not sure." That much was true. "I've been so wrapped up in getting this project completed, I haven't thought that far ahead." He had Lori on his mind. "I know I'd like to stay here, of course, but until I get this custody mess taken care of, I'm still in limbo."

"Like I said, let me know if I can help." Justin slapped him on the back. "Just don't let Shelly get away with anything."

"Believe me, I won't." She'd taken him to the cleaners once. No more. "Besides, Paige is handling it all for me."

Justin nodded. "Yeah, my sister-in-law is one of the best. She'll do everything she can to straighten this out."

God, he hoped so. Jace wanted nothing more than to end Shelly's threats.

They walked out of the office space and Justin said, "If you think you'd be ready to start another project by March, let me know."

Jace stopped. He was definitely interested. "What kind of project?"

"It's an idea I've had in the works awhile. I waited until I had the right partner in place, and now, it's in the designing stages."

Jace was more than intrigued. "So what is it?"

"A mountain bike racing school and trails. I bought several acres of land about five miles outside of town and plan to build a track. I'm bringing in a pro racer, Ryan Donnelly, to design it."

"I don't do landscaping."

Justin smiled. "I know. I want your company to handle the structures, cabins to house the students and instructors, including a main building to serve meals and a pro shop."

They walked through the main area of the building as Justin continued. "Eventually, I hope to work with Ryan to design bikes. I want the plant to be right here in Destiny." Justin arched an eyebrow. "I want you to handle it all, Jace."

This was a dream come true. "And I want the project, Justin. By early spring I could have the subs and crew in place to start." He worked to hold in his excitement. "But I'll need the plans by February."

Justin nodded. "Shouldn't be a problem."

Now if his personal life straightened out by then. With this new project he could move forward, make a fresh start. He thought about Lori. He couldn't wait to tell her. Tonight. This could be their new beginning.

* * *

By six o'clock, Lori had gathered her things and left the office. She went home, showered and changed into a nice pair of slacks and white angora sweater. Excited about spending the evening with Jace, she took extra time with her clothes and makeup.

Her pulse raced as she realized how badly she wanted to be with him. He was everything she'd ever dreamed the man she loved could be. Handsome, caring and a good father. What woman wouldn't dream about forever with him?

She walked back into the connecting bedroom to find Gina.

"Sorry, Lori, I didn't mean to disturb you. I know you plan to go out tonight."

"You never could disturb me," Lori assured her sister. "Is something wrong?"

Gina smiled. "No. For the first time in a very long time, everything is going right." She went to her sister. "Thanks to you. I never thought I could feel this happy again. And Zack…"

Lori hugged her, praying that continued. That Eric would leave them alone. "We're family, Gina. Besides, it's Lyle's money."

"No, you were there for us long before you inherited the Hutchinson money. You were always there for me."

"You're my sister and Zack is my nephew. Where else would I be?"

"Having a life?" Gina said. "And finding someone special."

Lori wanted to believe. "I think that has already happened."

Her sister smiled. "If Jace Yeager is as smart as I think he is, he'll snatch you up."

Of course, Lori hoped that tonight the man would make some kind of commitment, but she also knew he had to tread cautiously. They both did. "Let's just see what happens."

About eight o'clock that evening, Jace had put Cassie to bed, but she made him promise when Lori got there she would come up to say good-night. He was happy that his daughter got along with her.

He smiled, knowing he'd have Lori all to himself for the rest of the evening. There were so many things he wanted to tell Lori tonight. He wanted them to move ahead together.

He checked on the dinners he'd picked up from the Silver Spoon. Then he took the wine out of the refrigerator and got two glasses from the cupboard. He looked around his half-finished kitchen.

Okay, this place had been neglected too long. It was going to be his top priority. He could probably make some headway by Christmas. Thanksgiving at the Hutchinson house, and maybe, Christmas dinner at the Yeager house. That would be his goal.

He hoped to have the rest of his life in order by then, too. His daughter with him and Lori with them. He'd made a start with the custody hearing.

He saw the flash of headlights as a car pulled into the drive. His heart began to pound when he saw Lori climb out and walk up the steps to the back porch. He opened the door and greeted her with a smile.

"Hi, there."

She smiled. "Hi. Sorry I'm late."

Jace drew her into his arms because he couldn't go any longer without touching her, holding her. "Well, you're here now and that's all that matters. I missed you." He kissed her, a slow but intense meeting of their mouths, only making him hungry for more.

He didn't want to let go of her, but he promised himself he'd go slow. He tore his mouth away. "Maybe we should dial it down a little." He tugged at her heavy coat. "At least until I feed you."

She smiled. "I am a little hungry." She brushed her hair back and looked around. "Where's Cassie?"

"I'm losing out to the kid, huh? She's upstairs in bed." He led her into the kitchen. "I told her you'd come up and say good-night. I hope you don't mind."

"Of course not." Lori started off, but he brought her back to him for another intense kiss. "Just remember you're mine for the rest of the night."

"I'll be right back."

Jace's heart pounded as he watched the cute sway of her hips as she walked out of the kitchen and up the stairs.

He sighed and worked to get it together. "You got it bad, Yeager." He turned down the lights, and put on some music from the sound system, then lit the candles on the table. Back at the kitchen counter, he opened the chilled bottle of wine and filled the glasses at the two place settings.

It was impossible not to remember their dinner together at the cabin. He wanted nothing more than to have a repeat of that night. But that couldn't happen. Not with Cassie here. He blew out a breath. There was no doubt in his mind, they'd be together again. And soon.

Smiling, Lori walked down the steps and it turned into a grin when she saw Jace in the kitchen. "That's what I like about you, Yeager. You're just not a handsome face, you're domestic, too."

Jace turned around and tossed her a sexy smile. "I can be whatever you want."

Her heart shot off racing. *How about the man who loves me?* she asked silently as he came to her and drew her against him. She wanted nothing more than to stay wrapped in his arms, to close out the rest of the world.

She looked up at him. "Kiss me, Jace."

"My pleasure, ma'am." He lowered his head, brushing her mouth with his. She opened for him, but he was a little more playful and took nibbling bites out of her bottom lip.

With her whimper of need, he captured her mouth in a searing kiss. By the time he pulled back, her knees were weak and she had trouble catching her breath. "Wow."

He raised an eyebrow. "That was just an appetizer." He stepped back. "But before I go back to sampling you again, we better eat."

She was a little disappointed, but knew it was better to slow things down a little. She accepted the wine he offered her.

She sipped it and let the sweet taste linger in her mouth. She caught Jace watching her and smiled, then took another sip. "How was your day at the site?"

"Oh, I meant to tell you that Justin stopped by. Besides the office space, he wants to lease a loft apartment. I gave him Kaley's number."

"Good." She raised her glass. "The first of many, I hope."

"You and me both. Justin might want more than one apartment. I'm hoping Kaley can convince him of that.

Maybe give him a few incentives like a six-month re-
duction in the rent."

"That sounds good. Is that usually done in real estate?"

He nodded. "All the time." He walked her to the table
and sat her down, then began filling their plates with
roast chicken and mashed potatoes. "The Silver Spoon's
Thursday night special."

Lori took a bite. "It's very good."

"Come spring," he began, "I'll barbecue us some
steaks on the grill. That's my specialty."

She paused, her fork to her mouth. He was talking
about the future. "I'd like that."

He winked and took a bite of food as they continued
to talk about Mountain Heritage, then he told her about
Justin's offer for the racing bike school.

"Oh, Jace, you have to be excited about that."

Jace wanted to be, but there were still problems
looming overhead. Like getting permanent custody of
his daughter. He prayed that Paige could pull this off.
"There's still a lot to work out."

Lori nodded.

He didn't want to talk about it right now. This was
just for them. No troubles, no worries, just them. Yet,
he knew he couldn't make her any promises. He'd never
thought he'd find someone like Lori, someone he'd want
to dream about a future together.

The meal finished, they carried the dishes to the sink
and left them. He offered her coffee, but she refused it.

A soft ballad came on the radio. He drew her into his
arms and began slowly dancing her around the kitchen
and into the family room, where soft flames in the fireplace added to the mood. He placed his hands against

her back, pulling his swaying body against hers. "I want you, Lori," he whispered. "Never have I wanted a woman as much as you." His lips trailed along her jaw, feeling her shiver. He finally reached his destination. "Never." He closed his mouth over hers, and pushed his tongue inside tasting her, stroking her.

His hands were busy, too, reaching under her sweater, cupping her breasts.

"Jace," she moaned. "Please."

"I definitely want to please you." He kissed her again and was quickly getting to the point of no return.

"Well, well. Isn't this cozy?"

Jace jerked back and caught sight of Shelly standing in the doorway. He immediately turned Lori away from view. "What are you doing here?"

The tall brunette pushed away from the doorjamb and walked into the room as if she had every right to be there.

"Since no one was answering the phone, I came to see what the problem was." She gave Lori a once-over. "Now I know why. You're having a little party here while our daughter is asleep upstairs."

"That's my business, Shelly. And that doesn't give you the right to come into my house without an invitation. And you weren't invited."

"I don't need to be. I have custody of Cassie." She shot an angry look at Lori. "In fact I think I should remove her from here right now."

Lori gasped.

Jace got angry. "I wouldn't try it, Shelly."

"Try and stop me."

When she started to move past him, Jace stepped in

front of her. "You can't. I have an injunction that says she stays with me until the court hearing."

She glared. "I know. I got served today."

So that was why she showed up. "And this should be settled in court."

"I want my daughter. Now!"

"Stop it! Mommy, Daddy, don't fight!"

They all turned and saw Cassie standing at the bottom of the stairs.

Lori wanted to go to the child, but it wasn't her place.

Jace took over and went to his daughter's side. "Oh, baby. I'm sorry we woke you."

"You and Mommy were fighting again?"

"I'm sorry. We're trying to work something out and we got a little loud."

"Please, I don't want you to fight anymore."

Jace looked at Lori. "Will you take Cassie back to her room?" With her nod, he glanced down at his daughter. "I'll be up in a minute."

Shelly came over and kissed her daughter and sent her along.

Once they were alone, Jace took Shelly's arm and walked her out to the utility room. "I'm not going to let you come here and upset Cassie like that."

"You're just mad because I interrupted your rendezvous with little Miss Heiress."

"Leave Lori out of this. She's a respectable person in this town."

"And you're sleeping with her."

Jace had to hold his temper. "We've done nothing wrong. If you think so, then talk to the judge. I'll see you in court, Shelly."

Shelly's face reddened in anger. "Don't think you've

won, Jace Yeager. This is not going to end in your favor."

He held on to his temper. "Why, Shelly? Why are we arguing about this? You know Cassie is better off here. She's made friends and is doing great in school. I have a job that has me home every night." He stopped in front of the woman he once loved, but now he only felt sorry for. "When you get married, Shelly, I will let you see her anytime you want."

"That might not happen. So the game plan will change."

"Oh, Cassie."

Lori cradled the small form against her as they sat on the bed. She inhaled the soft powdery smell and realized how much Cassie had come to mean to her. She could easily become addicted to this nightly ritual.

She silently cursed Shelly Yeager. How could anyone drag a child into this mess? "I wish I could make it better, sweetheart."

The child's lip quivered as she looked up. "Nobody can. They always fight."

"I'm sorry. That doesn't mean they don't love you. They just have to work out what's best for you."

A tear ran down the girl's cheek. "I want to live here with Daddy, but if I do, Mommy will go away." Cassie's big blue eyes looked up at her, and Lori could feel her pain. "And she's gonna forget about me." She started to sob and Lori drew her into a tight embrace.

"Oh, sweetheart, have you told your father how you feel?"

The child pulled back, looking panicked. "No! I don't

want them to fight anymore." Her face crumpled again. "So please don't tell Daddy."

"Don't tell me what?"

They both looked toward the door to see Jace. "Nothing." Cassie wiped her eyes. "I'm just talking to Miss Lori."

Lori got up and Jace sat down to face his daughter. "Sweetheart, I'm sorry."

The little girl suddenly collapsed into her father's arms. Lori backed out of the room, not wanting to intrude. She realized right away how much this custody battle had affected the child.

And Cassie had to come first.

Lori couldn't help but wonder if they could get through this situation unscathed, or would Shelly follow through on her threats?

Lori's chest tightened. She'd never forget the heartache she'd felt when she had to leave her childhood home. Her father standing on the porch. That had been the last time she'd ever seen Lyle Hutchinson. Oh, God. She couldn't let that happen to this little girl. No matter what it cost her.

Cassie finally went to sleep and Jace walked out into the hall, but he didn't go downstairs yet. Heartsick over his daughter's distress, he needed some time to pull himself together. Cassie had been dealing with problems he and her mother had caused. No child should have to choose which parent to love, which parent to be loyal to.

He sighed, knowing he had to do something about it.

Jace made his way down the steps and found Lori standing in the kitchen. He went to her and pulled her into a tight embrace. "I guess we should talk." He released her and walked around the kitchen in a daze. "You want something to drink?"

"No," she said. "Is Cassie asleep?"

He nodded, feeling the rush of emotions as he went and poured himself a glass. "I'm so angry at Shelly for starting all this."

"Divorce isn't easy for anyone, kids especially." Lori closed her eyes momentarily. "Cassie needs constant reassurance that her daddy's going to be around."

Jace tried to draw a breath, but it was hard. "And I have been right here for her. I've been doing everything possible to keep her with me."

He immediately realized the harshness of his words. "I'm sorry, Lori, that you had to witness this." He pulled her close, grateful that she didn't resist. "I'm so frustrated." He held her tightly. "I've worked so hard to have a good relationship with my daughter."

Lori pulled back, knowing there wasn't any simple solution. "I know, but Cassie is still caught in the middle."

"This is all a game to Shelly."

It wasn't for the rest of the people involved. "Well, she is here and you have to deal with her. For Cassie's sake."

"I've been doing that," he told her. "Paige has gotten a court date for a custody hearing with a judge in Denver."

Lori was surprised by Jace's news. "That's good. When?"

"This coming Monday."

She told herself not to react, not to be hurt that he hadn't said anything before now. "So soon?"

He studied her with those intense blue eyes. "If we

don't do it now, the holidays are coming up. It could be delayed until January. By then Shelly might have taken Cassie to Europe." He paused. "I was going to tell you about it tonight."

That didn't take away the pain of his leaving. "How long will you be gone?"

"Probably just a few days. Don't worry, Toby has the project under control."

She shook her head. "You think I'm concerned about that when Cassie's future is in jeopardy?"

He shook his head. "Of course not, Lori. I know you care about her."

"I care about both of you. I want this to work, because she should be with you."

He looked at her, his blue eyes intense. "I'm going to see that happens no matter what the judge's decision is."

Lori felt her heart skip a beat. "Does that mean you'll move back to Denver?"

He nodded slowly. "I hope there's another way. I don't want to leave here, but if that's the end result of this hearing…there's no choice."

He might be going away, she thought, fighting tears. "Cassie's your daughter, so of course you have to go there. You have to fight for her."

"I care about you, Lori. A lot. I know you have a year commitment here, or I'd ask—"

"Then don't, Jace," she interrupted, forcing a smile. "Neither one of us is ready to jump into a relationship. Like you said, we both have other commitments."

His gaze locked on hers. "I want to say the hell with all of Shelly's games, but I can't. Bottom line is, I can't give you any promises."

And she couldn't beg him to. There was too much

at stake here. Most importantly, a little girl. Lori had once been that little girl whose father let her go. Cassie deserved better.

Lori couldn't meet his eyes. She fisted her hands so he wouldn't see her shaking. "It's too soon to make plans when we don't know the future."

"Is it? What about what happened between us at the cabin? Unless it didn't mean anything to you."

She swallowed hard. "Of course it did." She'd always have those incredible memories. "It was…special."

"Seems not as special for you as it was for me."

She had to get away from him. "I'm sorry, Jace. I need to go. I hope everything works out for you and Cassie." She headed toward the door and paused. She took one last look at the man she loved. "Goodbye, Jace."

When he didn't say anything to stop her, she hurried out the door and got into her car. Starting the engine, she headed for the highway. He hadn't even asked her to wait it out. Tears filled her eyes, blurring her vision, until she had to stop.

She cried for her loss, for letting this between her and Jace to get this far. She never should have let herself fall in love with this wonderful man. A man she couldn't have. She'd finally opened herself and let love in, only to be hurt again.

She brushed away more tears, praying that the pain would stop. That the loneliness would go away soon. This was what she got for starting to dream of that happy ending.

The only consolation was she wouldn't let another little girl go through the misery she had. She would never prevent Jace from having his daughter.

CHAPTER TWELVE

THAT night, sleep eluded Lori.

When she'd gotten home earlier she'd made up an excuse to go to her room. She hadn't been in the mood to talk about her evening with Jace. Not even with Gina. And what good would it do? Neither one of them had a choice in the matter. There was nothing to say except they couldn't be together.

But after several hours of tossing and turning, she got out of bed. Restless, she ended up wandering around the big house. She checked in on her sleeping nephew and pulled the covers around him, knowing Jace would do the same thing with Cassie. Smiling, she realized that had been one of the reasons she'd fallen in love with the man. His relationship with his daughter was part of that. She would miss them both so much if they couldn't come back here. What were Jace's chances of getting custody? Probably slim.

Lori walked down the hall, passing her childhood bedroom. She stopped, wanting nothing more than to shake the feeling of abandonment she'd had since her mother took her away from here.

She slipped inside, waiting as the moonlight coming through the window lit her path to the canopy bed.

Loneliness swept through her as more memories flooded back. Her absent father had been too busy for her. He'd been too busy making money and that meant he hadn't been home much.

Then long-forgotten images flashed though her mind. There had been some happy times. She remembered sitting at the dinner table, hearing her parents' laughter. Lyle wasn't very demonstrative, but she would always cherish the time he'd spent with her. Guess he'd been as loving as he was able to be.

She smiled, thinking of those good-night kisses she would treasure. She brushed away a tear as she turned on a bedside lamp and caught sight of the stuffed animals lined up on the windowsill.

Another memory hit her. "Oh, Daddy, you gave me all of these."

"Lorelei?"

Lori turned to find Maggie standing in the doorway. She was wearing her robe over a long gown. "Oh, Maggie, did I wake you?"

The housekeeper walked in. "No, I was up getting something to drink. This old house has a lot creaks and I know them all. When I heard someone walking around, I thought it might be the boy." The older woman eyed the stuffed animals. "Land sakes, child. You can't keep coming in here and getting all sad."

"No, Maggie. Really, I'm fine." She smiled as she wiped away the tears and held out one of her childhood animals. "Look. I remembered that Dad bought this for me." She reached for another. "He bought these, too." She gathered all them in her arms.

Maggie smiled. "I'm glad you remember those times."

And so much more. "Every time he went on a business trip, he came home with a toy for me." Another memory. "And when he was home he would come into my bedroom and kiss me good-night." Tears flooded her eyes. "He loved me, Maggie."

"Of course he loved you. You were his little girl, his pride and joy."

"Then why, Maggie? Why didn't he want me?"

The housekeeper shook her head. "It wasn't that." She hesitated, then said, "You never knew your grandfather Billy. If you had you might understand your father better."

"Kaley Sims mentioned him. She said he'd gone into a nursing home after a stroke."

Maggie made a huffing sound. "It was probably better than he deserved. That man was a terrible example as a parent. What Lyle went through as a child was... Let's just say, Billy wasn't much of a human being, so I won't go into his fathering skills."

"Wouldn't that make Lyle a better one?"

Maggie took hold of Lori's hands and they sank down to sit on the window seat. "I believe your dad did the best he could, honey. When Billy nearly lost all the family money, and that included the bank, this town almost didn't survive. Your father spent a lot of years rebuilding the family wealth, and trying to get Billy's approval."

Maggie continued, "Your mother didn't like being neglected, either. She wanted all of her husband's attention. I think she left hoping Lyle would come after both of you. Your father took it as another rejection and just shut down."

Lori had no doubt Jocelyn Hutchinson would do that to get attention. "But he had a daughter who loved him."

Maggie looked sad. "I know. I wish I had a better answer for you. I recall a few phone conversations between your mother and father. He asked Jocelyn to bring you here. She refused. When your mother remarried, he told me that you'd do better without him."

She felt a spark of hope. "He wanted me to come back here?"

Maggie nodded. "For Christmas that first year. He told me once how much you loved the tree lights in the town square."

A tear ran down Lori's cheek. She had no idea he would remember.

Maggie pulled her into a comforting embrace. "He kept this room the same, hoping to have you back here. So keep hanging on to the good memories, child. I know that was what your father did."

Lori pulled back. "How can I?"

The housekeeper brushed back Lori's hair. "Because your father knew he caused enough pain over the years." Maggie smiled through her own tears. "Think about it, Lorelei. Your father finally brought you home. No mistaking, he wanted you here."

Lori began to sob over the lost years that father and daughter would never get back. The tears were cleansing, and she had some answers.

"Lori?"

Lori looked at the open door to find her sister. "Oh, Gina. Sorry, did we wake you?"

"I was just checking on Zack."

Maggie hugged them both. "Share with your sister, Lorelei. It will get better each time." The older woman left.

"Should I be worried?" Gina asked once they were alone.

"Not any longer. I've learned a lot about my father. Lyle wasn't perfect, but he loved me in his way." Lori went on to explain about her discovery.

"I'm so glad," Gina agreed. "Every child needs those good memories." She hesitated. "That's what I hope for Zack."

"He'll have those good memories. I promise," Lori told her, thinking about Cassie, too.

Lori never wanted that child to go through what she had. So that meant she had to accept it. Accept she might not be able to have Jace Yeager.

Gina's voice broke into her thoughts.

Lori looked at her. "What?"

"Something else is bothering you. Would it have anything to do with Jace? Did you two have a fight?" Gina asked, frowning. "Oh, no, it's his ex-wife causing trouble, isn't it?"

Lori agreed. "Jace has to go back to Denver for the custody case. If he loses, he wants to live close by Cassie. That means he'll have to move back there."

"I wish I could hate the guy, but he's a great father." Gina suddenly grinned. "So move to Denver."

Lori would in a minute. "I can't until I fulfill Lyle's will. If I leave before the year is up, the town might not survive."

"That doesn't mean you can't go visit Jace for long weekends."

She could go for that. Would Jace want a long-distance relationship? "He hasn't asked me."

Gina jumped up. "Of course he hasn't. He doesn't know anything yet. Lori, I believe Jace Yeager loves you. And if he can, he'll do whatever it takes to get Cassie and come back here to you."

Lori was heartened with her sister's enthusiasm. "You sure seem to have a better outlook toward men these days."

Her sister shrugged. "Maybe they aren't all jerks like Eric. I've met a few here in town that seem really nice. Now, that doesn't mean I want to get involved with any of them. I'm happy concentrating on raising Zack."

If one good thing came out of returning to Destiny it was helping Gina and Zack have a chance at a new life. "And we have each other."

"Always." Gina nodded. "Now, we need something to do to keep you busy." She looked around what once had been a little girl's room. "This entire house, at the very least, needs a fresh coat of paint. We should redecorate the master suite, so you can move in there."

Lori knew Gina was trying to distract her, and she loved her for it. "The place is a little big for us, don't you think?"

"Of course it is. It's a mansion."

Lori turned to her sister. "What about moving into a smaller place?"

Her sister blinked. "Are you going to sell this house?"

She shook her head. "We have to live here for now. I think maybe Hutchinson House can be rented out for weddings and parties and the proceeds could go to the town." She couldn't help but wonder if Jace and Cassie would be living here in Destiny, too. "What do you think of that?"

"Lori, I think that's a wonderful idea." She hesitated.

"And you've been generous to Zack and me. But I feel I need to contribute, too. I know this mess with Eric still has me frightened, but thanks to you, I've felt safer than I have for years."

"I'm glad." Lori had already checked on her ex-brother-in-law. She'd contacted the police detective on the case. Eric had been staying with his family in Colorado Springs.

"I need a job," Gina blurted out. "It's not that I'm not grateful to you for everything, but I want to be more independent. I have to set a good example for my son. I don't want him to think he has an easy ride in life."

Lori hugged her, knowing the hell she'd gone through for years. "So you want a job. I just happen to have one."

Her sister frowned. "Lori, you can't make up a job for me."

"I hate to tell you, sis, but most of the people in Destiny work for Hutchinson Corp. And honestly, I'm not making this job up. Kaley Sims is going to advertise the Mountain Heritage spaces to rent and she needs to stage them. You're the perfect decorator to do it. So what do you say?"

Gina gave her a big smile. "I say, when do I start?"

"I'll talk to Kaley in the morning." Lori smiled, but inside she was hurting. Everyone was moving forward, but she couldn't, not knowing what her future held. "Come on, we both need to get some sleep."

They walked back to their rooms. Lori climbed in bed just as her cell phone rang. She reached for it off her nightstand.

She glanced at the familiar caller ID. "Jace," she answered. "Is something wrong?"

"No, nothing's wrong. I'm sorry I called so late. I just wanted to let you know that Cassie and I are leaving."

She already knew that. "When?"

"First thing in the morning."

So soon.

Jace went on. "Toby has everything under control at the site. There are only a few finishing touches before the last walk through. Kaley Sims is now handling the Heritage project. I'll pass on the news to her."

"I appreciate that," she told him. "Is there anything else?"

Lori begged silently that he'd ask her to wait for him. At least tell her he cared.

"I hated the way we left things last night," he finally said. "God, Lori, I wish it could be different."

She swallowed back the lump in her throat. "You're doing what's right, Jace."

"I know. I just needed to hear your voice," he told her and there was a long pause. "Goodbye, Lori." Then he hung up.

The silence was deafening. She lay back in her bed, pulling up the covers to protect her from the loneliness. It didn't help. Nothing would help but Jace.

"Why are you dead set on making my life hell?" Jace demanded as he stepped through the door into his one-time Denver home the next day. Something else that Shelly had gotten from their divorce.

He glanced around the spacious entry of the re-furbished Victorian. The hardwood floors he'd refin-ished himself, along with the plaster on the walls. He stopped the search when unpleasant memories of his marriage hit him. He turned back to Shelly to see her stubborn look.

"You're the one who had me served with papers."

"Because you came to Destiny and disrupted Cassie's life. I'm done with your games, Shelly. It's time we settle this."

"Well, that's too bad." She strolled across the room to the three windows that overlooked the street. "I'm Cassie's mother, and after today, the judge will see that I should have our child permanently. Where is our daughter?"

"She's in good hands." Paige had offered to watch her back at the hotel while he tried to straighten out a few things. "She's with Paige Larkin."

Shelly frowned. "So what are you willing to give up to spend time with Cassie? Your little girlfriend?"

"I'm not willing to give up anything. Besides, my personal life is none of your business." He prayed he still had one. Not only couldn't he make any promises to Lori, but he also couldn't even tell her his feelings.

"It is if you're living with her with our child. Maybe the judge should know, too."

"Stop with the threats, Shelly." He walked toward the front door. He opened the door and glanced out at the man on the porch and motioned to him to come inside.

Shelly looked at Jace suspiciously. "What are you up to?"

"You're the one who plays games, Shelly. So if I can't talk any sense into you, maybe he can." He prayed that all his hard work would pay off and not backfire in his face.

"Don't push me, Jace. You'll only lose." She gasped as Edmund Layfield stepped through the front door.

The distinguished gentleman was in his early fifties. He was dressed in a business suit and had thick gray hair. Jace had spent only an hour with the man and realized that he truly loved Shelly. Edmund also liked Cassie, but didn't particularly want to raise another child full-time, since his kids were grown.

Shelly came out of her trance. "Edmund, what are you doing here?"

"I came to see you, love. And I'm not leaving here until I convince you that we're meant to be together." He reached out and pulled her into his arms. That was when Jace made his exit.

For the first time in days, he realized that maybe they could come to a compromise. They all might get what they wanted. His thoughts turned to Lori. And that included him.

Tim parked the small SUV next to several other cars at Hutchinson House. It was Thanksgiving and half the town had been invited to have dinner here.

"Are you okay with this?" he asked Claire.

She smiled. "Normally no, but I can share this special day with Lori and Gina. It's important they feel a part of Destiny." She sighed. "Besides, all the kids and grandkids will be here." She smiled. "It's all about family being together. If only we would hear from Jace. You'd think our own daughter could give us some information."

He reached across the car and took his wife's hand. "Come on, Claire, you know Paige is Jace's lawyer."

"I know, I know, client/lawyer confidentiality." She frowned. "But I've seen how sad Lori is. If two people should be together, it's them."

"And if it's meant to be it will work out."

"I've been praying so hard for that."

It had been a week, and not a word from Jace. Lori had tried to stay positive—after all, it was Thanksgiving.

She looked around the festive dining room. The long table could seat twenty. There were two other tables set up in the entry to seat another twenty. And with the kids' table in the sunroom off the kitchen, everyone would have a place.

Maggie had cooked three turkeys and with Claire's two baked hams and many side dishes from everyone, she couldn't imagine not having enough food.

"Miss Hutchinson."

Lori turned to see Mac Burleson. "Mac, I asked you to call me Lori."

"Doesn't seem right," he told her.

"It seems very right to me. Unless you don't consider me a friend."

His eyes rounded. "You're a very good friend. I'm so grateful—"

"You did it," she interrupted. "You proved yourself at every job you've taken on. You make us all proud."

"Thank you…Lori." He smiled. "Is there anything else you want me to do?"

Some laughing kids ran by, chasing each other. She smiled at their antics. Her father would probably hate this. "Enjoy today. We have a lot to be thankful for." She knew she was so lucky, but two important people weren't here to share it with her.

"Hurry, Daddy, we're gonna be late for Thanksgiving."

Jace smiled, but it didn't relax him as he drove his

truck down First Street toward Hutchinson House. "We'll get there, sweetheart."

He glanced toward the backseat where his daughter was strapped in. They'd been gone a week, having stayed in Denver longer than planned. With the lawyers' help, they'd worked out the custody issue without a judge having to make the decision.

And in the end, it had been Cassie who'd told her mother that she wanted to live in Destiny with her daddy and all her friends and her horse. Shelly finally agreed, but wanted visitation in the summers and holidays. So Jace became the custodial parent. There was only one other thing that could make him happier. Lori.

"I just can't wait to see Ellie and Mrs. K. and Miss Lori, to tell everybody that I get to live here and be in the Christmas pageant."

"I can't wait, either," he told his daughter, praying that a certain pretty blonde felt the same about the news.

"Daddy, are you gonna ask Miss Lori today?"

On the flight home, Jace had told her how he felt about Lori and about her being a part of their lives. That was crazy, considering he hadn't even talked with Lori yet.

"Not sure. There's going to be a lot of people there today. It might have to wait, so you have to keep it a secret, okay?"

"Okay, but could I tell Ellie about Mommy's wedding? And that I'm going to go visit a real castle this summer?"

He smiled. "Yes, about the wedding, but the castle is only going to happen if I can get time off work." He was definitely going with her. He hoped Lori could go, too.

His heart began to race as he pulled up and climbed

out of the truck. He grabbed the wine and hurried after his daughter to the front door.

When they rang the bell, the door opened and Zack poked his head out. "Hi, Cassie. Hi, Mr. Jace."

"Hi, Zack. We came for Thanksgiving."

The boy grinned and opened the door wider and allowed them into the entryway filled with a long table decorated with colorful flowers and a paper turkey centerpiece. Cassie took off before he could stop her.

Jace was soon greeted by Justin and Morgan, then Tim Keenan and Paige and Reed Larkin joined them. He wanted to join in the conversation, but his eyes kept searching for a glimpse of Lori.

"She's in the kitchen."

He glanced at Justin. "Who?"

"As if you two are fooling anyone," his friend said. "You need to go to Lori before she comes out here and sees you."

Jace nodded and took off toward the kitchen. He knew his way around this house, but there were so many people here it was hard to maneuver. How was he going to be able to get her alone?

He saw Maggie at the counter. Without asking anything, she nodded toward the sunroom. He walked there as kids ran past him. Okay, so they weren't going to have any privacy.

Then he saw her and everyone else seemed to disappear from view. She was seated on the floor with some of the little kids. She was holding a toddler who'd been crying, and she managed to turn the tears into a smile before the child wandered off. Jace fell in love with her all over again.

Lori stood. Dressed in black slacks and a soft blue

sweater he ached to pull her close and just hold her. Tell her how much he'd missed her. How much he wanted her...

She finally turned in his direction. Her hair was in an array of curls that danced around her pretty face. Her chocolate eyes locked on his. "You're back."

That was a dumb thing to say, Lori thought as she looked up at Jace. So much for cool and calm.

"Hello, Lori."

"Hi, Jace." She didn't take a step toward him. "Is Cassie with you? Please tell me that she's with you."

He beamed. "Yes, she is." He glanced around. "I need to talk to you. There are so many things I have to tell you."

Just then Maggie broke in. "Sorry to interrupt but dinner is on the table. And Tim Keenan is ready to say the blessing."

Lori glanced back at Jace. "I'm sorry. Can we talk later?" Without waiting for an answer, Lori took off and headed toward the front of the house. She felt Jace following behind her as they reached the dining room. Hopeful, she added an extra place at the table for him.

She smiled at all her family and the new friends she was sharing today with. That included Jace and Cassie.

It grew quiet and someone handed her a champagne glass. "First of all, Gina, Zack and I want to thank you all for coming today. I hope this is the first of many visits to Hutchinson House. I want you all to feel welcome, so you'll come back here." She raised her glass. "To friends, and to Destiny." After everyone took a drink, she had Tim Keenan say the blessing.

The group broke up, and mothers went off to fill

their children's plates and settle them in the sunroom. Maggie stood by, watching for any emergencies. Lori ended up back at the head table, while Gina was seated at the entry table. Somehow Jace was seated at her table, but at the opposite end. Every so often, he'd smile at her.

She kept telling herself in a few hours they could be alone. After dinner, she went into the kitchen to check on dessert and finally saw Cassie.

"Miss Lori." The girl came and hugged her. "I got to come back."

"I know. Your daddy told me."

"Did he tell you about the wedding?" Cassie's tiny hand slapped over her mouth. "Oh, no, I wasn't supposed to tell you about that."

"Whose wedding? Your mommy's?" When Cassie didn't answer, she asked, "Your daddy's?"

The child giggled. "Both of 'em. But don't tell Daddy I told you. It's a surprise."

Lori could barely take her next breath. Was that why Jace said he got Cassie? He had to remarry Shelly?

She couldn't do this. She turned and found Jace behind her, holding her coat. "Okay, we need to get out of here and talk." He grinned. "I know just the place."

She gasped. "There's no need to tell me. I already heard from Cassie about the wedding. I hope you and Shelly will be happy."

He frowned. "What? You think that Shelly and I…" He cursed.

Lori held up her hand to stop him, but he took it in his.

"We're definitely going to talk about this," he began. "We need to get a few things straightened out. Now."

"I can't leave now."

"So we should just talk here. I'm sure all your guests would love to hear what I have to say," he said, and held out her coat.

"Why are you doing this?" she asked, keeping her voice low.

"I hate the fact that you even have to ask. I hope I can change that." When she hesitated, he asked, "Can't you even give me a few minutes to hear me out? To listen to what I have to say."

Lori wasn't sure what to do, only that she didn't want a scene here. She slipped on her coat and told Maggie she was leaving for a little while.

The housekeeper smiled and waved them on saying, "It's about time."

CHAPTER THIRTEEN

TWENTY minutes later, Jace was still furious as he pulled off the highway. The sun had already set, but he knew the way to the cabin.

"Why are you bringing me here?" Lori asked.

"So we can talk without anyone interrupting us." He glanced across the bench seat. "But if you want, I'll take you back home."

He watched her profile in the shadowed light. She closed her eyes then whispered, "No, it might be good if we talk. At least to clear the air."

"Oh, darlin', I plan to do more than clear the air."

Lori jerked her head around and even in the darkness he could see she was glaring. She opened her mouth but he stopped her words.

"Hold that thought. We're here." He pulled into the parking space and climbed out. No more snow had fallen since the last time he'd followed her here. It hadn't gotten any warmer, either.

He pulled his sheepskin coat together to ward off the cold as he went around to Lori's side. After helping her out, they hurried up to the lit porch. He took the key from his pocket and rushed on to explain, "I stopped by earlier." He unlocked the door, pushed it open and turned on the light inside the door.

"After you," he told her, watching surprise cross her pretty face. "Come on, let's get inside where it's warm."

Lori felt Jace's hand against her back, nudging her in. Once inside she stopped and looked around, trying not to think about the last time they'd been here. It didn't work. Memories flooded her head. How incredible it had been being in Jace's arms, making love with him.

"Just let me get a fire started." Jace went straight to the fireplace, where logs had been placed on the grate. He turned on the gas and the flames shot over the wood. He lit the candles that were lined up along the mantel, then turned to her. "You should be warm in a few minutes."

She recalled another time he hadn't waited for the fire to warm her. She pushed away the thought and walked to the table where she saw a vase of fresh flowers. Red roses. She faced him. "You bought these?"

He nodded.

"So you'd planned to bring me here?"

He pulled off his jacket and went to her. "I've been thinking about it since I left Denver. I want to be with you alone, to talk to you."

With her heart racing, she returned to the fire and held out her hands to warm them. Mostly, she wanted to gather her thoughts, but she was overwhelmed by this man. She wanted to be hopeful, but she also recalled what Jace had told her. He didn't want to get involved with another woman.

"Are you ready to listen to what I have to say?"

She stared into the fire. "So now you want to talk?

Why didn't you call me before? Let me know what was going on."

"Because I didn't know myself until recently. I was in mediation during the day with Shelly and her lawyers. At night, I was trying to ease my daughter's fears." His sapphire gaze met hers. "And I guess I've been so used to doing things on my own, I didn't know how to depend on someone else."

"You didn't have to be alone. I was here for you."

"I know that now. Yet, in the end, I had to make the decision based on my daughter's well-being. It was hard to know what was best for Cassie. Was I being selfish wanting her with me?"

Hearing his stress, she turned, but didn't go to him. "Oh, Jace. No, you weren't being selfish. You love Cassie enough to want to give her stability. I also believe that you love your daughter enough that if Shelly could give Cassie what she needed, you'd let her have custody."

He smiled. "It always amazes me how you seem to know me so well."

That wasn't true, she thought, praying he wanted the same thing she did. To be together. "Not so. I have no idea why you brought me here, especially since I haven't heard a word in the past week. And what about this wedding?"

This time he came to her. He stood so close, she could inhale his wonderful scent. The only sounds were the logs crackling in the fire as she waited for an explanation.

Then he took her hand. "I might have helped a little with a nudge to Edmund. He took it from there and went to see Shelly. They were married yesterday by the same judge who helped with the custody case. I escorted Cassie to her mother's wedding."

"Shelly got married?"

"Yes. I thought things would go smoother if I helped Shelly settle her problem with her now-husband. I contacted him the day I arrived, and got him to come with me to Shelly's place." He shrugged. "They took it from there, and now they're headed to England for their honeymoon and his family."

Jace met her dark eyes and nearly lost his concentration. "Before Shelly left we managed to sit down and decide what would be best for our daughter. In the end, Cassie told her mother she wanted to live with me in Destiny."

"That had to be hard on Shelly."

Jace nodded. "But she gets visitation, summers and holidays. She can't take Cassie out of the country until she's older." He studied Lori's pretty face and his stomach tightened. He wanted her desperately.

"It all finally got settled yesterday, and Cassie and I caught the first flight back here...and came to see you."

He reached for her hand and tugged her closer. "I want more, Lori. More than just having my daughter in my life. I also want you. No, not just want you, but need you."

Not giving her a chance to resist, his mouth came down on hers in an all-consuming kiss. He couldn't resist her, either. His hands moved over her back, going downward to her hips, drawing her against him.

With a gasp, she pulled back. "You're not playing fair," she accused.

"I want you, Lorelei Hutchinson. I'll use any means possible to have you."

"Wait." Lori pushed him away, not liking this. "What are you exactly talking about? Seduction?" She deserved more. "I won't be that secret woman in your life, Jace, that you pull out whenever it's convenient."

He frowned. "Whoa. Who said anything about that…" He stopped as if to regroup.

"First of all, I'm sorry that I ever made you feel that way. I asked a lot of you when I left here, and I know I should have called you. Believe me I wanted to, but I was so afraid that if I did, I'd confess how I felt about you. I didn't have a right yet. I needed all my concentration on Cassie. You and I both know what it's like to lose parents. I would do anything not to have that happen to my daughter." His gaze bore into hers. "No matter how much I care about you, Lori, I couldn't abandon my child and come to you." He swallowed. "No matter how much I wanted to. Not matter how much I love you."

She closed her eyes.

"No, look at me, Lori. I'm not your father. I'm never going to leave you, ever. How could I when I can't seem to be able to live without you. Even if I had to move back to Denver because of Cassie, I would have figured out a way to come and be with you, too."

"You love me?"

He drew her close and nodded. "From the top of your pretty blond hair, to your incredible brown eyes, down to your cute little ruby-red painted toes." He kissed her forehead, then brushed his lips against each eyelid. His mouth continued a journey to her cheek, then she shivered as he reached her ear. "I'll tell you about all your other delicious body parts later," he promised, then pulled back and looked down at her. "If you'll let me."

"Oh, Jace. I love you, too," she whispered.

"I was hoping you felt that way." He pulled her into his arms and kissed her deeply. By the time he released her they were both breathing hard.

"We better slow down a minute, or I'll forget what I was about to do." He went to his coat and pulled a small box out of his jacket pocket, then returned to Lori.

Her eyes grew round. "Jace?"

He felt a little shaky. "I want this to be perfect, but if I manage to mess up something, just remember how much I love you." He drew a breath. "Lorelei Hutchinson, I probably can't offer you a perfect life. I have a home that's still under construction. A business that isn't off the ground yet." His eyes met hers. "And a daughter that I'm going to ask you to be a mother to."

A tear ran down her cheek. "Oh, Jace, don't you know, those are assets. And I couldn't love Cassie any more than if she were my own."

"She loves you, too."

"So she's okay with me and you?"

He nodded. "She even approved of the ring." He opened the box and she gasped at the square-cut diamond solitaire with the platinum band.

"Oh, my. It's beautiful."

That was his cue. He got down on one knee. "Lorelei Hutchinson, you are my heart. Will you marry me?"

She touched his face with her hands and kissed him softly. "Yes, Jace, oh, yes."

With her mouth still against his, he rose and wrapped his arms around her as he deepened the kiss. He couldn't let her go. Ever.

He finally broke off the kiss, then slipped the ring on her finger. He kissed her softly, then pulled back. "Give me one second, then we'll have the rest of the night."

Lori nodded and looked down at her ring. She couldn't believe this was really happening. "Good, I'm going to need your full attention the rest of the night to convince me that this isn't a fairy tale."

He grinned, took out his cell phone and punched in a number. "You got it." He put it to his ear. "Hi, sweetheart," Jace said into the receiver. "She said yes." He looked at Lori and winked. "Yes, we'll celebrate tomorrow. I love you, too." He ended the call. "I hope you don't mind. Cassie wanted to know what your answer was."

"I don't mind at all. I think we have enough love that I can share it with your daughter." She wrapped her arms around his waist. "But maybe tonight, I'll let you show me."

"Not just tonight, Lori. Always. Forever."

EPILOGUE

IT WAS nearly Christmas in Destiny.

This year, the town council had asked Lori to light the big tree in the town square. She was honored, to say the least. Of course, she didn't do it alone. She'd invited Zack and Cassie to help throw the switch that lit the fifty-foot ponderosa pine.

While enjoying the colorful light show and the children's choir singing carols, she recalled the first day she'd arrived in Destiny. She felt so alone, then she started meeting the people here. That included one stubborn contractor who made her heart race. Made her aware of what she'd been missing in life.

For Lori there were bittersweet memories, too. Her father was gone and she'd never had the chance to have a relationship with him. But with her new family, she wasn't going to be alone. Not only Gina and Zack, but also her future husband, Jace, and a stepdaughter, Cassie.

Suddenly she felt a pair of arms slip around her waist from behind. She smiled and leaned back against Jace's broad chest.

"So are you enjoying your big night?" he said against her ear.

"Oh, yes." She smiled, recalling the last time she'd been here with her father. She called them treasured memories now. "But I have to say, I'm glad the school play is over."

"Until next year," he reminded her.

"Very funny. I'm planning to be really busy."

"You do too much as it is," he said as they watched the children's choir singing beside the tree. He tightened his hold, his large body shielding her from the cold night. "Between the mortgage and college scholarship programs, you have no free time."

She and Jace had made the decision together about taking only a small part of the inheritance to put away for the kids; the rest would go back into the town. They both made an excellent income from Hutchinson Corp properties.

"I want to get the programs up and ready for when my father's money comes through next fall." She stole a glance over her shoulder at him. "You'd be proud of me. I've turned over my job on the mortgage committee to Erin. She'll go to all the meetings, and I'll work from her recommendations."

"However you get it done, you're a pretty special lady to be so generous to this town."

She turned in his arms. "I only want to be your special lady."

He grew serious. "You are, Lori, and will always be." He kissed her sweetly. "How about we ditch this place for something a little more private."

"Oh, I'd like that, but you know we can't. For one thing, Cassie and Zack are singing." They both looked at the children. "And we're all invited back to the Keenan Inn for a party and to finalize our wedding plans. It's going to be a big undertaking for Claire and Gina to pull this off, especially with the holidays."

"I know, the first wedding at Hutchinson House," he said.

"The first of many, I hope," she reminded him.

Jace had to smile. With the exception of Cassie's birth, he couldn't remember ever being this happy. Now he had it all, the woman he loved and his daughter permanently. "So I guess a wild night together is out of the question."

"Of course not. It's just postponed for a few weeks."

"Until New Year's Eve," he finished. The date they'd chosen for their wedding. "That's a long three weeks off." Even longer since they'd spent most of their time with Cassie trying to help her adjust to the new arrangement. He hated having to send Lori home every night.

"You sure we can't sneak off to the cabin tonight?"

She gave him a quick kiss. "Just hold that thought and I promise to make it worth your while after the wedding."

"You being here with me now has made my dreams come true."

Hutchinson House never looked so beautiful.

On New Year's Eve Lori stood at the window of the master suite. She could see over the wide yard toward the front of the property.

The ornate gates were covered with thousands of tiny silver lights and many more were strung along the hedges. It was only a prelude for what was to come as the wedding guests approached the end of the circular drive and the grand house on the hill.

The porch railings were draped in fresh garland, and

more lights were intermixed with the yards of green-ery that smelled of Christmas. White poinsettias edged the steps leading to the wide front door trimmed with a huge fresh-cut wreath.

Lori smiled. The Hutchinson/Yeager wedding was going to be the first of many parties in this house.

Gina came in dressed in a long dark green grown. "Oh, Lori. You look so beautiful."

Lori glanced down at her wedding dress. She'd fallen in love with the floor-length ivory gown the second she'd seen it at Rocky Mountain Bridal Shop, from the top of the sweetheart neckline, to the fitted jeweled bodice with a drop waist and satin skirt. Her hair was pulled back, adorned with a floral headband attached to a long tulle veil.

"I hope Jace thinks so."

Gina handed her a deep red rose bouquet. "He will."

She felt tears forming. "I'm so lucky to have found him, and Cassie."

Gina blinked, too. "They're lucky to have you." She gripped Lori's hand. "I love you, sis. Thank you for al-ways being there for us."

"Hey, you were there for me, too. And nothing will change. We're still family. I'm only going to be a few miles from your new place." Lori frowned, knowing they had arranged to live in their own house. "You feel okay about the move?"

Her sister nodded. "Zack and I are going to be fine."

Lori knew that. Her sister was working with Kaley, having hours that enabled her to be home when Zack got out of school. She still worried about Eric showing up someday, but they'd all keep an eye out.

Gina straightened. "Okay, let's get your special day started."

They walked into the hall toward the head of the stairs where Charlie was waiting. She couldn't lie, every girl dreamed of walking down the aisle escorted by her father. She wasn't any different. At least now she'd been able to make peace with it all.

She whispered, "I'll always miss you, Dad."

Smiling, Charlie had tears in his eyes when she arrived. "Oh, Miss Lorelei, you are a vision. I'm so honored to escort you today."

She gripped his hands. "Thank you, Charlie."

The older man offered her his arm. "I know there's an anxious young man waiting for his bride."

The music began and Cassie and Zack, the flower girl and ring bearer, started down the petal-covered stairs. The banister entwined with more garland that wound down to the large entry. Next Gina began her descent. Once her sister reached the bottom the music swelled.

Holding tight on to Charlie, Lori's heart raced when she made her way down. Once she touched the bottom steps, she took it all in.

The room was filled with flowers: roses, carnations and poinsettias, all white. Rows of wooden chairs, filled with family and friends, lined either side of the runner that led through the entry and into the dining room and ended at a white trellis covered in greenery. And underneath stood Jace. The man who was going to share her life.

Jace's breath caught when his gaze met Lori's. She was beautiful. His heart swelled. He never knew he could love someone so much.

She made her way to him and he had to stop himself from going to her. Finally she arrived and he took her hand. When he locked on her big brown eyes, everything else seemed to fade away. There was only her. It was just the two of them exchanging vows, making the life commitment.

The minister began the ceremony and the vows were exchanged. Jace listened to her speak and was humbled by her words.

Then came his turn. He somehow managed to get the emotional words past his tight throat. Then Justin passed him the ring, and he slipped the platinum band on her finger. He held out his hand so she could do the same.

He gripped both her hands and the minister finally pronounced them husband and wife. Jace leaned down, took her in his arms and kissed her.

There were cheers as the minister announced, "It's my pleasure to introduce to you, Mr. and Mrs. Jace Yeager."

Jace held his bride close, never wanting to let her go. She was his heart, his life, the mother of his future children.

It had been a long journey but they had found each other. He pulled back and looked at his bride. "Hello, Mrs. Yeager."

With tears in her eyes, she answered, "Hello, Mr. Yeager."

Together they walked down the aisle hand in hand past the well-wishers toward their future together. It was their Destiny.

* * * * *

MELTING THE ICE
QUEEN'S HEART

AMY RUTTAN

This book is dedicated to one of my best friends, Diane. You are so strong and my awe and admiration of you is so much I can't even begin to explain it. Love you.

And to a great friend, Chris. There are friends you make who you feel like you've known your whole life in just a few short moments upon meeting. You were one of them. My family and I miss you every day, Mr. Baxter.

CHAPTER ONE

"WE HAVE A state-of-the art facility here at Bayview Grace and we're staffed with some of the top surgeons in the country." Dr. Virginia Potter gritted her teeth, but then flashed the board of directors and investors the best smile she could muster.

She hated this aspect of her job, but as Chief of Surgery it was par for the course. She'd rather have her hands dirty, working the trauma floor with the rest of the emergency doctors, but she was used to schmoozing. Earning scholarships and being on countless deans' lists had helped her perfect the fine art of rubbing elbows. It's how she'd got through school. Her childhood certainly hadn't prepared her for that.

Still, Virginia missed her time on the floor, saving lives. She still got surgery time, but it wasn't nearly as much as she used to get.

This is what you wanted, she reminded herself. It was career or family. There was no grey area. Her father had proved that to her. He had spent more time with his family instead of rising up in his job and because of that and then an injury he had been the first to be let go when the factory had moved its operations down south. Virginia had learned from that. To be successful, you couldn't have both.

It was the values her father had instilled in her. To always strive for the best, go for the top. Again, that was a sacrifice one had to make. It was a position she wanted.

To not make the same mistakes in life he had. Keep a roof

over your head and food on the table. That was what she had
been taught was a mark of success.

Others have both. She shook that thought away. No. She
didn't want a family. She couldn't lose anyone else. She
wouldn't risk feeling that pain again.

"I'd really like to see the hospital's emergency department,"
Mrs. Greenly said, breaking through Virginia's thoughts.

Anywhere but there, her inner voice screamed, but instead
Virginia nodded. "Of course. If you'll follow me?"

Why? Her stomach felt like it was about to bottom out to
the soles of her feet. Virginia had planned to steer clear of the
emergency room. There were so many more "tame" departments at Bayview Grace.

Departments with Attendings who were more polished and
less dangerous to her senses.

Bayview Grace's ER Attending was the quintessential bad
boy of the hospital.

She led the investors and the board of directors towards the
emergency department and tried to think back to the posted
schedule and whether Dr. Gavin Brice was scheduled for the
day shift, because even though Dr. Brice was a brilliant surgeon he and the board of directors didn't see eye to eye.

Maybe he's not working?

Oh, who was she kidding? He was always working and
she admired him for that, except this one time she wished he
wasn't so efficient.

Virginia had been the one to push for them to hire Brice.
They hadn't been impressed with his extensive CV. The board
had wanted a more glamorous, "citified" surgeon. Not one
who'd gotten his hands dirty and lived rough.

"It's all on your head, Dr. Potter. If Dr. Brice fails, you fail."

The threat had been clear.

At first Virginia had been nervous, because hiring Dr. Brice
had put her job on the line, but then she'd realized she was
being silly. His work with Border Free Physicians, practicing surgery in developing countries around the world, was an

experience in itself. His survival rates were the highest she'd ever seen.

There was no way Dr. Brice would not succeed at Bayview Grace.

She'd see to it, but the board still wasn't impressed with him.

His survival rates were still high. Topnotch, in fact, but Gavin was unorthodox and a wild mustang on the surgical floor.

He had no patience for surgical interns. No patience for anyone really.

Gavin followed his own rules when it came to practicing medicine. He was the perpetual thorn in Virginia's side.

Please, don't be on duty. Please, don't be on duty.

The board of directors and their investors headed into the emergency department.

"Get out of the way!"

Virginia just had time to grab Mrs. Greenly out of the line of fire as a gurney came rushing by from one of the trauma pods.

Speak of the devil.

Gavin Brice was on top of a man, pumping an Ambu bag and shouting orders to a group of flustered interns.

"There's no time, he has a pneumothorax. We have to insert a chest tube." He climbed down and handed the operation of the manual respirator over to a resident.

Oh. My. God. Did he just say what I thought he said?

"Dr. Brice," Virginia called out in warning.

Gavin glanced over his shoulder and didn't respond, effectively dismissing her presence. "Get me a 20 French chest tube kit." One of the interns ran off.

"Dr. Brice," Virginia said again. "Think about what you're doing."

The intern returned with the chest tube kit, handing it to Dr. Brice as he finished wiping the patient's side with antiseptic. "Ten blade."

Virginia gritted her teeth, angered she was being ignored. She spun around and gauged the expressions of the board members. Most had nasty pallors. Mrs. Greenly looked like she was about to pass out.

"Dr. Brice!"

"I said ten blade! Have you actually studied medicine?" he barked at an intern, ignoring Virginia.

She stepped towards the gurney. "You can't place that chest tube here, Dr. Brice. Take him to a trauma bay or an OR, stat!"

"Dr. Potter, there are no rooms free and I don't have time to mince words. As you can see, this man has sustained crush injuries and has pneumothorax from a motor vehicle accident. He could die unless I do this right here, right now."

"I really think—"

Gavin didn't even look at her as he cut an incision in the man's chest and inserted the chest tube. "Come on, damn you!"

Virginia watched the patient's vitals on the monitor. It didn't take long before the man's blood pressure and systolic regulated and for the fluid to start to drain through the silicone tube.

"Great. Now we need to clear an OR, *stat*." Gavin shot her a look. One of annoyance. He shook his head in disgust as the trauma team began to wheel the man off towards the operating rooms, his hand still in the patient's chest.

All that was left in his wake was a spattering of blood on the floor from where he'd made the incision to insert the tube.

Virginia rubbed her temples and turned to the board and the investors. "Well, that's our ER. How about we end this tour here and head back to the boardroom?"

It was probably the dumbest thing she'd ever said, but she didn't know how to recover from this situation. In her two years as Chief of Surgery this had never happened to her before. She'd never had an emergency play out in front of the board in the middle of a tour.

Investors had never had to watch a chest tube be inserted in front of them before.

The stunned members nodded and headed out of the department, except for Mr. Edwin Schultz—the tight-lipped head of the board. Another thorn in her side. It was no secret that he thought the hospital was bad from a business perspective. He was the one holding Bayview Grace back, because as far as Virginia was concerned, Edwin Schultz wanted to drop the axe on her hospital.

"Dr. Potter, I'd like to speak with you about Dr. Brice in private."

"Of course," Virginia said, rolling her eyes when his back was turned. She opened a door to a dark exam room, flicked on the lights and ushered Mr. Schultz inside. When she had closed the door, she crossed her arms and braced for a verbal onslaught of tsunami proportions.

"What was that?" Mr. Schultz asked.

"A pneumothorax. The chest tube insertion probably saved the man's life."

"Can you be certain?"

"If Dr. Brice hadn't have performed that procedure, the patient would've certainly died."

Mr. Schultz frowned. "But in the middle of the ER? In front of the investors and other patients?"

"It wasn't planned, if that's what you're implying." Virginia counted to ten in her head. Her whole body clenched as she fought back the urge to knock some common sense into Edwin Schultz's addled brains.

"I didn't say it was, Dr. Potter." He snorted, pulling out a handkerchief to dab at his sweaty bald head. He folded it up again and placed it in his breast pocket. "I'm suggesting that maybe you should have a talk with him about the proper place to perform a medical procedure."

She wanted to tell Schultz that sometimes there was no time to find a proper room or an OR in trauma surgery when a life was at stake, only that wasn't the diplomatic way and she'd worked so hard to become one of the youngest chiefs at Bayview Grace, heck, one of the youngest in San Francisco at the age of thirty. She wasn't about to give that up. Job stability was all that mattered.

Her career was all that mattered.

"I'll have a talk with Dr. Brice when he's out of surgery."

Mr. Schultz nodded. "Please do. Now, let's go take care of the investors because if they don't invest the money we need, the emergency department will have to be cut."

"Cut?" Virginia's world spun around, her body clenching again. "What do you mean, cut?"

"I was going to speak to you later about this, but the hospital is losing money. Many members of the board feel that Bayview Grace could make a lot more money as a private clinic. The emergency department is the biggest detriment to the hospital's budget."

"We're a level-one trauma center." And they had just got that distinction because of two years of her blood, sweat and tears.

Mr. Schultz sighed. "I know, but unless we get the investors we need, we have no choice."

Virginia cursed under her breath. "And how do you feel, Mr. Schultz?"

"I think we should close the emergency department." The head of the board said no more and pushed past her.

Virginia scrubbed her hand over her face.

What am I doing?

As a surgeon, she wanted to tell Mr. Schultz what she thought about shutting down Bayview Grace's ER, but she didn't. She held her tongue, like she always did, and her father's words echoed in her ear.

"Don't tick off the boss man, darling. Job security is financial security."

And financial security meant food, home and all the necessities.

Virginia wanted to hold onto her job, like anyone did. She wouldn't wish a life of poverty like she'd endured as a child on her worst enemy.

So she was going to hold her head up high and make sure those investors didn't walk away. She was going to make sure Bayview's ER didn't close its doors so the people who worked in trauma didn't lose their jobs.

Though she respected Dr. Brice and his abilities, she knew she had to rein him in to keep control of her hospital.

She just didn't know how she was going to do that, or that she really wanted to.

"Where's the family?" Gavin asked the nearest nurse he could wrangle.

"Whose family?" the nurse asked, without looking up from the computer monitor.

Gavin bit back his frustration. He knew he had to be nicer to the nurses. At least here he had them.

"Mr. Jones, the man with the crush injuries who had the pneumothorax."

The nurse's eyes widened. "In the waiting room. Mrs. Jones and her three teenage sons. They're hard to miss."

"Uh, thank you…"

The nurse rolled her eyes. "Sadie."

"Right. Thanks." Gavin cursed inwardly as he ripped off his scrub cap and jammed it into a nearby receptacle. He should really know her name since he'd been working with her for six weeks, but Gavin couldn't keep anyone's name straight.

Except Virginia's.

It wasn't hard to keep her name straight in his head. The moment he'd met her, his breath had been taken away with those dark brown eyes to match the dark hair in a tidy chignon. She was so put together, feminine, like something out of a magazine, and then she spoke about all the rules and regulations, about everything he was doing wrong, and it shattered his illusion.

No wonder the staff called her Ice Queen. She was so cold and aloof. There was no warmth about her. It was all business.

The woman was a brilliant surgeon, he'd noticed the few times they'd worked together, but she was always slapping his wrists for foolish things.

"It's not sanitary. Legal is going to talk to you. The hospital could get sued," Virginia had stated.

In fact, when he had a moment, he planned to discuss the functionality and the layout out of this emergency department with her and the board.

It was horrendous.

When he'd been working in the field, in developing countries, everything he'd needed had been within arm's reach, and if it hadn't been then he'd made do with what he'd had and no one had complained. No one had talked about reprimanding him.

He'd been free to do what he wanted to save lives. It's why he'd become a trauma surgeon, for God's sake.

If he wasn't needed in San Francisco, if he had any other choice, he'd march into Virginia's office and hand in his resignation.

Only Lily and Rose stopped him.

He was working in this job, this suffocating, regimented environment, because of them. He didn't blame them; it wasn't their fault their mother had died. It's just that Gavin wished with all his heart he was anywhere but here.

Although he liked being at home with them. He wanted to do right by them. Give them the love and security he'd never had.

Gavin stopped at the charge desk and set Mr. Jones's chart on the desk to fill out some more information before he approached the family with news.

"You know that was the board of directors you traumatized today," Sadie said from behind the desk.

Gavin grunted in response.

What else was new?

Board of directors. He pinched the bridge of his nose. "I suppose Dr. Potter wants to have a little word with me?"

"Bingo." Sadie got up and left.

Gavin cursed under his breath again. "When?" he called after her.

"Ten minutes ago," she called out over her shoulder.

Damn.

Well, Virginia would have to wait.

He had to tell Mrs. Jones her husband, who'd sustained severe crush injuries in a car accident, was going to be okay.

All thanks to his minor indiscretion over the chest tube insertion in front of the board.

Only he wouldn't get any thanks. From Mrs. Jones, yes, but from the people who ran this place, no.

It would be another slap on the wrist. Potter would tell him again how he was skating on thin ice with the board of directors.

It would take all his strength not to quit. Only he couldn't.

No other hospital in San Francisco was hiring or had been interested in him. He didn't have a flashy CV after working as a field surgeon for Border Free Physicians.

He didn't make the covers of medical journals or have some great research to tempt another hospital with.

All he had were his two hands and his surgical abilities.

Those two hands had saved a man today, but that wasn't good enough for the board. The bottom line was the only thing that mattered and it made him furious.

If it wasn't for the girls, he'd quit.

He couldn't uproot them. He wouldn't do that to them, he wouldn't have them suffer the same life he and Casey had endured as army brats, moving from pillar to post, never making friends and having absentee parents who had both been in the service.

Although he understood his parents now. He respected them for serving their country and doing their duty. He lived by the same code, only he wasn't going to raise a family living out of a backpack, and because he loved his life and his work he'd never planned on settling down.

He planned to die doing what he loved. Like his father had done.

Working until he'd dropped.

Of course, that had all changed seven months ago when Casey had called him.

Casey wanted stability for her girls and that's exactly what Gavin was going to give them.

Stability.

He picked up Mr. Jones's chart and headed towards the waiting room.

Virginia could wait a few moments more and he'd smooth things over with the board. Mrs. Jones, however, wouldn't wait a second more.

CHAPTER TWO

HE'S GOOD PR for the hospital.

Virginia felt like she was running out of ways to praise Dr. Gavin Brice to the board of directors. None of them were physicians.

None of them understood medicine.

And because none of the board understood medicine she constantly had to explain to them the actions of Dr. Brice; just like she'd done for the past hour.

Virginia rubbed her temples, trying to will away the nagging headache that gnawed her just behind her eyes.

It'd been grueling, but she'd managed to smooth things over. By again reminding them of Dr. Brice's phenomenal survival rate. It was probably that way because of the unorthodox techniques he used.

Of course, what was the point when the head of the board seemed so keen to shut down the hospital's emergency department and make Bayview Grace a private hospital? Private meant only for the wealthy.

And catering only to the wealthy made her sick.

When she'd first decided to become a doctor she hadn't just want to help those who could afford it. It was one of the reasons she'd chosen Bayview to do her intern and residency years. Bayview, back then, had had a fantastic pro bono fund and a free clinic.

The free clinic had been closed two years ago when she'd

done her boards. When she'd become chief she'd tried to get it back, but that would have meant dipping into the pro bono money and that money had been needed.

Mr. Schultz had feigned regret, but Virginia had seen those dollar signs flashing in his eyes. It made her feel a bit sick.

Her stomach knotted as she thought about the countless people from all walks of life who came to her hospital. The pro bono budget was dwindling and she wished she could help more, because at one time in her life she'd been in the poorest of the poor's shoes, getting by on only sub-par medical care.

It was why her sister Shyanne had died.

Shyanne had hidden her pregnancy from her parents, knowing they couldn't afford to help her with medical bills, but the pregnancy had turned out to be ectopic. Virginia had happened to be home on a school break in her first year of medical school and had kicked herself for not seeing the signs early enough.

By the time the ambulance had come to take Shyanne to the hospital, she was gone. Ruptured fallopian tube. She'd bled out too fast.

It was one reason why Virginia donated so much time to the pro bono cases, why she didn't want Bayview's ER closed, like the free clinic had been closed.

There was a knock on her office door, but before she could answer the man in question swaggered into the room and she had to remember herself. She had to control the flush that was threatening to creep up her neck and erupt in crimson blooms in her cheeks.

It was a damn pain in the rump that she was basically his boss and that he was so devilishly sexy. Reddish-gold hair, green eyes like emeralds. Even the scar on his cheek, which just grazed that deep, deep dimple, made the young woman she'd buried under her businesslike façade squeal just a little bit. He was the quintessential bad boy and she'd always had a soft spot for bad boys. Even though her mother had warned her not to give them the time of day.

Virginia and Shyanne had listened. Shyanne had got involved with a good boy. One who had been a golden son of De Smet, South Dakota. A golden son who had knocked Shyanne up and taken off on a football scholarship, leaving Shyanne in the lurch.

"You wanted to see me, Dr. Potter?"

"Yes. Please, take a seat." Pulling at the collar of her blouse, she motioned to the seat in front of her desk. When he moved closer she caught a whiff of his scent. A clean scent of something spicy but rugged and the smell made her insides flutter. With a calming breath she folded her hands neatly in front of her on her blotter. "The board has asked me to speak with you."

A brief smile quirked on his lips as he sat down. "Again?"

"Yes. Are you surprised?"

"Not really. I did happen to catch the expression of some of those investors today."

"You think it's funny?"

Gavin cocked his head to one side. "A bit."

Virginia bit her lip and silently counted to ten. "I managed to smooth things over."

He rolled his eyes. "Look, can I lay something out for you, Dr. Potter?"

She was stunned. "Of course, by all means."

"I don't care what the board approves or disapproves of. I don't care if they think the way I practice medicine is barbaric."

"I don't think they actually said barbaric, Dr. Brice."

He grinned. "Please, call me Gavin."

Virginia swallowed the lump in her throat. It was the first time since they'd met that he'd asked her to use his first name. Not that they'd had much social interaction, besides work-related conversations, and these seemingly frequent discussions about the board and his disregard for following hospital policies.

"Gavin, if you're unhappy, perhaps there's something we can do, or I can do, to make your practice here better?"

"There's nothing you can do. Frankly, I wouldn't be happy anywhere outside Border Free Physicians."

Intriguing. "Then can I ask you a personal question?"

"Of course, but I may not answer."

Touché. "Why did you leave Border Free Physicians and apply here?"

Gavin's easy smile faded and his mouth pressed into a thin line, his brow furrowing. Virginia couldn't help but wonder if this was something he wasn't going to answer. In his few weeks here she'd ascertained he was a private man. He didn't socialize with many people, ate his lunch alone and did his job efficiently, as far as Virginia was concerned. Maybe not to the board's approval, but as long as the patients lived and there were no lawsuits she was happy.

"I'm needed here," he said finally. Only that's all he said. No explanation about why he'd applied for the job or why he'd told her he wasn't happy here and wouldn't be happy anywhere but with Border Free Physicians.

So why had he left?

"You look confused," Gavin said, the teasing tone returning to his voice.

"Not confused." *Oh, who am I kidding?* "Okay, a bit confused."

"I'm sorry. I didn't really want to put you in this position."

"You haven't put me in a position, Dr. Brice."

"Gavin."

Heat bloomed in her cheeks. "Gavin. I only want to help you, even if this position is not the one you want."

Gavin nodded his head. "I thank you for that."

"For what?"

"For trying to help, but I really don't think I need it."

"I know it's difficult, you came from a job where you worked in rough conditions and had to think on your feet and quickly, but the board of directors has to protect the hospital's best interests."

"Isn't that basically what all trauma surgeons do?"

Virginia smiled. "Yes, but there are certain rules and regulations that have to take place in a hospital setting. They feel what happened today was inappropriate."

He snorted. "Inappropriate to save a man's life?"

"There are rules and the board is protecting the interests of the hospital."

"So you keep reiterating."

"It seems I have to." She crossed her arms. "Do you understand what I'm saying?"

"The bottom line." That look of disdain returned and he shook his head slightly.

Virginia knew and understood what he was feeling, but what choice did they have?

"Unfortunately."

Gavin stood. "I have to protect my patient's best interests, Dr. Potter. I won't change the way I practice medicine."

"I'm trying to help you." Now she was getting irritated. How could she help someone who didn't want her help? Easy. She couldn't. She was losing an uphill battle when it came to Dr. Brice.

He pulled out his pager and glanced at it. Not looking at her, thus silently ending their conversation. "I appreciate that, but I'm needed back in the ER."

Stunned, Virginia stood as he left and then watched through the glass as he jogged down the hall towards the ER.

What just happened?

She slowly sank back down into her chair, feeling a bit like a deer caught in headlights, like someone had just pulled a fast one on her.

The board wouldn't be happy with her for not reining him in, but then again she didn't really want to. Dr. Brice was someone who moved to the beat of his own drum. He annoyed the nurses because he couldn't remember their names, didn't have much time for interns and, yes, performed a medical procedure in front of a bunch of rich investors, but the point was he saved lives.

His curriculum vitae was impressive. As far she was concerned.

His image, his work in Africa, doing surgery on refugees, brought in good press for the hospital. People had a soft spot for good Samaritans.

Even if the board thought he was a bit of a rogue surgeon.

Virginia rubbed her temples. Her tension headache was becoming stronger. Couldn't he see how she was trying to make his transition to a metropolitan hospital setting just a bit easier? There was one thing Virginia took away from this meeting today and that was that Dr. Gavin Brice was a bit of a pompous ass.

Dammit.

Gavin glanced at his wristwatch and noticed the time. He was late and Lily was going to kill him. Rose wouldn't, though, she was so sweet, but Lily was a force to be reckoned with. This was the third time he'd missed taking her to ballet lessons and he'd pinky-sworn that he'd be the one to take her this time instead of Rosalie, the sitter.

He had no idea what he was doing and he was a terrible father figure, but that was the crux of the matter—he wasn't Lily's and Rose's father. He was their uncle, but as he was their only caregiver since their mother, his sister, had died of cancer, he was no longer cool Uncle Gavin who sent them postcards from new and exciting locations as he traveled to different developing countries with Border Free Physicians.

Now he was Mr. Mom and not very good at it. Lily, who was eight, had reminded him of it every day for the last couple of months.

"That's not how Mom did it."

Rose was four, all smiles, but she didn't say a single word.

It's why he was here, in San Francisco, instead of continuing with Border Free Physicians. He hated not being where he wanted to be, but he'd do anything to take care of those girls.

To give them the home life and stability he and his late sister, Casey, had never had.

After all his nieces had been through, there was no way he could drag them from pillar to post, living rough while he worked. He'd had to give up his life as a field trauma physician and get something stable, reliable and in the girls' hometown.

He needed to give them structure and not rip them away from all they knew. Especially not when their world had been shattered after their mother's recent death and their father's when Rose had been only an infant.

He had to be reliable or he could lose the girls to their paternal grandparents. He'd promised Casey he wouldn't let that happen. It had been only three months since Casey had died and though he'd always said he didn't want to be tied down, he wouldn't give the girls up for anything.

Even though he was a hopeless failure.

A cool breeze rolled in off the bay and Gavin shivered. He pulled his coat tighter. Even though it was August, there was a nip in the air and he still wasn't acclimatized to anything that wasn't subtropical.

He stuffed his hands in his pockets and headed for the grey minivan he'd inherited from Casey. His motorbike was sitting alone and forgotten under a tarp in the garage, because you couldn't ferry kids to and from various dance rehearsals, art classes and Girl Scouts' meetings on the back of a motorcycle.

As he made his way across the parking lot he caught sight of Virginia walking toward her dark, sleek-looking sedan. Gavin paused a moment to watch her move. She was so put together and she moved with fluid grace. Even if she seemed tight, like a taut bowstring most days.

Her dark hair was piled up on her head, not a strand of hair loose. There was a natural look to her and she didn't need to wear garish makeup to accentuate those dark, chocolate eyes or those ruby lips. Her clothing was stylish and professional but sexy. Today it was the pencil skirt, paired with a crisp shirt and black high heels that showed off her slim but curvy figure in all the right places.

She climbed into her car, and just as she was sitting down her skirt hiked up a bit, giving him a nice view of her stocking-clad thigh.

Gavin's pulse began to race. If any woman could emulate the princess Snow White it was Dr. Virginia Potter.

He let out a hiss of disgust; he'd been reading Rose far too many fairy tales if he was comparing the chief of surgery to Snow White.

Did that make him a dwarf? Though the way some of those surgeons and nurses moved through the hospital, it was like they were on their way to the mines for the day.

Virginia drove away and Gavin scrubbed his hand over his face. He needed a beer and to veg out in front of the television for a while.

One of the perks of being in the city.

He drove through the streets in a trance, letting the day's surgeries just roll off his back. When he pulled up into his sister's pink-colored marina-style home in the outer Richmond district, a twenty-minute commute from the hospital, he finally let out a sigh of relief mixed with frustration.

It had to be pink.

His whole life seemed to be wrapped up in various shades of pink from coral to bubble gum. At least his scrubs weren't pink.

The lights were all on in the living room above the garage, which meant the girls were home from dance rehearsal. Rosalie's car was on the street outside. The garage door opened and he pulled the van inside, next to his tarp-covered Harley.

I know, baby. I miss you too.

He sighed with longing, pulling the garage door down and locking it. Rosalie, having seen him pull up, was leaving as he opened the locked gate onto the street that led to the front door.

"Dr. Brice, how was your day?" Rosalie asked, brightly.

"You don't really want to know. How's Lily?"

Rosalie gave him a broad, toothy grin as she heaved her bag over her shoulder. "You don't really want to know."

"That bad?"

"It's been a rough day for her." Rosalie moved past him to the car. "When is your next shift?"

"Tomorrow, but then I'm not on call this weekend. I don't go back until Wednesday afternoon."

"Ah, a four-day weekend. *Que bueno.* I'll see you tomorrow, Dr. Brice. Have a good night." Gavin waited until Rosalie was safely in her car and had driven away before he locked the gate and headed inside.

The stairs from the entranceway to the main level were scattered with various dance paraphernalia and pink things. As he took a step something squished and squeaked under his feet, causing Rose to materialize at the top of the stairs, scowling with her chubby little arms crossed.

Gavin peeled the rubber giraffe from under his foot. "Sorry, I didn't mean to step on Georgiana."

Rose grinned and held out her hand. Gavin placed Georgiana in Rose's hand. "How's Lily?"

Rose rolled her eyes and then skipped off. Gavin groaned inwardly and dragged himself up the last few steps.

He found Lily sitting at the kitchen table, her chin resting on the table with a dejected look on her face. The same face Casey had made when he'd been taking care of her when their dad and mom had left them while they did their duty to their country.

It made his heart hurt just to think about how much he missed his sister.

"Lily."

Lily glanced at him sideways, her blue eyes so like Casey's. "I know. There was an emergency. I get it."

Gavin took a seat opposite to her. She talked so much like a little adult. "There was an emergency, in fact, a car accident. I had to perform surgery."

"Did you save the person's life?"

"I did."

Lily sat up straight. "Then I guess that's worth it."

At least someone thinks so.

"Very mature of you, Lily. Look, after tomorrow's shift I have the next four days off. I'm not on call and I can spend it with you and Rose."

Lily chirked up. "Really?"

"Really. We can go down to the piers, watch the sea lions." Rose skipped into the room then and crawled up on his lap.

"Can we get some clams?" Lily asked brightly.

Clams? I was willing to offer ice cream...

"You girls like seafood?"

"Yeah, Mom used to take us down to the fish market all the time. We'd get some seafood and she'd make her famous chowder."

Gavin nodded. "Sure. I'll try to make you guys some chowder. How about you two get ready for bed?"

"Sure." Lily got up and took Rose by the hand, leading her towards the front of the house. When Gavin had made sure they were out of earshot he laid his head down on the table. He had never thought he would be a father because he had always been afraid he would be terrible, like his own father was. Oh, his father was a hero all right, but he'd never hugged them, never complimented them and had never been there. It was the same with their mother and it terrified Gavin to his very core. He didn't want to become like them.

Only Casey had had the same fears about becoming a mother and she had been one of the best.

God, I miss her.

He just hoped he was doing right by his nieces.

He owed Casey that much.

CHAPTER THREE

VIRGINIA PICKED UP Mr. Jones's chart and read Gavin's notes quickly. When she glanced up she could see Gavin through the glass partition in Mr. Jones's room. Mr. Jones was still unconscious, so he needed to be in the ICU, but Gavin was speaking to Mrs. Jones.

At least Virginia assumed it was Mrs. Jones, as the woman had been by Mr. Jones's bedside all night. Which was what the night charge nurse had told her when she had started her shift at five that morning.

"Is everything okay, chief?" the charge nurse at the desk asked.

"Yes, Kimber, everything's fine." Virginia smiled and handed the binder back to her. "Just checking on the ER's newest celebrity before I head into surgery."

"Who?"

"Dr. Brice."

Kimber grinned. "Oh, yes, I heard about the excitement in the ER yesterday. I always miss the drama when I'm off."

Virginia cocked an eyebrow. "Is that so? What did you hear?"

"That Dr. Brice inserted a chest tube in front of the investors." Kimber shook her head and chuckled to herself. "I bet they were impressed."

Virginia didn't say anything else as Kimber walked the file back to where it belonged. Before Virginia had been the Chief of Surgery, she'd had friends and comrades she'd been able to talk to about anything. Now, because of her position, she had to be careful of everything she said.

There was no one she could blow off steam with. No one to vent to.

Except the cactus in her apartment.

Even then it wasn't the most animated of conversations.

She missed the days when she could go down to the cafeteria and sit down with fellow attendings and residents and shoot the breeze.

Heck, she could even talk to the nurses back then.

Now they all looked at her for what she was. Their boss.

Their careers were in her hands.

Kimber returned back. "Chief, really, is there anything I can do?"

Deal with the board for me? "No, why?"

"You were staring off into space."

"Thinking."

"About?"

Virginia cocked her eyebrow. "What do you think of Dr. Brice?"

"Dishy." Kimber waggled her eyebrows, but then she instantly sobered. "Sorry, chief."

"Professionally, what do you think?"

"Oh, well…" Kimber hesitated.

"Go on," Virginia urged.

"He's pretty brusque with nurses, doesn't remember our names. Refers to most of us as 'hey you'. Rarely says thank-you. But he's good with the patients and he's a great surgeon."

"Thank you, Kimber."

"Is Dr. Brice in trouble, chief?"

Virginia shook her head. "No, I just wanted to see how well he was getting on with the other members of the staff."

"The answer to that is not well." Kimber walked away from the charge desk, just as Dr. Brice left Mr. Jones's room.

He was staring at his pager, headed right for her. Finally he glanced up and saw her there and his eyes widened momentarily. "Dr. Potter, what brings you to the ICU today? I thought you'd be in more investor meetings."

Virginia gritted her teeth. "No. No meetings today, Dr. Brice."

"Gavin." He flashed her a smug smile, which she wanted to wipe off his face. Instead she ignored him.

"I'm headed for the OR, actually."

"Amazing, I didn't think chiefs of surgery were able to operate."

"I'm a surgeon first and foremost. Now, if you don't mind, I'll be off." She turned from him and headed for the OR suites, but Gavin followed her, keeping pace.

"What surgery are you preforming?"

"A routine cholecystectomy."

"I thought you were a trauma surgeon."

"I'm a general surgeon, but I did work in trauma during my fellowship years. Besides, our ER is staffed with several capable surgeons."

Gavin chuckled. "Not me, though."

Virginia cocked an eyebrow, but continued toward the ORs. "What do you mean?"

"We had this talk yesterday, Virginia. I'm not an asset to Bayview Grace."

"Dr. Brice—"

"Gavin," he interrupted.

She took a calming breath. "Gavin, who said you weren't?"

"You did."

"When?"

"Yesterday, after I saved Mr. Jones's life in front of the board, or have you mentally blocked that catastrophe of public relations proportions from your brain?"

Virginia chuckled. "I never said you weren't an asset. You're a fine surgeon, Gavin, you just have to work on your interpersonal skills." The doors to the scrub room slid open and she stepped inside. Gavin followed her.

Lord. Just let me be.

All she wanted to do was this surgery. Here she could clear her head and think.

"Interpersonal skills?" A smile quirked his lips. "In what ways?"

"I don't have time to talk the semantics over with you. I have a choly to attend to, that is, unless you want to scrub in?"

Please, don't scrub in, one half of her screamed, while the other half of her wanted to see him in action. To work side by side with him.

"I haven't done a routine choly in…well, probably not since my residency, and it wasn't done laparoscopically. The attendings and indeed the hospital where I obtained my residency weren't up to par with Dr. Mühe's ground-breaking procedure."

"I would love to have you assist, Gavin." Virginia stepped on the bar under the sink and began to scrub.

Gavin grinned, his eyes twinkling in the dim light of the scrub room. "Liar."

"Pardon?"

"You don't want me in your OR. I think you've had enough of me."

"That's true. You've been a thorn in my side since I hired you."

He laughed. "I know."

Virginia shook her hands and then grabbed some paper towel. "I would like to see you work, though. I haven't had the chance to observe you, and the nurses tell me you're a brilliant surgeon."

He raised his eyebrows. "I didn't think the nurses cared much for me."

"They don't." She smirked. "You really need to work on remembering their names."

"Not at the top of my priority."

Virginia shook her head and moved towards the sliding door that separated the suite from the scrub room. "Make it a priority, Gavin. You'll find things run a lot smoother if you do. Are you joining me?"

"I think I'll pass, Dr. Potter. I may be needed in Trauma."

"Virginia." She shot him a smug smile and headed into surgery, both relieved and disappointed that he wasn't joining her.

I should've gone into surgery with her.

Gavin was beating himself up over not taking the opportunity to sit in on a surgery with Virginia, the ice queen, even if it had been a routine one.

Emergency had been quiet. Eerily so. He'd resorted to charting, though secretly he was trying to learn the nurses' names but couldn't.

He could remember the most complicated procedure, but when it came to mundane, everyday things like dry-cleaning or remembering a name he couldn't.

What was wrong with him?

Something was definitely wrong with him, because he'd turned down the chance to get to know Virginia by operating with her. She'd been so uptight every time they'd spoken, but this time there had been something different about her.

She was more relaxed, more receptive to gentle teasing.

He'd enjoyed his verbal repartee with her, even if it'd only been for a moment. Gavin had seen the twinkle in her eyes before she'd entered the operating room, that glint of humor, and he'd liked it.

And it had scared him.

He had no time to be thinking about women. The girls were his top priority.

"I won't say what you're thinking, because if I say it we'll be bombarded with a bunch of trauma."

Gavin looked up from his chart to see Dr. Rogerson leaning over the desk, grinning at him. Moira Rogerson was another trauma surgeon, but only a fellow as she'd just passed her boards.

"Pardon?" Gavin asked.

"You know, like how actors don't say 'Macbeth' in the theater."

"Oh, I get what you mean."

ER physicians never remarked on a slow day. If they did it was bad juju and they'd have an influx of patients. Gavin returned to his charting, dismissing Moira.

At least he hoped it gave her the hint. The woman had been pursuing him like a lioness hunting a wounded wildebeest since he'd first set foot in the hospital.

"I was wondering if you'd like to grab a bite to eat with me after work?"

The lioness obviously couldn't take a hint. It wasn't that there was anything wrong with her, she was pretty, intelligent and a brilliant surgeon, but he wasn't interested in her.

He didn't like to be pursued and he wasn't interested in starting a relationship with anyone at the moment.

"I can't."

"Why?"

Gavin sighed in frustration. "I just can't."

"I know you're new to this city. What can you possibly have to do?"

Gavin slammed the binder shut and stood up, perhaps a bit abruptly. "Things." He set the chart down and headed towards the cafeteria. Maybe grabbing some lunch would clear his head.

Moira, thankfully, didn't follow.

Sure, he'd been harsh with her and, yeah, he had an itch that needed to be scratched, but since the girls had come into his life he had to be more responsible.

A year ago he would've taken Moira up on her offer and then some. As long as she hadn't wanted anything serious.

She was attractive.

Now that he had his nieces, he just couldn't be that playboy any more. His dating life could be summed up in two words. Cold. Showers.

In the cafeteria he grabbed a ready-made sandwich and a bottle of water. He was planning to take them outside and get some fresh air when he spotted Virginia on the far side of the cafeteria. It surprised him, as he never saw her in here.

She was sitting in the corner of the cafeteria at a table for two, but she sat alone. She was reading some kind of medical journal as she picked at a salad.

The cafeteria was full of other doctors, nurses, interns, but Virginia sat by herself.

She's the chief of surgery. The boss.

The ice queen.

No one would want to sit with their boss at lunch. They wouldn't feel comfortable, and he felt sorry for her. She was so young and she didn't have it easy.

Just like me.

He crossed the cafeteria and stopped in front of her. "May I join you, Virginia?"

She looked startled and glanced up at him. "Of—of course, Dr. Potter. I mean Gavin."

Gavin took the seat across from her. "How was your choly?"

"Routine." She smiled and his pulse quickened. He liked the way she smiled and especially when it was directed at him, which wasn't often. "How was the ER?"

"I think you can guess."

"I know. I won't say it."

"I'm trying to work on interpersonal skills, but I'm having a hard time putting faces to names."

She cocked an eyebrow. "You don't seem to have that problem with patients."

He nodded. "This is true."

"You're agreeing with me? Amazing." The twinkle of humor appeared again.

"You're mocking me now, aren't you?"

Virginia stabbed a cherry tomato. "So what's the difference between the nurses and the patients?"

"The patients aren't all wearing the same kitten-patterned scrubs."

Virginia chuckled. "Not all the nurses wear kitten scrubs."

"Well pink, then." Gavin snorted. "Always pink."

"What do you mean by that?"

"Nothing." Gavin didn't want to talk about his nieces. His private life was just that. It was his and private.

"What did you do in Africa? How did you remember names there?"

"It was easy. There were only ten of us at the most at any given time."

"It's a number thing, then."

Gavin swallowed the water he had taken a swig of. "There are so many nurses. I think they're multiplying and replicating in the back somewhere."

Virginia laughed. It was a nice one, which made him smile. "Please, don't tell them you think they're cloning themselves. You're a good surgeon, Gavin, and I'd hate to lose you to a pyre they'd light under the spit they'd tie you to."

Gavin winked. "I'm trying."

"Good." She leaned forward and he caught the scent of vanilla, warm and homey like a bakery. He loved that smell. Gavin fought the sudden urge to bury his face in her neck and drink the scent in. "I have a secret."

"Do tell."

"They wear nametags."

Gavin rolled his eyes. "Ha-ha. Very funny."

Virginia just laughed to herself as she ate her salad. "So, do you have any plans for the weekend?"

He cringed inwardly and then picked at the label on his bottle of water. "Nothing in particular. Are you off this weekend?"

"Yes, surprisingly."

"And do you have plans?"

"I do."

Gavin waited. "Not going to tell me?"

"Why should I? You don't divulge aspects of your personal life."

"Touché." He downed the rest of his water and stood. "I'd

better get back to the ER. It was nice chatting with you, Virginia."

"And with you, Gavin. I hope the ER remains quiet for you for the rest of the day."

A distant wail of an ambulance could be heard through an open window of the cafeteria. Several people raised their heads and listened.

Gavin groaned. "You had to jinx it, didn't you?"

And all that minx did was grin.

CHAPTER FOUR

VIRGINIA WAS TIRED of sitting in her apartment alone. Not even the cactus could get her mind to stop racing.

The two things on her mind were the board's threat to close the ER and Gavin.

After lunch yesterday she had felt the eyes of the other staff members boring into the back of her skull. They had obviously been shocked that the lone wolf, Dr. Brice, had sat with the ice queen of Bayview Grace, and the kicker had been that they'd both seemed to enjoy each other's company.

Well, ice queens could get lonely too.

Virginia couldn't let a slip up like that happen again. She couldn't afford to have rumors flying around about them.

She'd eat in her office from now on.

At least, that's what she'd decided on during her drive down to the pier in the calm serenity of her car.

Virginia had forgotten how crowded and noisy the pier was. It was a Saturday and it was August.

Tourist season.

The height of it.

All she wanted to do was get some fresh produce and maybe some shrimp down at the pier for dinner later, but she'd forgotten how jam-packed Fisherman's Wharf could be. If she had a nickel for every middle-aged guy in an Alcatraz T-shirt wearing sandals with dark socks hiked to their knees who had bumped into her today, she'd have twenty bucks. At least.

Virginia moved through the crowd towards the pier. Her favorite vendor had a stall right near the edge of the market. Nikos knew her by name, knew what she liked and had her order ready every third Saturday of the month.

She liked the conversation and the familiarity, but it also reminded her of how utterly alone she was. How much it sucked that she'd be returning to her apartment in Nob Hill with only the echo of her own voice, her mute cactus and cable television to keep her company.

You can't have it all, Virginia.

At least, that's what she kept telling herself. She needed to keep her job so she could keep a roof over her head and send checks to her parents in De Smet. She'd make sure her younger siblings had a better childhood than she and Shyanne had had. Money was what her family needed. Not her presence, even though her mother begged her to visit all the time. A pang of pain hit her. She missed her twin sister and her family with every fiber of her being.

Only she couldn't earn the money her family needed and take time off to visit them.

A shriek across the market shook her out of her dull reverie and she glanced to the source of the sound. A flurry of pink could be seen in the midst of the crush of locals and tourists.

The cloud of pink, in the form of a very puffy and frilly tutu, was attached to a golden-haired cherub on the shoulders of someone one could only assume was her father.

A pang of longing hit her and hit her hard.

Kids weren't part of the plan. It was why she was single, but in that moment Virginia couldn't remember for the life of her why.

Right, because I don't want to have to worry about anyone else. I don't want to lose any one else.

Another girl was pulling on the man's arm and he turned around.

Virginia let out a gasp of shock to see a very familiar face peeking out from under the tutu. None other than the lone wolf Dr. Gavin Brice.

She hadn't known he was married and with his vehement stance on where he'd rather be practicing medicine, Virginia would never have pegged him for a family man.

The pained expression on his face also confirmed her assumptions. Why hadn't he mentioned his children before? Or the fact that he was married?

Virginia knew she shouldn't get involved, that she should just turn the other way, but, dammit, Nikos would have her shrimp ready. She wasn't going to change her plans just because it might avoid an awkward conversation.

No. She was going to stay on her present course.

Besides, curiosity was getting the better of her.

"Curiosity killed the cat!" Her mother's voice nagged in her ear.

Shut up, Mom.

"Lily, I think we have everything we need." Gavin's voice was pleading.

"No way. You're missing the key ingredient. Besides, you said we could go watch the sea lions after this."

"Dr. Brice, what a surprise to find you here," Virginia said, interrupting them.

Gavin's eyes widened as he looked at her. His eldest daughter inched closer to him, her keen blue eyes probing her, picking out her weaknesses.

Virginia recognized the look because she'd done the same many a time when she'd been younger. Only Gavin's daughter was giving the stare dressed in a ballet leotard and tutu. Virginia envied her, because ballet was something she'd always wanted to do as a little girl but her parents couldn't afford it.

"Dr. Potter, what a surprise to see you here."

"I always come to the market when I have a Saturday off." Virginia grinned at the little cherub who was peeking out from the top of Gavin's hair. The cherub had a very messy blonde bun on the top of her head, like whoever did her hair had no idea what they were doing. Virginia could feel her heart turning into a great big pile of goo, which was starting to coat the insides of her chest cavity like warm chocolate. "Are you going to introduce me to your daughters, Dr. Brice?"

The eldest snorted. "He's our uncle, *not* our dad."

Gavin nodded. "Yes, these are my nieces. This is Lily. Lily, this is Chief of Surgery at my hospital, Dr. Potter."

Lily's eyes widened, obviously impressed. She stuck out her hand; the nails were a garish color of red, sloppily painted on. Virginia took her hand and it was a bit sticky. In fact, both girls looked a bit of a mess. Just as Gavin appeared to be, which was so different from his put-together appearance at the hospital.

"Nice to meet you, Dr. Potter."

"Likewise."

"And this little one who's latched herself to my brain, apparently, is Rose." Gavin poked at the chubby cherub, but she wouldn't release her death grip on her uncle.

Virginia smiled. "Nice to meet you, Rose."

Rose didn't utter a word, just continued to stare.

"Sorry, Rose doesn't talk," Gavin explained, and then sighed in exasperation.

"Shy?" Virginia asked.

"No," Lily said, piping up. "She hasn't talked since our mom died."

Gavin wished Virginia hadn't run into them. Mainly because he didn't want any of his work colleagues to know about his private life. On the other hand, he was glad he had run into her and she didn't even bat an eyelash after what Lily had blurted out. Not that he would've even recognized her from the polished businesswoman who graced the halls of Bayview Grace Hospital.

Her dark hair, usually pinned up and back away from her face, hung loose over her shoulders, framing her oval face perfectly.

Instead of a tight pencil skirt, crisp blouse and heels, she wore a bulky cardigan, jeans and ballet flats, but the rest, well, it suited her. He liked the relaxed, affable Virginia.

The cardigan he could do without. It hid too much of her curvy figure, which Gavin liked to admire on occasion, like when she wore those tight pencil skirts and high heels. Just thinking about that made his blood heat.

Get a hold of yourself, Gavin.

"I'm so sorry to hear that," Virginia said, and he could tell by the sincerity in her voice she really meant it. It wasn't one of those polite obligatory outpourings of grief. Virginia meant it.

Lily was growing bored with the conversation and was gazing around the teeming market. Rose had released her death grip on Gavin's head and was wiggling to get down off her perch to join her sister.

"Thanks," Gavin said, depositing Rose down on the ground beside Lily. He breathed a sigh of relief and stretched his neck.

"Well, I'd better go. I'm going to pick up some shrimp and head back to my apartment."

"That's what we need, Uncle Gavin. Shrimp," Lily piped up.

"Shrimp? I thought it was clams?" he asked.

Lily rolled her eyes impatiently. "Mom *always* added shrimp to her clam chowder."

Virginia chuckled. "Sounds like quite an undertaking."

Gavin lifted the cooler he was holding with his one arm. "This clam chowder is becoming more and more complicated."

"So it seems." Virginia smiled and warmth spread through his chest. He liked the way she smiled. "Well, I'd better go," she repeated.

"Can I come with you, Dr. Potter? I'll get the shrimp we need, Uncle Gavin."

Gavin watched as Virginia's eyes widened, but only for a moment. She appeared nervous.

"Uh, it's Lily, right?"

"Yep! So, can I come with you?"

"Okay," Virginia said, her voice shaking and her expression one of utter shock. Like a deer in headlights.

"That sounds great!" Lily took Virginia's hand and Gavin took a step back, surprised by his niece's familiarity with a perfect stranger. Gavin handed Lily some money and watched as Virginia guided her to a booth on the outskirts of the market. Virginia, though still looking stunned, handled it well.

They were in view the whole time, so there was nothing for Gavin to be worried about. He shook his head over Lily's behavior. She wasn't that open or friendly with strangers usually. Lily didn't like change. She was a creature of habit, but here she was seemingly at ease with his boss and buying shrimp with her.

A tug on his shirt alerted him to the fact Rose needed his attention. "Yes?"

Rose nodded in the direction Lily had gone with Virginia and shrugged. Gavin chuckled and rumpled her hair. "Got me, kiddo."

Gavin wandered closer to the stall. He watched in awe as the old Greek fishmonger doted on Lily. Virginia was so affable, laughing and totally at ease with his niece. There was a natural connection between Lily and Virginia. It made him a bit nervous. He didn't want or need a relationship. He wasn't looking for a mother for his nieces.

Aren't you? a little voice niggled in the back of his mind.

It made his stomach knot.

This was not the life he'd planned, but it was what he'd been dealt.

A bag of shrimp was passed over, Lily handed the old man his money and they turned and headed back. Gavin looked away quickly, not wanting to be caught staring at them. Like he was studying them or something.

"Got the shrimp!" Lily announced triumphantly. Gavin set the cooler down and she placed the plastic bag in beside the clams and the container of scallops.

Virginia knelt down. "That's quite a catch."

"I don't think it'll be clam chowder any more," Gavin said under his breath.

Virginia chuckled again and stood up. The scent of vanilla lingered and as she brushed her hair over her shoulder, he was hit with it again.

He loved the scent of vanilla. It reminded him of something homey. Something he'd always longed for as a child.

"I think you're past the realms of a simple clam chowder and headed toward a seafood chowder or a bisque." Virginia grinned.

"What's the difference?" Lily asked.

"Bisque is puréed and chowder is chunky," Virginia replied.

"Definitely chunky," Lily said.

Gavin just shook his head and shut the cooler. "I guess we're making seafood chowder."

Virginia crossed her arms. "Have you ever made chowder before?"

"Does making it from a can count?"

Virginia cocked a finely arched brow. "No, it doesn't."

"Dang." He grinned and was shocked by the next words that were suddenly spewing from his mouth. "Would you like to come over for dinner?"

Virginia was stunned.

Did he just ask me to dinner?

How was she going to respond? Well, she knew what she had to say. She had to say no, she was his boss.

"Please, come, Dr. Potter! Hey, maybe you could walk down to pier thirty-nine with us and watch the sea lions?" Lily was tugging on her hand, her blue eyes wide with excitement.

How can I say no to that?

She couldn't, but she should.

"I'm not sure, Lily. How about I just walk down to the pier with you? Then I should go home and get these shrimp into the fridge."

"Want to place them in my cooler?" Gavin asked, popping the lid.

Now she had no excuse to bolt. "Sure. Thanks." Virginia set her bag in the cooler. They made their way through the crowd and onto the boardwalk, heading away from Fisherman's Wharf and toward the loud barking sounds of San Francisco's famous occupants.

Lily and Rose rushed forward and climbed up on the guard rail to watch the sea lions lounge on the docks, surrounded by sailboats lining the pier.

"I've been here six months and I haven't come to see these guys yet. They're pretty loud."

"They are." Virginia winced as the sea lions broke into another course of barking. Lily laughed outright, but Rose didn't make a sound. She just beamed from ear to ear. Rose was such a little angel, or at least appeared to be. "How did your sister die?"

"Cancer," Gavin answered.

"I'm so sorry for your loss." And she was. If anyone understood, it was her, but she didn't share her own pain. She couldn't.

"Thank you." He gazed at her and butterflies erupted in her stomach. He looked so different today. The navy-blue fisherman's sweater accented the color of his hair and brought out the deep emerald of his eyes. His hair was a bit of a mess from Rose's handling, but the tousled look suited him.

It made her swoon just a bit.

Get a hold on yourself.

"Well, I'd better head back to my place." She bent down, opened his cooler and pulled out her bag of shrimp, dropping it in her canvas carryall. "Good luck with the chowder."

Virginia turned to leave, but Gavin reached out and grabbed her arm to stop her from leaving. "I'd really like it if you came to dinner tonight."

"Gavin…" She trailed off, trying to articulate one of the many excuses running through her brain.

I'm your boss.

Do you think it's wise?

People are already talking.

Of course, all those excuses were lame. What did she have to lose? Yeah, she was technically Gavin's boss, but it wasn't like he was an intern or even a resident. He was an attending, the head of trauma surgery, so why couldn't they be friends?

Who cares what other people think?

"Okay. Sure, I'd love to come to your place for dinner." She pulled out an old business card and a pen. "Write down your address."

Gavin did just that and handed it back to her. "I know Lily and Rose will be excited to have you join us tonight. We haven't had a real house guest since the funeral."

"What time should I be there?"

"Five o'clock. The girls are on a schedule for sleeping and since it takes me ten hours to get them to fall asleep once they're in bed…"

Virginia laughed with him. "Five o'clock it is. I'm looking forward to it."

Gavin nodded. "So am I. I'll see you then." He picked up his cooler and walked to where the girls had moved down the boardwalk for a better view of the sea lions.

Virginia glanced down at the card. Gavin didn't live very far from her apartment. The shrimp linguine she had been planning to make for herself tonight could wait until tomorrow.

Tonight she'd actually have company to talk to instead of four walls and a cactus.

The first thing Virginia noticed about Gavin's house was it was pink. Very pink. She parked her car and set her emergency brake. She'd been passing time for the last couple of hours, waiting for five o'clock to come.

The thing that struck her was that she was very nervous, like she was a teenager again, going on her first date.

She'd even done her hair and her makeup. So different from her usual Saturday attire of yoga pants, no bra and a tank top.

With one last check in the rearview mirror she got out of the car and opened the back door. Before she'd left the market she'd managed to pick up four small sourdough loaves. She was going to hollow them out so they could serve the soup up in them.

She hoped Gavin was a good cook, but she didn't have much faith in that. The thought made her laugh as she headed towards the gated front door. She pushed the buzzer and waited. As she was waiting she noticed a flicker of the drapes in the bay window above her and she spied quiet little Rose peering at her through the lace.

Poor little soul.

The door was unlocked and opened and Gavin opened the gate. "Welcome."

Virginia stepped over the threshold as Gavin locked the gate and then the front door again. He was dressed the same as he had been earlier, but at least his hair wasn't as messy. Still, he looked handsome and it made her heart beat just a bit faster.

"Are you afraid I might escape?" she teased, hoping he didn't hear the nervous edge to her voice.

"No, just force of habit. I'm not used to living in a big city."

"You live in a pretty nice neighborhood but, yeah, I can understand your apprehension." She regretted suggesting he might be nervous when he furrowed his brow.

"You live in a very pink house, Gavin," she teased, changing the subject.

"Yes, well, that's my sister's taste. She always loved the color pink." He began to walk up the steps. "You can leave your shoes on—actually, I'd advise it as I'm not the niftiest cleaner. My maid has the weekend off."

Virginia chuckled and followed him up the stairs to the main floor. Rose dashed out from the living room at the front of the house and wrapped herself around Gavin's leg.

"You remember my boss, Rose?"

Rose nodded and then gave Virginia a smile. It wasn't a verbal greeting, but at least it was a start. It was then Virginia noticed that there was no lingering scent of dinner cooking.

"Did you have some problem starting the chowder?"

"Yeah, as in I have no idea what I'm doing."

"I guess it's a good thing I decided to come tonight. Show me to the kitchen."

Gavin grinned and led her to the back of the house where the kitchen was. Lily was in the kitchen with a battered old recipe book in front of her and looked a bit frantic.

"I can't find it," Lily said, a hint of panic in her voice.

"What?" Virginia asked, setting down the bag of bread.

"The recipe my Mom used. I can't find it." Lily was shaking and Virginia wanted to wrap her arms around the little girl and reassure her that everything would be okay. Only she couldn't. She had never been very good at hugging.

"It's okay. Look, why don't we try out my recipe for tonight? What do you think?"

Lily nodded her eyes wide. "Okay."

"Virginia, you don't have to do that. You're our guest."

"It's okay, Gavin. I don't mind." Virginia hung her cardigan on the back of the chair and pushed up the sleeves on her top. "Lily, you want to help me?"

"Of course!" Lily jumped down from the chair where she was sitting and whipped open the fridge, pulling out various items.

"I didn't know you could cook." Gavin watched as Lily plopped the bags of clams, shrimp and the container of scallops on the kitchen table.

"I have hidden depths." Virginia winked. "Do you have any cream, Lily?"

"Yep!" She ran back to the fridge and pulled out a carton.

"Where are your pots?"

Gavin pulled out a stainless-steel saucepan. "Is this good?"

"Not in the least. Do you have a stockpot?"

"A what?"

Virginia rolled her eyes and began to open random cupboards, finally locating a stockpot in a bottom cupboard. She held it up. "This is a stockpot!"

"Impressive." Gavin pulled out a chair and sat down. Rose was there in a flash and climbing in his lap. "Mind if I watch?"

"Why?" Virginia asked skeptically.

"It's how we surgeons learn, by observation, is it not?"

"Perhaps I'll employ the Socratic method on you while I'm dicing the potatoes." Virginia reached down and began to peel one of the potatoes Lily produced.

"I don't think that's fair. I know nothing about cooking."

"He really doesn't," Lily said. "All he can make is grilled cheese. Rosalie does most of the cooking."

Virginia cocked an eyebrow. "Who's Rosalie?"

"My housekeeper slash nanny slash cook." Gavin poked at the bread. "What's in the bag?"

"Ah, that's a surprise that will have to wait until the chowder is ready." Virginia finished peeling the potatoes and began to dice them. Then she went to work on the onions and carrots. When the vegetables were diced she placed them in the stockpot with some salted water and set them to boil.

"Why would I put potatoes on to boil, Gavin?" Virginia asked as Lily grabbed Rose's hand and led her out of the kitchen. They'd obviously lost interest in making dinner.

Gavin shook his head. "I told you, I'm an observer. I don't adhere to the Socratic method."

"And how do you teach your interns?"

"Shut up." There was a twinkle of humor in his eyes.

"Did you just tell me to shut up?" She picked up the knife and pointed it at him. "Very dangerous, my friend." Virginia went to work on the clams, scrubbing them and shucking them. "I'm afraid your strict bedtime rule will be kyboshed tonight. This is going to take some time to cook."

Gavin sighed. "Well, at least it's Saturday and the summer break, so no school. Would you like some wine?"

"I would love some. I actually brought a bottle."

"We'll save yours for dinner." She took a seat at the table as he set a wineglass down in front of her and poured some red into the glass.

He sat back down and poured some into his own. "I'm glad you came tonight. The girls were so excited."

"Thank you for inviting me." Virginia took a sip of wine. It was good, from a local winery in Napa. "So, where is the girls' father?"

Gavin sighed and fingered the stem of his wineglass. "Dead. He was a soldier, he died in Afghanistan just after Rose was born."

Well, that explained why he'd left Border Free Physicians and taken a job in the city as a trauma surgeon. It hadn't been his choice, he was just doing his duty to his sister and his nieces. It was quite admirable of him to give up his career for two little girls.

"How terrible."

Gavin nodded. "I was on a leave from my work in Africa at the time. I spent a couple months helping Casey out. She was a rock, though, and of course my brother-in-law's parents helped too."

"Do they see the girls often?"

"They do. Their grandfather is a marine and they're stationed in Japan, but they come to San Francisco as often as they can to see them. Last time they were here I just worked double shifts at the hospital and allowed them free rein of the house."

She'd sensed a bit of bitterness when he'd mentioned the grandparents and she thought it best to change the subject.

"What about your parents?"

Gavin's lips pressed together in a firm line and Virginia wondered if she crossed some sort of line. "My parents are dead."

"I'm sorry," she said, trying to offer some sort of apology for prying.

"Don't be."

Virginia was stunned by the way he shrugged it off and cleared her throat nervously.

"I'm sorry. I know I sound heartless but they weren't the most loving of parents."

"No, I'm sorry, Gavin. I shouldn't be prying. It's none of my business."

"You're right. It's not."

CHAPTER FIVE

HIS GAZE WAS intense and riveting, making her feel very uncomfortable, but not in a bad way. In a way that was dangerous. If she hadn't been his boss and if he hadn't been working under her she could almost swear he was going to kiss her, or strangle her maybe.

If she hadn't been his boss she might even have kissed him back, but she was and she wasn't looking for a relationship.

Not now. Not ever.

Why not?

The question surprised her because she'd never entertained the notion before. The fact Gavin made her question the life path she'd chosen for herself was scary.

Virginia had had passing flings, not many, but the moment the man wanted to take it to the next level and become serious she'd break it off, put up her walls and plug the plug.

All her relationships had a DNR lifeline attached to them.

It was so easy, but looking at Gavin now, feeling the blood rush through her like liquid fire, her stomach bottoming out like she was on a roller coaster, she knew once she'd had a taste of him she'd want more.

Much more, and it frightened her to her core.

A hiss from the pot broke the connection and she got up to stir the potatoes and turn down the heat, hoping he didn't notice the blush rising in her cheeks.

"I hope I didn't offend you, Virginia."

"Why would that offend me? I have a tendency to pry to get to the truth." She looked over her shoulder at him. "It's a bad habit of my job unfortunately."

"I bet it's a pain in the rump to have to deal with all that bureaucratic nonsense that goes on behind closed doors at the hospital."

Virginia snorted and checked on the potatoes bubbling in the pot, before draining half the water away. *You don't know the half of it,* she was tempted to say. Only she had to keep those thoughts private. She couldn't be blabbing about hospital politics to another physician. Not when she was the head honcho. Instead she said, "I'm sure you had to deal with red tape with Border Free Physicians."

"To an extent. Of course, I wasn't getting my fingers slapped for inserting a chest tube in the ER in an emergency situation. Life over limb was the motto."

"Touché." Virginia started stirring the soup. The old first-aider motto was how all doctors should practice in a hospital setting. Lawyers, board members and insurance companies thought differently. Though they wouldn't come right out and say it. She changed the subject. The last thing she wanted to do was talk about work. "Too bad you didn't have any crab. This would be great with some fresh bay crab."

Gavin set down his wineglass, headed to the fridge and pulled out a container. "Left over from dinner last night."

"Awesome." Virginia dumped the crab into the pot. "You're quite a seafood connoisseur."

"Yes, lately I am. It's what the girls like and I try to make them happy."

"You're a good uncle."

"I try to be."

Virginia got lost in his riveting gaze again. This had to stop or she was going to forget her rules completely.

"So, are you going to tell me what's in the bag you brought?" he asked, breaking the silence, much to her relief.

"Sourdough bread. It's the secret ingredient to any good seafood chowder, especially in San Francisco."

"I'm not originally from San Francisco. I'm from Billings, Montana."

"That's…"

"Not exciting in the least." Gavin grinned, that dimple she liked so much puckering his cheek. Heat flushed in hers. She cleared her throat and went back to stirring the soup. "Well, I'd better make sure Rose is still conscious and hasn't passed out from hunger."

When he left the kitchen, Virginia let out a breath she hadn't even realized she'd been holding. What was she doing? This wasn't her. If only her mother could see her now, cooking for a man and two young girls. Her mother would be pleased, because her mother felt she worked too much.

"You never come home."

Though there was nothing much to go home for and her parents' double wide trailer in rural South Dakota was quite cramped when everyone was home.

If her mother could see her, she'd be pleased. Especially if she knew how much she was actually enjoying the company.

Gavin watched Virginia from across the table. This was not the cool, aloof and businesslike professional he'd been dealing with yesterday. This woman was not the ice queen.

This Virginia was warm and kind. She had an easy rapport with them. At the hospital there was a tangible barrier between Virginia and the other surgeons. A mix of fear and respect. The woman currently sitting in his dining room was not Dr. Virginia Potter, Chief of Surgery.

Only she was.

He was amazed at how well she got on with his nieces. Lily had been so closed off and cold with strangers since Casey had got sick and died. Even with him it had taken some time for Lily to warm up and trust him.

And you couldn't blame Lily for that reaction. Death had hit her hard, twice, in her young life.

With Virginia, Lily was chatting happily and engaging her in conversation. A smile touched his lips as he watched the two of them talk. Virginia was asking Lily about dancing and school. Was this what it was like to have a real family dinner?

He wouldn't know.

His parents had never been around. Casey and he had lived off of cereal and peanut-butter and jelly sandwiches. Sometimes, when Mom hadn't gone shopping, there would only be enough bread or cereal for one. Those were the nights he'd gone to bed hungry, because he had been taking care of Casey.

Now he was taking care of Casey's girls, making sure they wanted for nothing and that they were happy. It was why he was in the city instead of some far-flung country.

"I think your sister is out for the night. What do you think, Gavin?"

"What?" Gavin asked, shaking those painful childhood memories from his head. "What's up?"

"Uncle Gavin, Rose is passed out in her chair." Lily gazed at her little sister lovingly.

Lily and Virginia were right. Rose was sound asleep, curled up on her chair with her arms tucked under her chubby cheek and her bottom up in the air.

"Lots of excitement today." Gavin pushed out of his chair and scooped his younger niece into his arms. She let out a small huff of air but didn't wake up. "I'll be back momentarily."

"At least she ate her soup, but she didn't get a chance to finish off her bowl," he heard Lily say with an excited giggle as he walked down the hall toward Lily's and Rose's shared bedroom. He smiled again as he remembered the look of pure excitement on the girls' faces when their chowder had been served up in their own individual bread bowls.

"Bowls we can eat? No dishes!" Lily had chirped excitedly.

Rose hadn't said a word, but the twinkle in her eyes and the smile on her face had spoken volumes. She had been excited too. He'd salvage what he could of the bread bowl so she could have some tomorrow. Rose would be so disappointed in the morning to find out she'd missed out on her dinner bowl.

Gavin tucked her into the bottom bunk. Lily would climb in beside her sister later. The bunk beds were fashioned for a single on top and a double underneath. Though Lily's bed was technically the top bunk, that's not how they slept.

If they weren't waking up in the night, as far as Gavin was concerned, that sleeping arrangement was fine with him.

He tiptoed out of the girls' bedroom, stepping on the darned rubber giraffe again, but Georgiana's pitiful squeak didn't even cause Rose to stir. Gavin just cursed silently under his breath and made his way back to the kitchen.

When he got there, he could see that Lily wasn't far behind her sister. Her eyelids were beginning to droop and she was leaning pretty heavily on her elbow.

"Hey, kiddo, why don't you get ready for bed?" Gavin suggested.

"Aw, do I have to?"

"I think you should. You were an awesome help to me today, Lily. Thank you," Virginia said, standing and starting to clear the table.

"Okay." Lily got up and dragged herself down the hall to the bathroom.

"Brush your teeth!" Gavin called, and Lily's response was a groan of derision.

Gavin picked up the remainder of Lily's and Rose's dinners and took them into the kitchen. Virginia was filling the sink with water.

"You don't have to do that," he said. "You were our dinner guest and I made you cook."

"I don't mind."

"No, seriously. Come and have another glass of wine while I put the leftovers away."

"One more glass. I do have to drive home."

Gavin chuckled and poured her another glass. "The girls really enjoyed the dinner tonight."

Virginia smiled and warmth spread through his chest. She had a beautiful smile, with her full red lips. If it was any other woman, he'd be putting the moves on her.

She's my boss.

"I enjoyed tonight too." She took a sip. "I think there's one thing you need to learn about managing a house full of girls."

"Are you critiquing my parenting skills?" he teased.

"Just a bit."

"What can I approve on, then?"

"Don't take this the wrong way, but you seriously have no idea when it comes to a little girl's hair."

Gavin laughed and she joined in. It was the first time he'd really heard her laugh, a deep, throaty, jovial laugh, which not only surprised him but delighted him too.

"And you do?"

"Yes," she stated confidently. "First, because I was a little girl at one point in my life and also I have two younger sisters."

It was the first time she'd opened up to him. It was the first nugget of information he'd got from her.

"Sisters, eh?"

"Yes." She smiled. "And even though you may have grown up with a sister, you really don't know anything about hair."

"Little girls' hair baffles me. Actually, it drives me squirrely," he said, and he meant it. No matter how many scrunchies or ties or pins he used, he couldn't put their hair up in a bun or braid to save his life, but it was a necessity for dance class. "Anything else?"

"Also the nails. That red color is not flattering on Lily and it's pretty messy."

"Yes, I admit I need some boning up on those finer aspects, but she wanted to paint her nails and I get home from the hospital tired and some nights I don't have any fight in me. I just give in."

Virginia nodded. "I understand about giving in."

Tension settled between them. He wanted to ask her what was stressing her out, but he knew it had something to do with him and what the board deemed his crazy, unorthodox methods. The last thing Gavin wanted to do was talk about work with *this* Virginia.

The laid-back, affable, warm and caring Virginia who had just spent part of the day and the evening with him and the girls.

The Virginia who made him forget about his worries. How he feared he was a terrible father figure to his nieces. That he'd lose them to their paternal grandparents. The girls were all he had left. Only he felt like he was failing them.

Not once since his sister had died had he and the girls enjoyed an evening like this together. It had been nice and he found himself wanting it all the time, even though a long time ago he'd sworn he'd never have a family or a wife, because of the lifestyle he wanted. Living rough and always traveling.

"I should go," Virginia said, breaking the silence that had settled between them. She got up and picked up her purse from the kitchen counter. "Are you sure you don't need a hand with those dishes?"

"Positive. I'll walk you out."

Gavin escorted her to the front of the house and down the stairs. He unlocked the outside gate and stood with her for a few moments. The night was clear and the moon full. The water on the bay was still, like a mirror.

You could see the lights from across the bay, twinkling in the darkness; the two bridges dominating the San Francisco skyline.

"What a beautiful night." Virginia let out a little sigh, which sounded like one of regret. "I should go. Thank you for a lovely evening."

"Thank you for coming." He wanted to say that he'd really enjoyed getting to know her somewhat better, but instead said, "The girls really enjoyed it."

"I enjoyed meeting them." Virginia hesitated and then

ducked her head. "Well, I'd better be going. I'll see you on Wednesday afternoon, Dr. Brice."

And just like that it was no longer Gavin and Virginia.

It was Dr. Brice and Dr. Potter and he didn't like that connection at all.

She turned and walked away from him, heading towards her car. "Wait!" he called out, surprising even himself.

Virginia paused and turned. "Yes, Dr. Brice?"

"What are you doing tomorrow?"

CHAPTER SIX

WHAT AM I doing? What am I doing?

Virginia was standing in the middle of Union Square in the evening, waiting for Gavin and the girls. She'd been so flabbergasted that he'd invited her out, but it wasn't like a date. It was just another outing with Gavin and his nieces. Just an innocent outing between friends.

At least, that's what she kept telling herself.

The plan was to walk up from Union Square to Chinatown and have some dim sum. She had nothing better to do and it was a nice August evening.

Virginia nervously glanced at her watch. They were late, only five minutes but she'd been waiting for twenty, because when she was nervous she was always early, or, as she liked to call it, overly punctual.

Relax. They'll be here.

What if they didn't show? She'd appear like a real dork. Virginia shook that thought away. No one knew where she was. No one at the hospital knew she was meeting Gavin and his nieces here.

She needed to get a grip.

"Sorry I'm late."

She turned and saw Gavin, without the girls, behind her. He was dressed in jeans, a sport jacket and a nice button-down shirt. His hair wasn't a complete mess but still stuck up here and there from a troublesome cowlick.

He had a nice five-o'clock shadow, but she liked scruffiness on a man. She could smell the spicy scent of his soap, which made her feel a bit weak in the knees. Gavin presented a neat and tidy appearance but there was a hidden depth of ruggedness to him that appealed to her.

She'd always had a penchant for bad boys, wild boys, but she tended to date respectable, clean-cut men.

For some reason, when she saw Gavin, she pictured him on a big motorcycle clothed in leather and denim as he rode down the California coast. That brief little thought caused a zing of anticipation to race through her, but it was just a fantasy. She knew Gavin drove his late sister's minivan.

"Where are the girls?" she asked, her voice cracking. She winced, worried that she was probably sounding as dumb as she felt at the moment.

"Ah." He rubbed the back of his neck. "Their grandparents flew in unexpectedly from Japan. They have a layover for a couple of days, so the girls are spending time with them."

Virginia just nodded, suddenly feeling really nervous, like a shy teenage girl standing at the edge of a dance floor, waiting for someone, anyone to ask her to dance.

Why isn't he saying something?

"Maybe we should schedule this for another night, when the girls are able to join us?"

"Why?" he asked.

Virginia's cheeks flushed. "Do you think it's appropriate for the chief of surgery to go out with an attending?"

"We're going to have dinner, as friends. Just think of it that way, if you're nervous. I think a boss can have a friendly dinner with an employee." He grinned. "We'll save Chinatown and the dim sum for the girls. How about we catch the streetcar and head down to a diner on the Embarcadero?"

Virginia hesitated. "I don't know."

"Come on, Virginia, help me out. I want to give the girls space with their grandparents. Don't make me be a fifth wheel to their time together and I rarely have a moment free without them."

Go on. Live a little.

"What the heck. You're right. Lead the way."

Gavin took her hand, her heart beating just a bit faster at the intimacy. His hand was warm and strong as it squeezed hers gently. "Come on, then." He pulled her through the square as they jogged down to catch the F Market streetcar and she was glad she'd decided to wear flats instead of wedges or boots. Flats helped her keep up with Gavin's long strides.

When they crammed onto the streetcar, Virginia finally caught her breath. "Where are we going?"

"Fog City Diner."

"I hope you made reservations. That place is a San Francisco institution."

Then he grinned deviously, like a Cheshire cat. "We'll just have to play it by ear, won't we?"

She was going to say more, but more people got onto the streetcar and they were separated in the crowd.

When their stop came she got off and met him at the back exit. "It was a bit of crush in there, wasn't it? Seeing how you're not from around here, I thought you might miss your stop."

"I'm a pro at public transportation and large crowds. I rode a train across India and stood for six hours. Not fun."

"No, I bet."

They walked toward the diner and from the look of the crush of people going in and out of the doors Virginia knew it would be busy, and there weren't many other options around. The other couple of restaurants nearby would be overflowing with rejects from Fog City.

"Why don't we catch the next streetcar and head down to the wharf?" Virginia suggested.

"You have so little faith." He took her hand again, making her pulse race and her palms sweat.

Great. Sweaty palms are so alluring.

"It looks busy," she said nervously.

"Appearances can be deceiving." He pulled her inside and walked up to the seating hostess. "Reservations for two, Gavin Brice."

The hostess checked her list, smiled and grabbed two menus. "Ah, right this way."

Gavin grinned at Virginia with smug satisfaction. "After you."

Virginia shot him a dirty look as she followed the hostess to their booth overlooking the Embarcadero. He slid in across from her, the polished black tabletop reflecting his smug pleasure.

"You had reservations."

"I did. As you said, Fog City is a San Francisco institution."

"It's almost as if you planned this."

"Well, when the girls' grandparents flew in early this morning I made the reservation. I would've told you but I don't have your home number."

"You have my pager," Virginia teased. "Everyone in the hospital has my pager."

"You carry your pager around when you're off duty?"

She pulled it out of her purse and flashed it at him, like the big nerd she was. "I'm Chief of Surgery. What if there was some kind of freak accident and the press swarmed the hospital?"

"High-profile cases don't go to Bayview Grace."

Virginia bit back the feeling of annoyance that was threatening to rise. It was always a bit of a sore spot for her. She'd raised Bayview Grace to a level-one trauma center, but other hospitals still got all the press.

"That's part of my five-year plan for the regeneration of Bayview Grace Hospital. I plan to make it the top hospital in San Francisco. It's well under way."

Gavin leaned back against the cushioned seat. "Does it matter? We're a level-one trauma center and we practice good medicine. Who cares if we're not the top?"

"I care," Virginia snapped. When she'd become Chief of

Surgery at Bayview Grace the hospital had been in a sorry state and it had ranked low on the list of hospitals nationwide and statewide. It had been her mission to change that, to bring back its glory days.

It was what she'd lived and breathed for the first two years in her position. She would fight to the bitter end to keep Bayview open.

Two lonely, busy years and now Gavin was suggesting it didn't matter?

That her life didn't matter?

Gavin regretted the words when he saw the change of expression on Virginia's face. When they'd first got to the diner she'd been smiling so brightly and had been so at ease, just like she'd been the night before.

As soon as he'd brought up the hospital, that amiable woman had been replaced by the workaholic, tight-lipped and controlling chief of surgery that most staff at Bayview Grace avoided.

Virginia was not the most popular surgeon in the hospital, but it was hard to be popular when you were responsible for budget cuts, staffing and all the other mundane administrative stuff that Gavin wouldn't wish upon his own worst enemy.

Tonight wasn't supposed to be about work.

Then what's it supposed to be about? You're out with your boss.

It was supposed to be about fun. A night away from the girls and the responsibility of fatherhood.

"Are you saying the hospital's standing isn't important?" she asked, her voice rising an octave.

"That's exactly what I'm saying." No, he didn't care about the hospital's standing. He'd spent years in dirty holes of medical facilities, trying to bring medicine to those people who had no access. He'd worked in sweltering temperatures, monsoons, festering cesspools to treat people.

That's all that mattered when it came to medicine, as far as he was concerned. A hospital rating meant nothing, as long as people were being cured.

"I think I should go." She slid to the edge of the seat, but he reached out and grabbed her.

"Don't go. Look, I know it's important to you, but it's not important to me. I come from a different world."

She eyed him with misgiving but slid back to where she had been sitting.

"I don't want to talk hospital politics."

"Isn't that what coworkers do?" she asked.

"How about, just for tonight, we don't. Let's just forget about it all and enjoy ourselves."

Her expression softened. "You're right. I'm sorry too, for what it's worth."

"Why are you apologizing? You have nothing to apologize for."

"I do. You see, I don't go out. I live and breathe that hospital. I've forgotten what it's like to talk to another adult human being."

Gavin chuckled. "I understand. How about we take it slowly? Hi, my name is Gavin Brice and I'm a fishmonger."

Virginia laughed. "You're a what?"

"You know, one of those guys down at the wharves that monger fish."

"Do you know what monger means?" she asked, cocking a thinly arched brow.

"Doesn't it mean clubbing the fish to death or something?" He made a gesture of beating a fish against the table. "Like bashing in their brains?"

She laughed again. "That's not what a fishmonger does and that's not how you use that word properly in a sentence. It means to peddle, to sell or stir up something that's highly discreditable."

"Well, thank you, Merriam-Webster." He winked.

"What would you like to order?" the waitress asked, interrupting their conversation. Gavin quickly glanced at the menu and ordered the catch of the day and Virginia did the same.

When the waitress was out of earshot he continued.

"So, as I said. I'm a fishmonger. I like screwball comedies and aspire to own a macadamia farm in Hawaii one day and populate it with llamas."

"That's the most absurd thing I've ever heard anyone say."

Gavin grinned. "Come on, play along. Tell me who you are."

"Dr. Virginia Potter."

"No."

"No?" she asked in shock.

"No, you're…" He paused, trying to think of some crazy name.

"Fifi La BonBon?" she offered.

"I like it. It's very French and naughty."

A pink blush colored her cheeks and she cleared her throat. He didn't mean to get so personal with her, but he couldn't help himself. Virginia intrigued him and he wanted to get below the surface of her prim and proper exterior.

Beneath that cool professionalism he knew someone warm existed, a passionate woman, he hoped. By the way her cheeks flushed he was positive one did and his blood fired as he thought about exploring that woman.

Gavin fought the urge to run his fingers through her silky brown hair, to crush those rose-colored lips under his, bruising them in passion as he peeled those crisp, pastel-colored clothes from her body. He cleared his throat and fidgeted in his seat.

She's your boss.

It'd been some time for him; yes, that was a fitting explanation for his sudden infatuation with Virginia. A woman who had been a thorn in his side since he'd arrived at Bayview Grace. Always calling him into her office to tell him what he was doing wrong.

It's not her choice. It's the board.

But he knew the reason. She didn't chase him like other women did.

"Okay," Virginia said, breaking the silence between them. "I'm Fifi La BonBon and I'm a tank cleaner at the Monterey Bay Aquarium. I spend my day avoiding sharks and tickling starfish."

Now it was his turned to look stunned. "Really? A fishmonger and a tank cleaner, what an interesting pair we make."

The waitress brought them their drinks and caught the tail end of his sentence, shooting them both a quizzical look before disappearing again.

"The waitress is going to think we're nuts." Virginia swirled the wine in her glass. "I've never lived on the edge like this."

"What, wine in a diner?" Gavin teased, taking a sip of his Scotch. "You rebel, you."

Virginia leaned forward across the table and he caught a whiff of her perfume, vanilla. So different from when they were at the hospital, where scents were banned due to allergy reasons. Everything was so antiseptic and sterile.

So not like his work with Border Free Physicians, where every scent known to man seemed to trudge in and out of his clinics. Some intriguing, some not so much.

"No, this fantasy talk. I guess I'm not used to lying."

"Oh, come on, Virginia. You must have to bend the truth to some of your employees sometimes. Don't we bend the truth to our patients one time or another to make the blow sting just a little bit less?"

Her smile disappeared, but only for a brief moment, and he was worried he'd crossed some invisible line again. "Whatever do you mean? I clean tanks."

Gavin laughed out loud, surprised by the way she broke the tension and eased into the icebreaker conversation he'd started. It surprised him and pleased him. The waitress brought their meals and they chatted about their fake personalities, coming up with the weirdest stuff they could imagine, until it was time to leave the diner.

There was a chilly breeze coming off the bay when they headed outside and walked along the Embarcadero towards the next pier, where they could pick up the streetcar and head back to Union Square. It was where he'd parked his motorcycle.

"Did you drive down to Union Square?" he asked, because he didn't know exactly where she lived.

"No. I walked. I only live in Nob Hill, not far from Union Square."

Damn. He was disappointed. He'd wanted to offer her a ride on his bike, take her to her door, like a proper gentleman would.

This is not a date, he reminded himself for the umpteenth time, but who was he kidding? It was. He knew it and he was pretty sure she knew it too. Only it didn't have to be anything more than just this.

They wandered along the Embarcadero in silence. The only sounds were traffic, the waves and the wind, and they finally stopped when they could see the Coit Tower clearly.

"We've wandered quite a piece away from Market Street," she said, and she turned to look out over the water. The sun was setting, just behind the Golden Gate Bridge, in a fiery ball of liquid gold.

"It's been a while since I was able to enjoy a sunset." She let out a sigh. "I've been so busy, so damn busy."

Gavin wondered if he was supposed to hear that last admission, but if he wasn't supposed to be privy to that thought, he was glad he was.

He liked this Virginia. Very much.

"It's a nice sunset," he said. "But it's not my favorite."

"Where was your favorite sunset, then?"

Gavin leaned against the railing of the boardwalk. "Egypt. The sun setting behind the pyramids as the full moon rose above them. It was…magical."

Virginia sighed. "You've been so many places. I envy you."

"You haven't traveled much, I take it?"

She shook her head. "I went to Harvard and then came here. Like I said, I was too busy trying to fix Bayview Grace."

"What about summers off from school?" he asked.

"I worked. Scholarships and what I could save myself paid

my way through. My parents couldn't afford to send me." A blush crept up her neck, as if she was embarrassed by that admission.

"That's a shame."

"You're going to bring up this again?" she asked, annoyance in her tone.

"No, it's just that you haven't traveled or cut loose. I can't imagine not. It's hard for me to stay put and take care of my sister's kids. My wandering foot is itchy."

"You're doing the right thing, giving them the stability they deserve."

Gavin nodded, even if it was a bitter pill to swallow. He knew all about wanting that stability and craving it in his childhood, but it was hard to do when you spent most of your adult life living out of a rucksack. The whole world was your home.

"I can't tear them away from their home. I won't."

Virginia nodded. "I do envy your travels, though."

"You should try it, at least once or twice."

She smiled and ducked her head, tucking a strand of hair behind her ear. "Perhaps one day."

There was a sparkle in her eyes. Maybe it was the way the fading light from the sun reflected on the water but Virginia seemed to glow and Gavin couldn't help himself. He wrapped his arms around her, tipped her chin and kissed her.

He cupped her face in his hands; her skin felt like silk. Virginia softened a bit. The taste of the wine she'd drunk still tainted her lips. It was sweet, like her. He wanted to press her body against his, feel her naked under him. When he tried to deepen the kiss, Virginia pushed him away.

Her cheeks were flushed and she wouldn't look him in the eye. "I think…I think I'd better go."

"Virginia, I'm sorry."

"No, it's okay. There's no need to apologize and there's no need to mention it again." She hailed a cab and it pulled over. She turned, but still wouldn't look him in the eye, obviously mortified by what had happened between them. "I'll see you Wednesday, Dr. Brice. Thank you for the lovely evening."

And with that she climbed into the cab and was gone.

CHAPTER SEVEN

VIRGINIA LOOKED DOWN and realized she'd been holding the same file for a while. Janice would be furious, because all the "sign here" stickies were still void of her signature. Since Sunday when Gavin had kissed her she'd been walking around in a bit of a haze.

More like a stupor. His kiss had been like nothing she'd ever experienced. It had made her melt and if it had been anyone but Gavin she would've taken it a little bit further.

Since their stolen kiss and her panicked reaction to it, she'd tried to get her mind off it. Only she couldn't. All she thought about was the feel of his lips against hers, his stubble tickling her chin, his tongue in her mouth, his fingers in her hair.

Her knees knocked and she felt herself swooning like some lovelorn heroine in a romance novel.

She'd been berating herself for walking away, and she couldn't face being alone in her apartment, reliving that kiss over and over again. So she went back to work on Monday instead of taking the rest of her time off. Janice didn't even question her early return to work. Virginia often came in on her days off.

Truthfully, Virginia didn't want to admit to her or anyone else that she just couldn't stand the oppressive loneliness of her apartment and Gavin invading her dreams, her thoughts, her every waking moment.

One kiss had made her realize how lonely she was.

Dinner had been so wonderful, as had the company. The walk along the waterfront had been the same. She'd gone on other casual dates with men, but nothing compared to the time with Gavin. Usually she couldn't stop thinking about work.

For one stolen moment she'd forgotten she was Chief of Surgery. She'd forgotten about all her duties, all the problems, everything that made up the core of her existence.

Gavin made her forget everything, made her think of traveling, something she'd always dreamed of, though she'd never entertained the idea of doing it for real. Travel was expensive and a luxury. That was just it, Gavin made her feel frivolous, like doing something more than being a surgeon and working her fingers to the bone.

She couldn't remember the last time she'd enjoyed herself so much.

I shouldn't have left him. I should've taken a chance.

Only she knew why she had walked away. It'd been a one-off. When she'd got home and thought about it, she'd realized she shouldn't have done it.

She shouldn't have let him kiss her.

She was Gavin's boss. Nothing could happen between them. They couldn't date.

It was better to put an end to it now, before the girls became attached to her or something, and there was no way she could hurt those girls.

They'd already been put through the wringer enough.

Only a part deep down inside her wanted to risk it all to get to know them better. Gavin was handsome, but it wasn't his looks that attracted her to him and it definitely wasn't that pompous air he had when he marched through the halls of Bayview Grace. Far from it. That Gavin was a jackass.

It was the Gavin she'd briefly got a glimpse of on Saturday at his house. The Gavin who'd kissed her down by the water.

The man who had been thrust into fatherhood appealed to her greatly and that thought scared her. Kids weren't in the plan, she reminded herself for the umpteenth time.

Why can't they be?

She was a doctor, she wasn't going to end up poor, like her parents. Even though she could give a child what they needed, she didn't want to risk it.

What if something changed and she couldn't support a child any more? What if something happened to that child? She'd witnessed the pain and suffering her mother had gone through when Shyanne had died. It had almost killed their mother and she never wanted to experience that kind of loss.

It was far too risky.

Her pager went off in her pocket and she pulled it out. She was wanted in the trauma department. For one moment her courage faltered, because it was Wednesday and Gavin would be back on duty and, like the shy wallflower she'd been in high school, she cringed inwardly over the thought of facing him.

Get a grip.

Virginia pocketed her pager. She was Chief of Surgery. This was her hospital and she was first and foremost a surgeon.

Just because she was chief and did a lot of paperwork, it didn't mean she didn't belong in the trauma bay, getting her hands dirty.

And she had nothing to be ashamed about.

Nothing to be embarrassed about, because nothing had happened between her and Dr. Brice and that's the way it had to remain.

She had to forget about the kiss. It'd been a mistake and thankfully no one knew about it.

When she entered the trauma bay her gaze naturally gravitated towards Gavin, but she took a step back when she realized he wasn't in his scrubs but in his street clothes. Of course, it was only ten in the morning. He wasn't due to start until two. He also wasn't leading the paramedics, he was traveling with them and on the gurney was a little figure.

Virginia's heart skipped a beat and she ran towards them.

"What happened?" she asked as she followed the gurney into the trauma pod.

"Female age eight, fell off the monkey bars at the playground. No obvious head trauma, but there appears to be a fracture of her right ulna," the paramedic stated.

Lily was on the gurney, her face grey with pain. Virginia looked at Gavin and his pained expression said it all. Suddenly she saw her twin sister Shyanne on the gurney in agony, bleeding out. Lily had a fracture. She was not hemorrhaging because of a ruptured fallopian tube.

Get a grip, Virginia.

"Glad you could come, Dr. Potter," Gavin said.

"Of course. I'm the trauma surgeon on duty."

Gavin nodded, but didn't look at her.

Lily's gaze met hers. "Dr. Potter?"

"Hi, Lily."

"Wow, the chief of surgery." Then she sat up and retched into a basin.

I feel the same way some days.

"Let me just do an examination of your arm." She turned to the nurse and fired off instructions for an X-ray and pain medication.

Lily winced as Virginia gently palpated the site.

"It hurts." A sob caught in Lily's throat, but she kept up her stiff upper lip.

"Yeah, I'm sure it does." She leaned down and whispered, "You can cry if you want. Breaking a bone is a huge deal."

Lily shook her head and glanced at her uncle. "I told him I'd be brave."

Virginia glanced over her shoulder at Gavin and then back at Lily. "We're going to do an X-ray and check out what kind of fracture it is, and Nurse Jo here is going to give you some pain medicine in a moment."

Lily nodded and Virginia walked over to Gavin. "Is she allergic to anything?"

"No. Nothing."

"Good. Where's Rose?"

"With her grandparents. They were supposed to fly out, but

then Rosalie called as I was getting ready for work." Gavin scrubbed a hand over his face. "I appreciate you coming down, but couldn't one of your ortho attendings handle this?"

"No, Lily knows me. I'll make this as painless as I can for her."

Gavin's eyes narrowed. "You don't have to."

"I want to. She's frightened, though she doesn't want you to know it."

Gavin sighed and mumbled thanks before pushing past and sitting next to Lily. A pang of longing hit her, and hard, watching him sitting next to Lily, stroking her hair as Nurse Jo administered pain medication.

Her parents and other siblings were so far away. If she got hurt or sick no one would be here for her. Her parents couldn't afford to come see her.

There was no one.

No boyfriend, no kids and no family.

I want that.

The thought frightened her and she looked away, stepping out of the trauma room. She was just being emotional. It was not part of the plan.

She wanted to bring Bayview Grace to its former glory. That's what she wanted. That was the plan she'd crafted for herself the moment she'd taken her Hippocratic oath.

"Can you page me when Lily Johnson's X-rays come in?" she asked the nurse at the desk.

"Do you want someone from Ortho to handle it, Chief?"

Instead of snapping, Virginia just shook her head and smiled. "No, I'll see to the patient personally. Thanks, Deborah, and this is pro bono. Don't charge them for my services."

The nurse looked stunned, but only for a moment. "Of course, Dr. Potter."

It wasn't often Virginia dealt with minor fractures, let alone wrote off her time, but Lily was a staff member's ward and Gavin had enough to worry about without having to deal with billing. He'd have to fill out the forms, but at least he wouldn't have to deal with his insurance.

"Thank you." Virginia headed back towards her office. She had to put a safe distance between herself and Dr. Brice.

Gavin was fighting hard not to take over the situation. He was after all a trauma surgeon, his life in this hospital was running from room to room and assessing the most serious cases. He wanted to help Lily and it was killing him but he couldn't. He was family and there was a strict rule about physicians and family members.

He'd been shocked to see Virginia come into the room.

It had made his pulse race when she'd walked into the trauma pod, but the woman he'd kissed on the waterfront was gone, replaced by the austere chief of surgery.

And for a moment, when she'd been talking to Lily, she hadn't been that cold professional he'd first met when he'd come to Bayview Grace. For one brief moment he'd seen the woman from this last weekend.

The one he'd kissed.

Stop thinking about her.

He had to get her out of his mind. Virginia had made it quite clear what she thought about his kiss when she'd climbed into that cab and left him standing alone on the Embarcadero.

Of course, she'd made it clear to him that she was uncomfortable with the thought of it being a date and he'd promised her it was nothing more than coworkers going out for a quick bite.

And, honestly, that's what he'd thought when he'd shown up at Union Square.

They had just been going out as friends, but as the evening had worn on, he'd been unable to help himself. He was setting himself up to fall for a girl like Virginia.

She was his boss, she was taboo and he was like a moth to her flame. He always liked a challenge, the woman who was hard to get.

He was so rusty, though, when it came to dating women like Virginia. When he'd been traipsing around the world with Border Free Physicians there had been little time for romantic notions. There'd been the odd fling, but that had been all.

Just enough to relieve the itch, and even those had been few and far between.

This is not part of the plan, he reminded himself again for the ten thousandth time. He couldn't settle down and bring a strange woman home to the girls. The girls were his life now.

The girls like Virginia.

Gavin watched her walk out of the emergency department. Her chestnut hair was in a tight twist again, instead of falling loose over her shoulders. Her white lab coat was crisp, without a crease, the colors she wore were dark, professional, and her black pumps were flawless, without a single scuff.

Even the scent of vanilla was gone from her. Only the antiseptic scent of the hospital burned his nose.

This weekend the Virginia who made his heart race had been soft, both in the colors she'd worn and the scent of her hair.

"I feel funny," Lily said, her eyes wide and a bit dazed.

Nurse Jo chuckled and looked at Gavin. "It's the pain medication."

Gavin smiled and smoothed back the hair from Lily's forehead.

"I can feel my eyeballs, Uncle Gavin. They're round and b-i-g." Lily dragged out the word "big."

Gavin laughed. "It's right about now I should start filming, something to blackmail her with later when she hits those teen years."

"That's about right, Dr. Brice." Jo smiled. The woman had never smiled at him once since he'd started working here. Then again, he'd never really conversed with her before.

"We're ready for her in X-Ray," the orderly said, stepping into the room. "Hey, Dr. Brice."

Gavin nodded to Chet the orderly. "Should I go with her?"

Jo shook her head. "Nope, you know the rules. No family in Radiology. You get to take a seat in the waiting room."

"I'm a doctor here. In fact, I'm head of this department."

Jo crossed her arms. "Are you really going to try and challenge your head nurse, Dr. Brice?"

Gavin held up his hands. "Nope, you're right. I'll just head to the cafeteria. Page me when she gets out of Radiology."

"Will do, Dr. Brice."

Gavin leaned over and pressed a kiss against Lily's forehead. "I'm going to call your grandparents and check on Rose. She was pretty upset when you went to the hospital."

Lily nodded, still wide-eyed.

Gavin had left the room so they could prep Lily for Radiology. He was veering off towards the cafeteria when the charge nurse called after him.

"Paperwork, Dr. Brice. Lots of nice forms for you to fill out."

Gavin groaned. "I'll give you fifty dollars to fill them out for me."

The charge nurse gave him a look that would have made hell freeze over and handed him a clipboard.

"Well, it was worth a shot."

"It was, but no dice, Dr. Brice, and make sure it's legible. I'm *very* familiar with your handwriting."

Gavin rolled his eyes and headed towards the cafeteria, clipboard in hand. He too busy flipping pages and wasn't watching where he was going until he ran smack into a warm, soft body and was spattered with lukewarm coffee.

"Dammit!"

When he glanced up he was standing in front of Virginia, whose crisp white lab coat and blouse were now stained and drenched with coffee.

"Why don't you…?" She trailed off when she realized who it was and her cheeks flushed crimson. "Of course, it had to be you."

CHAPTER EIGHT

VIRGINIA STEPPED INTO a boardroom as a janitor came to clean up the mess of the two coffees that had just been dumped down her front. Gavin followed her with a roll of paper towels. She could feel the eyes of most of the staff and the patients in the trauma bay boring into the back of her skull. She was absolutely humiliated.

This was the last thing she needed. She peeled off her lab coat and tossed it on the table.

Gavin set down the clipboard beside it and then ripped off a sheet of paper towel, about to mop up the front of her chest.

"I'll take care of that, thanks." She tried not to snap at him, but she was more than annoyed. She had a board meeting later.

"I thought you were heading back to your office."

"I was, until I thought I'd bring you a coffee. You looked like you need a pick-me-up." She dabbed at her shirt, but there was no saving it at the moment. She'd have to change into her scrubs and attend the board meeting like that.

She was sure she'd get comments from some of the snootier members of the board about it.

Forget about them.

"It was nice of you to go to the trouble," Gavin said.

"It was no trouble. I was at the coffee cart and thought of you."

Gavin picked up the clipboard and grinned. "So I was an afterthought?"

Virginia sighed impatiently and tossed the soiled paper towel in the garbage. "I told you, you looked a bit pale."

"Well, thanks for the thought."

"You're welcome."

"By the way, I'm not going to be in to work later today." The twinkle in his eyes returned, that mischievous look that she liked so much.

"I assumed that. Your niece happens to be my patient." She eyed the clipboard. "Patient forms?"

Gavin *tsked*. "Yeah, and I've been given dire warnings from the charge nurse about curbing my terrible handwriting."

"Ah, Sara can be a bit of a bull about that. Why don't you fill out the forms here?"

"Only if you keep me company."

"I have a hospital to run," Virginia said. "I have a VIP patient who needs my help."

"She's in Radiology." Gavin pulled out a seat and sat down at the table, beginning to fill in the forms.

"I thought you'd be down in Radiology with her."

"They wouldn't let me. Jo, I think that's her name, can be a bit of a bull when it comes to that."

"Good to know you're learning names."

"Well, someone gave me a hint about name tags."

Virginia chuckled. "Do you want me to talk to them, get them to bend the rules?"

Gavin shook his head. "Nah, I don't want to ruffle any feathers." He cursed under his breath and slammed down his pen.

"What's wrong?" she asked as she pulled another sheet off the roll of paper towels.

"I know none of this information." He dragged his fingers through his hair, making it stand on end. "Dammit."

Gavin stood and stalked toward the far end of the room, muttering and cursing under his breath. She felt sorry for him. Of course he wouldn't have all this information memorized. A mother would, but an uncle who had been thrust into a fatherhood role wouldn't.

"Dammit, what good am I if I can't even remember something simple like her date of birth? Terrible. I shouldn't be doing this."

Virginia closed the boardroom door. "Gavin, what're you talking about?"

"I don't know Lily's birthday!" he snapped, and his hands fisted at his sides. "I know nothing. Everything is at home, in a file, and I've been so damn crazy at work and just trying to get the girls on schedule."

"It's not your fault."

"It is my fault, Virginia. I should know this by now." He cursed again and kicked the wastepaper basket.

Virginia wanted to reach out and hug him, to reassure him that it was okay he didn't know, only she didn't know how. Instead, she picked up the clipboard and began to fill in what she could.

"What're you doing?" he asked.

"Filling out what we can. The rest can come later, we know where you live." Virginia winked at him.

"You don't have to do this."

"It's okay, Gavin. I don't mind."

"Well, maybe I mind."

Virginia set the pen down. She was overstepping her bounds. What right did she have to help him? None. She'd made that clear on Sunday when she'd pushed him away and climbed into that cab.

"I'm sorry," Gavin said, as he scrubbed a hand over his face. "I didn't mean to snap. You were just trying to help."

"It's okay, Gavin." She stood and picked up her soiled lab coat. "Fill in what you can, bring the forms to me and you can phone me with the rest of Lily's information later."

"Don't go. Please stay."

"I have to." Her pager went off and she pulled it out of her coat pocket. "Besides, they're back from Radiology and I have a fracture to assess. Bring the paperwork. Come on."

Gavin nodded and followed her out of the boardroom.

She stopped and realized she needed to change. There was no way she was going to apply a cast to Lily's arm with a coffee-soaked shirt.

"Lily's in room 2121A. I'm going to change and I'll meet you there."

"Sure. See you there." Gavin turned and walked in the other direction towards the ortho wing. Virginia took a deep breath, trying to calm the emotions threatening to overtake her.

And for the first time since meeting Gavin and learning about his situation, she realized that the life he'd fashioned for himself, his plan, had been torn asunder.

Her plan was still sound. She was where she wanted to be. *Am I?*

She shook those thoughts away as she changed in her office bathroom. She put on her green scrubs, replaced everything in the new lab coat and tossed her soiled lab coat in the hospital laundry bag. As for her clothes, she left them in the sink. She'd take them to her dry cleaner's after work.

Janice cocked an eyebrow as she came out of her office in her scrubs.

"What happened to you?" Janice asked.

"Don't ask."

"Did it involve Dr. Brice?"

What? Virginia panicked inwardly. "No, why would it?" she asked cautiously.

"The man is a brilliant surgeon, but he's a bit of a klutz. He walks around these halls with his head in the clouds. If you see him barreling towards you, you'd best get out of his way because he won't see you."

"He has a lot on his mind."

Janice's eyebrows arched again in surprise. "You're defending him. Well, this is a first."

Virginia pinched the bridge of her nose. "I have to go put a cast on a little girl. Hold my calls."

"Can't someone from Ortho do that?"

"I can too."

Janice grinned. "I know, but usually minor cases like this you don't bother with. Especially ones involving a child."

Virginia rolled her eyes. "Why are you grinning like that?"

"Because I like this side of you. Could the ice queen be melting?"

Virginia groaned. "Just hold my calls, will you?"

"Of course, Dr. Potter."

Virginia headed off toward the ortho wing, cursing Janice and her uncanny ability to talk about the last thing Virginia wanted to discuss, and that was Dr. Brice. She was sure Janice would interrogate her later about her change of heart when it came to Gavin, because Janice had been listening to Virginia moan and gripe about Gavin since his arrival.

Now she understood him. Gavin wasn't just a faceless jack-ass, trying to make her life as Chief of Surgery impossible.

She understood where he was coming from, from a certain point of view.

Her life plan was still on track. Gavin's had been derailed.

The first thing Virginia noticed when she entered the room was that Lily wasn't as pale as she'd been before.

"How are we feeling, Lily?" Virginia asked, as the nurse handed her the films.

"Great!" Lily chirped.

Virginia hid her smile as she slid the films onto the light box to study the fracture. "It's just a greenstick fracture. Easy-peasy to fix."

Lily craned her neck to take a look. "Cool, but what do you mean by greenstick?"

"It means your bones are soft and you need to drink more milk," Gavin teased.

Lily rolled her eyes at her uncle. "Do I get a cast?"

"Yes, it's closer to your elbow, so you'll get a fancy cast you'll have to wear for a month."

"Awesome." Lily's eyelids fluttered.

"The pain meds are making her a bit loopy." Gavin rubbed

his eyes. "Damn, I need to call her grandparents. I forgot before. They'll be worried sick."

"Go," Virginia said. "I've got it here."

"Thanks." Gavin left the room and Virginia readied the supplies to make the cast. Lily opened her eyes again.

"Rose is upset."

"I bet she is," Virginia said. "You broke your arm. Was she there when it happened?"

Lily nodded. "She hates hospitals."

"Why?"

"Mom died in one. This one, actually."

Virginia's chest tightened. "I'm sorry to hear that."

"She was worried I was going to die."

"Did she tell you that?" Virginia asked, hopeful Rose only had selective mutism.

"No, but I know what she was thinking when the ambulance came. I was worried too."

Virginia bit back the tears that were threatening to spill. Even though she'd only known these girls for a couple of days, they tugged at her heartstrings. She knew all too well what Rose was feeling for Lily.

Virginia recalled when Shyanne's fallopian tube burst. She'd ridden in the ambulance with her sister, clutching her hand, trying desperately to hold onto Shyanne's life as if life was something tangible you could hold onto.

No matter how hard she'd squeezed, Shyanne had slipped away, like sand through her fingers, bleeding out.

Virginia cleared her throat. "You have a very minor fracture. You'll live, but you're not allowed to hang from the monkey bars again for a while. Now, why don't you tell me what color you want for your cast? I have lots of colors."

"I want pink, please."

"You really have a thing for pink, don't you?" Virginia teased.

Lily grinned. "Pink drives Uncle Gavin bonkers. Personally, I like blue."

"Why do you want to drive your uncle bonkers? I thought you guys loved him."

"Oh, we do, but it's just so funny."

Virginia bit back her chuckle and nodded. "Pink it is."

"Do you have any sisters, Dr. Potter?" Lily asked.

"I do."

"How many?"

Virginia bit her lip and hesitated. "I have two, but I did have three."

"What happened to the third?" Lily's eyes were wide.

"Promise you won't say anything."

"I do," Lily whispered.

"She died."

Lily's face fell. "Were you close?"

Virginia nodded. "Very close. She was my identical twin."

Lily nodded. "I was really close to my mom."

Virginia swallowed the lump in her throat. "I'm sure you were."

"Is your mom still alive, Dr. Potter?"

"Yep, someone has to take care of my other sisters and my two brothers." Well, financially anyway. She hadn't seen them in a long time. It was too hard. Virginia winked and continued finishing up the cast. "There, nice and pink. Do you think that'll drive your uncle bonkers?"

Lily smiled. "Yep."

"Good."

Gavin hung up the phone after his call to the girls' grandparents. They were relieved it was a minor fracture but they were hinting again about taking the girls, about suing for custody again. There were moments when he thought about it, not even bothering to fight it.

Moments like in the boardroom when he didn't even know something as simple as Lily's birth date. He knew generally when it was, he wasn't a total monster, but when Lily had been born he'd been in India.

Then it hit him and he remembered exactly when her birth date was.

Thank God.

Joss and Caroline had expressed again what kind of parenting they could provide the girls, but of course halfway around the world, and even then Joss could be transferred somewhere else until he planned to retire from the navy. He had no plans to take a commission in San Francisco.

That was not the life Casey had wanted for her daughters, even though she'd married a military man, they had bought the house outright and she had planned to stay there no matter where her husband was going to be sent.

Casey had been determined she wasn't going to drag her kids from pillar to post.

She'd wanted to give her girls stability.

"Why did you pick me, Casey?" he'd asked her. *"I'm not stable. Have someone else take the girls."*

"You're stable enough for me, Gavin. You took care of me when I was young. Please, I need you to do this for me."

There was no way he could've said no to Casey. He'd loved her so much, but right now with Lily in hospital, getting a cast on her arm, he felt like he'd let her down. Big time.

Perhaps he should just sign over custody to Joss and Caroline? Maybe that would be for the best.

He didn't know what to do.

He was confused.

He was lost.

Gavin headed back into the room and groaned when he saw what Virginia was doing to Lily's arm, but then he smiled and knew exactly what he was going to do.

There was no way in hell he was going to sign over custody of his nieces. He'd fight the custody issue again and again.

"It had to be pink, huh?"

Virginia grinned as she continued to wrap the cast and Lily shared a secret smile with her that made Gavin instantly suspicious.

"What's going on?" he asked as he took a seat next to Lily.

"Just girl talk," Virginia said absently, but winking at Lily, who giggled.

"If I didn't know better, I'd think you two were conspiring against me or something."

"Oh, please." Virginia snorted. "There, she's all done. I'll write up the discharge papers and you know the drill about cast care."

"Of course," Gavin responded.

"I'll write up a script for pain medication too. Take the rest of the week off, Gavin, if you need to." She turned and left the room.

Gavin knew he should be appreciative that she was willing to give him the rest of the week off, but he wasn't a baby.

"I'll be right back, Lily."

"Okay." Lily closed her eyes and drifted off to sleep, her pink cast propped up.

Gavin chased after Virginia, who was at the charge desk, writing up the papers. "Hey, I don't need the rest of the week off."

Virginia's brow furrowed. "You don't? I thought with Lily…"

"No, she'll be fine with Rosalie. I have a job to do and the girls have to get used to it. Lily's fall wasn't a cry for help or anything."

Virginia's eyes widened, obviously stunned. "I never said it was."

"The implication was there." Gavin's voice rose.

"I really think you should bring your issues up with me later, in private," Virginia whispered.

"I don't need the week off."

Virginia shrugged. "Fine." She pullled the discharge note off the clipboard and handed both it and the script to Gavin. "We'll see you tomorrow. Keep her arm elevated."

Gavin regretted confronting her and he let out a sigh as he watched her walk away. What the hell was wrong with him?

I'm an idiot.

With another sigh of regret he folded the note in half and returned to Lily's room to take her home.

CHAPTER NINE

I SHOULDN'T BE here. What am I doing here?

Virginia had been having this argument with herself for the last twenty minutes as she'd sat in her car on the street outside Gavin's home, debating with herself about whether she should ring the doorbell.

This morning he'd been so irrational. Though she really couldn't blame him. He was under a lot of stress.

She was also a bit mad at him for accusing her of thinking Lily had broken her arm on purpose. The child was level-headed and mature, given her age and the fact she'd lost both her parents. Lily had fallen off the monkey bars. Greenstick fractures were the most common fractures in kids.

Heck, she'd sent money last month to her parents because her youngest brother, who was sixteen, had done just the same jumping off the roof of the trailer.

So why was she sitting in her car outside Gavin's house? He was a doctor, he could handle it.

He'd forgotten to fill out his patient forms, at least that's the excuse she'd used to rationalize her appearance outside his house.

Really, she need to get her clothes to the dry cleaner's, have some dinner and get to bed early because she'd managed to reschedule the board meeting until tomorrow.

But, no, she was sitting in her car, mentally arguing with herself.

When had life become so complicated?

The moment I hired Dr. Gavin Brice.

With a sigh she got out of the car and headed towards the door. The gate was locked so she rang the bell. The moment the bell rang, the curtains twitched and she saw little Rose standing in the living-room window in her pajamas.

Virginia smiled and waved and Rose waved back before disappearing, just as the door opened. Gavin opened the door in a ratty old T-shirt and pajama pants. There were dark circles under his eyes and his hair was sticking up on end.

"Dr. Potter?"

"I didn't wake you up, did I?" She glanced at her wristwatch. It was only seven o'clock in the evening.

"Yes, but it's okay. I must've dozed off during the movie." He unlocked the gate. "Come on in."

"No, it's okay. I just brought the patient forms. You forgot to fill them out and both our asses are on the line from Jo and my assistant Janice."

"Thanks." He took the forms and his gaze roved her from head to toe. "You're still in your scrubs?"

"Well, my street clothes are still covered with coffee."

Gavin chuckled and rubbed the back of his neck. "Again, sorry."

"I'll be going." She turned to leave, but he grabbed her arm.

"Come in for a few minutes and check on your VIP patient."

"I don't think that's wise, do you?"

"As friends. I promise, nothing else will happen. Scout's honor."

"I don't know, Gavin."

"Look, don't make me stand out here in these ridiculous PJs any longer. I don't want my neighbors talking. Come in and say hi to the girls. Lily hasn't stopped yammering about her visit with you today and I think Rose is a bit jealous."

"Okay, for a few moments." Virginia stepped inside and Gavin locked up. "So why are PJs so ridiculous? They look quite comfortable to me."

"I sleep nude." He winked and headed up the stairs.

I had to ask. Heat flushed her cheeks and she tried not to picture Gavin naked, though she'd done that very thing since Sunday, when he'd kissed her and she'd almost forgotten who she'd been kissing.

She squished something rubbery under her feet and Rose materialized again at the top of the stairs, arms crossed and giving them the look of death.

Gavin rolled his eyes and scooped down to retrieve the rubber giraffe out from under her feet, yet again. "Rose, you have to stop setting booby traps on the steps. Here, take Georgiana and stop subjecting her to such horrible torture."

Rose caught her giraffe and rolled her eyes as if to say *puhleze* and walked away.

"She's got a thing about that giraffe on the steps."

Gavin groaned. "Every time I go out. I swear that damn giraffe wasn't on the steps when I went down."

Virginia chuckled. "It's okay."

When she walked into the living room she noticed Lily in the corner of the sectional sofa, propped up with pillows.

"Dr. Potter, what're you doing here?" Lily asked, but her voice betrayed her joy, which made Virginia's heart squeeze with pleasure.

Don't get attached.

"I've come to sign your cast. I forgot to do that before."

Lily beamed. "Sure!"

Virginia pulled a marker out of her purse and sat down next to Lily. She signed her name and drew a small cartoon frog. "There, now it's officially one of my casts. I always have to sign the casts I make. It's a rule."

"Thanks!"

Rose was frowning and Virginia could see a look of envy on her face. "Do you have a bear that needs a cast?"

Rose nodded and took off towards the back of the house.

"What're you doing?" Gavin asked.

"Saving you another trip to the hospital."

Rose reappeared with a bear and Virginia pulled out a roll of pink tape. "I presume pink, yes?"

Rose nodded vehemently and Virginia proceeded to apply a cast to her teddy's arm. When she was done, she signed the teddy's cast and drew the same goofy frog on it. "Now, make sure his cast doesn't get wet, keep his arm elevated and I'll see him in a month to get it removed."

Rose nodded solemnly and headed back to her bedroom.

"Nice move, Dr. Potter." Gavin grinned.

"Thanks." She put her pen away and stood up. "I should head for home. Long day of meetings tomorrow and I don't want to interrupt your..."

"We're having a sleepover pajama party tonight in the living room. Though we're not going to get to do manicures." Lily pouted for a brief moment and turned her attention back to the television.

Virginia cocked an eyebrow and eyed Gavin. "A sleepover. You're such a good uncle."

Gavin shrugged. "I try. I'm hoping her painkillers will kick in soon and I can carry them both back to bed."

Rose stormed back into the living room, wearing her pink tutu and curled up close to Lily. Virginia noticed it was really close, like Rose didn't want to let Lily out of sight for longer than she had to. Virginia knew how Rose felt. She missed Shyanne with every fiber of her being.

"Is Rose okay?" Virginia whispered.

"Yeah, I think she misses her grandparents. She was clingy when they went to the airport this afternoon." Gavin shrugged again.

Virginia glanced at the little girl in time to see an eye-roll and shaking her head in disagreement. "You think so?"

Virginia didn't think it was the grandparents' absence.

"What else can it be?"

Virginia pulled him into the hallway out of earshot. "Lily mentioned your sister passed away at Bayview Grace."

Gavin's expression softened and he scrubbed his hand over

his face. "Yeah, oh, hell. I didn't even think of that. Damn, and I go there every day to work. I never even thought of it. I started working there after Casey died."

Now it was Virginia's turn to feel guilty. She'd had no idea when she'd first hired Gavin that his sister had been an oncology patient and that she'd died in the hospital.

I'm the worst boss ever.

But, then, how could she have known? Gavin was such a private man.

"Gavin, I'm so sorry that I didn't know."

"No one knew, Virginia. I didn't want anyone's pity or condolences. I just needed the job. You know how I feel about the bureaucracy of my position."

Virginia nodded. "Still, if I had known…"

"Let's not talk about it. I'll mention this incident to Rose's counselor. Just another thing to add to the plate."

Virginia bit her lip and set her purse down on the hall table. "Why don't you have a shower or do something you like to do by yourself and I'll sit with the girls for a while? I'll give Lily and Rose a manicure, a nice-looking lacquer job."

"You don't have to do that. You have a busy day tomorrow."

"I insist. Besides, I'm not the only one. You took an unexpected day off and there was no head of trauma there to wrestle some of those residents in."

Gavin groaned and smiled. "Fine. I think I'll go have a shower or something. Thanks."

"No problem. Just bring me some nice pink nail polish."

He groaned. "Always with the pink."

Virginia laughed and headed back into the living room. The girls were watching a cartoon movie, something really annoying with terrible music.

"How about something a bit more fun? Something we can sing to? What movies do you have?"

"Mom's old DVDs are on the shelf there."

Virginia wandered over to the shelf and searched the titles, hoping Casey had had the DVD she was thinking of, and she almost shouted for joy when she pulled *The Sound of Music* out of the stack.

"Have you guys seen this movie?"

Lily and Rose shook their heads. "Isn't that Mary Poppins?" Lily asked.

Virginia grinned. "Yes, but this movie is awesome to sing to. I love singing to it. Whenever I was sick I would watch this movie over and over again."

She and Shyanne would sing the soundtrack at the top of their lungs. The last time she'd watched it had been a long time ago, with Shyanne right before she'd died. *The Sound of Music*, *Grease* and *Oklahoma!* to name a few had helped her while away many hours on the couch when she'd been feeling under the weather. It had also helped to drown out the sound of her parents fighting over money.

To this day, whenever she was feeling a bit rundown she'd pop on one of these old musicals and she'd feel like she was at home and comforted.

Julie Andrews had been more of a mother to her than her own mother had.

Gavin wandered in with the nail polish and, surprisingly, nail-polish remover, which caused Lily to squeal and Rose to jump up and down excitedly, because they knew what was about to happen.

He excused himself and Virginia put on the movie.

When the first number started Virginia took a seat between the two girls and started on Rose's nails first.

Gavin could hear the strains of the movie soundtrack drifting from upstairs. He retreated to the small basement and did some weights. Whenever he was stressed, he would work out. When he'd been traveling all over the world, working out had usually meant playing soccer, cricket or running. Exercising gave him the rush of endorphins he needed to put everything into perspective and he was still stressed about his run-in with the girls' grandparents when he'd brought Lily home.

They'd made it clear to him in no uncertain terms that they were going to petition for full custody of the girls.

Their reasoning was that he was a single man with no clue on how to be a proper father and they were the girls' grandparents, the closest the girls had to real parents.

He liked Joss and Caroline, but they had their faults.

Where had they been when Casey had been dying? Where had they been when Casey had been trying to fight the cancer that had claimed her life? When she'd been dragging herself to chemo appointments and raising two little girls on her own?

Then again, where had he been? He hadn't come back to the States until she'd called him to tell him she was dying.

Casey had been raising the girls on her own since Rose's birth and it broke Gavin's heart that he'd been halfway around the world, letting his sister fend for herself.

Joss and Caroline hadn't been there either.

When Casey had been dying they hadn't given up their lives, Joss hadn't retired from the service or tried to get a commission in San Francisco. No, but he had given up everything to be a father to these girls and he was damn well going to remain that way.

He'd fight Joss and Caroline tooth and nail to keep the girls.

Gavin continued to lift weights until he was exhausted and the sweat was pouring down his body.

After this he'd need to take another cold shower, because he couldn't get Virginia out of his mind.

He couldn't remember ever obsessing over one woman so much, but then again any woman he'd pursued for a brief dalliance hadn't brushed him aside and neither had he ever pursued his boss before.

Not that he'd really had a boss like Virginia before.

For a moment he fantasized that they were alone, that they weren't colleagues and were just two people who were attracted to each other. Two people who wanted one another and could give in to that passion.

He couldn't help but wonder what it would be like to take

Virginia in his arms and make love to her. She was so prim
and proper, but when he'd kissed her she'd melted just a bit
and he couldn't help but wonder if she'd ignite under his touch

Get a hold of yourself.

He was definitely going to need a cold shower and soon
First he had to get his mind off of her before he went upstairs
in his current state, which was a hard thing to do, given the
fact she was under the same roof as him.

When he set down the weights he realized the television
had gone strangely quiet and he glanced at the wall and balked
when he saw that it was close to midnight.

He'd let time get away from him.

He toweled himself off and headed back upstairs half
dressed. Everything was silent when he headed toward the
living room.

"Virginia—" Gavin stopped when he noticed that Virginia
was curled up on the couch, Rose was lying beside her and
Lily was snoring in the corner.

The television was on, but the DVD was frozen on the scene
selection menu. She looked so peaceful. They all did.

It surprised to him to see Virginia curled up with the girls,
but it also pleased him. The girls' nails were the color of bubblegum and then he noticed Virginia's neat, well-manicured
nails were also the color of bubblegum, and it wasn't a very
tidy job.

Which meant she'd let one of the girls do it.

A smile tugged at the corner of his mouth. She was so tender, so beautiful.

Don't think about her like that. She doesn't want you.

Virginia had made it clear. Nothing could ever happen
between them.

He moved to wake her up and then thought better of it. Virginia was exhausted; there were dark circles under her eyes
She'd had a pretty trying day herself.

Instead he shut the television off and then picked up the af-
ghan from the recliner and tucked all the girls in.

Only two of them were his.

And the other one he wanted desperately to be his too.

The incessant squeaking in Virginia's ear alerted her to the fact she wasn't in her apartment. She cracked open one eye to see a silent golden angel holding a rubber giraffe by the name of Georgiana in her face.

Rose gave it another long squeak, which sent shooting pain up Virginia's neck and behind her eyeballs. Then she realized she'd spent the night on Gavin's couch. She bolted upright.

"Oh, my God."

Rose wagged her finger and squeaked Georgiana again.

"Sorry, I didn't mean to curse." She glanced around the room until she spied the clock and realized she was going to be late for the board meeting.

Crap.

"I have to get to work." She stood up and realized she was still in the same scrubs she'd worn the previous day.

Double crap.

"Good morning," Gavin said, as he came into the room. He was dressed for work, coffee in his hand, and by the way his hair was glistening he'd obviously had a shower.

"Why didn't you wake me up last night?"

"You looked so peaceful."

Virginia groaned. "You should've woken me up. I need a shower and a change of clothes. I have an important meeting in an hour."

"There are some of Casey's clothes in the master bedroom and you can always borrow my shower."

"I don't think that would be appropriate."

Gavin took a sip out of his travel mug. "What's not appropriate about offering a friend some spare clothes and a shower?"

He had a point.

It wasn't ideal, but she really didn't have a choice. She hadn't become Chief of Surgery by attending meetings dressed as a slob.

"Point me in the right direction."

"Gladly."

She followed Gavin to the master bedroom. The room smelled distinctly like him. Masculine. A clean, spicy smell that she loved. The bed was made and she noticed a pile of blankets on the floor.

"What's going on here?" she asked as she stepped over the pile.

"Ah, I'm still not used to using a mattress. I've been sleeping rough for so long I find I can only get a good night's sleep on the floor."

"You've been in San Francisco for how long again?"

"Six months, but still no good. The bed is too soft and good for only one thing."

Virginia's pulse began to race, understanding his implication clearly.

"Clothes?" she asked, changing the subject.

He moved past her and opened up the closet. "Here's where Casey's clothes are."

"Why are you still keeping them?"

Gavin shrugged. "I haven't had the time to deal with her personal effects. Besides, they come in handy when I deliberately trap women here and force them to babysit my nieces."

Virginia rolled her eyes and snorted.

He opened another door. "There are towels in the closet. Feel free to use whatever."

"Thanks. I really appreciate this. I'll see you at work."

Gavin nodded. "See you."

When he left the bedroom Virginia peeled off the scrubs and climbed into the shower. The hot water helped work out the kinks in her back and neck.

She finished her quick shower and then dried herself off, towel-drying her hair. As much as she wished she had a straightener or a blow-dryer, she was just thankful she didn't smell like plaster or old coffee.

When she headed into the master bedroom she picked out

a simple blouse and pants, which were a little big on her but at least she wouldn't be in wrinkled old scrubs. She jammed the scrubs in her purse after tying back her hair.

As soon as she left the bedroom Gavin was standing there, holding a mug of coffee out.

"Please, don't dump that on me."

"You might want me to." He winced. "Your car was parked in a no overnight parking zone and was towed."

Virginia closed her eyes and took a deep calming breath. What she really wanted to do was let out a string of profanities that would shake the very rafters of Gavin's pink home, but there were children in the house, so she refrained from uttering them out loud and kept them to herself.

"How am I going to get to work?" she asked calmly.

"You can ride with me, but I hope you don't mind riding on the back of my bike. Rosalie needs the van for the girls today."

"You ride a motorcycle?"

He nodded. "I do. What do you say, Virginia?"

Her heart beat a bit faster in anticipation at the thought of riding behind the most stereotypical bad boy. She did have a thing for motorcycles.

Instead of saying *I'd love that* and letting him know how exciting the prospect was, she restrained herself. "Sure, I really don't have a choice."

"Don't sound so enthused," he teased. "Well, let's go."

Virginia downed the rest of her coffee and followed Gavin outside to the garage. He uncovered the Harley and dug out an extra helmet for her. She was really excited to ride behind him, but she also hoped no one from the hospital would see her arrive on the back of Gavin's motorcycle.

The gossip would be endless and she didn't want anything to get back to the board about it. It could put her career and Gavin's in jeopardy.

He secured her purse and his satchel in one of the panniers, before climbing on.

She climbed on the back of his motorcycle and wrapped

her arms around him. The moment she did so, her heart beat a bit faster and she hoped he didn't notice. What she really longed to do was press her body tight against his, but she kept her distance the best she could. Still, it felt so good to be so close to him.

"Hold on." He revved the engine and the purr of the bike drowned out the loud beat of her pulse. The vibrations rippled through her. He pulled out onto the street, parked and shut the garage door before climbing back on. "You ready?"

Virginia nodded and he turned on his signal and hit the streets of San Francisco. The moment he hit the road, she pulled him tighter as she held on for dear life. She'd lived in San Francisco for years, she learned to drive on its streets when she'd first moved here and had ridden the streetcars and trolleys up and down the hills, but until now those hills had never freaked her out.

She repressed the urge to cry out as Gavin maneuvered his way through the San Francisco streets towards Bayview Grace.

The ride terrified her, but it also thrilled her. As they crested a hill and raced down the other side she felt like she was on some crazy roller coaster.

For the first time in a long time she felt carefree and that feeling scared her. When they arrived at Bayview Grace Gavin parked in his reserved spot.

"What did you think of the ride?" he asked as she handed him her helmet.

Her knees wobbled a bit. "It was… Thanks for bringing me."

Gavin grinned. "Any time. If you want, I'll take you to the lot to retrieve your car after work."

"No, thanks, Dr. Brice. I'll take transit or a cab. I'm not sure how late I'll be working tonight."

"Sure. Thanks again for your help with the girls last night."

"My pleasure." She glanced at her watch and saw she was already five minutes late. "Look, I have to go. Thanks."

What she wanted to say was that it was no problem and that she would gladly spend another evening with the girls.

She also wanted to tell him how much she'd enjoyed the impromptu sleepover party with them and how good it had felt to have two sweet little angels sleeping next to her on the couch, but she didn't.

It wasn't her place.

She turned on her heel and walked briskly towards the hospital. Her legs were still shaking from the ride and her heart was shaking a bit from the feelings that were threatening to overpower her common sense.

CHAPTER TEN

WHEN VIRGINIA CAME out of the board meeting a few hours later, she had a pounding headache. Janice was waiting for her in her office with some files.

"You look like you've been run over by a steamroller," she remarked.

"Haven't I?" Virginia asked as she took a seat behind her desk. "More budget cuts."

"Ugh," Janice remarked.

"My sentiments exactly."

Virginia was frustrated. The board had hired her to bring this hospital back from the dead, but how was she supposed to do that when they constantly cut her budget?

Because they wanted a private clinic, at least some of them did, and she wasn't going to let go of her ER without a fight. So she'd proposed a hospital benefit. A glitzy affair showcasing their brilliant attendings and the innovative strides they were making in order to receive funding.

Her suggestion had pleased the board no end, but it meant she had a big party to plan. So instead of spending time with patients, doing innovative surgeries or research she was going to be planning a big party.

"That's an interesting color choice and I don't mean to be disrespectful, but who did your nails?"

Virginia glanced down at her hands and groaned inwardly. Rose had painted her nails, and they were horribly mangled, messy and now the enamel was chipping. It was also pink. No wonder she had been getting weird glances from some of the members of the board.

"I'm not on the top of my game today."

Janice cocked an eyebrow. "No kidding. Wild night last night?" There was a hint of hope in her assistant's voice. Janice was always hoping that Virginia would live a little and she voiced her opinions quite loudly at times.

"You're young. Don't spend your youth locked away. Go out and live a little."

Why couldn't they just let her be? It was her life after all.

She knew one thing: planning benefits and schmoozing hadn't been part of the original plan. Virginia wanted to be in the OR or researching.

The internal dialog in her head was turning into a bit of a broken record.

"Well, what were you up to last night?" Janice prodded.

"A bit of an impromptu sleepover." She groaned inwardly, regretting the admission, because when Janice got a hint of gossip, she was like a dog with a bone. Virginia was usually more aloof with Janice, but lack of a good night's sleep had caused a lapse in judgement and she'd let down her walls a bit.

"Oh, do tell." Janice was grinning from ear to ear.

"You know, it's funny. I have all this work to do."

Janice snorted and dropped the last file on her desk. "Fine, I can take a hint. Before I go, though, A&B Towing called and they had information on where your car is being held. The message is the pink slip on the top."

Janice shot her a knowing but smug look as she left the office.

Virginia groaned. She'd forgotten about her car. She only had an hour before the impound lot closed. Her paperwork could wait until she got back. She needed her car.

When she left her office, Janice was smiling secretly to herself as she worked. Virginia just shook her head and left for the lot.

* * *

"I heard you were looking for this." Gavin dropped the patient forms onto Janice's desk. He'd meant to drop them off sooner, but he'd had a surgery to attend. He'd literally just got out of the OR. All he'd had time to do was scrub out, and he was still wearing his scrub cap, because Janice had been paging him about the missing forms since he'd arrived.

"Thank you, Dr. Brice, and very neat handwriting too."

"Sorry I didn't drop them off straightaway."

Janice cocked an eyebrow and looked at him over her horned-rimmed glasses. "Well, I can be persistent when I need something done. I know how distracted you surgeons get."

Gavin lingered and he didn't know why.

You know why.

"Is Dr. Potter out of her meeting yet?"

Janice's eyes widened and then she grinned and leaned forward. "Yes, but she had to step out. Her car was impounded last night. So unlike Dr. Potter."

"Right. I forgot."

"Really? You knew about her car being impounded? Do tell." Janice leaned on her elbow, propping her chin on her fist and fluttering her eyelashes behind her tortoiseshell bifocals.

Gavin held up his hands. "I don't think it's any of my business to tell you. If Virginia didn't mention it, then I won't."

"Virginia? Usually other surgeons refer to her as Dr. Potter or chief. Didn't realize you two were so close." Janice grinned like the cat that had got the cream, or like the Grinch when he thought of his evil plan. So smugly pleased with herself.

Gavin cursed inwardly. "You're a bit of a pest, aren't you?"

"One of the best, Dr. Brice."

Gavin backed away. He didn't want to make Virginia angrier at him. "Well, I'm being paged. I'd better go."

Janice gave him a skeptical look. "Of course, Dr. Brice. Of course."

Gavin made a mental note not to cross swords with Janice, though some of the nurses had already warned him of that.

Janice was a force to be reckoned with. She'd been a charge nurse herself for years and was the keeper of the gates, more intimidating than Cerberus itself. Although it was Gavin's experience that women like Janice had barks that were worse than their bites. She had implied that there was something personal between himself and Virginia.

Though he wanted something more intimate, he knew if he went after Virginia it wouldn't be just a fling and he wasn't sure if he had anything to give Virginia because marriage and monogamy were something he had never pictured for himself.

When he headed back down to the trauma bay Dr. Rogerson popped out of a room.

Gavin liked independent, strong woman, but he didn't like being hunted down by overly forward women. To Moira Rogerson he was just a piece of meat and he didn't like it.

"How's your niece, Dr. Brice?"

Gavin frowned. "How did you know?"

He liked to keep his personal life just that—to himself. Especially with people he worked with.

"I was on duty yesterday. I was originally paged until the ice queen took over."

Gavin didn't like that nickname, knowing that was the name the other surgeons used when referring to Virginia. Ice Queen was far from the truth.

She might be a bit heavy-handed when it came to running the hospital, but Virginia wasn't that way outside work. He'd seen the softer side of her.

"Well, Dr. Potter is a trauma surgeon and my niece broke her arm." Gavin pulled out his phone and pretended to check for text messages, though he had none. Moira didn't get the hint that he wasn't interested in talking.

"I didn't know you were guardian to your nieces. That's really sweet." Moira grinned at him, a smile meant to devour a man whole.

"I don't talk much about them. I like to keep my private life private."

He walked into the lunchroom and got himself a drink of water. Moira followed him and he groaned inwardly, wishing she would just go away.

"How old are your nieces?"

Swallowing the water was like trying to down a cue ball at the moment. "Why do you want to know?"

"Just trying to make small talk." Moira took a step forward and placed her hand on his arm, gently squeezing it.

"I'm afraid I don't do small talk."

Moira smiled. "What do you do, then?"

"Surgery?" he offered, and Moira just laughed, which was annoying and high-pitched, and she clutched his arm tighter.

"You're so droll, Gavin."

He ground his teeth, not liking the way she said his name. "I don't know what's so funny about stating the truth."

"So would you like to have dinner sometime? Maybe tonight?"

Gavin was about to answer and glanced up in time to see Virginia walk back into the hospital. His heart skipped a beat as he watched her walk through the entrance and he was taken back to that stolen moment on Sunday, down by the water, when time had seemed to stand still and he'd pulled Virginia into his arms and kissed her.

The scent of her perfume, the touch of her lips still burned in his memory, as did the pointed rejection, which still stung him.

Virginia and he were coworkers, maybe even friends, but that's all they could be.

She'd made that pretty clear.

"Gavin?" Moira turned to see what had caught his attention. "Oh, the ice queen."

"Sure, why don't we go out tonight?" Gavin suddenly blurted out, trying not to look at Virginia as she headed towards them.

Moira grinned. "Yes, I'd love that. I'll page you later for the details." Moira winked and finally left him in peace.

Virginia nodded curtly to Moira as they passed in the hall

and then, as if knowing she was being watched, she glanced at him. Her dark gaze locked with his and he saw a faint pinkness tinge her skin as she walked into the room.

"You're still here. I thought your shift ended a couple of hours ago?" she said.

"Surgery. The closest hospital was packed and the ambulance rerouted here."

A brief smile flitted on her lips and he knew it wasn't because of the possibility that someone had been injured. Virginia was thinking in terms of business for Bayview Grace.

"I'm glad the ambulance thought to reroute here."

"We were the closest and the man was in no condition to wait for the ambulance to take him to the level two trauma. I don't think that's something we should be celebrating."

Virginia bit her bottom lip and gave him a quizzical look. "I'm not celebrating."

"Come on, I saw the brief smile that flitted across your face."

She pinched the bridge of her nose and sighed. He knew that response and he'd come to loathe it, especially after she'd had a meeting with the board of directors.

He moved past her and shut the door to the room then pulled the blinds to the room so they were in relative privacy.

"What's going on?"

Virginia shrugged her shoulders. "I don't know what you mean."

"I know that look. Very well."

This time she did smile and her shoulders relaxed from the tense hunch they'd had just moments before.

"It was just a long day and I didn't get the best sleep last night."

"What're you talking about? That couch is too soft."

Virginia cocked an eyebrow. "Says the man who sleeps on the hardwood floor."

"Did the meeting have something to do with me?" he asked. "You can tell me. I know for a fact you can tell me."

The smile disappeared and she sighed again. "Not you directly, just in general financial terms."

"That bad?"

"I have to organize a benefit for the end of the month. A real glitzy affair." She wrinkled her nose in disgust. "Not my most favorite job."

"I don't blame you." He rubbed the back of his neck. "Black tie, I suppose?"

"Yes, and mandatory for all Attendings. One month from today, so get yourself a sitter."

"Ugh."

Virginia chuckled and opened the door. "My sentiments exactly. Are you headed for home now?"

"I think so. I just dropped those forms off to Janice."

"Good."

They walked out of the room together.

"Hey, if you need help planning the gala or benefit, whatever you want to call it, just ask."

"You have hidden depths, Dr. Brice. I thought you were a roughneck sort of physician?"

"That may be, but I've attended many, many, many mandatory galas on behalf of Border Free Physicians."

"Well, maybe I'll take you up on your offer. I hate party planning. I never had a party when I was young."

"Never had a party?" Gavin asked, intrigued by this insight into her.

"No, my parents couldn't stretch to that luxury."

"What did they do?"

"Unemployed, for the most part. I grew up in a trailer in South Dakota with two brothers and three sisters."

"That's a surprise."

"Really? Why do you say that?"

"You don't seem the trailer type."

Virginia crossed her arms. "Is there a trailer type?"

Gavin rubbed the back of his neck. "Sorry, no, there isn't

unless you count what's on television. I didn't mean to make assumptions."

"It's okay. I have hidden depths. Ugh, I hope someone can help."

"A surgeon as a party planner?" Gavin asked in disbelief. "Surgeons usually aren't social types."

"You'd be surprised around here." Virginia tucked a wayward lock of brown hair behind her ear. "I saw you talking to Dr. Rogerson. She's a bit of a social butterfly."

Is she jealous?

Gavin was amused, pleased she'd noticed, but he didn't want to talk about it. He'd let her stew a bit. "Well, I'd better head for home. The girls get anxious when I'm late."

"Of course. Have a good evening and send them my best." Virginia turned and walked away from him towards the office.

Gavin watched her walk away.

And then a horrible thought crept into his mind. If the hospital needed to throw a benefit, one that would cause the chief of surgery a large amount of stress, how bad a shape was the hospital in and would he even have a job in the near future?

CHAPTER ELEVEN

GAVIN MANAGED TO finagle Rosalie into babysitting. He owed that woman a large Christmas bonus.

Now he was standing in the middle of Union Square, waiting for Moira to arrive. He glanced over and saw the place where Virginia had been waiting for him. When he'd seen her there, he'd been mesmerized by her simple beauty and he'd known he'd have a hard time keeping his hands off her.

Virginia occupied his mind constantly, made him think things he shouldn't.

Was that why he'd agreed on this date with Moira and suggested this location, re-creating the date he and Virginia had gone on? Was he trying to prove to himself that he could find that spark with anyone, that Virginia wasn't special?

He didn't have time to contemplate it further as Moira walked over to him. She was dressed nicely, different from her scrubs. She was dressed as prettily as Virginia, only the color was a deep emerald, which suited Moira's hair. It was also more seductive and instead of ballet flats she wore heels, which were impractical for the date he had in mind. Of course Moira wasn't to know that.

"Hi," she said, her smile bright as she stopped in front of him. She leaned over and gave him a peck on the cheek. Her perfume was a bit overpowering and floral. Not homey like vanilla and certainly not subtle.

"Hi, yourself."

"Where are we going? I hope it's not far." Moira pointed to her heels and then lifted the hem of her dress slightly, showing off her leg. "These are murder on my feet, but they're so pretty."

"I was actually thinking of the Fog City Diner."

"Oh." There was a hint of disappointment in her voice.

Gavin didn't know what she'd expected. Obviously something fancier as she was decked out to the nines.

"Is there something wrong with that restaurant? I've been told it's a San Francisco institution."

"For tourists, yes."

"I made reservations."

"Sounds good." Gavin could tell she was lying by the way she forced a smile. "Is your car nearby? I took a cab here as mine's in the shop."

"No, I'd thought we'd take the streetcar."

"You're kidding me, right?"

I guess I am. "No, I'm not kidding. I thought we'd take the streetcar and enjoy the sights."

"How about I pay for a cab? No offense, but these heels are a little much for a streetcar."

"Sure." What could he say to that, no? Gavin trailed behind Moira as she marched over to a taxi stand at a nearby hotel. It didn't take long before they were both settled into the back of the cab. Moira snuggled up next to him, her floral scent mixed with the spicy smell permeating the cab, making his stomach turn.

Virginia had had no problem riding the streetcar. In fact, it had seemed to enhance the experience of that night. It had been fun. Virginia wasn't high-maintenance. He had an inkling, going into this date, that Moira was high-maintenance.

Did he really want to date someone who was?

This wasn't for the long term, he reminded himself again. This was just a fling. Who cared if Moira preferred different things to Virginia? This wasn't a comparison between the two women. He wasn't looking for something long term.

Though maybe he was and that thought scared him.

On that short cab ride to the Fog City Diner, Gavin finally admitted to himself how lonely he'd been and maybe he did want to settle down and have it all. The thought was extremely unsettling. Having custody of the girls had changed his perspective entirely.

The conversation at the diner was one-sided and stilted. Moira chatted away, but Gavin just couldn't clear his head from his jangled thoughts. It'd been so easy to talk to Virginia.

"Gavin, are you listening?"

"Sorry, what?"

Moira frowned. "You're a bit out of sorts."

"A bit. What were you saying?"

"I was just telling you how some staff members think the ice queen is melting. That her demeanor is softening around her cold, hard exterior. Can you imagine? I wonder what brought that on, though I have my suspicions."

"Softening? How do you mean?"

"Well, she's been behaving differently lately. I think it's a man."

Gavin's heart stuttered, but then he shrugged, feigning indifference. "Maybe she has a lot on her mind."

"Who knows? But she's been more…I don't know…approachable. More relaxed and nice. Not so aloof. The nurses like the change."

"I don't quite see the problem, then."

Moira leaned forward. "I've heard talk of the ER getting the axe."

Now she had Gavin's full attention. He'd been sure something was up with Virginia planning that gala.

"Who told you that?"

Moira grinned. "Ah, so you've heard it too."

"Nothing concrete, just rumors. Especially rumors involving a certain fundraising event."

"The gala! Yeah, it had me worried too. My source is on the board of directors."

Gavin cocked an eyebrow. "Go on."

"There are threats to close the ER, but Dr. Potter is fighting tooth and nail to keep it open."

Gavin grinned, pleased to hear it. They called Virginia the ice queen. How little they knew when she was working so hard for them and they had no idea. "Is she?"

Moira sighed. "It won't do her any good. It's why I applied to another hospital and got a job."

"You're leaving Bayview?"

"Before it sinks. I have to protect myself and my career. If you're nice to me I can get you an interview." She slid her hand across the table, reaching out for his, and then her foot began to slide up his leg in a very suggestive manner. A move he would've welcomed six months ago.

"I think your thoughts on Bayview sinking are premature. I think Dr. Potter will save Bayview Grace."

Moira frowned, retracting her hand, and the game of footsie ended as well. "Why did you say yes to this date, Gavin?"

"What do you mean?"

She rolled her eyes. With a sigh she opened her purse and placed a twenty on the table. "You're clearly not interested in me. You're obviously hung up on someone else. I don't want to spend my evening talking hospital politics."

She slid out of the booth and stood. Gavin panicked and jumped in front of her, grabbing her by the shoulders and pulling her close to him before crushing her lips against his in a kiss. A kiss to prove to himself and her that he wasn't hung up on anyone.

Moira melted into his arms, a moan escaping from the back of her throat, then her tongue pushed past his lips.

Gavin felt nothing.

His kiss with Virginia had been so different. It had been gentle, sweet and it'd turned him on. This was rough, clumsy and evoked no response from him at all.

He didn't want Moira. He wanted Virginia.

Moira broke the kiss. She sighed and then frowned. "Goodbye, Dr. Brice."

Gavin didn't try to stop her this time as she walked past curious onlookers as she left the restaurant. He sank back down against the seat, before pulling out a couple of twenties to pay the bill.

When he walked outside a thick fog was rolling in and the sun was just starting to get ready to set, making the area glow orange in the haze. Gavin walked along the Embarcadero. August would soon be over. The girls would go back to school. He had to switch to nights so he could take them to and from school. Rosalie already said she'd take them during the nights he worked.

There would be no time for dating.

Not until the girls were older.

Only would it make a difference? Would he even have a job in a few weeks' time?

Was Moira doing the smart thing by jumping ship?

Gavin didn't know how long he walked, but he ended up in front of Bayview Grace. Virginia's car was still in the lot.

I need to know.

He had two little girls depending on him. He needed job security and stability in order to keep the girls. If he lost his job and had to move, the girls' grandparents would certainly sue for custody and possibly win. It would kill him to lose the girls now.

Virginia shuffled through more paperwork and glanced at the clock. It was almost eight. She should really go home, but what would she be going home to?

Nothing.

Then her mind wandered to Gavin. She knew he was on a date with Moira Rogerson. She'd heard it through the rumor mill—well, she'd actually heard it from Janice, who kept an ear to the grapevine.

It shouldn't bother her because she wasn't looking for a relationship, but it did. It made her feel jealous, just picturing him laughing and talking with Moira like he'd done with her.

If he started dating Moira she had no one to blame but herself. She'd pushed him away and it was for the best. She couldn't give him what he wanted because she was terrified to admit it was what she wanted as well, but she wouldn't put her heart at risk again.

She wouldn't lose anyone else she loved.

Virginia sighed and set down her papers. She stood up and stretched, deciding it was time to leave when the door to her office burst open. Virginia jumped and saw Gavin standing there, dressed in the same kind of clothes he'd worn when he'd taken her out.

"Dr. Brice, I thought you were out for the evening."

"I was, but I needed to talk to you."

The butterflies in her stomach began to flutter. "Oh?"

"I need to… I mean, I want…" Gavin rubbed the back of his neck and then shut the door behind him. "I need to switch to nights."

"Oh—oh, okay." Virginia took a seat, her knees knocking. She didn't know what she'd been expecting him to say, but it definitely wasn't that. She felt relieved and disappointed all at the same time. "Why?"

"The girls start school the first week of September and I want to be able to take them to and from school. It's Rose's first year there and I think it's important that I'm there."

Virginia nodded. "Of course. I would ask if you've talked to your superior but as you're head of that department there shouldn't be a problem. I'm sure someone will want to change."

"Jefferson is switching with me. He's young and he's looking forward to day shifts, even if it's only for the school year."

"Then it's all settled." Virginia watched him. He looked nervous and he stood there as if he wanted to say more. "Is that all you needed to talk about, Gavin?"

"No." His gaze met hers, those deep green eyes intense, riveting her to the spot. "Is the ER threatened?"

Virginia cleared her throat. "What're you talking about?"

"The gala. It's not just some fundraiser, it's to save the ER, isn't it?"

"It's a fundraiser for the ER, yes."

Gavin scrubbed his hand over his face. "Is my job safe?"

Virginia wanted to tell him the truth, but she honestly couldn't. She was sworn to a confidentiality agreement.

"The ER isn't in danger."

It was a lie, one that made her feel sick to her stomach. Gavin walked over to her desk and sat down in front of her.

"You're sure?"

Virginia looked away. "Gavin, I wish I could tell you otherwise, but I'm bound by a legal agreement to keep it secret." Then she looked back at him, trying to convey everything she couldn't say in a look.

"I see." Gavin nodded. "I understand."

"I would tell you."

"I know you would."

"I'll write you a recommendation letter if you want to leave. I understand why you wouldn't want to stay."

"I don't need a letter." Then he reached across the desk and took her hand in his. "I have faith that you'll keep this hospital from going under. I'm not ready to jump ship."

His hand around hers felt so good. It calmed her and made her wish that it wasn't just their bare hands touching. That it could be more.

Virginia took her hand back. "Where did you hear this rumor?"

"Dr. Rogerson."

"Ah, well, that makes sense. She handed in her resignation this morning." Virginia cleared her throat. "I heard you were on a date with Moira. How was it?"

Gavin grinned and leaned back in the chair. "Fine."

Virginia's cheeks flushed. "Oh, that's great. She's a wonderful surgeon."

"Are you jealous, Virginia?" Gavin asked, his green eyes twinkling mischievously.

"Don't be ridiculous. I just wanted to know where the rumor started so I could quash it before it got out of hand. I don't care who you see or don't see, Dr. Brice. You've made it clear that your personal life is no concern of mine and it isn't."

Gavin's smile disappeared and he frowned. "Well, glad that's settled."

Virginia nodded and turned back to her paperwork, effectively dismissing him. "I'd better get some more of this paperwork done and I'll schedule your duty shifts for the evening starting on your next rotation."

"Great. Thanks. I appreciate it." He stood and she watched him as he walked across the room and opened the door. He turned and glanced back. "Good night, Dr. Potter."

"Good night, Dr. Brice."

CHAPTER TWELVE

"YOU'RE DOING A fantastic job with the benefit, Dr. Potter."

Virginia plastered on her best smile as she walked through the Excelsior downtown San Francisco. "I'm glad you approve, Mr. Shultz." That was what she said, but what she really thought was, I hope this is worth it, because this benefit is already costing the hospital precious amounts of money.

Money that could be used to keep the emergency department open.

She'd been carrying around that information for a month and it was eating her up inside. This benefit had to go off without any kind of hiccup in order to save the emergency department. There were so many people in the department who depended on their jobs. Especially Gavin.

She let her mind wander to him for a brief moment. She hadn't seen him since they'd spoken that night in her office. Though it wasn't unexpected. He'd transferred to nights and she'd been so busy with the gala that there hadn't been a chance to catch up. There had been a few times when she'd caught a fleeting glimpse of him coming in as she was leaving, but that was about it. Although she'd see him soon because she had an appointment to see Lily in about an hour.

Virginia glanced at her wristwatch. "If you'll excuse me, Mr. Schultz, I do have an appointment with a VIP patient."

"Of course, of course, but before you go I just wanted to

confirm with you that Dr. Gavin Brice will be speaking at the event."

"Dr. Brice?"

"Yes," Mr. Schultz said. "Many of the attendees are quite interested in hearing him speak. He may have started as a bit of a rogue, but he's starting to fit in with our hospital. We'd love to have him talk about his experiences with Border Free Physicians."

"Well, I can certainly ask him, but he's not one of the attendings I asked to speak. He's on nights now and I may not be able to pull him away from his duties."

Mr. Schultz frowned. "Then you need to ask him, Dr. Potter. I would advise you to tell him to speak."

Virginia plastered another smile on her face and excused herself from the hotel ballroom.

"Tell him to speak."

Like she could order her surgeons to do anything like that.

Still, she had to try and get Gavin onside for the sake of the benefit.

Would it really save the hospital?

Or was it just a temporary patch on the shredded artery?

When she got to the hospital, she changed into her scrubs. When she came out of her office Janice stopped her typing.

"Lily Johnson is waiting for you in exam room 2221A. Dr. Brice is with her."

"Thank you, Janice. Hold my calls."

"Of course."

When Virginia entered the exam room Gavin was sitting with Lily. As were Rosalie and Rose. Gavin was in his scrubs because he was on duty tonight, and it pleased her that he was making time for the girls.

He always had time for his nieces. She admired him for that. First she checked out the X-rays waiting on the light box for her. "Well, it looks like that ulna is all healed. How about we take care of your arm and get that cast off? What do you say to that?"

Lily smiled. "I'm really looking forward to getting it off."

"I bet you are." Virginia readied her tools and smiled at Rose. "How are you today, Rose?"

Rose shrugged but didn't smile.

"Nervous about your sister?" Virginia asked.

Rose nodded.

"There's no reason to be nervous." Virginia picked up the saw used to remove the cast and started it. Rose's eyes widened, her little face paling. "This saw won't cut her skin. You want to know how I know?"

Rose didn't nod but watched the saw in fascination. Virginia placed it against her palm, running the saw over her hand.

"See, it just tickles."

"Cool," Lily said. "That's so cool."

Virginia winked at Gavin, who was hiding his laugh behind his hand. "Okay, Lily, let's get this tired-looking cast off." She slipped goggles and a face mask on the little girl.

"What're these for?"

"It'll protect you from the dust. I have my own pair too."

Lily held her arm still. Virginia slipped on her mask and goggles and set the oscillating saw down through the fiberglass, cutting away at the fibers.

Lily watched, her eyes wide from behind the goggles, until the cast fell away from her pale arm.

"Yuck, it's all weird-looking and it stinks." Lily pinched her nose.

Virginia set down the saw and palpated Lily's arm and then moved it around, asking her if she felt any pain. "Well, your arm's been covered for a month. It hasn't seen the sun in four weeks. Your bone appears to be nice and healed, so I'm begging you, as your doctor, not to hang from any monkey bars at school. Promise me."

Lily grinned. "I promise. Can I keep my cast? I like all the signatures."

"Of course." She turned to Gavin. "Her skin is really dry.

Bathe it in warm water for twenty minutes twice a day and dry it by rubbing gently."

"I know how to take care of a limb after a cast comes off."

Virginia chuckled. "Of course."

"Rosalie, can you take the girls home now?" Gavin asked.

"Of course, Dr. Brice. Come on, girls, you'll see your uncle tomorrow morning."

Virginia helped Lily down and handed her the cast. "Take care of that arm, Lily."

"I will, thank you, Dr. Potter." Lily took Rose's hand and they walked out together.

Virginia watched the girls leave with Gavin's housekeeper. "Dr. Brice, before you start your shift, there's something I need to talk to you about."

Gavin crossed his arms over his chest. "Of course, shoot."

"The board has asked if you would speak at the gala benefit next week."

"No."

Virginia scrubbed her hand over her face. She had half expected that answer from him. "Please, would you do it for the hospital? You offered to help me before with the planning."

"Yes, but that was organizing it. I don't do well with crowds. I don't like giving speeches and I'm sorry but I'm not going to give one for this hospital." He turned to walk away but Virginia stepped in front of him, blocking him from leaving.

"I don't think you quite understand what I'm asking you."

"I do understand what you're asking me, Dr. Potter. The board wants me to talk about all the great adventures I had with Border Free Physicians, but the thing is they *really* don't want me to."

Virginia was confused. "What're you talking about?"

Gavin let out a heavy sigh. "It's not that I don't like speaking to crowds, not really. It's just that I would write a speech, telling all those tuxedoed people exactly what I experienced, the nitty-gritty details of developing countries and how they should be pouring their extra money into helping those less fortunate. Even here, in this city, there are countless missions. There are people living in this city, not necessarily on the streets, who need medical attention. They just can't afford it."

Virginia was stunned. "And you're saying that the board wouldn't want you to talk about it?"

He nodded. "Precisely. I've written my speech countless times in my head. Each time it's edited. I'm not allowed to actually talk about what's needed. The people who buy these expensive plates and bid on the silent auction don't care about what's happening under their noses, let alone in the wider world."

"I will let you speak about that," Virginia said.

Gavin gave her a half-hearted smile. "You say that now, but your hands are tied, Virginia. Don't make a promise that you aren't able to keep."

"I don't think you understand what's really at stake."

"Tell me, then. Tell me what's at stake."

Gavin waited with bated breath for her answer. Though he knew. He'd heard enough rumblings in the hallways about Bayview Grace bleeding out money like its carotid artery had been severed, that the emergency department would most likely be amputated, meaning that he would be out of a job. Moira had been right.

He wanted Virginia to tell him that. Though he knew she couldn't, he still wanted to hear it from her lips all the same.

The staff in the emergency department were stressed, worried about their futures, about their security, and when the staff were stressed, mistakes were made.

Gavin hated working in an environment like that.

What he wanted from Virginia, from his chief of surgery, was for her tell him that this benefit was a last-ditch effort to save the emergency department.

He wanted the truth.

So he waited, watching as Virginia thought of some kind of excuse or story to throw him off the scent.

He'd dealt with stuff like this in Border Free Physicians. He knew how to get around it and he wasn't going to back down until he had the truth.

"You need to speak at the benefit," she said, and straightened her shoulders, crossing her arms in that stubborn stance he knew all too well.

She was going to hold her ground, just as much as he was, and he admired her for that.

"I don't have to speak, Virginia. I'll attend the benefit, but I'm not speaking."

"Yes, you are."

He cocked his head. "I don't think you can force me."

"No, I can't and I really don't want to, but the board has made it clear that you will speak. Just like the other attendings who've been asked. You will speak at the benefit, Dr. Brice."

"Because my job depends on it?"

Virginia didn't utter a word but she nodded, just barely.

Damn.

"How bad is it?"

Virginia glanced over her shoulder and then shut the door to the exam room. "It's bad."

"So the emergency department really is on the chopping block?"

"You know I'm betraying a confidentiality agreement. I could get sued."

"I won't breathe a word." And he wouldn't.

She sighed and her face paled.

"How bad is it? Is it just the ER?" he asked.

"A few departments, actually."

Gavin leaned against the wall. The last thing he wanted to do was uproot the girls, but the other hospitals weren't hiring attendings, and there was no way he was going to take up Moira's offer to put in a good word at her new workplace. Anyway, he'd burned his bridges with her after she'd walked out on their date.

"I'll give a speech."

Virginia relaxed. "Thank you. It means a lot to me."

"I'm doing it for the hospital, for all the people who depend on their jobs, but can you do one thing for me?"

"It depends," she said skeptically.

"Promise me you'll do it."

"I can't blindly promise, Gavin."

"Oh, but you expected me to blindly promise to speak at an event I don't agree with?" he snapped.

"You're an attending. It's your duty."

He snorted. "It's not my duty to watch the board try and make a bit of money by throwing away what little they have to try and save this hospital, by hosting some snooty benefit."

"Gavin, I really don't want to argue with you."

"Look, I just want you to tell my staff what's on the line. They know something is up and not knowing is stressing everyone out."

Virginia shook her head. "I can't tell, Gavin. They can't know. I can't afford to have some of my staff leave. Not just yet. You promised."

"That's unfair to them. To those who've given Bayview Grace their loyalty."

"My hands are tied."

"No. They're not."

"Don't you think letting them know that their jobs are on the line would be more detrimental to them?" Virginia's face turned crimson, her voice rising. Gavin had never seen her like this before but, frankly, at this moment he didn't care.

He was damn mad.

His staff deserved to know.

"Tell them."

"No, and you'd better keep your word to me that you won't either." She turned on her heel and stormed out of the exam room.

Gavin let her go and let out a string of profanities. He didn't want to fight with her. She was his equal and she rubbed him the wrong way, because she was just as pigheaded as he was.

Put yourself in her shoes.

Only at this moment he couldn't do that rationally. He didn't envy her her job or her position one bit, but the way he was feeling now, if he was chief of surgery he'd be warning his employees that this hospital was in danger.

He took a deep calming breath and then saw her logic.

If she did tell the staff, they'd all leave or not care any more about doing a good job, because what was the point if the hospital was doomed?

He was a jackass.

"Hey, I saw you were having some words with the ice queen," Dr. Jefferson said as he wandered into the exam room. "She was on a rampage, from what I saw. What did you say to her?"

"She's not an ice queen. Show some damn respect, Jefferson."

Jefferson frowned. "What has gotten into you?"

"Nothing."

"You're absolutely stressed."

You think? Only he didn't respond to him, he just paced back and forth, trying to calm his nerves. "Is there something in particular you wanted, Dr. Jefferson?"

"Yeah, there's been a major crash on Van Ness. A streetcar and a bus. All hospitals are being braced for trauma. We'll most likely be getting the less serious cases…"

Gavin didn't listen to him further. He pushed past Jefferson, grabbing a rubber gown from the closet and heading out the emergency doors. The moment he stepped outside onto the tarmac he could see a large billow of smoke to the west. Most likely from the accident.

The sound of sirens pierced the air.

He just hoped Virginia's decision to keep his staff in the dark was worth it, and he hoped they remained focused enough not to make any mistakes today.

CHAPTER THIRTEEN

"So, DO YOU have a date?"

Virginia glanced up at Janice, who'd come into her office with a pile of files. "A what?"

Her lips twitched. "A date. You know, where you take someone out you're attracted to."

"No, I don't have a date."

Janice tsked. "I think the chief of surgery, who planned this event no less, should attend the gala with a hunky and gorgeous man on her arm."

Virginia shook her head. "This chief of surgery has been too busy trying to plan this gala and run a hospital to find a date."

"Well, I guess that's a good enough excuse." Janice dropped the pile of files on her desk with a flourish. "Your patient files to go over and report on. Records says you're behind on your reports."

Virginia groaned. "Can't you do it for me?"

Janice snorted. "Do I look like the doctor?"

"I'm not answering that on the grounds it might incriminate me." She grinned up at Janice, who looked unimpressed.

"However, if I was in your position I would be out wrestling me down some handsome hunk as eye candy for my arm."

"Thanks for the advice, Janice. I'll make a note of it." She rubbed her temples.

"You could use a drink," Janice remarked as she left the office.

I sure could.

Virginia checked her watch. It was almost seven in the evening. She'd been at the hospital since four that morning. Almost fifteen hours. It was then she realized how long she'd been bent over her desk, planning a party.

Was this what she'd signed on for?

No.

She'd bought a beautiful dress yesterday. Royal blue, but she hadn't gone out with anyone to get it, because she didn't really have any girlfriends. There had been no one to ooh and ahh over it. No one to tell her that her butt looked too big or what shoes would go with it.

And now she'd be attending the gala alone. No one to appreciate the dress, no one to dance with or make her feel sexy.

She couldn't remember the last time she'd gone on a date.

What about dinner with Gavin?

Her cheeks flushed at the memory of his kiss. The way his hands had felt around her. The way his eyes had twinkled in devilment, but that hadn't been a date.

Had it?

Who was she kidding? It had been, but like most dates she had, nothing had come of it. She and Gavin were friends, or quasi-friends. She hadn't had a chance to speak to him since she'd taken off Lily's cast and asked him to do the speech.

She hadn't asked. She'd ordered him to and he'd asked her to be up front with the staff, but she'd refused.

In her flurry of work Virginia had seen Gavin around the hospital and she couldn't help but wonder what had happened on that date with Moira Rogerson. Was he still seeing her? Before Moira had left it had been plain to everyone that Moira had had a thing for Gavin, and who could blame her really? Gavin was a handsome, accomplished and desirable man. Even if he was somewhat brusque.

Moira was a pretty woman and Virginia wondered if Gavin was interested in her.

A thought that irked her.

She had no claim on Gavin. He'd kissed her and she'd pushed him away. She'd made it clear that they could never be.

I have to get out of here.

Virginia closed her email and shut down her computer. She grabbed her purse and headed out. Janice had gone home for the evening, which was good because Virginia wasn't sure she could take any more teasing about "wrestling up" a man.

When she got outside she headed for her car and then stopped. There was a bar across the road. She'd never set foot in it but it looked like a respectable enough place.

What the hell?

She crossed the road and entered the bar. It was dark inside, even though it was still light outside for a quarter to eight. There were a few people in the bar, a couple playing darts, and she recognized a few people from the hospital, but they didn't acknowledge her and why would they? She was the ice queen of Bayview Grace.

Virginia took a seat at the bar.

"What'll it be?" the pretty blonde bartender asked.

"I honestly don't know."

She cocked an eyebrow. "Well, I've heard some strange things in here, but that's a first."

"Really?" Virginia asked. "I guess that fits as it's my first time in a bar."

"Wow." The young woman grinned. "You're a virgin, then."

Virginia noticed a couple of men down at the end of the bar perked up at the mention of the word "virgin."

"What would you recommend?" Virginia asked, changing the subject.

"How about a glass of wine? I have some nice local wines."

Virginia nodded and felt relieved. "That sounds good."

The bartender nodded. "I'll be right back with a nice red."

Virginia glanced around, not knowing where to look. There was a television over the bar, but it was on a sports channel and she had no interest in that.

"Here's a nice red from Napa." The bartender smiled at

her brightly and set the glass down on a napkin. "I hope you enjoy it."

Virginia handed her some money. "I'm sure I will."

The bartender nodded and headed down to the other end of the bar. Virginia took a sip of her wine and read the labels on the bottles of liquor lining the back shelf.

"Now, I would've pegged you for more of a Shiraz type of girl." Gavin sat down on the barstool next to her.

"Fancy seeing you here."

He chuckled. "I could say the same about you."

Virginia shrugged her shoulders. "Janice suggested I should go out and have a drink. Among other things."

"Other things?" Gavin asked. "Now I'm intrigued."

"Janice likes her opinions, however inappropriate or personal, to be known."

"That's for sure."

"What'll it be, Dr. Brice?" the bartender asked.

"The usual, Tamara. Thanks."

Tamara the bartender nodded and pulled out and filled a glass with beer, setting it down in front of him.

"You come here often?"

Gavin nodded. "Lately. Rosalie is a lot like Janice. She felt I needed some release on my night off. Once a week for the last month I've been coming here. I have a beer and then head home."

"You've been coming here enough to know the bartender's name," Virginia remarked.

"See, that's the interpersonal skills I've been working on."

"Kimber in Trauma says you don't know her name yet."

"Who?"

"She says you call her 'Hello Kitty'."

Gavin laughed. "It's her scrubs. She wears a lot of scrubs that remind me of something Lily or Rose would be wearing. I like her, though, she's a good nurse."

"I like her too."

"Was she offended?" Gavin asked.

"You care?"

"Of course." He took a sip of his beer. "I need my staff on the top of their game. I want to prove to your board that the ER is worth saving."

Virginia's stomach knotted. "You haven't mentioned that to anyone?"

Gavin frowned. "Why would I? It's not my job to tell them their jobs are on the line."

Tension settled between them.

"No, you're right, it's not." Virginia set her wineglass down and stood. "I should really get going."

Gavin grabbed her arm. "Where are you going? You haven't even finished your wine."

"I came here to relax, Gavin. I don't want to talk about the hospital."

"I'm sorry. I didn't want to bring it up either. Don't go."

Virginia sat back down. "How is your speech coming along?"

"No work, remember?"

"Sorry." Virginia took a sip of wine. "It seems like work is all I have time for."

"That shouldn't be your priority, but who am I to talk?"

"How are the girls?" She'd missed them and it surprised her how often she thought about them.

"Good." She noticed tension there, something in the way he pursed his lips and the way his brow wrinkled. "Lily hasn't gotten into any more scrapes."

"I'm glad to hear it."

"Do you have a date yet?"

Virginia tried not to choke on the wine in her mouth. Had he just asked her what she thought he'd asked her?

"Pardon?"

"I asked you if you have a date for the benefit." Gavin watched her face for a reaction and he got the one he was expecting. Her eyes widened and pink crept up her neck to form a delectable little flush.

Virginia cleared her throat and began to fiddle with the stem of her wineglass. "I—I haven't had a chance to ask anyone."

Good.

"Neither have I, though I've been asked."

She looked up at him through her thick, dark eyelashes. "Oh, who asked you?"

"Does it matter?" he asked.

There was a flash of something which flitted across her face. Jealousy, perhaps. Gavin certainly hoped so.

"How nice for you."

"I'm not going with them, though."

Their gazes met. "Oh, why not?"

Gavin shrugged. "I'm not interested."

"She's pretty, smart, what's not to like?"

"Who are you talking about?"

"Moira Rogerson."

Gavin cocked an eyebrow. "Moira's left Bayview. I haven't seen her since that night I asked you to switch me to the night shift."

"Why? As I said, she's pretty, intelligent…"

Gavin grinned. "Are you trying to convince me to take Moira to the benefit?"

"Well, when all is said and done, it's someone to dance with."

"I don't dance." Gavin finished off his beer and signaled Tamara for another one.

"What's wrong with dancing?" Virginia asked.

"I don't know how to dance. Do you?"

"I do, in fact." She chuckled. "Don't look so shocked."

"And do you like dancing?" he asked.

"Of course. It's one of the perks of this upcoming benefit. I can't stand stuffy dinners but the dancing after the speeches should be quite enjoyable." Virginia smiled at him, making his blood heat. He loved it when she smiled at him, which wasn't very often.

"Then you should have a date."

Virginia groaned. "Not you too."

"Who's been bugging you to get a date?"

"Janice." Virginia snorted. "Something about being the chief, wrastling and arm candy."

Gavin chuckled. "Wrastling?"

"Her words, not mine." Virginia finished off her wine and set the glass down. "I really should go. I have a long day again tomorrow."

"I'll walk you out." Gavin dropped some money on the bar and walked outside with Virginia. The sun was finally setting in the west. It was brilliant, reflecting off the Golden Gate Bridge. Everything around them was warm and tranquil, but soon fall would be coming, though he'd been told that autumn in San Francisco didn't bring with it that fresh crispness as a lot of other places did.

When he'd first arrived a taxi driver had remarked that sometimes October was hotter than the summer.

He slipped his arm through hers and escorted her across the street, dodging a streetcar as they crossed the slow street.

Virginia pulled out her car keys. "Thanks for the company."

"You should come to the bar more often. It's a frequent haunt of staff members."

"I doubt they'd want the ice queen gracing the darkened doorway of their favorite watering hole, then."

"I wouldn't mind." Gavin cleared his throat. "The ice queen isn't such a harridan anymore."

Virginia blushed again and looked away. "I'll see you later, Gavin. Give my best to the girls." She turned to walk away but he stopped her again. "Is there something else I can help you with?"

"Go with me." His pulse was thundering between his ears.

"Pardon?" she asked, stunned.

"Be my date to the benefit."

"You're serious?"

Gavin nodded. "I am. You need a date, I need one and I

can't think of someone I'd rather go with. I have a condition, though."

Virginia crossed her arms. "There's a condition to being my date? This I have to hear."

"Teach me to dance."

Virginia snorted and then laughed. "You're serious?"

"Well, I don't want to embarrass the chief of surgery by trying to whisk her around the dance floor with two left feet."

Her eyes narrowed. "You have a point, but I have to say I've never been asked out before and had to meet certain conditions."

"It's a date, but not really, you said yourself that you can't date someone you work with."

A strange look crossed her face and she appeared a bit disappointed. Just like he'd felt when she'd climbed into that cab after their dinner, but he wasn't doing this as revenge. Gavin wanted the blinders on Virginia to come off and see that it would be okay for them to date. He wanted to date her.

"You're right," she said, breaking the silence. "Of course."

"So is that a yes?"

"Perhaps." She grinned, a devious smile that made him cringe and wonder what he'd just got himself into. "I have a condition too, though."

"Are you in a position to demand conditions? I mean, I've had an offer."

Virginia punched him hard in the arm. "Hey, I can find a date."

"Okay, what's your condition?" Gavin rubbed his arm.

"I get to pick your tux."

"Tux?"

"It's a black-tie benefit. What were you going to wear?" There was apprehension in her voice.

"A nice suit."

Virginia rolled her eyes. "A tux and it'll be of my choosing. I'm not having you show up in your tuxedo shirt and jeans."

"Fine," Gavin agreed grudgingly. "So, do we have a deal?"

Virginia stuck out her hand. "We do."

Gavin took it, but pulled her close. "Since this is a deal on a sort of romantic notion, shouldn't we seal the deal in some other way?"

She was so close he could smell her perfume. Her body was flush against his, her lips soft, moist and beckoning.

"I think a handshake will do." Her voice was shaky as she took her hand back and stepped away. "Shall we go shopping for a tux after your next shift?"

"I'll check with Rosalie, but I'm sure it'll be fine."

Virginia nodded. "Good. Have a good evening, Gavin. I'll see you on Thursday morning."

Gavin watched her walk across the parking lot and he couldn't help but smile to himself. Sure, he'd manipulated her, but Virginia was a stubborn woman. She was a challenge and it'd been some time since he'd been challenged.

Now, if he could only deal with the other troubling aspect of his life and get the girls' grandparents off his case.

He let out a sigh and headed to his car.

Come hell or high water, he was going to get his life worked out.

One of these days.

CHAPTER FOURTEEN

"I FEEL RIDICULOUS," Gavin shouted from behind the curtain.

"I don't care." Virginia tried to suppress her laughter. "This is part of the deal." The salesman in the tuxedo rental shop shot her a weird glance from behind her, one he didn't think she'd see but which she saw clearly in the full-length mirror.

"I feel ridiculous."

"Shut up, you're just embarrassing yourself."

Gavin snorted and she laughed silently behind her hand. "I still don't understand what's wrong with my gray suit. It worked for other events I've attended in my career."

"It may have been fine for other events, but my benefit is black tie. It has to go off without a hitch." She paused and her stomach knotted as she tried not to think of the reason why her benefit had to go off without a problem.

The ER's head was on the chopping block.

She got up and wandered toward the curtain. "Are you going to let me see or do I have to come in there?"

"You could come in." And then he laughed from the other side of the curtain, which made Virginia's cheeks flush at the thought of him naked behind a thin curtain.

"I can get you a set of tails," she countered.

"No, thanks. I'm coming out."

Virginia stepped back as the curtain slid to one side. Gavin stepped out and her breath caught in her throat just a bit.

The black tuxedo suited him. Finally, she understood that

expression "fits like a glove," because it was like the tuxedo had been made for him. It made her swoon, her stomach swirling with anticipation. He was a fine specimen.

"Well, how do I look?" Gavin straightened his collar a bit and turned. "Better than the scrubs?"

Much. Much better, was what she wanted to say. "You'll do."

He cocked an eyebrow. "Just do?"

"Well, I still think you should wear tails."

Gavin snorted. "No tails."

The salesclerk came over and took some measurements and Virginia watched, trying not to laugh. Gavin looked so unimpressed, but he looked so dashing. Like James Bond, but a more rugged Bond. Instead of the fancy British cars James Bond drove, this version of him drove a motorcycle.

"I'll get this order ready for you and you can change." The salesclerk rolled his eyes as he walked past Virginia.

"What did you do to the poor sales associate?"

Gavin grinned like a devil. "I coughed when he was doing my inner leg."

Virginia couldn't contain her laughter any more. "You're going to drive that poor man to drink."

Gavin shrugged. "I like having fun."

"Could've fooled me, the way you march around that ER."

His easy demeanor faded. "There's no time for frivolity there. If we relax even for a moment, a mistake might happen."

"I respect that kind of drive."

Gavin cocked an eyebrow. "It has nothing to do with drive, it's survival."

"Survival?"

"You've hinted in no uncertain terms that our department is poised to take the axe. We have to run like a well-oiled machine."

Virginia swallowed the lump that formed in her throat. "This benefit will change everything. If we raise enough money and get more investors on board, the ER won't close."

"Virginia, don't lie to me. The signs are on the wall. Mr

Schultz wants a private clinic to cater to the rich. He's just looking for an excuse to let the hammer fall."

She wanted to tell him he was wrong, but she couldn't because she'd thought the same thing more than once.

"Well, the tuxedo suits you. No pun intended." She hugged herself and walked away as he retreated back to the change room.

She wandered to the front window of the shop and watched the streetcars go by on Market Street. The light outside was getting dim and a fog bank was rolling in, but the fog bank was still high and wouldn't affect them as they were at the foot of San Francisco's many hills.

Gavin came out and paid his deposit and they walked outside together. The air was a bit nippy, but Virginia didn't mind this weather.

South Dakota, at this time of year, was a heck of a lot colder. She hadn't been back home in years. It was late September now and hunting season would be starting. De Smet was a sleepy town for the most part, except for the summer, when the Laura Ingalls Wilder pageants took over the town, and the fall, during hunting.

In a couple of months the temperature would drop and the snow would begin to fly and, boy, would it ever. The open vastness of the Dakota prairies would cause whiteout conditions that rivaled those of Alaska and Canada.

San Francisco didn't get snow like that and for the first time in a long time she was missing it. They walked along Market and then headed uphill towards Union Square. The place where they'd met on their first date.

After that she'd sworn to herself she'd never let that happen again, yet here she was, walking with him back to that same place.

What am I doing?

"What're you thinking about?"

"Home," Virginia said.

"Where are you from again?"

"De Smet, South Dakota."

"Not far from Billings, where I grew up." He winked. "Although I've lived in many other places. My parents' jobs always forced Casey and I to be uprooted. I hated constantly moving around."

"Yet you worked with Border Free Physicians?"

"I liked what they represent and I didn't have a family I was uprooting. I would never move the girls. San Francisco is where I'll stay."

"Most army brats aren't so bitter about being moved around."

Gavin sighed. "My parents weren't very… They loved us, but their military careers were their priority and they weren't overly affectionate. Casey and I had no other family. I took care of my sister a lot."

"How did they die?"

"My father was killed in the line of duty the year I went away to college. My mother—my mother committed suicide a year later. She had undiagnosed post-traumatic stress from Iraq. My father's death caused her to snap. Casey was fresh out of high school and married the girls' father the year that happened."

"I'm sorry."

Gavin nodded. "Thanks. It was hard."

"I can understand your devotion to your nieces and wanting to give them that stability. I can see why Casey chose you over the girls' grandparents."

"Yes." Gavin's brow furrowed and she wondered if she'd touched a sore spot. "What about your family? Why haven't you gone home in a long time?"

Virginia hesitated. She never talked about her family to anyone. She didn't want people to know about where she came from. She'd made that mistake before and once people knew they judged her, and she didn't want that.

And she didn't go home because of Shyanne. Everything

reminded her of Shyanne and it hurt too much, even after all this time.

The day Shyanne had died, a piece of her had died too.

"My parents live in a trailer, remember? There wouldn't be room for me to visit." Only her voice cracked with emotion she couldn't hold in.

"What's wrong?"

"It's too painful for me to go back."

They stopped in the square and she was glad for the bit of fog that rolled in as she blinked away the tears that were threatening to spill.

"What happened?" Gavin asked.

Virginia shook her head, but he wouldn't take no for an answer and he ushered her into a small café. The maître d' sat them in the back and Gavin ordered two coffees.

"What happened?" he asked again. "I've spilled some of my secrets so it's time for you to pay up."

She smiled, but barely. Her lips quivered slightly. "I'm a twin."

"Really?"

"Shyanne was my best friend, she was…" Virginia couldn't continue.

"How did she die?" Gavin asked, his voice gentle. His eyes kind.

"Ectopic pregnancy. Something so easy to take care of and diagnose, but I come from a very poor family. Shyanne got pregnant in the last year of high school. The guy took off and she didn't tell anyone because Dad couldn't afford health care insurance. He could barely afford to keep food on the table for the seven of us. Her tube ruptured and by the time they opened her up to do a salpingo-oophorectomy she was gone."

"I'm sorry. I'm surprised you didn't take up a job like I had, to help the underprivileged."

"Are you judging me now?" she snapped.

"No, I'm just curious."

"Who do you think pays for their health insurance now?"

Virginia played with an empty packet of sweetener lying on the table. "Besides, my dad told me to get a job and work hard and keep it."

Gavin nodded. "I understand you a bit better."

Virginia snorted. "Should I be worried?"

"No, but I'm surprised your dad still doesn't have a job."

Virginia sighed. "He's disabled. He was a welder but was hurt on the job. He gets disability checks."

"So how many siblings do you have?"

"Two sisters left and two brothers. The sisters have moved out, but my two brothers are still in high school."

"Must've been nice, having a big family like that."

Virginia smiled. "It was. It is."

"Do you miss them?" he asked.

"I do, but I haven't been back since Shyanne died. Let me rephrase that. I tried once or twice, but it was too hard."

"Don't you get lonely around the holidays?"

"I could ask the same about you, Gavin."

Gavin gave her a half-smile. "It's hard to miss family when you're working."

"Exactly."

And that made Virginia a little sad. Kids and family had never been part of her plan, just working hard and making sure that she had a decent roof over her head and that none of her other siblings would have to die the way Shyanne had. That was what drove her.

She worked holidays and she didn't mind.

Holidays hadn't been extravagant when she was a child and she blocked most of her childhood memories, but one hit her.

Shyanne and her creeping out to the living room in the trailer to see if Santa had come, and that year he had. Their little stockings had had a bulge in the toe.

They'd curled up together on the couch, huddled together while a blizzard raged outside, and just watched the glow of the Christmas lights dancing off the old orange shag rug in the living room, waiting until everyone woke up in the morning and they could see what Santa had brought them.

Santa had brought her a toy pony, with pink hair.

She still had it in her apartment, packed away.

Last Christmas she'd run the ER and racked up a considerable amount of time in the OR. She'd been so happy.

Until she'd got the messages on her phone when she'd got home after a long shift at the hospital. Her mother begging her to come home, her mother wishing her a merry Christmas and telling her how much she missed her.

"Sorry for depressing you," Gavin said, breaking the silence as they finished their coffees. "Must be the fog."

"Must be."

"So, you said you were going to teach me how to dance?"

Virginia smiled. "I'm off tomorrow. I can stop by your place."

"The girls would be happy to see you."

"And I them."

Gavin grinned. "Good, it's a date, then."

"You weren't kidding. You seriously suck at dancing." Virginia winced as Gavin stepped on her toe again. Good thing they weren't wearing shoes. Even with the heels she had picked out for her dress, Gavin would still tower over her, which made her feel dainty. She was five ten and hardly ever met a man who towered over her.

"I'm good at head-banging if you put on some heavy metal." He moved away from her and selected a rock song from his music player, one that you couldn't dance to. At least, that's what she thought.

Virginia crossed her arms. "How am I supposed to teach you to dance to that?"

Gavin grinned and took a step towards her. "Maybe we should practice with a slow song?"

A lump formed in her throat, her mouth going dry, and he was just inches from her. She was suddenly very nervous about his arms around her, about being so close to him. They'd kissed, that memory was burned into her brain, but they were alone in the house, not out on the Embarcadero in public view.

His hands slipped around her waist, resting at the small of her back with a gentle touch, and he took her right hand in his left.

"I think this is correct?"

"Well, in proper ballroom dancing your right hand should be just below my shoulder blade."

"I like it where it is."

"You want to learn this properly, don't you?"

"My apologies, Ginger."

Virginia rolled her eyes and he slid his hand up her back. "Thank you."

"Where did you learn the proper stance for ballroom dancing?"

Virginia winked. "Google."

Gavin laughed and she began to lead him in a slow dance, but soon she wasn't leading and it was Gavin waltzing them around the room.

"I thought you said you didn't know how to dance?" she accused him.

"I have hidden depths, Dr. Potter." He grinned. "I don't know how to fast-dance, but I do know some of the basic slow-dance moves."

"And where did you learn these basic moves?"

"Junior high."

"Junior high, huh? So who was the girl?"

"You know me so well." Gavin winked. "Her name was Kirsten and I wanted to take her to the semi-formal and impress her with my mad skills. So I signed up for dance class, which was taught after school by the aging and venerable Ms. Ward, who smelled keenly like beef vegetable soup and heat rub."

Virginia laughed out loud. "And did Kirsten appreciate your efforts?"

Gavin sighed. "No, she decided to go to the semi-formal with Billy Sinclair."

"The hussy!"

Gavin laughed and then dipped her, bringing her back up slowly until their faces were just inches apart. Virginia's pulse thundered in her ears, being so close to his lips, so close but so far away.

"You're a fine dancer, Dr. Potter. A better teacher than Ms. Ward was, and you smell better too."

"I hope I don't smell like soup." She grinned and gazed up into his eyes, and her heart stuttered just briefly, being pressed so tight against him.

This was a dangerous position to be in.

"You smell a million times better." He touched her face, brushing his knuckles against her cheek and causing a shudder of anticipation to course through her.

Virginia braced herself for a kiss, one she wanted, one that she hadn't stopped thinking about for a long time, but he moved away when the front door opened. This was soon followed by loud shrieking and what sounded like a herd of wild elephants storming up the stairs.

They broke apart as Lily and Rose burst into the living room.

"Dr. Potter," Lily said with enthusiasm that matched the bright smile on her face.

Rose just waved but still didn't say anything.

Rosalie came up next. "Sorry, Dr. Brice. I didn't know you had company."

"No, it's okay, Rosalie. I should be going."

"Aww." Lily pouted. "Can't you stay for dinner tonight, Dr. Potter?"

Virginia glanced at Gavin and he shrugged his shoulders. "It's just hot dogs and hamburgers on the barbecue."

"Please stay, Dr. Potter," Lily begged.

"All right," Virginia said, capitulating. It had been some time since she'd had a real home-cooked barbecue.

Lily shouted her pleasure and Rose jumped up and down excitedly.

"Come, girls, let's get washed up for dinner." Rosalie ushered Lily and Rose from the room.

"Is there something I can help with?" Virginia asked.

"There's a plate of hamburgers and a package of hotdogs in the fridge. If you grab them, I'll get the grill heated up."

"Sure." Virginia made her way to the back of the house where the kitchen was. She opened the fridge and pulled out the hamburgers and hotdogs. As she bumped the fridge door shut with her hip a piece of paper fluttered down to the floor.

She cursed under her breath and set down the meat on the kitchen table so she could pick up the piece of paper.

Virginia glanced at it and did a double take when she saw it was a petition for custody. The girls' paternal grandparents, who were stationed in Japan, were suing Gavin for full custody of the girls. Or had. Virginia's stomach sank when she saw the judgment was attached and was momentarily relieved when she saw they'd been denied, but only on the grounds that Gavin had a good steady job in the girls' hometown and uprooting them would be cruel.

If that changed, according to the judgment, Gavin would lose custody of Lily and Rose. Virginia folded the paper up again, feeling guilty for prying. If Gavin had wanted to tell her this, he would've.

She placed it back on the top of the fridge and sank down in a nearby chair. His job was what kept the girls in his custody. If he lost it and had to uproot the girls, their grandparents would get them.

And his job depended on her, the benefit and her ability to keep Bayview Grace from turning into a private clinic. She couldn't bear it if she was responsible for Gavin losing the girls.

"Hey, the barbecue is ready," Gavin called through the open kitchen window. "Bring me those dogs, chief."

"I'll be right there." Virginia took a deep, calming breath and headed outside.

Lily and Rose were kicking a ball back and forth while Rosalie sat in a lawn chair with a glass of iced tea.

She handed Gavin the plate.

"Are you okay, Virginia?" he asked.

"What? Yes, I'm fine."

"You seem like you're in a bit of a daze."

"I'm okay. Really." She wandered over to the table and poured herself a glass of iced tea. The sun was setting, making the whole scene in the backyard glow with warmth. Virginia smiled. Everyone was so happy and she couldn't understand why the girls' grandparents would want to destroy this.

She would do everything in her power to convince the board not to close the ER. *It wouldn't be my fault.*

Only it would. She was Chief of Surgery.

There was no way she was going to be responsible for tearing apart this family. A family she desperately wished she was a part of.

CHAPTER FIFTEEN

VIRGINIA WAS STARING off into space again when her inbox pinged with a new email. She wasn't going to bother with it, except she saw it was from Boston General. An old colleague from her intern years was working there.

Out of curiosity she opened it and her breath caught in her throat when she realized it was a job offer.

It was for the head of their level-one trauma center. It wasn't Chief of Surgery, but the salary was good and there would be an extensive amount of research money at her disposal. Her friend had recommended her for the job. Boston General wanted her. They were impressed by how she'd managed to salvage Bayview Grace and it was a tempting, tempting offer.

And then guilt assuaged her. Her career path was secure, but Gavin's and those of the rest of the ER staff were not.

"You're still here?" Janice asked, barging into Virginia's office.

"Of course. Why wouldn't I be?"

Janice raised her eyebrows. "Have you seen the time?"

Virginia glanced at her phone and realized it was a quarter to three. "Darn." She was running late for her hair appointment. The benefit was tonight, the very benefit that was going to make or break this hospital.

"Thanks for the reminder, Janice." Virginia grabbed her purse.

"So, you still haven't told me what piece of hot man flesh you managed to wrangle up to take you to the benefit."

Virginia rolled her eyes. "Sometimes I think you take too many hormones."

Janice snorted. "Cheap shot, Ice Queen. Now, come on and spill the beans."

Virginia tried to suppress her smile. "Dr. Brice is accompanying me to the benefit."

"As in Dr. Gavin Brice?" Janice's mouth dropped open like a fish gasping for air. "You're joking, right?"

"No, I'm not. Dr. Brice is my date for tonight. Why is that so hard to believe?"

"I guess because of how many times he's been hauled into the principal's office." Then she grinned. "Perhaps that's *why* he has been."

Virginia shook her head. "I'm going to be late."

"Please, tell me you're wearing something drop-dead sexy."

"What is up with you?" Virginia asked as she put on her coat.

"Just living vicariously. Now, tell me about the dress."

"You're the one who told me I was going to be late."

"I guess I'll have to wait to see it tonight." Then she grinned, one of those grins like the Cheshire cat in *Alice in Wonderland* would give.

Virginia shook her head. "I'm going to send you for a tox screen. I swear sometimes you're dipping into the sauce."

Janice laughed. "Hey, as I said, just living vicariously. I'm glad for you."

"Glad?"

"I like you and I want to see you happy." Janice shrugged. "Now, go on, get out of here and get all made up. Knock his socks off."

Virginia smiled and left. Janice may be all up in her business at the best of times, but the woman really was the closest thing she'd had to a friend since she'd become Chief of Surgery and the closest thing to an overbearing and overprotective mother since she'd moved out here.

The next shift of physicians was arriving. Physicians who were going to work the night shift while a lot of the department heads were at the benefit.

Virginia avoided making eye contact with anyone. She was tired of being stopped and asked questions about the future of Bayview Grace and whether this benefit would help.

As far as she was concerned, she didn't believe it would. She felt like she was delaying the inevitable, but the board was very keen on the idea and she knew it was for them. The rich investors who liked to have a good party. Having this benefit and raising money would make them feel good later when they dropped the axe on the trauma department of the hospital.

"*Que bueno,* Dr. Brice!"

"Yeah, you look handsome," Lily gushed. "And I bet she won't recognize you since you shaved off your scruffies."

Rosalie laughed and Rose grinned.

"Why are you laughing, Rosalie? Uncle Gavin's scruffies were weird and patchy. He looks good with a shaved face."

Gavin sighed and straightened the black bow tie. He felt like an overstuffed penguin in this tux, but when he'd tried it on, Virginia's face had flushed and he'd known she approved.

"I'm uncomfortable," he muttered.

"Of course you are, Dr. Brice, but just think how your *querida* will light up when she sees you."

"Dr. Potter is *not* my *querida.*" Though he wanted her to be.

Rosalie cocked an eyebrow in disbelief. "Sure. Lily, don't you have a present for your uncle?"

"Right!" Lily leapt down from the bed and ran out of the room. Gavin heard the fridge door open and Lily came running back with two clear boxes and handed him one. "It's your boutonniere."

"My what?"

Rosalie stepped forward and took the box from him, opening it and then pinning the spray on his lapel. "I did this for my son when he was going to prom."

"I'm not going to prom," Gavin said. "It's a benefit."

Rosalie tsked under her breath. "Let them have their fun. They were so excited to buy you one."

Gavin felt a bit goofy with the small white carnation and spray of baby's breath pinned to his lapel, but overall he felt uncomfortable. He was used to jeans and a T-shirt, not this penguin suit. He glanced at Rose, who was sitting cross-legged on the floor in front of the full-length mirror.

"How do I look, Rose?"

Rose grinned and gave him a thumbs-up, before scrambling to her feet and leaving the room.

"I'll take that as a compliment," Gavin murmured. "What's the other box for?"

"It's for Dr. Potter," Lily said, holding it out. "It's a wristlet."

Gavin ruffled Lily's head. "Thanks, I'll tell her it's from you."

"No, you can't do that, Uncle Gavin. You have to tell her it's from you." Lily handed him the box. "You look worried."

"I'm a little worried that you're getting so excited about this. It's a work thing really."

"Don't worry, Dr. Brice. The girls just aren't used to you getting all dressed up and going out." Rosalie straightened his tie. "You look good. Go and have some fun. Don't come home until after your shift tomorrow."

"Fun is not something I'm planning on having."

Rosalie shook her head. "Dr. Potter is a very attractive woman."

Gavin cleared his throat and patted his jacket. "Shoot, have you seen some cue cards? My speech is written on there."

"On your dresser," Rosalie said. "Now, come, Lily, let's leave your uncle in peace to finish up and we'll watch for the limo."

"Limo?" Gavin asked. "I didn't order a limo."

Rosalie grinned deviously. "I know, Dr. Brice. You were going to pick up the chief of surgery in the minivan. I think not."

"Rosalie, you're going to be the death of me."

Rosalie just laughed and shut the door to the bedroom. Gavin let out a nervous breath he hadn't realized he'd been holding and smoothed down his hair again. His usual cowlick of hair wasn't standing on end. It was actually tame tonight. It was weird that he'd shaven off his "scruffies," as Lily so eloquently put it, but he wanted to make a good impression.

And not on the board.

Everything he was doing was for Virginia.

"The limo is here, Uncle Gavin!" Lily shouted down the hall.

"Thanks." Gavin picked up the wristlet Lily had picked out for Virginia. It was a bright bubblegum hue of pink.

Always pink.

The limo had better not be pink.

He said his quick goodbyes to the girls and headed outside, breathing a sigh of relief when he saw the limo was black. It was sleek and sophisticated. Even though he planned to give Rosalie a stern talking to for hiring a limo, he decided that it had been a smart thing to do.

He gave the driver Virginia's address and climbed into the back.

It was a short drive to Virginia's Nob Hill apartment and he realized he'd never been to her place before.

Her apartment was in a modern-looking building halfway up the steep hill. He pushed her buzzer.

"Who is it?"

"It's me. Gavin."

"Come on up."

The door unlocked and Gavin entered the lobby. Her apartment was on the third floor, so he didn't bother waiting for the elevator. Instead he took the stairs, trying to calm his nerves.

Virginia's apartment was at the end of the hall. He took a deep breath and knocked.

Virginia opened the door and his breath was taken away at the sight of her. He'd known she was going to be dressed up, but he hadn't mentally prepared himself for what he was seeing. Her hair was swept up off her shoulders in a French twist at the back, but it wasn't the hairstyle that caught his attention. It was the creamy long neck that was exposed to him, thanks to the dress she was wearing.

The color was a deep royal blue, which set off her coloring perfectly. It was a one-shoulder dress, but it had lace across the shoulder and the bodice. There was beige fabric underneath to hide any nudity, but you couldn't tell was fabric there. The intricate lace flowers looked like they were painted on her skin.

There were a few sequins that made the dress sparkle in the light. The dress hugged her curves, clinging to her in all the right places, and there was a slit up the left side, almost to her thigh.

Her legs were long, lean and he had a mental image for a brief moment of them wrapped around his waist.

His breath was literally taken away and he knew he wouldn't be able to mumble any two words together coherently.

What he wanted to do was scoop her up and take her to the bedroom to show her just how much he liked her dress.

"How do I look?" she asked, and did a spin.

"Wow." It was all he managed to get out.

Virginia cocked an eyebrow. "Wow? That's it?"

"I—I don't know what else to say." *I could show you exactly what I think about you wearing that dress.* "You look stunning."

She blushed. "Thank you."

"The color is becoming."

Virginia gave him a strange look and then shut and locked her door. "So, should we take my car?"

"No, I have that taken care of."

Gavin held out his arm and she took it as they walked to the elevator.

"Well, I guess no one will see us arrive in the minivan."

Gavin snorted. "It's not the minivan."

"The motorcycle?" She frowned. "I don't want to ruin my hair."

He shook his head. "You'll see."

As they walked into the elevator she cocked her head to one side and then touched his face gently. "You shaved! I don't think I've ever seen you without…"

"Scruffies, as Lily calls them. Yes, she was quite impressed I'd shaved my scruffies off."

Virginia chuckled. "You do clean up nice, Gavin."

"As do you."

They rode the elevator down to the lobby and she gasped in surprise when she saw the limo. "Oh, Gavin. Wow."

"Now who's using wow?" he teased, and opened the door for her. As she climbed inside, Gavin caught another glimpse of her creamy-white leg and took another deep breath. He slid in beside her and shut the door.

"Can you take us to the Excelsior on Market, please?" Gavin asked.

"I will, sir, but I was told to take you on a small little drive first. There's some complimentary champagne in the bucket. We'll arrive at the Excelsior at six-thirty." The driver put up the privacy screen.

Gavin looked at Virginia apologetically. "Are we going to be late?"

She shook her head. "No, the happy hour is from six to seven and it's only five-thirty. Let's enjoy ourselves."

"Okay. Oh, but first I have something for you." He reached for the clear box. "I'm sorry, it's bright pink."

Virginia giggled. "The girls?"

"I'm not supposed to say. You don't have to wear it."

"No, I love it. Pink goes with blue." She held out her hand. "Besides, I didn't get to go to prom. This is fun."

Gavin opened the box and then slid the wristlet onto her, but before he let go of her hand he brought it up and pressed his lips against her knuckles.

"Gavin," she whispered. "You know…"

"I know." He knew her feelings on dating, but he couldn't help himself. He was falling in love with Virginia, in spite of everything. He'd never thought he'd feel this way about a woman, but he was falling head over heels for her.

"How about we have some of that champagne? It might take the edge off for your upcoming speech."

"Good idea." Gavin found the champagne and handed Virginia a flute. He popped the cork and poured them both a glass. "To a successful benefit tonight."

"Cheers."

He hated champagne, preferring beer, but he downed it as quickly as he could. He wanted the alcohol to numb him from the nervousness he felt about his upcoming speech, about the security of his job at Bayview Grace, and to keep him from pressing Virginia down against the leather seat and taking her, like he desperately wanted to.

Tonight was going to be a long night.

The limo driver took them up the long figure-eight length of Twin Peaks Boulevard. Gavin didn't really enjoy the twisting and turning. They were gripping the seat of the limo tightly, jostling back and forth from the drive up the Eureka North Peak.

"Whose idea was this?" Virginia asked.

"Most likely Lily's. She said Casey used to speed up this hill and it was like being on a roller coaster."

Virginia chuckled. "I can see why."

One sharp turn caused her to slide across the seat and fall against his chest, her hand landing right between his legs.

"Gavin, I'm so sorry." She moved. "I wasn't expecting such a sharp turn."

"Don't apologize. I understand." What he wanted to tell her was he didn't mind in the slightest. It was nice having her so close, even if her hand had landed dangerously close to possibly injuring him.

The limo driver took them to Christmas Tree Point, which had the best vantage point over the entire city and the bay. The driver got out and opened the doors. Gavin grabbed the champagne glasses as Virginia wandered over to the railing. The wind, surprisingly, was not strong and there was no fog rolling from the Pacific to obstruct the view.

There was a breeze and it whipped at Virginia's dress, making it swirl and ripple like deep blue waves. A smile was on her face and she sighed as he handed her a full glass of champagne.

"Whatever happens tonight with the benefit, you should be proud. It's quite a feat for a prairie girl."

She grinned and took a sip of her champagne. "Lily's idea was good. You'll have to mention it to her."

Gavin chuckled and moved closer. "I will."

"I love this view." She sighed again. "So different from vast prairie."

"I've been through South Dakota, there are some rolling hills."

"The Wessington Hills. Yes, to the west, but where I come from it's just prairie. Don't get me wrong, I love it but I think I love this more."

Gavin leaned on the railing. "It is quite beautiful. I can see why my sister chose to settle here."

"Have you ever been up here before?" Virginia asked.

"No, this is my first time." He straightened and took her empty glass from her, setting it down on a bench so he could cup her face. "I'm glad I could share it with you."

"Me too," she whispered. Her cheeks were rosy and he wasn't sure if it was the nip in the air, the champagne or whether she was feeling something for him.

Gavin hoped it was the latter.

He tipped her chin so she was forced to look at him. Her

eyes were sparkling in the fading sunlight. The sun was going down behind her, giving her the appearance that she was glowing.

"Gavin…"

"I know what you're going to say."

"You do?"

He nodded. "I do, but I'm going to do it anyway."

Before she could interrupt him again he kissed her, gently. Though it took all his strength to hold back the passion he was feeling for her right now. There was something so right and perfect about this kiss and he hoped it wasn't going to end up as badly as the first one had.

Virginia moved in closer, her hand touching his cheek and then sliding around to the nape of his neck, her fingers tangling in his hair. It made his blood heat.

He wanted her. Right here. Right now.

Virginia broke off the kiss and leaned her forehead against his. "I think—I think it would be wise if we head back downtown."

Gavin nodded and fought the desire coursing through him. "You're probably right."

She grinned, her eyes still twinkling. "I know I'm right. You're a dangerous man, Gavin." Then she blushed again and moved past him towards the limo. The driver, who'd discreetly returned to the driver's seat while they'd been making out, jumped out and opened the door for Virginia.

Gavin watched her climb back into the limo, catching just a glimpse of her bare leg through the slit in her dress.

What does she mean by saying I'm a dangerous man?

A grin broke across his face as he thought about the possibilities, but the one that excited him most was that he affected her just as much as she affected him.

He wanted her. More than that, he was almost sure that he was falling in love with her. Maybe he wasn't the only dangerous individual here tonight.

Virginia was just as dangerous as he was.

CHAPTER SIXTEEN

VIRGINIA COULDN'T TAKE her eyes off Gavin. When she walked in on his arm, she saw the looks of envy and admiration from the other women in the room. Gavin cleaned up nicely. She liked him all rough and rugged, but she liked him this way too, in a tuxedo, looking svelte.

When Virginia caught Janice's eye from across the room, Janice winked and gave her a thumbs-up, which made Virginia blush, but Janice was right. Gavin was a fine specimen and it was taking all her strength not to jump into his arms like some kind of teenage girl.

And that kiss up on Christmas Tree Point was burned into her lips. And into her mind. And it was all she could do to keep her wits about her. All she wanted to do was drag Gavin out of the room and have her way with him.

Which shocked her.

Get a hold of yourself.

Instead, she made sure they were mingling, that they weren't alone together, and she was pleasantly surprised at how charming and affable he was to the board members and investors. Even Mrs. Greenly, who'd nearly been trampled by Gavin on a gurney just a couple of months ago, was conversing with him and then checking him out when he wasn't looking.

Though she couldn't blame Mrs. Greenly one bit.

Gavin looked so fine.

He was up on the stage now, talking to the board about his

work and how important trauma medicine was to Bayview Grace, but Virginia couldn't make out a word. All she heard were muffled sounds like Charlie Brown's teachers would make on the old cartoon specials.

It has to be the champagne.

The stuff they'd had in the limo was top-end champagne and she'd had a couple of glasses. Well, more than a couple. She'd had four and she was feeling happy at the moment. Not drunk, just relaxed. She hadn't planned on drinking so much before the benefit, but being trapped in that limo with Gavin as they'd gone on a little scenic drive up the twin peaks had been more than Virginia could handle.

The whole time she'd just wished that the driver would make himself scarce so they could make out in the backseat. Like teenagers.

She'd fallen in love with Gavin. She didn't know when or how, she just realized it now, but she really didn't have any chance with him because every time he'd tried with her, she'd shot him down.

The sensible side of her, the chief of surgery side, had turned him down flat.

As long as they worked at Bayview Grace and she was chief, there was no way they could date.

Unless she took that job, but that new job was across the country and Gavin had already stated he wasn't going to up-root the girls and she didn't blame him one bit.

There was applause and Virginia realized the speech had come to an end. She clapped in enthusiasm and moved up on the stage to give her little spiel and thank the people who had spoken this evening.

Gavin passed her on the stairs and flashed her an encouraging smile, one that made her knees knock together and her blood heat.

She only hoped no one would see her blush up on stage.

"Thank you, Dr. Brice, for your impassioned speech about trauma care at Bayview Grace. I want to thank all my esteemed colleagues for taking time out of your hectic schedules and speaking here tonight about our hospital. I also want to thank the board of directors and their guests. Bayview Grace runs on the generosity of caring individuals such as yourselves. Our hospital has come a long way in the two short years I've been Chief of Surgery and I know with your continued support we can go much further. The dance floor is being cleared and our band is ready. Please, enjoy your evening here and thank you all again." Virginia smiled and acknowledged the applause as she left the stage.

"You're very good at PR, Dr. Potter," Gavin teased as she took a seat beside him.

"It's all part of the job." They were alone at the table, as everyone was getting up to mix and mingle as the band warmed up.

"Do you enjoy it, though, or would you prefer to be in surgery?"

"That's not a fair question, Gavin."

He cocked an eyebrow. "Why not?"

"I like being Chief of Surgery," she stated, and only because no one else was sitting at their table at that moment. "I would like it even more if I had more OR time. Are you happy?"

Gavin grinned. "Very."

"I find that hard to believe."

"Why?" he asked.

"Because you're not off trekking around the world. You made it very clear to me several times you'd rather be anywhere but here."

Gavin hung his head in defeat. "That was before."

"Before what?"

Gavin opened his mouth to say something else but Mr. Schultz approached the table. "Excellent speech, Dr. Brice. I didn't think you had it in you."

Gavin plastered a fake smile across his face. "Neither did I, Mr. Schultz. If you'll excuse me for a moment, I think I'll check on the girls."

Virginia watched Gavin leave the room and wished she could go with him, but Mr. Schultz took his empty seat.

"You did a fine job, Dr. Potter."

"Thank you."

Mr. Schultz sighed. "I hope you'll be able to do the same when we transform Bayview Grace into a private hospital."

Virginia's stomach knotted. "You can't have made the decision already—we haven't even tallied any of the donations and the silent auction isn't even finished."

Mr. Schultz shrugged and downed the glass of Scotch he had in his hand. "The board wants what it wants."

"I think you'll be pleasantly surprised by what we achieve tonight, Mr. Schultz."

He gave her a petulant smile. "We'll see, Dr. Potter. We'll see."

Virginia shot him figurative daggers as he got up and left to schmooze with some rich potential investors.

She was annoyed.

Mr. Schultz didn't care how much money they brought in. In his eyes, the ER was deadweight and he wanted it gone.

A private hospital specializing in plastics and sports medicine would bring in so much more money and all Mr. Schultz saw was the dollar signs. He didn't care about the poor people on the street who came into the ER every day.

Those without insurance or funds to pay for the medical help they needed. Like Shyanne.

What am I doing?

Having a good job and security was one thing, but not living by your principles was another. If the ER closed, she would quit. There was nothing else for it. There was no way she could work at a private hospital, treating only the privileged few. That's not why she'd become a doctor and she couldn't help but wonder when her course in life had left that path.

"Are you all right? You look a little pale." Gavin sat down and then poured her a glass of water from the carafe. "Here, have a drink."

"Thanks. It's a bit hot in here." She took a sip of the water, but the lump in her throat made it hard to swallow.

The band started up by playing an old rock ballad from the eighties. One she'd always liked as a child.

"Come on." Gavin took her hand and pulled her to her feet. "Let's dance. You look tense."

Virginia didn't argue as he pulled her out onto the dance floor. Only he didn't hold her in the proper stance she'd lectured him about only a couple of nights ago. His hand rested in the small of her back and this time she didn't argue. She liked the feeling of his strong hand there, guiding her across the dance floor.

"What's wrong?" he asked.

"I told you, it's the crush of people. I'm not good with large crowds."

"You live in the city," he teased.

"I grew up on the prairies." She laughed. "It's so silly."

Gavin shook his head. "No, it's not."

"And you're used to a mad crush."

"I traveled across India by train, remember? This is nothing compared to that."

Virginia shuddered. "I wouldn't like that."

"I wouldn't let you do that. Not dressed the way you are." He leaned in close, his hot breath fanning her neck. "You look good enough to devour."

Her pulse quickened. "Devour?"

"Yes, it's what I've been fighting all evening."

"The urge to d-devour me?" Her voice caught in her throat. Even though she shouldn't press it further, she wanted to. Badly. "Tell me how."

Gavin moaned and held her tighter, her body flush against his. She could feel every hard contour of his chest through their clothes and she wondered what it would be like to feel nothing between them. What it would be like if they were skin to skin, joined as one? The thought made her knees tremble and her stomach swirl with anticipation.

"I would take out the pins in your hair so I could run my fingers through it." The words were whispered close to her ear, making her skin break out in gooseflesh. "Then I would kiss you. I want to taste your lips again."

Virginia closed her eyes and recalled the way his lips had felt pressed against hers. She wanted him. What did she have to lose?

"Go on," she urged.

"Virginia, I don't think I can. Not in decent company." He pulled her tighter and she felt the evidence of his arousal pressed against her hip.

"Come on." Virginia moved away and pulled him off the dance floor.

"Where are we going?"

"I was offered a gratis suite for booking the function at the hotel." She pulled out the key card the hotel had given her this morning when she'd finalized details. Virginia swiped it in the elevator and then glanced nervously at Gavin.

"Are you sure?" he asked.

Virginia kissed him then, showing him exactly how sure she was. She was tired of being alone and for once she wanted to live a little. Take a chance, and Gavin was worth the risk.

The elevator doors opened, but they didn't break their kiss. She just dragged him in, letting her fingers tangle in the hair at the nape of his neck. His tongue pushed past her lips, twining with hers.

The elevator doors opened with a ding and they broke off their kiss. Virginia was glad no one was waiting on the other side, but even that wouldn't have stopped her from her present course.

"Which way?" Gavin asked, his voice husky and deep, rumbling from his chest.

Virginia took his hand and led him down the hall to the suite. She swiped the keycard and opened the door, but before she could cross the threshold Gavin scooped her up in his arms, claiming her mouth again. He kicked the door shut with his heel.

The room was dark, except for the thin beam of city lights through the blackout curtains. Gavin set her down on the floor, her knees back against the edge of the bed. It made her feel nervous, but exhilarated her all the same. It felt like the first time all over again.

If only it was. Her first time hadn't been all that memorable and the guy hadn't made her feel the way Gavin was making her feel right now.

She wanted Gavin.

All of him.

She wanted him to possess her. For once she didn't want to be the boss and she was giving it all to him.

Gavin reached up and undid her hair from the twist, letting it fall against her shoulders. He ran his fingers through it.

"I've been longing to do this since you opened the door to your apartment and I saw you in that dress."

He kissed her again, just a light one, then he buried his face against her neck. His hot breath fanned against her skin, making goose pimples break out. A tingle raced down her spine and she let out a little sigh.

Air hit her back and she realized he was undoing the zipper in the back of her dress. She shivered, from nerves and anticipation.

His lips captured hers in a kiss, his tongue twining with hers. Gavin's fingers brushed against her bare back before he trailed them up to slip the one shoulder off. Her dress pooled on the floor. All she was wearing now was her bustier, lace panties and heels.

It was so risqué.

It thrilled her. Virginia's heart was racing.

"God, you're beautiful. More beautiful than I imagined."

Virginia kicked her heels off and sat down on the bed. "Come here." And she reached out and pulled him down.

"You'll wrinkle my suit."

"I do hope so." She undid his bow tie and tossed it away. Then helped him take off his tuxedo jacket.

"No throwing that." He stood up, laying the jacket neatly on a chair, and began to undress for her. Her body was awash with flames of desire. She leaned back to watch as he peeled away the layers.

His chest was well-defined and bare. Then he toed off his shoes and socks before he undid his trousers, stepping out of them and hanging them over the chair as well. He was wearing tight boxer briefs and Virginia could see the evidence of his arousal.

Gavin approached the bed and Virginia pulled him until she was kneeling in front of him. His eyes sparkled in the dim room. "I wanted you the moment I saw you, Virginia."

"Even with all my nagging?"

Gavin moaned and then stole a kiss, his fingers tangling in her hair, pulling her closer. "Especially with the nagging."

"Me too," she whispered. Reaching for him, she dragged him into another kiss. His hands slipped down her back, the heat of his skin searing her flesh and making her body ache with desire. Gavin made quick work of her bustier.

Knowing that she was so exposed to Gavin sent a zing of desire through her. He cupped her breasts, kneading them. Virginia let out a throaty moan at the feel of his caresses against her sensitized skin.

Even though he was a surgeon, his hands were surprisingly calloused. Probably from all his years in Border Free Physicians.

Virginia ran her hands over his smooth, bare chest, before letting her fingers trail down to the waist of his boxers. He grabbed her wrists and held her there, before roughly pushing her down on the bed, pinning her as he leaned over her. He released her hands and pressed his body against hers, kissing her fervently.

"Virginia, you drive me wild."

She kissed him again, letting his tongue plunder her mouth. Her body was so ready for him.

Each time his fingers skimmed her flesh, her body ignited, and when his thumbs slid under the sides of her panties to tug them down, she went up in flames.

He pressed his lips against her breast, laving her nipple with his hot tongue. She arched her back, wanting more.

"You want me?" he asked huskily.

Make me burn, Gavin.

His hand moved down her body, between her legs. He began to stroke her, making her wet with need.

"I want to taste you. Everywhere."

Virginia didn't even have a chance to reply. His lips began to trail down over her body, across her stomach and down to the juncture of her thighs. When he began to kiss her there, she nearly lost it.

Instinctively, she began to grind her hips upward; her fingers slipping into his hair and holding him in place. She didn't want him to stop. Warmth spread through her body like a wildfire across the prairie.

She was so close to the edge, but she didn't want to topple over. She wanted him deep inside her.

"Hold on, darling."

Virginia moaned when he moved away. He pulled a condom out of his trouser pocket and put it on. She was relieved. Being with him had made her so addle-brained she'd completely forgotten it.

"I see you've planned for all contingencies," she teased.

"Honestly, I just remembered it was in there. Thank goodness, it is. It's a force of habit from my wilder days."

"I'm glad that's a habit you haven't broken."

"Damn straight. Now, where were we?"

He pressed Virginia against the pillows and settled between her thighs. Gavin shifted position and the tip of his shaft pressed against her folds. She wanted him to take her, to be his.

Even though she couldn't be.

He thrust quickly, filling her completely. She clutched his shoulders as he held still, stretching her. He was buried so deep inside her.

"I'm sorry, Virginia," he moaned, his eyes closed. "You feel so good." He surged forward and she met every one of his sure thrusts.

"So tight," he murmured again.

Gavin moved harder, faster. A coil of heat unfurled deep within her. Virginia arched her back as pleasure overtook her, her muscles tightening around him as she came. Gavin's thrusts became shallow and soon he joined her in a climax of his own.

He slipped out of her, falling beside her on the bed and collecting her up against him. She laid her hand on his chest, listening to his breathing.

"That was wonderful," she whispered.

"It was."

As Virginia lay beside Gavin in silence, the only sounds the city of San Francisco and his breathing, she couldn't help but wonder what she'd done. She'd made a foolish mistake. She'd slept with a fellow employee. Something on her no-no list, but right here, right now she didn't regret it.

This was where she wanted to be and for the first time in a long time she didn't care what happened to her job, and that thought terrified her.

CHAPTER SEVENTEEN

INCESSANT BUZZING WOKE him from his slumber. When Gavin opened his eyes a crack, the light from the rising sun filtered in through a gap between the hotel room's curtains, blinding him, and he winced. The buzzing continued and he reached over for his phone. He glanced at the clock. It was only five in the morning. It took him a few moments to focus enough to read the words.

"Large incoming trauma. Please report to hospital stat."

Damn.

He sent off a quick text to Rosalie about being called in for a trauma, but Rosalie wouldn't mind. She'd take the girls for the whole weekend, she'd said so last night.

It was as if Rosalie had known what was going to happen. He usually hated it when she was right, because she loved to lord it over him, but in this instance he didn't mind.

Not in the least.

Gavin placed his phone back on the nightstand and let out a groan. He rolled over and looked at Virginia, sleeping with her dark hair fanned out over the thick pillow. She looked so peaceful nestled amongst the feather pillows and the feather top. A tendril of her brown hair curled around her nipple and he groaned inwardly as he ran his knuckles gently over her arm.

He remembered every nuance of her. It would be burned on his brain forever. Virginia had been so responsive in his arms.

So hot.

Being buried inside her had been like heaven. He hadn't realized how much he'd wanted her until he'd been joined with her.

When everything else had been pulled away and it had only been them.

Vulnerable. Naked.

Exposed.

Just thinking about her made his passion ignite again. He was so hard and ready for her. Gavin groaned and moved away.

As much as he wanted to spend the morning in bed with her, he couldn't.

A trauma was coming in. All part and parcel of being head of Trauma and he didn't want to give Mr. Schultz any more reason to close the ER.

He'd do anything to help Virginia and make her job easier.

He leaned over and pressed a light kiss against her forehead. Virginia stirred and opened her eyes, but just barely. There was a pink flush to her cheeks. She looked very warm and cozy.

"What time is it?" she mumbled.

"It's five. I have to go to the hospital." He kissed her bare shoulder, groaning inwardly again, not wanting to leave.

She sat up quickly. "What's wrong?"

"A trauma is coming in and they need all hands on deck." Gavin cupped her face and kissed her again. "I'm sure if they need the chief of surgery, they'll page you. For now, why don't you just lie back and rest?"

Virginia snorted. "As if. If there's a trauma coming in, I'll be there."

Gavin watched as she scrambled out of bed, the sheet wrapped around her. "You know, you don't have to be so coy with me in the morning. Not after last night."

Virginia's cheeks flushed pink. "It was dark last night."

"You're a prude." He winked.

"Not at all." Then, as if to prove her point, she dropped the sheet, showing off every inch of her naked body to him.

Gavin's sex stirred and he groaned. "You're killing me."

"You're the one who called me a prude." She slipped on her lace panties and then pulled on her dress. "Are you going to just lie there with a trauma coming in?"

"Turn around."

"Now who's the prude?" she asked, teasing him.

"Fine." He stood up and her eyes widened at the sight of him, naked and aroused. Her blush deepened and she turned away.

"A little warning would've been nice."

"I warned you." He waggled his eyebrows when she glanced back at him.

"Get dressed and I'll meet you downstairs." She grinned at him as she collected her purse and left the room.

Gavin quickly pulled on the necessary components of his tux and carried the rest. Virginia was downstairs and was just finishing with the check-out.

A cab was hailed by the doorman and they slid in the back together. The atmosphere became tense and Gavin couldn't figure out why, but Virginia was barely glancing at him and she was sitting ramrod straight almost right against the opposite door.

"Are you okay?"

"Fine," she said, but there was a nervous edge to her voice.

"What changed between the hotel room and here?"

"The taxi driver." Virginia winked and then she lowered her voice. "Last night was wonderful, Gavin, but right now there's a huge trauma coming in and we need all our wits about us."

"I think coffee is in order. I didn't get much sleep last night."

The cab driver smirked in the front seat and Virginia shot him a warning look.

"This is me being a prude again. Seriously, we can't have people gossiping."

He was tempted to say, "Who the heck cares?", but he didn't. He knew Virginia as the chief of surgery had a professional image to keep up.

"Okay, you have my word. I'll be good…for now." And then he snatched her hand and kissed it.

Virginia smiled and touched his face. "Your scruffies are back."

Gavin laughed. "Well, I didn't have time to shave."

When the cab driver pulled up to the emergency room doors at Bayview Grace there were already four ambulances pulled up out front.

"Go," Virginia said. "I'll take care of this. I have to swing around to the front to change. You'd better change into scrubs too. That's a rental."

Gavin nodded and jumped out of the cab. He ran into the emergency room and headed straight for the locker rooms. He peeled off his tux, jammed it into his locker and pulled out a fresh set of scrubs and his running shoes.

Once he was suitably dressed he headed back out into the fray.

"What do we got, people?" he shouted over the din.

"Multi-vehicle accident on the freeway." Kimber, the charge nurse on duty, handed him a clipboard. "The less critical cases are being sent here as the nearest hospital is full up."

Gavin nodded. A gurney was coming in and he ran to catch up to the paramedics. "Status?"

"Jennifer Coi, age thirty, was a restrained driver in a multi-car pileup. Vitals are good, but she's complaining of tenderness over the abdomen and pain in her neck."

"Take her to pod one," Gavin ordered.

He glanced around the emergency room, which was humming with activity. This was nothing as traumatic as the other hospital was probably getting, but he couldn't see how the board could or would close this department down.

Bayview Grace's ER was needed in this end of the city. Only truly heartless, greedy people would shut it down. He shuddered because that was the impression he got from Edwin Schultz. Greedy. If that man had been a cartoon character, he'd have permanent dollar signs in his eyes.

Dollar signs Gavin wanted to smack off his face.

Lives mattered more than the almighty dollar. That was what he'd learned in the field. Only more dollars would've brought better medicine to a lot of those developing countries.

It was a vicious cycle.

Focus.

Gavin shook those thoughts from his head. There was no time to think about budgets and politics. Right now, Mrs. Coi was his priority.

Life over limb.

Mrs. Coi needed him to be alert and in the game.

This was why he'd become a doctor, to save lives.

This was all that mattered to him.

Before he ducked into pod one to deal with his patient he caught sight of Virginia coming from the direction of her office, in scrubs and with her hair hastily tied back, examining individuals on the beds in the main room. They hadn't paged her and she could've just stayed in bed, but she'd jumped into the fray without complaint.

It was just one more thing he loved about her.

Mrs. Coi's condition was a lot worse than original triage at the accident site had indicated. Her spleen had been on the verge of rupturing, so Gavin and Dr. Jefferson had wheeled her into emergency surgery.

Gavin had got to the woman just in the nick of time. He'd removed her spleen and was now closing up.

"How was the benefit last night?" Jefferson asked as they worked over Mrs. Coi. The question shocked him. He was not one for idle chitchat in the operating room.

"It went really well." He cleared his throat. "Why?"

"I heard your speech was something to hear, that's all," Jefferson said offhandedly.

"Clamp." He held out his hand and the scrub nurse handed it to him. "I don't know about that."

Jefferson's eyebrows rose. "I've heard nothing but great

things about your speech, Gavin. I only wish *I* could've been there to hear it personally."

Gavin just shot him a look of disbelief as he really couldn't frown his disapproval behind a surgical mask. He wasn't going to get into this with him.

"More suction, please, Dr. Jefferson."

Jefferson suctioned around the artery and Gavin began to close the layers.

"I did hear something very interesting last night, though." The way he'd said "something very interesting" made Gavin's hackles rise.

What had he heard? Had anyone seen him and Virginia going to the elevator or had someone seen them this morning, leaving in a cab together?

"Did you?" He was hoping his tone conveyed that he wasn't in the least bit interested in pursuing this topic of conversation.

"Yes, according to Janice, the ice queen is leaving Bayview Grace."

"What?" Gavin paused in mid-suturing. "Sorry. Dr. Potter is leaving Bayview Grace?"

Jefferson's eyes narrowed. "Dr. Brice, are you going to continue to close?"

He shook his head. "Yes, but continue what you heard. I'm all ears."

"Ice Queen was offered a job at some fancy Boston hospital. They're offering her a huge salary and lots of research grants. It's also a level-one trauma center."

Gavin's stomach dropped to the soles of his feet and his head began to swim. How many times had Virginia reiterated that her career was important to her? Her job was everything, and if a Boston hospital was offering her a heck of a lot more, why would she stay?

Maybe that's why she seduced me.

That thought angered him, but it made sense. She'd constantly rebuffed him, telling him they couldn't be in a relationship because she was essentially his boss, but last night she'd been the one to drag him upstairs to the room.

The one who'd kissed him. She'd been the one who'd wanted him last night. Oh, he'd wanted it too, but he hadn't been going to press her. He hadn't wanted to scare her off, especially after how she'd made it so clear that they couldn't be together in that way.

"Did she accept the job?"

"I don't know, but I heard Janice talking about it to another nurse last night. Janice was gushing to anyone who would listen about how proud she was of Dr. Potter and how she was going to miss her." Jefferson snorted. "Well, I'm not going to miss the ice queen. Good riddance, as far as I'm concerned."

Gavin gritted his teeth and took a deep calming breath, because he was suturing up the subcutaneous layer and because he didn't want Jefferson or any of the other staff to know this news affected him.

Only it did.

After what they'd shared last night, Gavin was positive something was going to come of it, but if she was going to move to Boston...

You don't know that. It's all hearsay.

"Would you finish closing for me, Dr. Jefferson?"

"Of course, Dr. Brice."

Jefferson took over the suturing and Gavin left the operating room. He tossed his gloves in the medical waste and jammed his scrub gown in the laundry basket. After he'd finished scrubbing out he headed straight for Virginia's office, hoping she'd be there.

What Jefferson was saying could be just idle prattle. The only one who could confirm it was Virginia. He hoped it was just a rumor.

He hoped she hadn't just slept with him because he was one last fling and that it was okay to have sex with him because she was going to leave Bayview Grace and San Francisco.

There was no way he could go to Boston. He wasn't going

to uproot his nieces on the off chance Virginia wanted more from him.

And he wasn't going to go through another custody battle with their grandparents. The only reason he'd won the last one had been because he planned to remain in San Francisco and give them the stability Casey had so desperately wanted for them.

Gavin wasn't going to risk all of that for idle gossip, or for someone who'd just used him. Who didn't really want him.

Janice wasn't at her desk, but he could see that Virginia was in her office, bent over her desk and working on files.

He didn't knock, he just barged in. She looked up at him, momentarily surprised, but then grinned. "Gavin, I heard you were in surgery for a ruptured spleen. How did it go?"

"It went fine," he snapped.

"Is something wrong?" Virginia frowned and set down her file.

"Are you taking that job in Boston or what?"

Virginia's mouth dropped open. "What're you talking about?"

Gavin shut her office door. "I heard you were offered a nice job in Boston. One with lots of nice research funding."

She frowned. "Where did you hear that?"

"Dr. Jefferson."

"And how did Dr. Jefferson find out?"

Gavin's stomach twisted. "So it's true. You've been offered a position."

"I'm not going to deny it, so yes. Yes, I have, and it's a very nice offer."

Gavin crossed his arms. "I see."

"A friend recommended me for an opening."

"So it's a good offer?"

"Yes," Virginia said. "It's tempting."

"Did you accept?"

Her mouth opened and she was about to answer but her office phone rang. "Dr. Potter speaking. Yes, Mr. Schultz. Of course, I'll be up momentarily."

"The board?"

"Yes, they want to meet with me." Virginia didn't look at him as she picked up her white lab coat and slipped it over her scrubs. "I have to go, Gavin. Can we talk about this later?"

"I think I have all the information I need."

Gavin left her office. She hadn't denied or confirmed anything, meaning that she probably was going to take the job and move across the country. He was angry at himself for letting her in when he'd known he shouldn't have. Virginia was career driven, but mostly he was angry that he'd allowed the girls to get to know her.

And that rested solely with him. It was his fault and the guilt of allowing that to happen was eating him up inside.

"First off, Dr. Potter, we'd like to thank you for organizing such a great benefit last night. Even though it was a huge success, the investors still feel like their money would be better put to use if we turned Bayview Grace into a private clinic." Mr. Schultz gave her a pat on the back and then returned to his seat at the end of the long table. "We're cutting the trauma department. We've decided to turn the emergency room into a plastic day-surgery suite."

"Plastic day surgery?" she said.

"Botox and skin-tag removal. Clinics like that prove to be the most lucrative." Mr. Schultz grinned and started going on and on about his plans for turning her emergency room into a spa.

Botox and skin tags? Virginia had to repeat the words in her mind again because she couldn't get a grip on the reality of it.

Was that what her emergency room was being reduced to? Two years of hard work, late nights and sacrifice to salvage a wreck of a hospital, to bring it up to national standards, and it was all being wiped clean. Excised like a blemish on the face of San Francisco.

Virginia's heart sank, but she was also angry. She didn't know why she bothered wasting her time and wasting the time of all those surgeons who had given such excellent speeches. It had been an exercise in futility. Just like she'd feared it would be. "I see, and what other departments will be cut?"

"Just the emergency department. It's the one that bleeds the most money. We have people just wandering in off the streets and there's no guarantee that billing could track them down and get them to pay."

"And what of the staff in the trauma department?"

Mr. Schultz tented his fingers, the sunlight filtering through the slatted blinds reflecting against his shiny bald head, making him look like one of those evil villains from an old cartoon or an old James Bond movie. "They'll be given a generous severance package as per their contracts. We really don't have the spots for them. We're planning to recruit some of the top plastic surgeons in the country. We are aware you're primarily a trauma surgeon but we'd like you to stay on as Chief of Surgery."

Virginia closed her eyes and all she could see was Shyanne's face in her casket. She couldn't afford the health care she'd needed and it had cost her her life. Then she thought of Gavin and the girls. What would become of them?

She couldn't work for a hospital like this, for a board of directors who only wanted to help people who had the money to pay. Growing up in a poor family—well, she'd been a victim of such exclusivity before and she wasn't going to work for an employer who believed in it.

It went against everything her father had taught her, but she knew for the first time she was going to have to quit without the promise of another job, because she wasn't going to take that job in Boston either.

She wanted to stay in San Francisco with Gavin. Maybe she'd open up her own urgent-care clinic somewhere down in the Mission district, where she could give help to those who needed it. It frightened her, but also gave her a thrill.

"I'm sorry, Mr. Schultz, but I'm going to have to decline."

"Pardon?" he said. "What do you mean, decline?"

"I mean I'm quitting. I'll give you my six weeks' notice, but after that I'm done. I can't work for a private hospital."

Mr. Schultz shrugged. "Very well, but before you go you have to tell the trauma department what the board's decision is. We want the ER closed by the end of this week."

Virginia's stomach twisted. She'd never had to fire so many people in her life, but she had little choice. The axe was dropping on Bayview Grace and there was nothing she could do about it. "Fine, I'll tell them tomorrow. They're still dealing with a large trauma that has come in."

Mr. Schultz wrinkled his nose. "Yes, I'm aware of that."

Virginia nodded and left the boardroom. Mr. Schultz didn't thank her for her years of service, or anything else for that matter, and she didn't care. She never had liked the head of the board.

Janice was at her desk when Virginia returned and she looked anxious.

"Well, what's the word, Dr. Potter?" she asked in a hushed undertone.

Virginia just shook her head.

Janice's face paled. "No."

"I'm afraid so."

"When?" Janice asked, her voice barely more than a whisper.

"By the end of this week. I have to tell the staff tomorrow."

"That's—that's crappy."

"Your words, my sentiments."

"I'm sorry, Dr. Potter. Truly I am. I wouldn't wish that job on my worst enemy."

"Thanks, Janice." Virginia scrubbed her hand over her face, feeling emotionally drained and exhausted. She let out a long sigh. "If anyone wants me, I'll be in my office. I need some time to think."

"Speaking of enemies, Dr. Brice is in there. He's been waiting since you went up to your meeting. He looks quite agitated."

Virginia groaned inwardly. "Thanks, Janice." She opened the door and Gavin spun around to face her. He'd been looking out her window, the one that overlooked the garden courtyard.

"What did the board say?"

"If I tell you, you can't say anything to your staff until I make my announcement to them tomorrow. I mean it, Gavin."

His brow furrowed. "You can't be serious. After everything that happened last night, they're going to axe the trauma department?"

Virginia scrubbed her hand over her face. "Yes."

Gavin cursed under his breath. "You're going to tell the rest of the staff tomorrow?"

"Yes, everyone is being let go in that department. The board wants to start fresh and they want the budget to hire top-of-the-line plastic surgeons to come to Bayview Grace."

Gavin snorted. "Plastic surgeons?"

"They're going to turn the ER into a plastic day-clinic/spa thing."

"Just what the city needs, more botox clinics. Of all the stupid, moronic… It's just plain dumb. What a bunch of heartless money-mongers."

Virginia sat down in her chair, suddenly completely exhausted. "Your words, my thoughts exactly. I'm sorry this had to happen to you, Gavin. Hopefully, you won't lose custody of the girls."

"What?" he snapped, his eyes narrowed and flashing with anger. "What did you say?"

Virginia cursed inwardly, knowing she'd overstepped her bounds by reading that document, but there was no going back now.

"The custody battle with the girls' grandparents. I saw the

judgment stipulated that you had to remain in employment here in San Francisco or you could lose custody of the girls."

"How do you know that?" Gavin demanded, his voice rising in anger.

"I read the judgment."

"How dared you read that? That was private."

Virginia stood up. "It fell off the fridge and I picked it up. If you wanted to keep it private you shouldn't have left it in your kitchen, where anyone could see it."

"It doesn't matter where it was, that was none of your business."

Virginia pinched the bridge of her nose. "Why are you making such a big deal about it?"

"Because it was private. You're not part of my family or the girls'. You had no right to go prying."

"I'm sorry."

Gavin snorted. "Sorry doesn't cut it."

"I thought we meant something more to each other."

"Yeah, well, that was before your job offer in Boston and you prying into things you had no business to." Gavin strode across the room and opened the door. "I won't say a word to the staff, but I hope you enjoy the east coast, Dr. Potter."

"I'm not taking the job, Gavin. I want to stay in San Francisco."

"You should take that job in Boston. There's nothing left here for you." And with those parting words he slammed the door to her office and to her heart.

Virginia didn't sleep well. When she dragged herself into the hospital she saw that the notice was already taped to the ER's doors. Last night when they'd had a slow period she'd called Ambulance Dispatch and told them that Bayview Grace was closing its emergency room. Then she'd asked Security to lock all the doors and tape the notices up.

The nurses and doctors on duty had been dumbfounded.

When all the patients had left, she'd told them she'd speak to them in the morning when the morning shift came in.

She hadn't even gone home that night. Instead she spent the night on the couch in her office, but sleep hadn't come to her. Her mind had just kept racing. Two thoughts plagued her. The layoff speech and Gavin's dismissal of her.

"You should take that job in Boston. There is nothing for you here."

It had stunned her and broken her heart.

Why did I read that judgment?

She kept chastising herself over and over again. In the early hours of the morning she'd finally realized she had been in the wrong for reading the custody judgment, but Gavin had totally overreacted. He'd won the judgment. There was nothing to be ashamed about.

Closing her out and ending what they'd had was immature. Especially without giving her the benefit of an explanation.

She deserved to have her explanation heard after all they'd had.

What had they had?

That was the crux. There had been no firm commitment in their relationship. All they'd had was one night of wanton abandon and the odd pleasant discourse.

No. Not just the odd conversation. Virginia had thought at the very least they were friends. She didn't have many girl-friends, but from what she understood, friends gave friends the benefit of the doubt.

Virginia shook her head in the bathroom mirror and then finished brushing her teeth. She'd thought Gavin had at least been her friend, but apparently she'd been wrong.

It was just better for her when she had no connections. When it was just her and the pathetic cactus in her apartment.

Relationships were messy and needy. Virginia didn't have time for all this stuff.

Only she'd never felt more alive or happy as she had these

past few weeks that she'd been with Gavin, and now it was all gone.

Janice knocked on the door and opened it. "Dr. Potter?"

Virginia rinsed her toothbrush and walked out of her office bathroom. "Yes, Janice."

"The trauma department staff are waiting for you in boardroom three." Janice gave her a weak smile and turned to leave, but then stopped and walked toward her.

"Is there something you need, Janice?" Virginia asked, confused by Janice's demure manner.

"I just wanted to tell you that I'm going to miss you, Dr. Potter. I've enjoyed working with you."

Virginia was confused. She hadn't told Janice about her decision to leave. She had been planning to tell her after she dealt with closing down the ER. She didn't want the trauma staff to think she was playing the martyr for them.

"Where did you hear that I was leaving?"

"Mr. Schultz asked me to post an advertisement for your position amongst the other senior attendings who are staying."

Virginia pinched the bridge of her nose. "I was going to tell you."

Janice nodded. "I know, and I understand why you were keeping it a secret, but now the staff know."

Virginia sighed and then two arms wrapped around her. It was Janice hugging her. Just that simple act of human contact caused Virginia to break down in tears. She'd never mourned her sister properly. She'd never had time, but even that was coming out of her.

It was like a dam had exploded and everything she was feeling, that she'd pent up inside for too long, came gushing out of her, washing her clean.

Janice just held her, patting her back and whispering soothing words to her. How everything was going to be okay and that she understood Virginia had to do it.

When the sobbing finally ceased, Janice let go of her firm grip on Virginia and smoothed back her hair.

"I know it's not my place, you being my boss and all, but I do think of you as a daughter, Virginia."

It was the first time Janice had really used her name. Virginia returned the wobbly smile. "Thanks, Janice."

"No, I mean it. I remember when you came in for your interview as a resident. You were so aloof and like a robot. That's where you earned the nickname Ice Queen. You displayed no emotions, no empathy, but these last couple of months…" Janice shook her head and smiled. "You're not an ice queen any more. You don't deserve that name. The Dr. Virginia Potter who first started here wouldn't be as compassionate about what she has to do now. I like you so much better this way and I'm really going to miss this woman."

"Janice, I don't think I can do this. I fought so hard to bring that department up to level-one standards and now I'm pulling the plug on it. The board signed a DNR and I'm unhooking it from life support."

Janice's brow furrowed. "That's the corniest thing you've ever said to me."

Virginia laughed and brushed away a few errant tears with the back of her hand. "Sorry, my brain is a little fried."

"I noticed, but something else is going on."

"I slept with Gavin."

Janice's eyes widened and then she nodded. "I thought so. The way he looks at you and the way you look at him. Look, I don't think he'll be angry at you, he'll understand why you have to lay him off. He's a bit of an ass and clueless when it comes to social interactions with the staff, but I don't think he's cold-hearted."

Tears stung Virginia's eyes again. "It's over; it was over before it really got started."

"I don't understand."

"Gavin overreacted to something I did and basically rejected me."

Janice cocked an eyebrow. "What did you do?"

"I can't say what it was. It was nothing bad. I just read something private that I shouldn't have. It fell off the fridge at his place and I picked it up and read it. He was livid."

Janice snorted. "Then he shouldn't have left it on the fridge. What is wrong with men? The next time I see him I'm going to give him a piece of my mind."

"No, don't do that," Virginia said. "Then he'll get angrier that I told someone about it. Just let it be. It was never meant to work out anyway. I can see that now."

"Okay," Janice said. "You know, you really look wiped."

"I didn't get much sleep last night and I feel like I've aged about ten years."

"You've got some deep shadows around your eyes. I'd put on some concealer if I were you." Janice winked. "It won't be smooth sailing today, I'm not going to lie to you, but don't let them bully you."

Virginia gave Janice a peck on the cheek. "Thanks."

"You're welcome." Janice opened the door and turned. "If you set up another practice somewhere I can be bought for the right amount of money and vacation time." Janice winked and left.

Virginia scrubbed her hand over her face and headed back to the bathroom. Her face was blotchy and red. Her eyes were bloodshot. She looked and felt like she was a hundred years old. She couldn't help but wonder how many gray hairs from this ordeal she was going to get.

At least it would soon be over. The ER doctors and staff would get their severance packages and they'd be gone.

All she would have to do was paperwork and tie up some loose ends. Then she could walk away from Bayview Grace.

And go where? She didn't know.

She had no interest in going to Boston.

She felt like she was in limbo and it terrified her.

Virginia splashed some water on her face and pulled her hair back into a ponytail. She held her head high when she left her office, Janice giving her an encouraging smile, which she appreciated immensely.

Shoulders back and head held high, Virginia.

Her hand paused on the knob of the boardroom door. She could hear the rumbling murmurs from those who were about to lose their jobs, through the door.

You can do this.

Steeling her resolve, she pushed open the door and stepped into the room. The large boardroom was full. All the seats were taken and there were several people standing along the walls. In the crowd she picked out Gavin right away. He was looking at her, but there was no warmth to his gaze.

It was like she was looking at a stranger. A cold, distant stranger, and that made her heart clench.

The room fell silent and every eye in that room was on her. She could feel them boring into her back. She walked up to the front of the room.

"I'm glad you could all make it. I want to discuss the reasons I closed down the emergency room last night. The board of Bayview Grace Hospital has decided to turn Bayview into a private hospital. One that doesn't have a trauma department."

"What?" someone shouted, and an explosion of angry voices began to talk amongst themselves and at her.

Virginia held up her hand. "I know. I understand your frustrations."

"But what about that benefit?" Kimber asked. "I don't understand. I heard that it went well."

Virginia nodded. "It did, Kimber, but the investors who signed on agree with the board's decision to turn this into a profitable private hospital."

"So what's going to happen to the ER?" Dr. Jefferson asked. "Is it just going to be wasted space?"

"It will be turned into a plastic surgery-day spa."

"What does that mean?" someone shouted angrily from the back.

"It doesn't matter what it means. It's done. The board is hiring plastic surgeons this minute and Dr. Watkinson from Plastics is being made head of that department."

"What's going to happen to us?" Kimber asked, her voice tiny in the din.

Virginia glanced at Gavin. His eyes looked hooded and dark from across the room, but then she saw a momentary glimmer of sympathy.

She looked at Kimber. "I'm afraid, effective immediately, you've all been made redundant here at Bayview Grace."

Kimber's face fell and she looked like she was on the verge of tears. Tears Virginia herself was trying to hold back. The angry voices increased, but she kept her focus on Kimber.

Or, as Gavin had referred to her, Hello Kitty. She was wearing those scrubs now. Virginia had always liked Kimber. She was one of the many staff Virginia liked and was sad to see go.

"Tomorrow you may all pick up your severance packages. You will each find a letter of recommendation from me."

"You tried, Dr. Potter," Kimber said.

Virginia paused as she tried to leave the room and met Kimber's gaze.

"We know how hard you worked to save our jobs."

Virginia glanced at the faces of her staff and, except for the odd irate doctor, all she saw was sympathy and compassion. Even gratitude for what she'd tried to do. It made tears well in her eyes, but when she looked for affirmation from Gavin, the one person she cared about, she found none.

Gavin had left the room.

What did you expect?

Virginia then knew it was definitely over. He was done and so was she.

CHAPTER EIGHTEEN

Six weeks later

"YOU NEED TO get out of this funk, Dr. Brice," Rosalie chastised him. "You're seriously starting to depress me. I don't understand what you're so upset about. Your urgent care clinic is running smoothly and you have more hours now to spend with the girls."

Gavin sighed and poured himself another cup of coffee. She was right. He'd been in a funk since his *stupid* fight with Virginia.

He'd thought about calling her but hadn't. He'd been such an idiot.

"You're right, Rosalie. I'm sorry for bumming you out."

Rosalie *tsked* under her breath. "It's Dr. Potter, isn't it? Have you talked to her?"

"No. I haven't spoken to her since I was handed my severance package." Even then it hadn't been Virginia who'd handed him the severance package, it had been Janice, who'd given him the stink-eye when she did it.

"I still don't understand what happened." Rosalie shook her head. "I could've sworn that woman cared for you. I'm usually never wrong about these things."

"I overreacted. I was tired, emotionally drained and I overreacted. I blew my chance because of my temper." And then he proceeded to tell Rosalie the entire story of what had happened between him and Virginia the last time they'd spoken.

Rosalie let out a string of Spanish curses, all of which he was sure were aimed at him and were probably different words for idiot.

When her tirade subsided she crossed her arms over her ample bosom and glared at him. Her dark eyes were flinty. "You need to go and see her before she leaves San Francisco and you never see her again."

"She won't want to see me."

"Ah, you're so stubborn. It drives me crazy." Rosalie began to curse again and then marched over to him and pinched his cheek, shaking him hard. "You need to apologize to her. So what she read the judgment? She was right. You left it in a stupid place and, frankly, I think it meant she cared."

"She was offered a job in Boston and slept with me on the same night. Don't you find that suspicious?"

"No, I don't. I saw the way she looked at you and the way you looked at her. The job offer and you two finally getting together were just coincidences. I know she cared for you. It's just you're a man, you're *stupido*."

"*Stupido* I will take. You could've called me worse."

A smile cracked on Rosalie's lips. "Believe me, I want to."

Gavin groaned. "I miss her."

"So do I."

Rosalie let out a shriek and Gavin spun around, spilling coffee down the front of his shirt. Rose had climbed out of bed and was standing in the doorway of the kitchen. In her hand was Georgiana.

"Rose, what did you say?" Gavin asked as he knelt down in front of her.

"I miss Virginia." Then she gave Georgiana a little squeak right in his face. Gavin pulled his niece tight against him, hugging her. She'd spoken. The last time he'd heard her voice had been just before Casey's death.

"I want my mommy."

"I know you do, Rose."

It was the last thing she'd said. It had haunted him daily since she'd gone silent. He'd been worried she'd forget how to talk or, worse, that they'd forget what her voice sounded like.

The doctors called it selective mutism, but no matter what Gavin had done, he hadn't been able to coax Rose to talk.

Right now, her voice had a lilt of a thousand angels.

"I'm hungry and you're squishing me." She squirmed out of Gavin's arms and climbed up to the table.

"What do you want for breakfast, *querida*?" Rosalie asked through some choked sobs.

"Cereal."

"Then that's what you shall have." Rosalie covered her face with her hands and sobbed silently, her back to them, her shoulders shaking.

"What's wrong, Rosalie?" Rose asked. "Why are you sad?"

Rosalie laughed. Her voice was wobbly. "I'm not sad, *querida.* You make me so happy. Now, what kind of cereal?"

"Chocolate!" Rose's eyes twinkled as Rosalie grabbed a bowl and poured Rose a bowl of chocolate puffs.

Gavin brushed away a few of his own tears as he stood up.

Rose had made perfect sense and had stated the obvious. And Lily had been in a foul mood for a long time, as had he.

Virginia had brought a light to their lives. One he couldn't deny any more.

He'd never thought he'd find someone he wanted to settle down with, but then again he'd never thought he'd be raising children. When he'd pictured his life, he'd imagined that he'd be working until he died in some far-flung country.

Now that life was not one he wanted.

He wanted the stability that Casey had achieved. He wanted family and someone he loved to come home to.

He wanted Virginia.

"I'm going out."

Rosalie grinned. "Are you going where I think you're going?"

Gavin nodded. "Yeah, I'm going to go make things right."

Virginia worked her last shift at Bayview Grace in the evening, only because she didn't want to face Janice and all the others during the day. She didn't want them to see her cry. She tied up the loose ends she needed to in the peace and quiet of the night shift. There was no one in the trauma department. All of the staff were long gone.

Word about her leaving Bayview Grace was actually met, for the most part, with sorrow. No one wanted to see her go.

The board had hired Dr. Watkinson as their chief of surgery and he was already out ordering people around and making changes, all with Edwin Schultz's glowing affirmation.

Even though, technically, Virginia was still Chief of Surgery, she just let Dr. Watkinson have his way, because she'd emotionally disconnected herself from the hospital the moment she'd laid off all those employees.

Dr. Watkinson had hired some of them back, nurses he was fond of, but not everyone. Kimber, for instance, was gone. There was no smiling face down in the ER any more. No more "Hello Kitty" scrubs directing paramedics where to go.

Of course there was no ER.

And as she walked through it on her last day the scene with Mr. Jones and the board replayed in her mind and now she could laugh about it.

She could see it all so clearly. Gavin cracking that man's chest with such skill and precision. Not caring that the board and a handful of investors were watching with horror on their faces.

"Life over limb."

It was his motto and it was a good motto. Mr. Jones had survived.

Maybe if Shyanne had got herself to a hospital when she'd first started having shoulder pain she would've come across a trauma surgeon like Gavin and her life might have been spared by a simple operation. They just would've removed the fallopian tube.

Virginia sighed and left the ER. Heading back to her office, or rather Dr. Watkinson's office. When she got up there she could see him in her old office, measuring something.

She just shook her head.

Janice stood. "I couldn't keep him out of there a moment longer. I took your box and purse out. I figured you wouldn't want to go in there and talk to him."

"I appreciate that, Janice. I've talked to him enough this week about the job." Virginia rolled her eyes.

"What're you going to do now? I know you turned down that job in Boston."

Virginia shrugged. "I don't know. Maybe I'll open a private practice somewhere, but first things first. I'm going to go home and visit with my family."

"South Dakota?"

"Yep." Though it was not really home to her anymore. San Francisco, Gavin and the girls felt like a real home to her, but that was all gone. She hadn't seen him in weeks. Not since the layoffs and their gazes had locked across the room. She'd thought she'd seen a glimmer of sympathy there, but she must've been wrong.

"How long have you been away?" Janice asked.

"I haven't been back there…" She hesitated like she always did when she came close to mentioning Shyanne. "I haven't been home since my sister died. It was too painful, but now I feel resolved. I feel like a huge weight has been lifted from my shoulders."

Janice hugged her. "I'm really going to miss you, Dr. Potter."

"I'm going to miss you too, Janice."

Janice nodded and smiled. "Don't worry. I won't make things easy on Dr. Watkinson." With the mischievous glint in Janice's eyes, Virginia was prone to believe her.

"Well, I'd better be going. I'm officially no longer an em-

ployee here." She handed over her hospital ID and key card.
"I'd better leave and make this less painful. The exit interview
was bad enough. Goodbye, Janice."

Virginia picked up her box of belongings. Throughout the
week she'd taken larger items home. All that remained were
the few things she'd needed to get her through until the end.

And now it was here.

As she walked through the halls of the hospital that had
been her passion, the very center of her being for so long, she
didn't feel sad.

When she stepped outside an unseasonably warm breeze
caressed her face and she sighed.

She turned back, only once, and looked up at Bayview
Grace, staring the hospital she'd tried to save. A few months
ago she would've been sad to walk away, but now she just felt
resolved to Bayview's fate. In retrospect there was nothing
she could've done.

She'd done everything right.

She'd done her best.

She felt nervous that she didn't have a job yet, but she was
sure she could find something in San Francisco. In the interim
she'd booked a trip to return to De Smet and visit her family.

It was something that was long overdue; she had to put the
ghost of her sister to rest.

And she wouldn't mind having the company of her large
family in a confined space for a bit. It would be better than
staring at the walls in her apartment. She hadn't realized how
much she'd miss Gavin until he was gone.

She wasn't angry at him any more, she just missed him.

They were both too stubborn and settled in their ways to be
together—at least, that's what she told herself.

Kids and a husband hadn't ever been in her original plans,
but life could change in an instant. Something she'd learned
from working in trauma her whole career, but she hadn't
really understood it until Gavin Brice and his two nieces had
come barging into her life.

The box under her arm was heavy and she shifted it, pulling out her car keys. With a sigh of resignation she turned around to head to her car and froze in her tracks.

Gavin was in the parking lot, leaning against his motorcycle and dressed in his leathers. He was parked right next to her sedan.

Her knees knocked with nervousness, while the rest of her body was excited to see him. She wanted to throw herself into his arms, but after his parting words to her she refrained from making such a fool of herself.

Instead she walked over to him, opened her car and shoved her box of belongings inside. "Hello, Dr. Brice."

"Dr. Potter," he acknowledged. "Coming off the night shift?"

"Yes."

"I'm glad it was the night shift. I didn't really relish waiting here all day."

"What are you doing here?"

Gavin took off his sunglasses. "I've come to apologize."

Her eyes widened in shock. She leaned against her car. "I'm listening."

"I'm sorry, I was just angry about losing my job and…well, I wasn't angry that you read that judgment. I was angrier about the fact that I could lose you."

"To the Boston job?"

"Yes, but by the time you told me you weren't taking it my temper had gotten away with me. I was an idiot."

A smile quirked her lips. "I agree with that."

Gavin chuckled. "I've been trying to apologize for a couple of weeks now. I just… As I said, I was an idiot."

"Yes, so you said. I'm sorry too, Gavin. I shouldn't have pried, but I care for you and the girls. So much."

"They care for you too. Rose said she missed you."

"What?" Virginia was stunned. "Rose spoke?"

Gavin nodded. "This morning. She said she misses you, and Lily has been in a foul mood for weeks."

A lump formed in Virginia's throat. "I miss them too. I never thought kids liked me too much and vice versa, but I do miss your girls."

Gavin took a step forward, taking her hands in his. "Is that all, just the girls?"

Her heart began to race. "I've missed you too, Gavin. So much."

He cupped her cheeks and kissed her. Virginia's knees went weak and she melted into him, her whole body feeling like gelatin, almost like the earth below her feet was shaking, but it wasn't an earthquake she was feeling. She was feeling relief, love and joy.

Gavin broke off the kiss and leaned his forehead against hers. "I've missed you, Virginia. I fought my feelings so many times. I didn't want to settle down, but I can't help it. I love you."

"I love you too, Gavin...against my better judgment," she teased.

He laughed and kissed her again, holding her tight against his body. "Why don't we head back to my place? We can come back for your car later. That is, unless you have any other plans?"

"No, nothing. Even though it terrifies me to the very core, I'm unemployed."

"I have an opening at my clinic."

Virginia cocked an eyebrow. "Your clinic?"

He nodded. "I took my severance money, got some investors and opened an urgent-care clinic not far from here. I hired as many staff members from Bayview's trauma as I could. Kimber is head nurse now!"

Virginia was pleased. "That's—that's wonderful. Kimber is an excellent nurse. What else do you have at your clinic?"

"We have an OR and can do most minor surgeries. I also have a generous enough budget to do pro bono work. So, what do you say? Would you like a job?"

This time Virginia kissed him. She couldn't remember the

last time she'd felt so happy, so free. The job he was offering wouldn't pay as much as Bayview or the Boston hospital would, but she'd be doing a job that would help out people like Shyanne and that was worth its weight in gold.

"When do I start?"

"I'm headed there right now." Gavin handed her a helmet. "But you're just coming off the night shift."

Virginia took the helmet and jammed it on her head. "I'm a surgeon. I'm ready. Although I will have to cancel my trip to De Smet next week."

"You were going to visit your family?"

"Yeah, but I can cancel it."

"No, you're going, and Lily and Rose could use a bit of a holiday. Don't they have a Laura Ingalls Wilder museum there?"

"They do."

"Then I think we should all take a trip out there."

"Are you sure? It'll be cold this time of year."

"Positive. I want to meet your family, because all I want is you, Virginia. Just you."

She wrapped her arms around his neck and kissed his scruffy face. "Did I tell you how much I love you and your scruffies?"

"Yes, but tell me again."

Virginia grinned and kissed him again. "So much."

Gavin nodded. "Ditto. Let's go check out your new job, Dr. Potter."

Virginia climbed onto the back of his motorcycle, wrapping her arms around his chest. "I'm ready, Dr. Brice."

And with him, she was. She was ready for anything.

* * * * *

HER PLAYBOY'S SECRET

TINA BECKETT

To those who dare to chase their dreams

PROLOGUE

One week ago

IT WAS A curse heard around the world. Or at least around the ward of the Melbourne Maternity Unit.

Everyone on the ward went silent and several heads cranked around to see what the normally easygoing Lucas Elliot could possibly be upset about.

Darcie Green already knew—had braced herself for this very moment, wondering what his reaction would be.

Now she knew.

Still facing the rotation roster hanging on the far wall, Lucas didn't move for several seconds. Then, as if he couldn't quite believe what his eyes were telling him, one finger went to the chart, dragging across it to follow the line that matched dates with names.

She cringed as he muttered yet again, slightly lower this time. A few sympathetic glances came her way as people went back to their jobs. Isla Delamere, her former flatmate—now heavily pregnant—mouthed, "Sorry," as she tiptoed out of firing range.

A perfect beginning to a stellar day. She rolled her eyes.

Nine months in Australia and Darcie was just beginning to feel a part of the team. Except for Lucas's very vocal reaction at having the rota that matched hers, that was. He'd evidently not seen the list until just now.

Did he even know she was standing not seven meters behind him at the nurses' station? Probably not.

Then again, it was doubtful he would even care.

It wasn't as if she felt any better about having to spend an entire rotation with the handsome senior midwife. She just hadn't been quite as "loud" in expressing her displeasure.

Yes, she'd given him an earful about his periods of tardiness a few months back. But that had been no reason to call her an uptight, snooty, English…

Her eyes closed before the word formed, a flash of hurt working through her yet again.

Was the thought of being paired with her so hideous that he had to make sure everyone on the ward knew what he thought of her?

Evidently.

And why not? Her fiancé hadn't minded letting a whole chapel full of wedding guests know that he'd fallen in love with her best friend, who just so happened to be her maid of honor. Tabitha had promptly run over to him, squealing with delight, and thrown herself into his arms, leaving Darcie standing there in shock.

And, yes, Robert had called her uptight as well, right before he'd dropped the bomb that had ended their engagement.

Lucas's left hand went to the back of his neck, head bending forward as he massaged his muscles for a moment. When he finally turned around his eyes swept the area, going right past her before retracing his steps and pausing.

On her.

Then his left brow quirked, a rueful smile curving his lips. "Sorry. Heard that, did you?"

Was he serious? "I imagine there were very few who didn't."

He moved forward, until he was standing in front of her—all six feet of him. "I bet you did some name-calling of your own when you saw the rotation." His smile faded. "Unless you requested we work this one together."

Sure. That's just what she would have done, left to her own devices.

She forced her chin up. "No, I didn't request it, but it doesn't bother me, if that's what you mean. I've had worse assignments." Before she could congratulate herself on keeping her response cool and measured, even when her insides were squirming with embarrassment, he gave her a quick grin.

"Touché, Dr. Green. Although since you almost had me fired the last time we interacted, I assume your 'worse assignment' didn't fare quite as well."

Since the assignment she'd been referring to had had to do with returning hundreds of wedding gifts courtesy of her ex, it would appear that way. "I don't know about that. I think he feels *quite* lucky not to have to deal with my—how did you put it?—'uptight English ways' any more."

Lucas's gaze trailed over her face, but instead of whipping off a sharp retort he leaned in closer. "Then maybe you should consider some behavior modification courses."

Although the words were made in jest—at least she thought they were—they still stung. Darcie pulled the edges of her cardigan around herself to combat the chill spreading from her heart to the rest of her body and then forced every muscle in her chin go utterly still, so he wouldn't see the wobble. "You're right. Maybe I should."

His head tilted, and he studied her for a minute longer. He reached out a hand as if to touch her, before lowering it again. "Hey. Sorry. I was teasing."

Maybe, but a part of what he'd said was true. Men did seem to find her "chilly and distant"—words her ex had also used to describe her during the last troubled weeks of their engagement. And he had been right. Compared to her, Tabitha was warm and bubbly and anything but distant.

Darcie couldn't help the way she was made, though, could she? She dragged her thoughts back to the man in front of her. She hadn't tried to be unreasonable during their confrontation a few months ago, whatever Lucas might have thought. Was asking someone to be prompt and to keep his mind on his job so unreasonable?

Well, she didn't really have her mind on the job right now either.

"Don't worry about it." She fastened the buttons on her cardigan to keep from having to hold onto it and drew herself upright. "I'm sure, if we both remain professional, we'll come off this rotation relatively unscathed."

He gave her a dubious-looking smile. "I'm sure we will."

As he strode away, his glance cutting back to the chart and giving a shake of his head that could only be described as resigned, she realized that was the problem. Neither of them seemed able to maintain a calm professionalism around the other.

Two fortnights. That's all it was. Just because her rota corresponded with his, it didn't mean she had to stick to his side like glue. She could do this.

Doubt, like a whisper of smoke that curled round and round until it encased its victim, made her wonder if her ex-fiancé's cutting words were the hardest things she would ever face. She'd thought so at one time.

But as Lucas ducked around a corner and out of sight, she had a terrible suspicion she could be facing something much worse.

CHAPTER ONE

Present day

"CORA? WHAT'S WRONG, sweetheart?"

Lucas leaned a shoulder against the wall outside the birthing suite as his niece's voice came over the phone, dread making his blood pressure rise in steady increments. Every time he thought his brother was through the worst of his grief, he'd go on yet another binge and undo all the work he'd accomplished during therapy.

He took a quick glance down the hall. The coast was clear.

Lucas had worked hard over the last week to make sure his personal life didn't interfere with his job. As angry as he'd been at Darcie for giving him a public flogging over being late for work a couple of months ago, she'd been right. It was why he'd hired a childminder to help with Cora's care. Burning the candle at both ends was not only unwise, it could also be dangerous for his patients.

Had his parents still been alive, they would have been happy to help. But it had been almost ten years since the car accident that had taken their lives.

His niece's voice came through. "Nothing's wrong. I just called to tell you what Pete the Geek did today."

Cora's Belgian sheepdog. Muscles he hadn't been aware he'd contracted released all at once. "Can you tell me later, gorgeous? I'm working right now."

"Oh, okay. Sorry, Uncle Luke. Are you coming for dinner tonight?"

"I wouldn't miss it, sweetheart." He smiled, unable to resist the pleading note in her voice. "What are we having?"

"Prawns!"

Cora's birth was what had propelled him to change his career path from plastic surgery to midwifery. The lure of a glamorous life filled with beautiful women had faded away in a moment when Felix's wife had gone into labor unexpectedly. Lucas had delivered his own niece in the living room of his brother's home. As he'd stared down at the tiny creature nestled in his hands, Cora had blinked against the light and given a sharp wail of protest that had melted his heart. Seven years later, she still had the power to turn him into a soppy puddle of goo, especially since he and Felix were now the only family she had left.

He needed to get off the phone, but the ward was quiet—none of his patients were laboring at the moment. He cradled the device closer to his ear. "Prawns, eh? What's the occasion?"

She giggled. "Just because."

"You're going to spoil me." His chest tightened at how happy she sounded. He'd take this over those *other* phone calls any day.

"Oh," his niece said, "make sure you bring some briquettes for the barbie. Daddy forgot them at the store."

Felix had forgotten quite a few things lately. But at least he seemed to be pulling out of his current well of depression.

Footsteps sounded somewhere behind him, so he moved to end the conversation.

"Okay, Cora, I will. Looking forward to tonight."

"Me too. Love you bunches."

"Love you even more, sweetheart. Bye." He ended the call, only to have the very person he'd been hoping not to encounter stalk past him, throwing an icy glare his way.

Lucas sighed. The woman did seem to pop up at just the wrong time. He slid the phone into his pocket and decided to go after her. He had no idea why, but he liked trying to get a rise out of her. Within five steps he'd caught up with her. Matching her pace, he glanced to the side.

Not good. The obstetrician's lips were pressed together into a thin line, her expression stony.

He pushed forward anyway, throwing her what he hoped was a charming smile. "Were you looking for me?"

Her expression didn't budge. "I was, but I can see you're busy."

"Just taking a short breather between patients. What was it you wanted?"

She glanced at him, her eyes meeting his for a mere second. "Is Isla scheduled to see you this week?"

Isla Delamere was one of his colleagues as well as a friend.

"Yes, did you want to be there for her appointment?"

Her chin edged up in a way he was coming to recognize. "I'd planned to be. She's my patient as well."

Okay, he'd gotten a rise out of her, but not quite the kind he'd been hoping for.

He moved ahead of her and planted himself in her path before she could reach the door to the staff lounge. Why he was bothering he had no idea, but something in him wanted to knock down a block or two of that icy wall she surrounded herself with. "Listen, Dr. Green—Darcie—I know we got off on the wrong foot somehow, but can we hit the reset button? We have three weeks of our rotation left. I'd like to make them pleasant ones, if at all possible. What do you say?"

The tight lines in her face held firm for another moment, and he wondered if she was going to strike him dead for daring to use her first name. Then her eyes closed, and she took a deep breath. "I think I might be able to manage that." The corners of her mouth edged up, creating cute little crinkles at the outer edges of her eyes. "If we both try very hard."

Something in Lucas's chest shifted, and a tightening sensation speared through his gut. Had he ever seen the woman smile? Not that he could remember, and certainly never at him. The transformation in her face was...

Incredible.

He swallowed. That was something he was better off not thinking about.

Three weeks. He just had to get through the rest of this rotation. From what he understood, Dr. Green had only been seconded to MMU for a year, then she'd head back to England. He did some quick calculations. She had, what...three months left? Once their rotation was over she'd be down to two, which meant it was doubtful they'd be paired together again. He gave an internal fist pump, trying to put his whole heart into it. It came off as less than enthusiastic.

Because you still have these three weeks to get through.

He gave her another smile. "I think I can manage it as well."

"Well, good. Now that that's settled, when is Isla's appointment?"

He checked his schedule. "Next Wednesday at two."

Darcie pulled her phone out and scrolled through a couple of screens before punching some buttons. "I don't have anyone scheduled at that time, so I'll be there." She gave him another smile—a bit wider this time—and the wobble in his chest returned. And this time he noticed the crinkles framed eyes that were green. A rich velvety color. Sparkling with life.

Her lips were softer too than they had been earlier. Pink, delicate, and with just a hint of shine.

The tightening sensation spread lower, edging beneath his waistband.

What the hell? Time to get out of here.

"Great. See you later." He turned and started back the way he had come, only to have her voice interrupt him.

"Don't forget to call for a consult if anything unusual comes up."

He stiffened at the prim tone. "Yes, I know the protocol, thank you."

When she didn't respond, he turned around and caught something…hurt?…in the depths of those green eyes, and maybe even a hint of uncertainty. In a flash, though, it winked out, taking with it any trace of her earlier smile and, very possibly, their newborn peace accord.

While that bothered him on a professional level, it was what he'd seen in her expression in that unguarded moment that made him want to cross over to her and try to understand what was going on in her head. He didn't. Instead, he chose to reiterate his comment in a less defensive way. "I'll ring if I need you."

Then he walked away. Without looking back. Praying the next weeks sped by without him having to make that call.

That man should wear a lab coat. A long one.

Darcie tried not to stare at the taut backside encased in dark jeans as he made his way back down the hall, but it was hard. No matter how much she tried to look anywhere but there, her peripheral vision was still very much engaged, keeping track of him until he finally turned down a neighboring corridor.

The thread of hurt from his curt response still lingered, just waiting for her to tug on it and draw it tighter. Why had he acted so put out to have her assistance on a case?

Was it the professional rivalry that sometimes went on between midwives and obstetricians?

She sagged against the wall, pressing her fingers against her temples and rubbing in slow, careful circles to ward off the migraine that was beginning to chomp at the wall of her composure.

What was it about Lucas that put her on edge?

The fact that he was a man in a field dominated by women?

Or was it the fact that all the expectant mums who came through the doors clamored to be put on his patient list? Despite the run-ins they'd had over the past nine months, Senior Midwife Lucas seemed quite capable of doing his job with an ease and efficiency that only enhanced his good looks.

And they were good.

She tried to dredge up an unflattering image, like the time he'd come in late for work, dragging his fingers through his wavy hair, his rumpled clothes the same ones he'd had on when he'd left the previous afternoon. Nope. He'd been just as attractive then as the first time she'd laid eyes on him.

Ugh. She disliked him for that most of all.

Or maybe it was all those secretive phone calls she'd caught him making when he'd thought he'd been alone. Oh, those were definitely over the top. So many of them, right in the middle of his shift.

And he wondered why she was outraged when he came in late or took little side breaks to indulge in whispered conversations.

Could she be jealous?

She straightened in a flash. *No!* Just because Robert had decided she wasn't enough "fun", it didn't mean she should go ballistic over any man who wanted to indulge in a bit of pillow talk on the phone.

Maybe it wouldn't bother her so much if he didn't

use the same flirty tones when in conversation with the MMU staff and his patients. The tone he turned on this "Cora" person—a kind of I'm-not-willing-to-commit-but-I-still-want-you-at-my-beck-and-call attitude that grated on Darcie's nerves. Especially after the way her ex had led her down the rosy path, only to dump her for her maid of honor—who, actually, *was* a lot of fun to be with.

She sighed and went into the lounge to get a strong cuppa that she hoped would relieve the steady ache in her head and keep it from blooming into something worse.

As soon as she moved into the space, she knew it was a mistake. Lucas, it seemed, was the main topic of conversation among the cluster of four nurses inside.

"I swear one of his patients this morning had on false eyelashes. While in labor!" Marison Daniels blinked rapidly, as if trying to imitate what the woman had done. They all laughed.

If Darcie had hoped to slide by them, grab her tea and tiptoe back out of the room unseen, that hope was dashed when the nurse next to Marison caught Darcie's eye and gave the jokester a quick poke in the ribs with her elbow. The laughter ceased instantly.

Oh, Lord. Her face burned hotter than the kettle she'd just switched on.

"Sorry. Didn't mean to interrupt."

"You didn't interrupt," Marison assured her. "I was just headed back to the ward."

The others all echoed the same thing.

With a scurry of feet and tossing of rubbish, the four headed out.

Just what she needed. To be reminded that she was still very much an outsider when it came to certain things—like being allowed to let her hair down with the rest of them.

No, the pattern had been set from the moment she'd got off the plane. Oh, she'd made friends and people were nice enough, but to let her in on their little jokes? That didn't happen very often, except with Isla.

Worse, she'd even overheard Lucas making fun of her English accent while on one of his phone calls to Cora. It hadn't been in a mean way, he'd just repeated some of her colloquialisms with a chuckle, but it made her feel self-conscious any time she opened her mouth around him. So she made sure she spoke to him as little as possible. And now that they were sharing a rota, she was still struggling to maintain that silence.

Not that it was going to be possible forever.

She could still picture the confident way he strode through the hallways of the ward, his quick smile making itself known whenever he met a patient. She wrinkled her nose. More than one expectant mum would have probably given her left ovary to bat long sexy lashes and claim the child she was carrying was Lucas Elliot's.

Including his current paramour, Cora?

Probably, but not *her*. She was done with men like him.

Her fiancé had been handsome and attentive. Until he hadn't been. Until he'd grown more and more distracted as their engagement had progressed.

Now she knew why.

And Lucas had Cora. She was not about to smile and flirt with a man who was taken. She wasn't Tabitha.

She packed leaves into the tea ball and dropped it into a chunky mug—a gift from her dad to remind her that her favorite footballers resided in England and to not let herself get swept away by a handsome face, especially one who lived halfway round the world.

Lucas's quirked brow swam before her eyes, and she let out an audible groan, even as she poured boiling water into her cup. No matter how good looking he was or how elated she'd been to see the momentary confusion cross his expression when she'd smiled at him, she did not need to become like False-Eyelash Lady—the one Marison had carried on about.

There'd be a real corker of a reaction if someone caught her mooning after him. Or staring after him, like she'd done earlier.

She bounced her tea ball in the water and watched as the brew grew darker and darker, just like her thoughts. What she needed was to stay clearheaded. Like he'd said, they had three more weeks together.

He wanted them to be pleasant ones. She finished adding milk and sugar to her cup and then discarded the used tea leaves, rinsing the ball and leaving it on a towel for the next person who needed it.

"Pleasant" she could do, but that had to be the extent of it. Maybe she should be grateful for all those calls to Cora…maybe she should even hope the relationship stayed the course. At least for the next few weeks.

Which meant she would not go out of her way to put him at ease or cut him any slack if he came in late again. Neither would she give the man any reason to look at her with anything other than the casual curiosity his eyes normally held.

And once those three weeks were up?

Life would go back to the way it had been before they'd found themselves joined at the hip.

Joined at the hip. She gave a quick grin. That was one place she and Lucas would never be joined, even if the idea did create a layer of warmth in her belly. But it was not going to happen. Not in this lifetime.

With that in mind, she took a few more sips of the sweet milky brew, then, feeling fortified and ready to face whatever was out there, she headed off to see her next patient in what was proving to be a very interesting morning.

CHAPTER TWO

FELIX WASN'T AT HOME.

Arms loaded with items for their dinner, Lucas set everything down in the kitchen. "Where is he?"

Chessa, the childminder, shrugged and said in a quiet voice, "He went out an hour ago, saying he needed to buy prawns, and hasn't come back yet."

Damn. "And where's Cora?"

"Outside with Pete." The young woman's brow creased. "Should I be worried? He's been good for the last few weeks, but he did put some bottles of ale in the fridge. I haven't seen him drink anything, though."

"It's okay. It's not your job to watch him. If he ever fails to come home before you're supposed to leave, though, call me so I can make sure Cora is taken care of."

"I would never leave her by herself, Mr. Elliot." The twenty-five-year-old looked horrified.

"I know you wouldn't. I just don't want you to feel you have to stay past your normal time."

The sliding door opened and in bounded Pete the Geek in a flash of brown and white fur, followed closely by Cora, whose red face said they'd been involved in some sort of running game. The dog came over and sat in front of him, giving a quick woof.

Lucas laughed and reached in his pocket for a treat. "Well, you're learning."

He and Cora had been working on teaching Pete not to leap on people who walked through the door. By training him to sit quietly in front of visitors, they forestalled any muddy paw prints or getting knocked down and held prisoner by an overactive tongue. The trick seemed to be working, although if the tail swishing madly across the tile floor was any indication, Pete was holding himself in check with all his might.

Kind of like *him* when Darcie had smiled at him as he'd left the hospital?

Good thing he had more impulse control than Cora's dog.

Or maybe Darcie was training him as adeptly as Cora seemed to be training Pete.

"He wants his treat, Uncle Luke."

Realizing he'd been standing there like an idiot, he tossed the bacon-flavored bit to Pete and then bent down to pet him. "I think he's gained ten kilos in the last week."

He squatted and put an arm around both his niece and her dog.

Cora kissed him on the cheek, her thin arms squeezing his neck. "That's just silly. He doesn't weigh that much."

"No?" He gave her a quick peck on the forehead, grimacing when Pete gave his own version of a kiss, swiping across his eyebrow and half his eye in the process. "Okay, enough already."

He couldn't hold back his smile, however, despite the niggle of worry that was still rolling around inside him.

Where the hell was his brother?

Standing, he kept one hand on Pete's head and smiled at the minder. "Would you try ringing his mobile phone and seeing how long he'll be while I fire up the barbie and get it ready? I don't know about everyone else but I'm starving."

His voice was light, but his heart weighed more than the dog at his feet.

"Of course," Chessa said. "I'll bring you some lemonade in a few minutes."

As he was preparing the grill, she came out with a glass and an apologetic shake of her head. "There was no answer, but I left a voice mail."

"Thank you. Luckily I brought some prawns with me, just in case. Feel free to stay and eat with us, if you'd like."

She smiled. "Thanks, but if it's all the same to you, I think I'll head back to my flat. Do you need anything else?"

"No, I think we're good."

Twenty minutes later he had the briquettes going while Cora and Pete—worn out from a rough-and-tumble game of tug of war—lounged in a hammock strung between two gum trees, the dog's chin propped on his niece's shoulder. Both looked utterly content. Rescuing Pete had been the best thing his brother had ever done for his daughter, unlike a lot of other things since his wife's tragic death. In fact, the last four years had been a roller coaster consisting of more lows than highs—with the plunges occurring at lightning speed.

He went in and grabbed the package of prawns and some veggies to roast. Just as he started rinsing the shellfish, the front door opened and in came his brother. Bleary, red-rimmed eyes gave him away.

Perfect. Lucas already knew this routine by heart.

"Was our cookout tonight?" his brother asked, hands as empty as Lucas's stomach. "I forgot."

His molars ground against each other as he struggled with his anger and frustration. Was this what love and marriage ultimately led to? Forgetting that anyone else existed outside your own emotional state? Felix had a daughter who needed him, for God's sake. What was it going to take to make him look at someone besides himself? "Cora didn't forget."

His brother groaned out loud then mumbled, "Sorry."

"I'm just getting ready to throw it all on the barbie, so why don't you get yourself cleaned up before you go out there to see?"

The first two steps looked steady enough, but the next one swayed a bit to the left before Felix caught himself.

"Tell me you're not drunk."

"I'm not."

"Can you make it to your bedroom on your own?" The last thing Lucas wanted was for Cora to come in and see her father like this, not that she hadn't in the past. Many times.

Felix scowled. "Of course I can." He proceeded to weave his way down the hallway, before disappearing into one of the rooms—the bathroom.

Looks like you're spending the night on your brother's couch once again, mate.

Lucas had impressed on Cora the need to call him if her father ever seemed "not himself." The pattern was bizarre with periods of complete normalcy followed by bouts of depression, sometimes mixed with drinking. Not a good combination for someone taking anti-depressant medication.

He made a mental note to ask Felix if he was still taking his pills, and another note to make sure he arrived at work…on time! As he'd found out, it was tricky getting Cora off to school and then making the trek to the hospital, but if the traffic co-operated it could be done.

Otherwise that hard-won peace treaty would be shredded between pale English fingers.

Strangely, he didn't want that. Didn't want to disappoint her after he'd worked so hard to turn things around between them. Didn't want to lose those rare smiles in the process. So yes. He would do his damnedest to get to the hospital on time.

And between now and then he'd have to figure out what to do about his brother. Threaten him with another stint in rehab? Take away his car keys?

He cast his eyes up to the ceiling, trying not to blame Melody for allowing his brother to twine his life so completely around hers that he had trouble functioning now that she was gone.

Lucas never wanted to be in a position like that. And so far he hadn't. He'd played the field far and wide, but he still lived by two hard and fast rules: no married women and no long-term relationships. As long as he could untangle himself with ease the next day, he was happy. And he stuck to women who felt the same way.

No hurt feelings. And definitely no burning need to hang around and buy a house with a garden.

Finishing up the veggies, he faintly caught the sound of the shower switching on, the *poof* from the on-demand water heater confirming his thoughts. Good. At least Felix was doing something productive. He opened the refrigerator, pulled out the ale in the door and popped the top on every single bottle. Then he took a long gulp of the one in his hand, before proceeding to pour the rest of the contents down the drain, doing the same with every other bottle and then placing the lot in the recycle bin. If the beer wasn't here, Felix couldn't drink it, right?

Not that that stopped him from going out to the nearest pub, but at least that took some effort, which he hoped Felix didn't have in him tonight.

Lucas went outside and loaded the prawns into a cooking basket and set it over the fire, then arranged the vegetables next to them on the grate. Cora's empty glass of lemonade was next to his full one. She was still sprawled on the hammock and it looked like both she and Pete were out for the count. If only he could brush off his cares that easily, he might actually get a full night's sleep.

But maybe tonight would be different. He'd learned from experience that the fold-out cot in the spare room was supremely uncomfortable. He was better off just throwing a quilt over Melody's prized couch and settling in for the night there.

And he would wake up on time. He absolutely would.

And he'd arrive at work chipper and ready to face the day.

He hoped.

Something was wrong with Lucas.

He'd come through the doors of the MMU with a frown that could have swallowed most of Melbourne. She'd arrived at work armed with a smile, only to have him look right past her as if she didn't exist.

Ha! Evidently she'd been wrong about his reaction. Because there was nothing remotely resembling attraction in the man's eyes today. In fact, his whole frame oozed exhaustion, as did the two nicks on the left side of his strong jaw. He'd muttered something that might have been "G'day." Or it might just as easily have been "Go to hell."

She was tempted to chase him down and ask about his evening, but when she turned to do so, she noticed that the back of his shirt was wrinkled as if he'd... Her gaze skimmed down and caught the same dark jeans he'd worn yesterday.

Her stomach rolled to the side. The staff all had lockers, and the last time he'd come in like this he'd used the hospital's shower and changed into clean clothes. That's probably what he was headed to do right now.

The evidence pointed to one thing. That he'd spent the night with "Cora" or some other woman.

The trickle of attraction froze in her veins.

None of your business, Darcie.

Just leave the man alone. If she made an issue of this,

they would be back where they'd started: fighting a cold war that neither one of them would win.

But why the hell couldn't he drag himself out of his lover's bed in time to go home and shower before coming to work?

Unless he just couldn't manage to tear himself away from her.

An image emerged from the haze that she did her best to block. Too late. There it was, and there was no way to send it back again—the one of Lucas swinging his feet over the side of the mattress, only to have some faceless woman graze long, ruby fingernails down his arm and whisper something that made him change his mind.

She shook her head to remove the picture and forced herself to get back to work.

Just as she did so she spied one of her patients leaning against the wall, her hands gripping her swollen belly. Margie Terrington, an English transplant like herself, had just come in yesterday for a quick check to make sure things were on track. They had been.

At least until now. From the concentration on her face and the grey cast to her skin, something wasn't right. Darcie glanced around for a nurse, but they were still tending to the morning's patients. Darcie hurried over.

"Margie? Are you all right?"

Her eyes came up. "My stomach. It's cramping. I think it's the baby."

"Let's get you into a room."

Alarm filled her. No time to check her in or do any of the preliminaries. This was the young woman's second pregnancy. She'd miscarried her first a little over a year ago, and she was only seven months along with this one. Too soon. The human body didn't just go into labor this early unless there was a problem.

Her apprehension grew, and she sent up a quick prayer.

Propping her shoulder beneath Margie's arm, they headed to the nearest exam room. One of the nurses came out of a room across the hall, and Darcie called out to her. "Tessa, could you come here?"

The nurse hurried over and got on the other side of their patient.

"Once I get her settled, can you see if you can find Lucas? He arrived a few minutes ago, so he might be in the lounge or the locker area. Let him know I might need his help."

"Of course."

The patient was sweating profusely—Darcie could feel the moisture through the woman's light maternity top. Another strike against her. If she had some kind of systemic infection, could it have crossed the placenta and affected the baby? A thousand possibilities ran through her mind.

Pushing into the exam area, the trio paused when Margie groaned and doubled over even more. "Oh, God. Hurts."

"Do they feel like contractions? Are they regular?" They finally got her to the bed and helped her up on it.

"I don't know."

Tessa scurried around, getting her vitals, while Darcie tried to get some more information. What she learned wasn't good. Margie had got up and showered like normal and had felt fine. Forty minutes later she'd got a painful cramp in her side—like the kind you got while running, she'd said. The pain had grown worse and had spread in a band across her abdomen. Now she was feeling nauseous, whether from the pain or something else, she wasn't sure. "And my joints hurt, as if I'm getting the flu."

Could she be?

As soon as Tessa called out the readings, the nurse went out to get the patient's chart and to hunt down Lucas.

"Let's get you into a robe and see what's going on."

"Wait." Margie groaned again. "I think I'm going to be sick."

Grabbing a basin, she held it under her patient's mouth as she heaved. Nothing came up, though.

"Did you eat breakfast?" Darcie started to reach for a paper towel, only to have Lucas arrive, chart in hand. He took one look at the scene and anticipated what she was doing. Ripping a couple of towels from the dispenser, he glanced at her in question. "What've you got?"

"This is Margie Terrington from Southbank. She's cramping. Pain in the joints. Nausea."

"Contractions?"

"I'm not sure. I'm just getting ready to hook her up to the monitor."

He tilted his head. "Theories?"

"None." She laid a hand on the young woman's shoulder. "Are you up to telling Lucas what you told me?"

Even as she asked it, Margie's face tightened up in a pained grimace, and she gave a couple of sustained breaths, dragging air in through her nose and letting it out through her mouth. A second or two later she nodded. "Like I told you, I took a shower this morning. Then I started getting these weird sensations in my side."

"What kind of weird?"

"Like a pulled muscle or something." She stiffened once again. She gritted out, "But now my whole stomach hurts."

"Where's the father?" Lucas asked.

"He's at work. I—I didn't want to worry him if it's nothing."

Lucas frowned. "I think he should be here." He glanced at Darcie. "Can you get her hooked up while I ring him?"

If anything, Margie looked even more frightened. "Am I going to lose this baby too?"

Darcie's heart ached for the woman, even as her brain still whirled, trying to figure out what was going on. "Let us do the worrying, love, can you do that?"

"I think so." She wrote her husband's phone number on a sheet of paper and handed it to Lucas.

While he was gone, Darcie got Margie into a hospital gown and snapped on a pair of gloves. Then she wrapped the monitor around her patient's abdomen. Wow, she was really perspiring. So much so that it had already soaked through the robe on her right side.

And her abdominal muscles were tight to the touch. "Are you having a contraction right now?"

Margie moaned. "I don't know."

She started up the machine and the first thing she heard was the quick *woompa-woompa-woompa-woompa* of the baby's heart. Thank God. Even as that thought hit, a hundred more swept past it. A heartbeat didn't mean Margie's baby wasn't in distress, just that he was alive.

She stared at the line below the heart rate that should be showing the marked rise and fall of the uterus as it contracted and released. It was a steady line.

Placing her hand on Margie's abdomen again, she noted the strange tightness she'd felt before. But it seemed more like surface muscles to Darcie. Not the deep, purposeful contraction of a woman's uterus.

Lucas came back and glanced at the monitor. "Your husband's on his way."

"Thank you." Another moan, and her hands went back to her stomach.

Lucas sat next to the bed and held the patient's hand, helping guide her through the deep breathing.

"She's not contracting." Darcie's eyes were locked on the monitor where a series of little squiggles indicated that something was happening, but it was more like a series of muscle fasciculations than the steady rise and fall she would expect to see. Could she have flu, like Margie suspected?

"When did you start sweating like this?"

Lucas's voice drew her attention back. He eased Margie's robe to the side and stared at the area where moisture was already beading up despite just having been exposed to the chilly air of the ward. Strange. Although Margie was perspiring everywhere—Darcie gave a quick glance at her face and chest above the gown— there was a marked difference between her moist upper lip and her right side, where a rivulet of liquid peaked and then ran down the woman's swollen belly.

"I don't know. An hour after my shower? Right about the time I started to hurt."

He peered at her closer. "You said you took a shower. Did you feel anything before or after it? A sting…or a prick maybe?"

A prick? Darcie stared at him, trying to figure out where he was going with this.

"No."

"Where did the pain start exactly?"

Margie pressed her fingers right over the area that was wet from perspiration.

He muttered something under his breath then glanced up at Darcie. "I need to make a quick phone call."

"What?" Outrage gathered in her chest and built into a froth that threatened to explode. Surely he was not going to make a personal call right now.

As if he saw something in her face, he reached out and encircled her wrist. "I want her husband to check on something at the house before he comes here," he said in a low voice.

The anger flooding her system disappeared in a whoosh as she stared back at him.

Margie's panicked voice broke between them. "What's wrong?"

"I'm not sure yet. But I don't think you're in labor."

"Then what?"

"I think you may have been bitten by a redback," Lucas said.

"A what?" Margie asked.

"It's one of our most famous residents," he said. "It's a spider. A nasty one at that."

A redback! Darcie had heard of them but had never

encountered one, and since she wasn't from Australia, it had never dawned on her that Margie could have been envenomed by something. Her patient was also from England. She'd probably never thought of that possibility either.

She glanced at Lucas. "Are they that common?"

"Quite." He patted Margie's hand. "If that's the case we have antivenin we can give you, which should help."

"If it is a bite, will it hurt the baby?" She gritted her teeth and pulled in another deep breath.

"I think we've caught it at an early stage." His gaze went back to the monitor, which Darcie noted still held steady. "I want to have your husband check the towel and your bathroom."

The patient's eyes widened. "I used the walk-in shower in the guest bathroom this morning. I almost never use that one because it's quite a long way from the bedroom. But my mother is due to fly in to help with the house and baby in a few weeks, and I thought I could tidy things and scrub the shower stall down as I was bathing."

"I'm just going to pull Dr. Green into the hallway for a moment. I'll send the nurse in to sit with you."

Once they were outside the room, and Lucas had rung the husband, asking him to shake out the towel and examine the bathroom, she spun toward him. "A redback. Are you sure?"

"Pretty sure. Most Australians know what to look for, but no one else would. I've seen this once before. A redback bite that comes in looking like preterm labor."

She sagged against the wall. "God. I would have never checked for that. I didn't see a bite. Didn't even think to ask."

"You wouldn't have. And as for the bite mark…" He shrugged. "Small fangs, but they pack quite a wallop."

He gave a smile that looked as tired as she suddenly felt.

"Can we give antivenin to her during pregnancy?"

"We've given it before. I can't recall anyone having a bad reaction, unless the patient is allergic to the equine immunoglobulin in the serum." He sighed. "There've been some conflicting reports recently about whether or not the antivenin actually works, but I've seen enough evidence to tell me it's worth a shot. Especially since she's miscarried once already."

Lucas's mobile phone buzzed, and he glanced at the screen. "It's him. Let's hope this is the answer we're looking for."

He punched a button asking a few questions before assuring the man that she should do well with the antivenin and telling him they'd be awaiting his arrival.

"He found the redback. It was still in the towel. A big one, from the sound of it." He dragged his fingers through his hair. "I'll need you to sign off on the medication. We'll go the intravenous route rather than administering the antivenin intramuscularly, since that's more favored at the moment."

"Of course." She closed her eyes with a relieved laugh. "God, I could kiss you right now. I never in a million years would have got that diagnosis right."

A few seconds of silence met her comment.

Hell. Had she really just said that? About kissing him?

Evidently, because when she dared to look at him again a thread of confused amusement seemed to play across his face. "I don't think now would be appropriate, do you, Dr. Green? But later…" He let his voice trail off in a way that gave her no question that he was definitely open to whatever later meant.

What? Hadn't he just come to work this morning all rumpled and sexed up?

Sexed up? Was that even a real expression?

Whether it was or not wasn't the point. It was unbelievable that he would roll out of one woman's bed and be ready and willing to kiss a second one. A perfect stranger, actually, since they barely knew each other.

Not likely, you jerk.

She gave the haughtiest toss of her chin she could manage and fixed him with a cold glare. "It's a figure of speech, Lucas, in case you haven't heard. I was just happy to know that Margie's symptoms have an explanation and a treatment. But get this straight. As grateful as I am for your help, I had no intention of *really* kissing you. Now…or ever. I have no interest in being part of a love triangle. Been there. Done that."

Before she could scurry away in horror over that last blooper, he murmured, "I stand corrected on the kissing, although you totally had me for a moment or two. But I'm intrigued by this supposed love triangle you envision us in. Care to enlighten me as to who the third party might be, or do I have no say in the matter?"

Was he serious?

She wanted to hurl Cora's name at him. Instead, by some superhuman force of will, she clamped her jaws shut before they had a chance to issue any other crazy statements. Then, without another word, she swung back into their patient's room to give her the news about the redback.

At least he hadn't asked her about the been-there-done-that part of her rant, because no one needed to hear her sad tale about the wedding that almost had been. Or the woman who'd stolen her fiancé's heart when he was supposed to be madly in love with her.

Since when had she become so reckless with her words?

Just like the ruby stripe on the infamous redback that warned of dire consequences to those who came in contact with it, the answer to her last question was inscribed with words that were just as lethal: Lucas Elliot.

He made her forget about everything but his presence.

The thing was, she had no idea how to go about scrubbing him—or the image of their lips locking in a frenzy of need—from her mind and finishing out the rest of her time in Australia in relative peace.

But she'd better figure out an antivenin that would work against his charm and inject herself with it. As soon as she possibly could.

CHAPTER THREE

"HOW'S CORA?"

Isla settled herself on the paper-lined exam table like a pro, despite the burgeoning evidence of her pregnancy.

A week after they'd successfully treated the redback spider victim, Darcie had somehow managed to keep her tongue to herself.

Ugh. Now, why did that thought sound so raunchy?

And why was it that every time she was around Lucas her mind hadn't quite stopped doing mental gymnastics over every word the man uttered, turning them over and over and looking for hidden meanings?

There weren't any, and he hadn't brought up the subjects of kissing, love triangles, or anything else of a personal nature, for which she was extremely grateful.

Here Isla was, though, bringing up the one person she had no desire to hear about.

Lucas's supposed lover.

As if hearing her thoughts, he glanced at her before looking back at their patient. "She's great. Wants me to buy her a sports car."

Darcie's eyebrows shot up, even though she tried to keep her facial features frozen into place. The woman had actually asked him to buy her a car? A pool of distaste gathered in the pit of her stomach. Just what kind of women did the man hang out with?

Isla, though, instead of castigating Lucas and telling him to kick the tramp to the curb, laughed as if she found that idea hilarious.

"Did you tell her she has to be tall enough to reach the pedals first?"

Her brain hit the rewind button and played those words over twice. Either he was dating a very short woman or…

"Yep. I also told her she has to be old enough to have her driving permit. So I'm safe for a few years."

Darcie couldn't help it. The words just came out. "Cora's not of legal age?"

"He hasn't talked your ear off about her yet? Wow." Her former flatmate blew out a breath. "She's his niece. And she gives him quite a bit of grief. Isn't that right, Lucas?"

The man in question studied Darcie as if he couldn't quite grasp something. "That's right, and…" The pupils in his eyes grew larger. "Oh, Darcie, I'm almost afraid to ask. Who did you think she was?"

"I—I…" She stammered around for a second then finally gave up.

He made a tutting sound then his lips curved. "I think I see. A love triangle, wasn't it? I don't know if I should be insulted or flattered."

"I just thought, she was—"

"My girlfriend?"

Isla's voice cut in. "Would someone like to clue me in on what you two are going on about? What's this about a love triangle?"

"It's nothing."

Lucas spoke at the exact same time she did. He then laughed, while Darcie's face flamed.

Their patient looked from one to the other of them. "Oh, this is definitely *not* nothing. But…" she patted her belly "…someone is starting to use my bladder as his own personal football. So unless you want to take a break while I visit the loo, maybe we should get on with this."

"Of course." Lucas pulled out his measuring tape and stretched it over the bulge of Isla's belly, writing the results on her chart. "Right on schedule. At this rate I think the baby will weigh in at a little over seven pounds. The perfect size for a first baby."

"Thank goodness, because right now my stomach looks to be the size of a football." She gave a light laugh. "I guess that's why this little guy feels like he's training for the World Cup."

"Anything out of the ordinary? Contractions?"

"No. Nothing. I feel great." She glanced at Darcie. "Except I have to break our date for the beach this afternoon. Someone called off sick, and they've asked me to fill in."

"Don't worry about it. Some other time."

"I know, but I promised to take you to see some sights, and with everything with Alessi and the baby, time has just slipped away." Isla slid a look at Lucas. "Aren't you two on the same rota?"

A pit lodged in her stomach. "Yes, why?"

"Well, because…" She gave the midwife a wide smile. "Would you mind going in my place? Darcie and I were going to make a list of things for her to see and do. If she puts it off too much longer, she'll go back to England without having visited anything."

Her unease morphed into horror. "Isla, I'm sure he has other things to do with his off time than go to the beach."

"Actually, I'm free once our shift is over." The smile he gave her was much slower than Isla's and held a touch of challenge that made her shiver. "I'll be happy to help her make her list. And maybe even tick an item or two off of it. Since we *do* have the same rota. Unless she doesn't trust me, for some reason."

Isla skimmed her hands over her belly and gave a sigh that sounded relieved. "Of course she trusts you. That would be brilliant, Lucas. At this point, I would only slow her down."

They were making plans that she hadn't even agreed to. And go to the beach with Lucas? See those long legs stretched out on the sand beside hers? A dull roar sounded in her ears as panic set in.

"I'll be fine—"

A quick knock sounded before she could blurt out the rest of her sentence, that she would be fine on her own, that she didn't need company.

Sean Anderson, one of the other obstetricians, poked his head into the room. "Sorry, guys, they told me Isla was here." He looked at the patient, his expression unreadable. "One of your teen mums-to-be projects is at the nurses' station, asking for you. And after that your father wants to speak with you about your sister. I have a few questions about her myself."

Poor Isla. Not exactly the kind of thing one wanted to deal with when heavily pregnant.

Charles Delamere—Isla's father and the head of the Melbourne Victoria Hospital—had given her friend nothing but grief over her older sister's mad dash to England and the reasons behind it. Sean hadn't been far behind in the question department. But according to Isla, she'd promised Isabel that she would never reveal her secret to anyone. Especially not to Sean, since his coming to the hospital nine months ago had been what had sent Isabel running for the door in the first place.

She tried to avoid the other man's gaze as much as possible, until Isla sat up and grabbed her hand. "Would you come with me, since you wanted to know more about the teen mums program?"

Her eyes said it all. She didn't want to be alone with Sean in case he grilled her again about Isabel. Darcie wouldn't have known about any of this except that Isabel's sudden departure had left an opening at both the MMU and in the Delameres' luxurious penthouse flat, which she'd shared with Isla until her friend's marriage to Alessandro.

Darcie had been all too happy to take Isabel's place, since she knew what it was like to run from something. In Darcie's case, it had been the right decision. In Isabel's, she wasn't so sure.

Isla hadn't told her much, but she knew Isabel was keeping something big from Sean. Maybe it was time for her to tell him the truth and see what happened.

But that wasn't her decision to make.

"Of course I'll come with you. It'll give me a chance to meet someone who's in the program."

As Isla threw her a grateful look and slid off the bed, Lucas, who'd been listening to their conversation without a word, wrapped his fingers around Darcie's wrist. "I'll meet you by the entrance after work. This'll give us a chance to discuss some things as well."

Like how she'd somehow managed to leap to the conclusion that his niece was some floozy that kept him out late at night and caused him to have a flippant attitude about work? Heavens, she'd misjudged the man, and she wasn't exactly sure how to make it right. But going to the beach with him was the last venue she would have chosen. For the life of her, though, she couldn't think of a way to get out of it. "If you're sure."

"More than sure." His thumb glided across the inside of her wrist, the touch so light she was almost positive she'd imagined it, if not for the cheeky grin that followed. Then he released her. "Give me a ring when you're done."

"'Kay."

Once out the door, she went with Sean and Isla to the waiting area, her shaking legs and thumping heart threatening to send her to the floor. It took several deep breaths to get hold of herself.

It turned out the expectant mum was there to introduce Isla to a friend of hers—also a teen, also pregnant—who wanted to be included in the teen mums program. Darcie's heart ached over these young women who found themselves facing the unthinkable alone. She glanced at her friend, who greeted the newcomer with a smile, handing her a brochure that explained the enrolment process for TMTB. Darcie might not be able to understand what they went through, but Isla and Isabel understood all too well. Her chest grew tighter as she noticed Sean still standing behind them.

Oh, the tangled webs.

Once the girls were off on their way, Sean stepped forward. Holding up a hand, Isla stopped him in his tracks. "Don't ask, Sean. I can't tell you." She hesitated, and her mouth opened as if she was going to say something else then stopped.

All the heartache with Robert came rushing back, and Darcie realized how much simpler it would have been if he'd told her the truth when he'd first realized he loved someone else, rather than dragging out the process. If he hadn't kept his feelings for Tabitha a secret, maybe things would have been easier on all involved.

That thought propelled her next words.

"Maybe you should call Isabel and ask her yourself," she suggested, grabbing Isla's hand and giving it a quick squeeze of reassurance. She was half-afraid Isla would smack her for sticking her nose where it didn't belong.

Sean's blue eyes swung toward her. "I tried when I heard she was leaving, but she wouldn't take my calls."

Instead of cutting her off, Isla nodded, wrapping her arm around Darcie's as if needing to hold onto something. "Maybe, Sean...maybe you should just go there. If you're standing in front of her, she can't ignore you."

"Go to England?" he asked.

That was a fantastic idea.

Lucas had planted himself in Darcie's path a couple of weeks ago, and she'd been forced to stand there while he'd had his say. Maybe Sean should do the same. Once everything was out in the open, they could decide what to do with the truth. Or at least Isabel would be forced to tell him to his face that she wanted nothing to do with him. Somehow Darcie didn't think that's what the other woman would say when it came down to it. But, whatever happened, it was up to the two of them to hash things out. It wasn't Isla's responsibility, and she shouldn't have to act as intermediary, especially with a baby on the way. The last thing she needed was any added stress.

"I can give you her address, if you promise not to tell her where you got it," Isla added.

"My contract at the hospital *is* almost up." He dragged a hand through his hair, tousling the messy strands even more. "I'll have to think about it."

Isla's chin angled up a fraction of an inch. "I guess it comes down to whether or not you really want to know why she left, or how much you might come to regret it if you never take the chance and ask."

"I'll let you know if I need that address." With that, he strode down the hallway as if the very hounds of hell were hot on his heels.

Darcie sighed. "Do you think he will?"

"I don't know. Maybe the better question would be… if he *should*."

Why had he agreed to take her to the beach?

Lucas paused at the entrance to the car park to roll down the long sleeves of his shirt and button the cuffs against the cool air—or maybe he was gearing up for battle.

Having seen Darcie's face go pink when she'd realized Cora was his niece and not his lover had made something come to life inside him…as had her comment about a love triangle. The fact that she'd envi-

sioned herself with him in that way was so at odds with
how she'd always treated him that her flippant words
had intrigued him. As had the thought of seeing her
outside her own environment. Would the woman he'd
come to view as an English rose—beautiful skin, green
eyes, and a set of thorns that would pierce the toughest
hide—turn into someone different once she stepped off
hospital property?

That was why he'd agreed. If she was going to make
any kind of transformation, he wanted to be there to
see it.

He glanced back inside the hospital as he waited. It
was spring in Melbourne, and the air definitely bore a
hint of that as it had been warmer than usual. Hence
Isla's suggestion of going to one of the beaches hadn't
seemed too crazy. In fact, the temperature was still
holding at almost nineteen degrees, and the sun was just
starting to ease toward the horizon, so they wouldn't
need jackets. Although in Melbourne that could change
at any time.

"Hi, sorry I'm late," Darcie said in a breathless voice
as the automatic doors closed behind her. "I wanted to
grab a cardigan."

She'd done more than that. She'd changed from her
dark trousers and white blouse into a long gauzy white
skirt and a knit turquoise top that crossed over her chest
in a way that drew attention to her full curves. Curves
that made his mouth go dry.

The transformation begins.

He swallowed, trying to rid himself of the sensation.
He'd expected her to let her hair down in a figurative

sense. He hadn't expected to see those soft silky strands grazing the upper edges of her breasts.

That he was still staring at.

Forcing his eyes back to her face, where the color of her shirt made her eyes almost glow, he blinked back to reality. "Don't worry about it. Do you want to take the car or ride the tram?"

"Oh, the tram, please. I haven't ridden it to the beach yet, and it sounds like fun."

When he'd called the house, Chessa had said Felix was home and was grilling burgers on the barbie. When he'd tensely asked the childminder if he seemed "okay" she'd answered yes. For once he appeared clearheaded.

Thank God. The last thing he wanted to do was skip out on his date with Darcie and ruin his reputation with her all over again.

Nope. This was not a date. Something he needed to remember.

"How do you usually get to the beach, then? Taxi?"

She glanced at him as they headed for the nearest tram station. "I haven't actually been yet. I hear they're beautiful."

"You haven't been to any of them?" Shock made him stop and look at her. Isla had mentioned taking her to see some sights, but surely she'd at least visited some of Melbourne's famed beaches.

"Nope. No time. That's why Isla suggested starting there and making a list of some other things."

They started walking again. Hell, she'd been here how long? Nine months? "Well, I'm glad she mentioned it, then. We can get a snack at one of the kiosks if you want. The beaches are prettier in the morning, though."

Maybe he should take her to see the sun rise over the ocean. Those first rays of light spilling onto the water and sand made them flash and glitter as if waking from a deep slumber.

Like him?

Of course not. He wasn't asleep. He was purposeful. Conscious of every move he made and careful to keep his heart far from anything that smacked of affection…or worse. He'd seen firsthand what had happened with Felix and Cora when Melody had died. He never wanted anyone to have to explain to a child of his the things he'd had to explain to his niece. That her father was very sad that her mother had gone away.

You mean she died.

Cora had said the words in her no-nonsense, too-adult-for-her-age manner that made his heart contract.

His niece needed him for who knew how long. He wouldn't do anything that would jeopardize his ability to be there for her.

Especially not for love.

That wasn't true. "Love" was exactly why he'd decided to remain single. He needed to expend all his emotional energy on a little girl who desperately needed a dependable, stable adult. Something that Felix couldn't be. At least not yet.

Buying their tickets, he eased them over to the queue, where a few people waited for the next tram to arrive.

Darcie's soft voice came through above the sound of nearby traffic. "I owe you an apology."

He glanced over in surprise to see her hands clasped in front of her, her eyes staring straight ahead. "For what?"

"For chastising you for being late all those months ago. I thought you were…that Cora was…" She shrugged.

The tram, with its bright splashes of color, pulled to a halt as he processed her words. They both got on and grabbed an overhead strap, since all the seats were full. As they did so, he suddenly saw the whole situation through Darcie's eyes. If she truly had thought his niece was a woman, then all those times he'd come rushing into work after sleeping on his brother's couch had to look pretty damning when viewed through that lens.

He stepped closer to prevent anyone from hearing and leaned down. "I should have explained, but I thought it was—"

"None of my business. And it wasn't. If I had questions, I should have asked you directly."

Whether the reasons had been valid or not, she'd been right in expecting him to be prompt and ready to work when it was time for his assigned shift. "I should have tried harder."

Except that sometimes there'd been no way to do that. He'd had to take Cora to school on mornings that Felix had been recovering from a bender or, worse, when he hadn't come home for the night. There'd been that worry on top of having to care for his niece. There had been days he probably shouldn't have come in to work at all. Except his sense of duty had forced him to march in there—late or not—and do what he'd promised to do.

After a while, though, all those promises had begun to bump into one another and fight for supremacy. His niece had to come first. And he would make no apologies for that.

The tram started up and Darcie lurched into him for a second. He reached out with his free hand to steady her, but she recovered, pulling away quickly and clearing her throat. "Does your niece live with you?"

His grip tightened slightly on the handhold, but he forced his voice to remain light. "She lives with my brother, but I help out with her every once in a while."

That was the understatement of the year. But he loved Cora. He'd give his life for her if he had to.

Sensing she was going to ask another question, he added. "Her mom died of cancer a few years ago."

She glanced up at him. "I'm so sorry, Lucas."

So was he. But that didn't change anything. "Thank you." He braced himself to go around a curve, and Darcie—not anticipating the shift—bumped into him once again. This time the contact sent a jolt of awareness through him. He just prevented himself from anchoring her against him, and instead changed the subject. "So how is it that you haven't seen any of our beaches? As busy as you are, surely you could have managed one side trip."

"It's no fun on my own." She gestured at the sights outside the tram, which were racing by with occasional stops to pick up or let off passengers.

With Isla busy building her own life, Lucas had never stopped to wonder how Darcie was faring now that she had the Delamere flat all to herself. That made him feel even worse. "You should have asked someone at the hospital to go with you."

"It's okay. I understand how busy everyone is."

Their bodies connected once more, and this time he couldn't help but reach out to make sure she didn't stumble or hit the passenger on her other side. She didn't object, instead seeming to lean in to brace her shoulder against his chest. Or that could just be his damned imagination since the contact seemed to be burning a hole through his shirt. Whatever it was, he was in no hurry to let her go again. Except they were nearing the Port Melbourne Beach, which was one of the best locales for a newbie tourist. "Let's get off at this one."

When the tram stopped, he reached for her hand and guided her to the nearest door. Stepping down and waiting for her to do the same, he glanced around. "I want to get a notebook."

"What for?" she asked, brushing her skirt down her hips.

"To make that list Isla mentioned."

She reached into her bag and pulled out a small spiral-bound pad. "I have this if that would work."

"Perfect. We can sit down and put our heads together."

She paused then said, "Oh, um…sure, that would be great. But you really don't have to go with me to see the city."

It was said with such a lack of enthusiasm that he smiled. "I told Isla I would. Besides, I want to. It'll be one way for me make amends."

"Are you sure? If anyone needs to make amends, it's me."

He allowed his smile to grow as he took the notepad from her and headed toward the paved footpath that led to the beach. "You were just trying to avoid that love triangle you mentioned."

Darcie laughed, a low throaty sound that went

straight to his groin and lodged there. "For all I knew, it could have been a love hexagon…or octagon."

"Hmm, that might be a little ambitious even for someone like me."

"Someone who jumps from woman to woman?"

He shook his head. "Nope. I don't jump. I just don't stick around long enough to make any kind of angles—triangular or otherwise."

And if that didn't make him sound like a first-class jerk, he didn't know what did. "That didn't come out exactly right."

"It's okay. I understand. You're just not interested in serious relationships. Same here."

"Really? No serious relationships back in England?"

"Not at the moment."

"So there was someone?" The pull in his groin eased, but a few other muscles tensed in its place. Why did the idea of her being with someone else put him on edge?

"I was engaged. I'm not any more."

Those seven words were somehow more terrible than if she'd gone through a long convoluted explanation about why she and her fiancé had come to their senses and realized they weren't meant to be together. They spoke of heartbreak. And pain.

All the more reason for him to stay out of the dating pool.

"I'm sorry it didn't work out."

"Me too."

So she still loved the guy? She must. What the hell had her fiancé done to her?

He reached down and squeezed her hand, and instead of letting go he held on as they reached the wide footpath that ran along the far edge of the beach where other people strolled, jogged or rolled by on skates or bicycles.

"Wow, it's busy for so late in the afternoon," she said.

"It's a nice day. Do you want to walk in the sand or stick to the path?"

"Definitely the sand. Let me take my shoes off." Stepping to the side and grasping his hand more tightly, she kicked off one sandal and then the other, reaching down to pick them up and tuck them into the colorful tote bag she carried. "Your turn."

He let go of her hand long enough to remove his loafers and peel off his socks, shoving them into his shoes. He then tucked the notebook under his right arm so he could hold his shoes with the same hand.

Once their feet hit the sand their fingers laced back together as if by magic, and Darcie made no move to pull away.

She was a visitor. Alone, essentially, and dealing with a broken engagement. He was offering friendship. Nothing more.

And if she offered to drown her sorrows in his arms?

All the things that had gone soft suddenly headed back in the other direction.

Hell, Lucas, you've got to get a grip.

It might have been better if she'd never shown him her human side. Because it was doing a number on him. Okay, so he could show her some things. Maybe he'd invite Cora along for the ride. He could make sure his niece was being cared for and have a built-in chaperone should his libido decide to put in more appearances.

Darcie stopped halfway to the shoreline, her arm brushing his as she took in the sights around her.

"What's that ship?" She motioned to where the *Spirit* was docked, waiting on its next round of travelers, its large sleek shape a normal part of the landscape here at the beach.

"It carries passengers and vehicles across to Tasmania. Maybe that's first thing we should put on your list."

"Maybe."

Darcie's hair flicked around her face in the breeze from the surf, the long strands looking warm and inviting in the fading rays of the sun. His fingers tightened around his shoes, trying to resist the urge to catch one of the locks to see if it was as silky as it appeared. Good thing both of his hands were occupied at the moment.

"It's lovely here," she murmured.

It was. And he wasn't even looking at the water. Why had he never noticed the way her nose tilted up at the end, or the way her chin had the slightest hint of an indentation? And the scent the wind tossed his way was feminine and mysterious, causing a pulling sensation that grew stronger by the second.

"I agree." He forced his eyes back to the shoreline and started walking again. "Are you hungry? We could grab something and sit on the sand. Then we could start on that list while we eat."

She reached up and pushed her hair off her face with her free hand. "That sounds good. I should have brought an elastic for my hair."

"I like it down."

Green eyes swung to meet his. She blinked a couple of times. "It's not very practical."

"Neither are a lot of things." Why was he suddenly

spewing such nonsense? He motioned to a nearby vendor. "How about here?"

They bought some ice-cream bars and ate them as they strolled a little further down the beach. By the time they'd finished they'd come across an area that wasn't packed with people. "Can we stop?" she asked.

"I didn't think to bring a blanket."

"It's fine." Dropping her shoes and bag onto the soft sand, she sat cross-legged, covering her legs with her skirt. Then she propped her hands behind her hips and lifted her face to the sky. She released a quiet exhalation, a sound that spoke of letting go of tension…along with a hint of contentment.

She was still transforming—losing some of those hard, brittle edges she had at the hospital. Maybe they were simply a result of working long hours with little or no downtime. Because right now she was all soft and mellow, her billowing skirt and bare feet giving her a bohemian, artsy flare he'd never have equated with Dr. Darcie Green. And he liked it. The hair, the pale skin, the casual way she'd settled onto the sand, curved fingers burrowing into it. That firm behind that had bumped against him repeatedly as they'd ridden the tram.

The list! Think about something else. Anything else.

He opened the notebook and riffled through pages of notes from what must have been a medical seminar until he came to a blank sheet. He drew a pen from his shirt pocket. "So what would you like to see or do while in Australia?"

Her eyes blinked open but she didn't look at him. Instead, she stared out at Port Phillip Bay instead. "Mmm. Travel to Tasmania on that ship we saw?"

His pen poised over the paper as she paused for a second.

"Do some shopping. Visit a museum." Her brows knitted together as she thought. "See some of the parks. Go to a zoo."

She glanced his way, maybe noticing he wasn't writing. Because he was still too damn busy looking at her.

He shook himself. "Those are all safe things—things every tourist does. You should have at least one or two things that are a little more dangerous."

"Dangerous?" Her eyes widened just a touch.

"Not dangerous as in getting bitten by a redback but dangerous as in fun. Something you never would have done had you remained in England. Something outrageous and wild." He leaned a little closer. "Something you'll probably never get a chance to do again."

There was silence for a few seconds then her gaze skimmed across his lips and then back up, her cheeks turning a luscious shade of pink.

Oh, hell. He was in deep trouble. Because if the most outrageous thing she could picture doing was pressing her mouth to his... Well, he could top that and add a few things that would knock her socks—and the rest of her clothes—right off.

"What are you thinking?"

She shook her head. "Nothing."

"Darcie." His voice came out low and gruff. "Look at me."

Her face slowly turned back toward him.

"If I write, 'Kiss a non-triangular Aussie' on this list, would you consider that wild and dangerous?"

There was a long pause.

"Yes," she whispered.

His gut spun sideways. He hoped to God he'd heard what he thought he'd heard, because he was not backing away from this. His brain might have come to a standstill, but his body was racing forward at the speed of light.

He set the notebook on the sand, one hand coming up to cup her nape. "Do you want to tick at least one thing off that list before we leave this beach? Because you have a willing member of the male Aussie contingent sitting right next to you."

"You?"

"Me."

He reeled her in a little closer, his senses coming to life when her eyes slowly fluttered shut.

He would take that as a yes.

His body humming with anticipation, Lucas slowly moved in to seal the deal.

CHAPTER FOUR

HE TASTED LIKE ice cream.

Darcie wasn't quite sure how it happened, but that tram ride must have messed with her head, muddled her thinking, because somehow Lucas was kissing her, his mouth sliding over hers in light little passes that never quite went away.

That was good, because once the contact stopped the kiss would be over.

And that was the last thing she wanted.

There were people walking on the path not ten meters behind them, but it was as if she and Lucas were all alone with just the beach and the sound of the surf to keep them company.

His lips left hers, and she despaired, but he was back in less than a second, the angle changing, the pressure increasing just a fraction. Her arms started trembling from holding herself upright, and as if sensing her struggle he eased her down, hand beneath her head until she touched the sand.

The flavor of the kiss changed, going from what she feared might be a quick peck—the thing of friends or family members—to a full-on assault on her senses... a *kiss*.

If he was out to prove that Aussie men were hot-blooded, he'd done that. He'd more than done that. There was a raw quality to Lucas that she didn't understand but which she found she liked. As if he were a man on the edge—struggling to keep things casual but wanting, oh, so much more.

So did she.

Darcie opened her mouth.

The kiss stilled, and she wondered if she'd gone too far or if he was trying to process what to do at this point.

You said wild and dangerous. I'm laying myself open to it so, please, don't make me sorry.

He didn't. His tongue dipped just past her lips, sliding across the edge of her upper teeth before venturing further in. Her nerve endings all came to life at once, nipples tightening, gooseflesh rising on her arms.

Maybe she could tick that item off her list multiple times…right here, right now.

She wound her arms around his neck, reveling in the sense of urgency she now felt in his kiss. His free hand went to her waist and tightened on it, his thumb brushing across her ribs in a long slow stroke.

Then he withdrew, pulling back until he was an inch from her mouth.

"Damn." His curse brushed across her lips, but he didn't sound angry. Not like he had when he'd seen the rotation schedule. More like surprised.

He sat up, using the hand behind her head to help her up as well. "We'd better start actually making that list or it's never going to get done."

Who cared about some stupid list?

His jotting things down, though, gave her a chance to

compose herself. Well, a little. Because nothing could
have prepared her for that kiss. Not her relationship with
Robert or any of her past dating experiences.

Lucas was... She wasn't sure what he was. But he
was good.

She glanced over at the sheet of paper where he'd
made a list of about ten things. "Kiss an Aussie" was
first on the list, but the tick mark he'd made beside it
was now scratched through.

"I thought we were going to cross that off."

The look he gave her was completely serious. "We
can't tick something off a list that didn't exist at the
time it happened."

"We can't?"

"No." His eyes went dark with intent. "Because if you
want to experience a real Aussie kiss, it has to be behind
closed doors—with no audience to distract you."

Distracted? Who'd been distracted? Certainly not her.

But if he wanted to kiss her again—like that—she
was more than willing to play along.

He scrawled a couple more words.

"Hey, wait a minute. I never said I wanted to bungee jump."

"Dangerous, remember?"

"But—"

"I have a friend who used to have a bungee-jumping
business. He closed it last year but still lets friends take
a dive from time to time. And I promised Cora—my
niece," he reminded her with a smile, "that she could
come out and watch me do a jump."

It was her turn to be surprised. "You bungee jump?"

"I have to get my adrenaline pumping somehow, since I don't have any love triangles to keep me busy."

That was something she didn't even want to think about, because she might end up volunteering if she wasn't careful.

She wouldn't mind meeting his niece, though. And it wasn't like *she* had to jump.

"Okay, I'll go. But I don't promise I'm going to do anything but watch."

"Oh, no, gorgeous, you're going to do a whole lot more than that. I promise."

Why had he invited her on his and Cora's day out?

Because he'd been too strung out on kissing her two days ago to think clearly when he'd written that item on her so-called list. She and Cora had been chatting the whole trip, with Darcie twisted around in her seat in order to talk to her. Why couldn't Cora have hated her on sight?

But she hadn't. And her "Are you Uncle Luke's girlfriend?" had turned Darcie's face the color of pink fairy floss. She hadn't freaked out, though. She'd simply shaken her head and said that she was just a friend.

Huh. He couldn't remember any friends kissing him the way she had.

And it had shocked the hell out of him. Prim and proper Darcie Green had something burning just beneath the surface of those cool English features. He had the singe marks on his brain to prove it.

As they stood on the edge of the tower suspended over a deep pool of water, Cora bounced up and down with excitement but Darcie looked nervous. "You don't have to do this, you know," he murmured.

"Are you sure it's safe? What if…?" She nodded toward Cora.

He understood. What if something happened in front of his niece? And maybe it hadn't been the smartest thing to bring her up here to watch. But she'd been begging to watch him do one of his jumps for a while now.

"Max Laurel is an engineer and a friend." He glanced over at where a stick-straight figure was adjusting some fittings. "He has his PhD in physics. I trust him. And at a hundred feet the tower isn't very high. Even if the bungee-cord snaps, there's a safety line. If that fails as well, I'll just go into the water."

He gave her a quick smile. "Like I told you earlier, he only does it for friends, he's not open to the public any more."

"What happens when you finish the jump?"

"Max will lower me the rest of the way into the water, and I'll undo the cables and swim to the side." He understood her nerves, but compared to what had happened between them back at the beach this felt pretty tame. No way was he about to admit that to her, though.

Neither was he planning on being the Aussie she checked off her list, despite his words to that effect.

Strung out on kisses.

Yep, there was no better way to put it than that. But it had to stop now. Because he had a feeling things could get out of hand really quickly with Darcie for some reason. And not just for him. She'd just come out of a bad relationship and he didn't want her to get the idea that anything serious could come of them being tossed together at work and for a few outside excursions. He had enough on his plate with Felix and Cora to risk complicating his life any further.

"You ready, Luke?" his friend asked.

"I am. Can you hold on just a minute?"

Going down on his haunches in front of his niece, he put his hands on her shoulders. "Are you sure you're okay with this? I don't want you to be scared."

"No way! As soon as I'm old enough, I'm going to do it too."

Lucas had told her she had to wait until she was eighteen before attempting it. He wanted to make sure her bones and joints were strong enough to take the combination of her weight and the additional force that came from the jump. He smiled at her bravado, though. "Then let's get this show on the road."

"Darcie is going to jump too, isn't she?"

He glanced up at the woman in question. "Depends on how brave she's feeling."

"I'm only feeling half-brave. Is that enough?"

The fact that she was here, at the top of the tower, said she was more than that. She could have backed out of the trip altogether and he wouldn't have stopped her. But here she was. "More than enough."

"I'll cheer you on," promised Cora. "I wish Daddy had come, though."

Lucas hadn't told Darcie why he helped so much with his niece, and he was glad to keep it that way. For Felix's sake.

His brother was supposed to be seeing his counsellor today. Lucas could only hope he was keeping his word. His behavior the other day seemed to have snapped him back to awareness. Then again, they'd been down that same road a couple of times.

So he settled for a half-truth. "I'm sure he'll come next time. He had some things he needed to do today."

When he glanced at Darcie a slight pucker formed between her brows before it smoothed away again.

Did she suspect things weren't quite right in the Elliot household? Time to shift her attention.

"Okay, Max, are you ready for me?"

"Just about."

The next several minutes were spent attaching a thick cable to his ankles and an additional safety line to a harness that went around his torso. If something happened to the first elastic band the second one was meant to catch him. He'd done this at least twenty times with no ill-effects. Then again, he'd never had his niece and a woman watching him go over the side. Something inside him poked at him to show off for Darcie—do a spectacular swan dive or something, but that was out of the question. Safety had to come first when it came to Cora.

He moved into position, and Max checked everything once again and then gave him the thumbs-up sign. Lucas counted to three in his head and then…

Over!

He catapulted out into the air, gravity pulling him into a smooth arc as he began his downward trajectory.

The wind whistled in his ears, and he thought he might have heard Cora shout, but it was all lost in the exhilaration of the jump. Although, as the elastic began to grab and slow his descent, he wondered if even this could top that kiss he'd shared with Darcie.

Damn.

The bungee yanked him halfway back up before letting him fall again. But the closer he got to the end of his jump, the more irritated he became. This had once filled his senses like nothing else ever could. And where he'd been happy to share it with her a couple of days ago, he was now not so sure that he'd done the right thing.

His bouncing halted, but unfortunately his wavering thoughts kept right on careening up and down, the whine of the motor as Max slowly lowered him down to the water failing to drown them out for once. Then he hit the pool and let his buoyancy carry him back to the surface, where he unhooked himself from the bungees and ankle straps, and did a slow side crawl to the edge of the pool.

He looked up and saw two faces looking down at him. One filled with an elation he recognized from years of seeing that same expression. One filled with uncertainty, as if the woman he'd known for less than a year had sensed what had been in his head as he'd done the dive.

This was not her fault. It was his own damn exhaustion and worry about Felix catching up with him. It had to be that. It couldn't be that Darcie had somehow struck a chord inside him that was still reverberating two days later.

If it was…then somehow he had to figure out a way to silence whatever she'd started.

Lucas was in the water at the far side of the pool. Waiting for her to jump so he could help her unfasten the bungees. Max told her he'd set the tension so that she wouldn't drop as far as Lucas had before it caught her up. Then the winch would let out the line until she slid into the water. Piece of cake.

Easy for him to say. Lucas hadn't come up to give her a pep talk or anything. He'd remained at the bottom, radioing up from a walkie-talkie on the side of the pool that he'd stay down and help Darcie.

Maybe it was just as well that he hadn't come back up because everything on her body was trembling. Even her hair follicles seemed to be vibrating in terror. She wasn't afraid of heights, but something about jumping and hoping an elastic cord would somehow stop her from hurtling headfirst into the water was a scary prospect.

"You can do it, Darcie." Cora's cheerful voice broke into her thoughts.

Not willing to let the girl see how scared she was, she pasted on a smile she hoped looked halfway real. "You'll be okay up here?"

"Oh, yeah. I'm going to take pictures of you as you go over."

Perfect. Just what she needed. For this moment to be recorded for all to see. She would have to find a discreet way to ask Max not to put it up on his wall of fame. Where Lucas's image appeared in several different sets of swim trunks his face was always filled with that same look of exultation, eyes closed as if taking in every second of the jump.

Speaking of jumps, she'd better go before someone got tired of waiting and pushed her over. "Okay, Cora. Count to three, and I'll jump."

"Woo-hoo!" The child yelled down to Lucas. "Get ready, here she comes. One...two...*three*!"

Darcie held her arms out from her sides and jumped as far away from the tower as she could, just as Max had instructed her. The fabric buckles of the ankle harness were where her every thought was centered right now, and she squeezed her eyes shut tight. She fell... and fell. Suddenly, she felt a firm tug that turned her so she was facing the water—at least she assumed so since she still couldn't bring herself to look. A squeal left her throat before she could stop it as she bounced several times, still with her head pointed straight down. Then she came to a halt.

Hanging. Upside down. In midair. Just like a bat.

She chanced a glance down and saw that Lucas was there, right below her. The sight of him made her pounding heart calm slightly as a mechanical hum sounded from the tower above her. Slowly, she started moving downward at a steady rate. Coming closer and closer to those familiar features.

His arms stretched up as she came within reach and he put a hand around her shoulders, keeping her from plunging headlong into the water. Her body made a curve before his other arm wrapped around her hips. He went under, still holding her. That's when she realized he was treading water and her weight was sending him down. She struggled to free herself, kicking with her legs to keep from drowning the man.

But he didn't come back up. Instead, she felt his hands on one of her ankles, and she stopped paddling to let him undo the carabiner that attached the bungee cord to her legs. She sank beneath the surface and opened her eyes. There he was, fingers undoing the shank that held her ankles together, before moving further up to unclasp the static safety line at her waist.

His eyes were open as well, and they looked into hers. He reached out to finger a strand of her hair that floated between them, making her exhale a stream of bubbles. Then he leaned forward and gave her a quick kiss before grabbing her hands and dragging her upward. A good thing, because suddenly she'd forgotten that she needed to breathe.

Once at the surface she dragged in a couple of ragged breaths while Lucas kept his arm around her waist and waited while she composed herself and prayed for her nerves to settle down just a bit.

"You did it."

"I can hardly believe I jumped." The elation was slow to kick in, but it was there now that she knew she was safely at ground level again.

"I can hardly believe it either." Lucas smiled and leaned in close to her ear. "Well, it looks like you got your first tick mark, Dr. Green. Congratulations."

Since she'd just jumped off a tower into the water, she assumed he was talking about the bungee-jumping item on the list they'd made together.

Which meant he wasn't counting that quick kiss in the water as having completed that other item on her list.

Because he was still waiting on the behind-closed-doors part to happen?

Oh, Lord. And she'd thought bungee-jumping was dangerous. It was tame compared to what her head conjured up.

The prospect of being with Lucas in a quiet, nonpublic place had to qualify as wild and outrageous, right? Because right now she couldn't imagine a scarier prospect than finding herself back in his arms.

CHAPTER FIVE

CORA WAS ASLEEP.

Glancing in the rearview mirror on the way back to the house, a shard of concern worked its way through his chest. He hadn't realized until after he'd helped Darcie from the pool that his niece had been taking pictures of their jumps. He wasn't quite sure what she'd been able to see from the tower, but he hoped that impulsive peck on the lips had been safely hidden beneath the water.

Why had he done that anyway? Kissed her. Again.

Because as he'd seen her sail toward him at the end of that bungee cord she had been so different from the person he'd imagined Darcie Green to be for the last nine and a half months. She'd seemed as free as a bird, tethered only by those safety cords. He'd halfway thought she'd back out of it once the time came. She hadn't.

He was happy for her in a way that was alien to him. And unsettling.

Maybe he should get some things straight with her. Only he didn't want to do that in front of his niece in case she wasn't really asleep.

"Do you mind if we drop Cora off first?"

"Of course not. But I can take a taxi if you want to just drop me off at the hospital."

"Your flat is on the way back, so it's not a problem. You're still at the Delamere place, right?" He'd been to the luxurious penthouse flat for a few parties thrown by Isla and Isabel.

"Yes, I'm there. Are you sure you don't mind?"

"Not at all." He glanced over at her, noting she'd gone back to her prim way of sitting with her hands clasped in her lap. "Did you have fun today?"

After he'd done a couple more jumps—Darcie demurring that once had been more than enough—they'd put on some dry clothes and had then had lunch with Max. That's when Cora had mentioned getting dozens of pictures and that she couldn't wait to show them to him and Darcie.

Showing them to him was one thing. But Darcie?

He was going to preview them first before that happened.

"I did, actually." Her eyes flicked to his and then back to the road in front of them. "I'll probably never get a chance to do anything like that again. Please, tell your friend thank you."

Darcie had already told him multiple times. In fact, she'd seemed to hang on his friend's every word during lunch. He'd been glad in a way, but watching her laugh over something Max had said had also caused a dark squirming of his innards he wouldn't quite call jealousy but it was something he didn't recognize. And didn't like.

"I noticed you exchanged social media information so you can do that."

She frowned and threw him a sharp glance. "Should I not have? He was the one who initiated it."

Yes, he had. And the last thing he wanted was to risk Max's friendship over a woman who would be gone in a couple of months.

He settled for saying the first thing that came to mind. "Max's a nice guy. He doesn't have a lot of experience with women."

Oh, and that sounded awful. Darcie evidently agreed because a dark flush came to her cheeks. "I think it would be better to let me off at the hospital, if you don't mind."

Prim. Uptight. Formal. All things he associated with the Darcie of three months ago. Not the warm, open woman who'd accompanied him today.

He took his hand off the wheel and covered her twined fingers. "I didn't mean that as a cut, Darce. I know you wouldn't do anything to lead him on." Why he'd felt the need to shorten her name all of a sudden he had no idea. But he liked it. Liked the way it rolled off his tongue with ease.

Another reason it would be good to talk to her. Because she was a nice girl. Just like he'd talked about Max being a nice guy. He didn't want to do anything to lead *her* on. And those two kisses they'd shared could have definitely made her think things were headed down the wrong path.

Weren't they?

Absolutely not.

"You're right. I wouldn't lead him—or anyone else—on, or make them think things that weren't true."

The words were said with such conviction that Lucas

glanced at her again and made an educated guess. "Your ex?"

"Yes." She paused for a moment. "Let's just say it's made me careful about how I interact with men."

Wow. Had that been part of those angry sparks that had lit up the maternity ward whenever he'd had dealings with her? He wasn't sure. But one thing he did know, he didn't want to go back to those days.

So maybe he should just cool the warning-her-off speech he'd planned. Wasn't he assuming a lot in thinking she was going to fall all over him because of his two lapses in judgment? Wasn't he being an egotistical jerk to think he was that irresistible?

Good thing the drive over to Felix's house gave him time to think before he did something else stupid.

Speaking of his brother's house… They were nearing the street. He put his hand back on the gear lever and downshifted as he turned at the corner. Five houses went by and they'd arrived.

Once in the driveway, he motioned for Darcie to wait while he got Cora out of the backseat. Unbuckling his niece and easing her from the car, he swung her up into his arms. She peered out of one eye then flicked it shut again.

"Cora, have you been pretending to sleep this whole time?"

"No." The word was mumbled, but there were guilty overtones to it.

Perfect. Good thing he'd decided not to tackle heavier subjects while driving.

And his comment about Max, and practically holding her hand a few minutes ago? Hopefully Cora's eyes had been pasted shut and had missed that.

But knowing his niece…

He gave an inner groan, his mind going back to the camera dangling on a cord around her neck.

Nothing he could do about that at the moment except take her inside and hope she forgot all about it by tomorrow morning.

The first thing he heard when he opened the door was a loud belch from somewhere inside.

Oh, hell. Not now.

He turned to Darcie. "Do you mind waiting here for a minute? I'll be right out."

Proving his point about his niece feigning sleep, her eyes popped open. "Oh, no. She has to come in. I want to take her back to see my room." She held up her camera. "We can look at the pictures I took on my computer."

"Luke? Is that you?" His brother's voice came from the living room, keeping him from commenting on Cora's suggestion. "I've been wondering when you were going to get home."

Felix *sounded* sober. Whether he was or not was another matter. "Yes, it's us."

Stepping in front of Darcie so he could enter first had nothing to do with being rude and everything to do with scoping out the situation. Cora was used to it—in fact, his niece had turned into a mother figure for her broken parent. But it was getting to the point where Lucas was going to have to intervene and take drastic action.

Again.

He set Cora on her feet but held her hand as they

made their way to the living room, Darcie just behind him. There his brother sat in a recliner, staring at the television. Lucas glanced at the floor beside the chair. There was no sign of beer…or any other alcoholic beverage, for that matter. Could he have heard them come home and got rid of it? That burp had sounded pretty damning.

"Hey, girlie, come over here and give Daddy a hug."

Cora rushed over to her father and threw herself into his arms. That's when Lucas noticed the picture. The one of Felix, Cora and Melody taken in this very living room shortly after their daughter's birth. It was on the end table next to Felix and not in its normal spot on the fireplace mantel.

And when his brother's eyes met his they were red-rimmed.

He was drunk…maybe not from alcohol but from the deep grief that he refused to let go of. He held onto it as tightly as he did his liquor.

Damn. Don't do this now, Felix.

Unaware of what was going on, Darcie shifted next to him. His brain hummed as he tried to figure out a way to get her out of there without her realizing something was very wrong. Cora slid from her father's arms and hurried back to Darcie with a smile. "Come see my room."

Darcie's gaze took in Felix and then Lucas, as he stood there, jaw tight, fingers itching to curl into fists at his sides. He forced them to stay still instead. "Sure," she said to the little girl. "Let's go."

The pair trailed off down the hallway, while Lucas stared at his brother. "Have you been drinking?"

"Only one." He reached behind his back and pulled out an empty beer bottle. At least, Lucas hoped it had been empty before he'd secreted it behind him. "Something happened to the rest of them."

Lucas thought he'd dumped all the bottles. Evidently not. "Did you hide this one?"

"Yep." His brother waggled his head. "Good thing, too. Someone must have drunk all the rest of them. I think Chessa might have a drinking problem. Maybe we should fire her."

The childminder wasn't the one with a problem. It was his brother, in all his bitter glory.

"I dumped them. She didn't drink them."

"What?" His brother got to his feet, gripping the bottle in his fist. "You've got no right, Luke."

His voice went up ominously, causing Lucas to glance down the hall where Cora's door was wide open.

"Don't do this, Felix." He kept his own tone low and measured, hoping to lead by example.

"Don't *you* do this." Felix bit out the words. "You have no idea what it's like to lose someone important to you."

Yes, he did. He was watching it happen right before his eyes. Felix was a shell of the man he'd once been. A sad, drunken shell.

He decided to divert the subject if he could. He didn't want Cora or Darcie to hear his brother at his worst—or listen to the tears that would inevitably follow one of his tirades. "Are you taking your medication? You're not supposed to drink with it."

"I'm not."

Lucas wasn't sure if he meant he wasn't taking his

medication or if he wasn't drinking. But since he was now shifting that bottle from one hand to the other, he would have to assume it was the latter. That he was off his antidepressants.

He took another quick look down the hallway then held his hand out for the beer bottle.

His brother surprisingly handed it over without an argument, probably because it was empty. He went over to the recycling bin and tossed it inside, hearing the clink as it landed on other bottles—hopefully the ones Lucas had emptied the other day.

When he went back he knew what he was going to say. "I love you, Felix, and I was hoping I'd never have to say this, but if you can't get your act together, Cora's going to have to come live with me for a while."

His brother shook his head, eyes wide. "You wouldn't take her from me. She's all I have left."

"I don't want to. But I can't leave her here to watch you spiral back down, not when you've worked so hard over the last several months."

Felix sank into his chair. "I know. I need to pull it together, but…" He glanced at the picture of his wife.

With a sigh, Lucas took the picture and put it back in its spot on the mantelpiece just as Cora and Darcie came back into the room.

Darcie's face was pink and her glance went from him to Felix. Her hair was a riot of curls from their day at Max's and the sea air. It framed her face in a way that made his breath catch in his lungs. Lucas glanced at the group of pictures on the ledge over the fireplace.

Was this how his brother had started down that dark

road? An initial attraction that had turned into an obsession that refused to let go, even after Melody's death?

Hell if he knew, but if that's the way it worked, he didn't even want to stop and glance at that road.

Hadn't he already? With both those kisses?

His jaw tightened and he glared at his brother. "Are you going to be okay tonight?"

"Yeah." Except Felix wouldn't quite meet his eyes. "Cora and I are going to be just fine. I've got big plans for us. Pizza and a movie. That one with all the singing and ice and snowmen."

His niece squealed. "I love that movie. You have to sing with me this time, Dad!"

"Yep, we're going to sing." He threw Lucas a defiant glare that dared him to argue with him.

He wouldn't, and his brother knew it. Not right now. But he would soon if Felix couldn't get back on track.

And if he had to take Cora away? What then for Felix?

That was one thing he didn't even want to think about. All he knew was that there came a time when the needs of his niece had to take precedence. And that time was drawing closer every day.

Darcie hadn't slept well. She wasn't sure if it was from looking at those pictures of her and Lucas frolicking in the pool or from the memories of him helping her take her restraints off.

That had to be it, because she certainly hadn't had a lot of restraint when it came to the man. And she needed some. Desperately. At least Cora hadn't captured that kiss they'd shared in the water.

She breathed a prayer of thanks.

Dressing quickly, she scowled at the dark circles beneath her eyes that told a tale of a long, hard night. There'd been those pictures, yes. But there'd also been something about Lucas's brother. He'd seemed just a little "off."

Not that she could pinpoint what made her think that. Cora had seemed happy enough when she'd interacted with him.

Maybe it was her coworker's behavior that had set her on edge and not Felix's.

Lucas had been tight-lipped the whole time he'd talked to his brother, and when she'd been in Cora's room, staring at those damning images, she'd thought she'd heard one of them raise his voice. She wasn't sure who it had been, though.

And it completely obliterated her view of Lucas as a self-indulgent playboy. His face had been deadly serious as he'd faced off with his brother. Were there hard feelings between the pair?

If so, he'd said nothing about it on the way back to her flat. And when she'd invited him up, he'd refused, saying he had an early morning. Well, so did she.

Another thing that had skewed her image of him. What man in his right mind would give up an opportunity to get into a woman's flat and into her pants?

Certainly not the Lucas she thought she knew.

Then again, she'd thought Cora was a full-grown woman back then. She didn't remember hearing Lucas talk about any other women over the months she'd known him. If anything, it was the other way around. Women talked about him. Wore false eyelashes for him. Threw themselves at him.

He hadn't taken the bait once that she knew of.

Maybe he's just not interested in you, dummy. He could have an unspoken rule about dating co-workers.

And kissing them? Did he have a rule against that too?

Not that she could tell. And she knew of at least a couple of the female species who would kill to have been in her shoes on either of those occasions.

Dwelling on this would get her nowhere. She tossed down the last of her tea with a sigh and went to finish dressing. At this rate, it was going to be one very long, depressing day.

Darcie made it to the maternity ward and signed in with just minutes to spare. Her eyes automatically tracked to the sign-in sheet, looking for Lucas's name. The space was blank. Strange. He wasn't here yet.

After all that blubbering about having an early day today? Irritation marched into her belly and kicked at its sides a couple of times. Maybe she'd been wrong after all. Maybe he did take the bait from time to time…just not when she was the one dangling it.

Fine. She wasn't going to wait around for him to check in.

Even as she thought it, she stood there and brooded some more, while the clock crept to three minutes past the hour, and the second hand began its downward arc, reminding her of Lucas's bungee jump yesterday. And, like yesterday, he was headed straight for the bottom… of her respect.

He was officially late. Again.

What was with the man? He never seemed irresponsible when you talked to him. But his actions? Another story.

Even as she thought it, Lucas came skidding around the corner, hair in glorious disarray, face sporting a dark layer of stubble. He took one glance at her and then took the pen and signed in. Five minutes late. Not enough to throw a fit about but he'd obviously not been home.

"Where were you?"

He flicked a glance her way then one brow went up in that familiar nonchalant manner that made her molars grind. "Keeping tabs on me, are you?"

She wanted to hurl at him, "You're late, and I want an explanation!" She wanted something other than his normal flippant response—the one that went along with the MMU's view of him: a charming playboy who took nothing seriously.

He'd diagnosed Margie Terrington, though, when she hadn't.

Because everyone in Victoria knew what redback bite symptoms were.

Except her.

"No, of course not. I just…" For some reason she couldn't get the words out of her mouth, not while tears hovered around the periphery of her heart.

She would not beg him for an explanation. Or ask him to reassure her that he wasn't this rumpled couldn't-care-less man who stood before her, as delicious as he looked.

He stepped closer. "I know I'm late. And I'm going to be later still once I go back and shower. But I'll make it quick." His jaw tightened. "All I can do, Darcie, is say I'm sorry."

Still not an answer. But at least all that glib cheekiness was gone.

She glanced at the patient board. "It's still quiet. I'll let Isla know you're here and that she can go home."

"Thanks." Warm fingers slid across her cheek and his glance dipped to her mouth before coming back up to her face.

Heat flashed up her spine. He wouldn't. Not here at work.

Before she could pull back—or remain locked in place, which was what her body wanted her to do—he withdrew his hand and took a step back.

"It would help me a lot if you didn't go all pink every time you saw me—peace treaty or not, a man's only got so much willpower."

"I don't go pink!" Even as she said it, heat flamed up her neck and pooled in her cheeks, proving her a liar. It also broke the bubble of anger that had gathered around her.

Lucas laughed and tapped her nose. "Like I said…" He let the sentence trail away and then headed for the locker area, dragging both hands through his hair and whistling as he went.

Whistling!

Passing him in the hallway, Isla turned to glance at his retreating back before her eyes came to meet hers. Warmth again flooded her face as her friend drew near. "Well, I see he got here." She looked closer. "Why are you so red?"

"I—I…" What could she say, except deny it again?

"Oh, God. You two aren't…" Isla lowered her voice

"…doing it, are you? I know I suggested he take you to the beach, but—"

Darcie reared back. "Of course not," she said in a loud whisper.

"Then why does the man look like he just rolled out of someone's bed? And why are we whispering? There's no one around."

Darcie cleared her throat and walked to the nurses' station. "We're whispering because I don't want any ugly rumors floating around about my personal life."

"Personal life?" Isla rubbed her belly. "You actually have one?"

The words might have stung had they not come from her friend. But Isla was right. "No. Can you blame me?"

Tessa came from a room with a chart in hand. She'd evidently overheard the last part of Darcie's declaration because she said, "You need to get out there and live it up a bit. Melbourne has some awesome nightclubs. Maybe we could make it a group outing."

"I don't know…"

Isla took up the cry. "Yes! You have to go at least once. I can't believe I didn't take you."

"You were kind of busy, remember?" An understatement if there ever was one.

Her friend laughed, hand still on her burgeoning stomach. "Maybe just a little. But, seriously, you can't leave Australia without seeing at least a little of the nightlife."

The three of them were still joking about it when Lucas appeared less than ten minutes later. Wow, the man was fast, she'd give him that. His hair was damp from his shower and he'd changed into fresh clothes.

"What are we talking about, ladies?"

"Oh…nothing." Even as she said it the slow flush rose in her face like clockwork. One side of his mouth lifted but, thank God, he said nothing about it this time.

Isla nudged her. "Darcie hasn't been to any of the nightspots. None. Zip. Can you believe it?"

"It seems there's quite a lot she hasn't experienced yet."

Lucas said it with a totally straight face, but she glanced sharply at him.

Tessa cocked her head, drumming her short fingernails on the counter. "Maybe I can get a group together to go to the Night Owl tonight. They have brilliant music and dancing. How does that sound, Darcie?"

"Well, I…" She didn't dance if she could help it. Another thing that had worn thin with Robert, who had loved it.

"If Darcie's going to make a checklist of things to do while in Australia, that should definitely go on it."

Great, just what she needed, to have him remind her of his challenge—that she pick things that were outside her comfort zone. Clubbing was definitely one of those. Not that any of them had suggested making the rounds and getting drunk.

She tried one last time. "I have to work tomorrow."

Lucas parried with, "We'll watch our step and make sure you're not arrested."

"Arrested!"

Isla put a hand on her arm. "He's kidding. You should go, Darcie. Especially since Lucas seems to be offering his services as a bouncer. You know, in case a thousand guys start hitting on you. I, unfortunately, am not allowed to have any fun for another month or so, even if Alessi would agree to let me go."

Darcie snuck a glance at Lucas, who didn't look at all put out with the idea of tagging along.

The nurse picked up a chart with a grin. "I have to go back to work now, unlike some of you. I'll ask around and whoever wants to come can meet up at the entrance of the hospital at eight, okay? Wear something sparkly."

And with that, Tessa and Lucas both walked away without giving her a chance to refuse. And the hunky midwife had left without actually confirming that he would be there—protecting her from unwanted advances.

Unfortunately, if he did come, Darcie had no idea who was going to save her from him—or from herself.

CHAPTER SIX

SHE'D WORN SOMETHING SPARKLY. And green. And clingy as hell.

That dress was probably banned in ten countries. There was nothing vulgar about it, but the neckline scooped far enough down that a hint of creamy curves peeked over the top of it. And it was snug around her hips and the sweet curve of her backside, exposing an endless length of bare leg. He'd been trying not to stare as the group of them had taken off from the hospital and headed toward the railway station. But, holy hell, it was hard.

"Did you go shopping?" Because he just couldn't see Darcie pulling something like this out of her wardrobe. Not that he was complaining. No, he was salivating. And thinking about all the men at that club who were going to see her in this dress was doing a number on his gut.

"No. Isla loaned it to me. I didn't bring anything suitable for a night on the town."

Suitable. That was one word for it. What it was suitable for was the question. Because in his mind he could see himself peeling the thing down her shoulders and right past all those sexy curves. They might just get arrested after all.

Why had he agreed to come again?

Oh, yes. To ward off any unwanted advances. If that was the case, he was going to have his hands full. Because he might end up having to fight off his own advances if he couldn't get his damned libido under control. Right now it was raging and growling and doing all it could to edge closer to this woman.

Thank God, the train ride was a short one. And there were seats this time, instead of having to stand and have her bump against him repeatedly. Within another few minutes they arrived at the Night Owl, a club frequented by young professionals looking to let their hair down.

The second the doors opened the music hit him between the eyes. Loud, with a driving beat, blast after blast of sound pumped out into the night air. Despite his cocky words earlier in the day, Lucas had not gone to a club since his early days at medical school. Life had been too hectic, and after Melody had died he just hadn't had much else on his mind except his brother and Cora.

Ten people in all had come with them. The rest of the group went in, but when Darcie started to pass through the door she backed up as if changing her mind, only to crash into his chest. Her backside nestled against him for a split second before she jerked away again.

His internal systems immediately went haywire.

That decided it. He wanted to be here. With her. For whatever reason.

Maybe it was just to escape the highs and lows that had become a normal part of life these last years. He'd enjoyed the bungee-jumping trip far too much. He was ready to repeat the energetic day. But in all-adult company this time. The club would do that and more.

Strangely, the noise would insulate them, keep their words from being overheard by those around them.

When she again hesitated he leaned down. "It's okay, Darce. I'm right here with you."

There was that short version of her name again, sliding right past his lips like it belonged there. He didn't know why that kept happening, but it did the trick. She stepped through the door. And as if he'd fallen down the rabbit hole in that old children's book, the inside of the club morphed into something from another place and time.

Darkness bathed the occupants, except for brief snatches of light that flooded his pupils. The extremes made it hard to focus on anything for more than a second at a time so bodies became puppets, moving in jolts and jerks as if controlled by outside forces. The sensation was surreal. Anything that happened in the club tonight would take on a dreamlike quality: had it happened, or hadn't it? Maybe that was for the best.

Tessa came back and grabbed Darcie by the arm, dragging her away and making a drinking motion with her hand, since it was probably impossible for her to yell above the noise.

When had it become noise? At one time in his life he would have been yelling for the DJ to turn the sound up. Not any more. He squinted, trying to see where the group from the hospital had gone. When he trained his eyes to capture the second-long flashes emitted by the strobe he could just make out the dim overhead lights of the bar at the far side of the room. At least those weren't blinking on and off.

A few minutes later he was there, squeezed between Darcie and some guy on her left—who shot him a look that could only be described as a glare. The man picked up his drink and moved on to another woman a few seats away. Tessa laughed and saluted him with her drink, while the glass in front of Darcie contained something that looked fruity and cold, with plenty of crushed ice—and probably a shot of something strong. The bartender came over with a quizzical lift of his brows.

"Just a lemonade," he yelled above the music.

Darcie threw him a wide-eyed glance. "I thought we were supposed to be living dangerously."

"I still have to get you home in one piece, so it's better for me to play it safe. At least for tonight." Lucas had had enough of Felix's drinking problems to last a lifetime. Except for that swig of beer he'd taken in his brother's kitchen, he hadn't touched the stuff in almost two years.

Some of their party had broken off into pairs and were already out on the dance floor—he squinted again—if that could be called dancing. The body parts moved, but they were disjointed...staccato. Although maybe that had to do with the lights blinking on and off.

Darcie put her straw to her mouth and took a sip of her drink then stirred the concoction while glancing around at the nightclub. The Night Owl was living up to its name, although it seemed a little early for the die-hard crowd. How much more packed could the place get?

"Are these kinds of things big in Australia?" she shouted.

This was ridiculous. They were both going to be hoarse by the time they got to work tomorrow if they kept this up. He drew her closer and leaned down to her ear. "I'm not a big nightclub person."

She tilted back to look at him then moved back in. "You bungee jump, but you don't go out drinking with the guys?"

Her warm breath washed across his ear, carrying the scent of her drink. Strawberries. Or mangoes. Okay, so maybe this wasn't going to be the disaster he was imagining because he liked having her close like this.

The guy from the seat next to him had evidently struck out with woman number two, because he was back. Bodily inserting himself between the two of them and turning his back to Lucas.

"Dance?"

He couldn't blame the guy. Darcie was beautiful. But if anyone was going to dance with her, it was going to be him.

Standing, he poked the intruder in the shoulder to get his attention. The man—a body-builder type with bulges and lumps that bordered on unnatural—didn't budge. So Lucas moved out and around until he was facing the competition.

Darcie was already shaking her head to the offer. Instead of taking the hint, the jerk held out his hand.

Lucas stared him straight in the eye. "She's with me, mate. So try somewhere else." Taking her hand, he said, "Come on, gorgeous. Bring your drink."

She grabbed her glass and went along with him, throwing the other man an apologetic look. What the hell? Had she wanted to dance with him?

This time it was Lucas who hesitated. He stopped and glanced down at her.

"Here, try some," she said, holding her beverage up to him. "It's really good."

As much as he did not want to try some girly-girl drink, he noted the creep from the bar was still glowering their way. Probably hoping to corner her alone. To send another message, he took the glass from her and sipped from the straw…and made a face. He couldn't help it. That wasn't a drink. That was some kind of smoothie or something. But the act of putting his mouth where her lips had been—where they had applied suction and…

He took another sip. A bigger one this time and let it wash down his throat. Not so bad the second time around.

Handing it back to her, he towed her further out onto the floor, where dark forms kicked and flapped and buckled, only to come up for more. It reminded him more of a fight scene from a movie than actual dancing.

Flashes of green from her eyes met his. "I'm not much of a dancer."

There was something about the way she said it. As if she expected him to be upset. Hardly.

She couldn't be any worse than what was going on around him. "Let's pretend the music is slow and not worry about what everyone else is doing." He'd had to swoop in again to be heard. "Can you dance with your glass in your hand?"

"No. Help me finish it." She took another drink, the contents of the large goblet dropping a quarter of an inch, then held it out to him again.

He was going to pay for this later, when the memories came back to haunt him in his sleep. But he drank anyway. Relished the slight taste of her on the straw.

When the glass was empty he motioned for her to wait and then deposited it on the nearest table, ignoring the surprised looks from its occupants. Then he strode back to Darcie and took her right hand in his, his other arm settling across her hips and pulling her close. When his attention swept the bar for the man who'd hit on her, he didn't see him. Good. Because tonight there would be no cutting in.

Darcie was all his. At least for a few hours.

If Cora didn't call.

Closing his eyes and settling her against him, he allowed his senses to absorb the feel of her curves, the scent of her hair and the way it slid like fine silk beneath his chin.

He tuned out the music…and tuned in Darcie instead. Only then did he allow his feet to sway, taking quarter-inch steps and allowing his inner rhythm to take over. Her arm crept up, her hand splaying across the skin on the back of his neck, fingers pushing into the hair at his nape.

Decadent.

Isla was right. There were some things that just shouldn't be missed. And dancing with Darcie was one of them.

She shifted against him with a sigh. "This is much better than what they're doing."

"Who?" His eyes cracked open, letting the chaotic scene back into his head.

"Everyone. I don't normally like to dance. But this feels okay."

"Yes, it does."

The song ended and the room paused for three or four seconds, while Lucas cursed silently. Then, as if the universe had read his mind, another song came on. This was slow and soothing and not quite as loud. The atmosphere shifted. The strobe went off in favor of dim, steady lighting.

Arms twined together and single dancers edged off the floor to let the couples have a turn.

"Is this better?" he murmured into her ear.

"Mmm, yes."

Lucas's hand tightened on her back, thumb skimming up her spine and drawing his palm along with it until it was between her shoulder blades, before gliding back down to her waist.

Hell, this was nice. Maybe a little too nice.

Darcie must have sensed it too because the fingertips that were against the lower part of his scalp brushed back and forth, sending a frisson of raw sensation arrowing down to his groin.

He willed away the rush of need that followed, trying to think about anything else but the pulsing that was beginning to make itself known in not-so-subtle ways.

Football. Kayaking. Hiking.

He dragged various activities through his head and forced his brain to come up with five important items about each one, before moving on to the next. Anything to keep from having to step back a pace or two in order to hide her effect on him.

Because he didn't want to go. Not until this song was over and done. And maybe not even then.

There. Things were subsiding. Slowly. But as long as she didn't…

Her fingertips dragged downward, emerging from his hair and sliding sideways across the bare skin of his neck.

"Darce, are you trying to make me crazy?" Because if he didn't say something, she was going to end up with one hell of a surprise.

Her cheek moved away from his chest and she glanced up at him. "I wasn't trying to. Why, am I succeeding?"

Something about the way she'd said that. As if surprised. Or curious. Or a whole lot of things. None of them good because it just stirred him to say more stupid things. They'd all agreed to leave separately, so they could each decide when they'd had enough. But no way was he letting Darcie leave there on her own.

"Yes." He let that one word speak for him, because it was true.

"So I can cross this off my list, right?"

"Driving me crazy?"

"No." She gave a soft laugh. "I was talking about coming to a nightclub."

His brows went up, and he realized without that godawful strobe light he could finally see her without the additional shock on his senses. Being this close to her was as heady as laying her down on the sand at the beach had been. "I thought you might be angling to finally cross something else off your list."

Her tongue came out, moistening that full lower lip. "What's that?"

She was going to make him say it, wasn't she? "Kissing an Aussie."

"But I thought you said that had to be behind closed doors in order to count." The breathiness of her response made him smile.

"It does. But that can be arranged."

Her fingers at the back of his neck tightened, and her eyes closed for a second.

Was she going to turn him down? His body started to groan and swear at him for screwing this up. Maybe he should limit it to just the kiss. But, hell, he didn't want just a kiss. He wanted to carry her down some dark hallway and toss her on a bed…expose every luscious inch of her. And *then* kiss her.

When her eyelids parted again she gave a nod. "Then yes. But only if it's a wild and outrageous kiss."

He couldn't resist. He leaned down and nipped the jawline next to her ear. "Trust me. I can make that happen."

The song ended, and Lucas realized he and Darcie were no longer dancing. In fact, they were just standing there in each other's arms, staring at each other.

"Let's go back to Isla's flat."

"What?" He pulled back, thinking he'd surely misunderstood. He wanted to be alone with her, not visit Isla and Alessandro.

She laughed, unwinding her arm from around his neck and grabbing his hand as she made her way off the dance floor. "I mean the Delamere flat, where I'm staying. Alone."

That was more like it. Besides, that end of town was closer than his own place. And his barely furnished flat left little to be desired as far as what she was probably used to. "That sounds like a plan. Lead on."

Darcie was somehow able to find her keys in the tiny glittery purse that she'd slung over her shoulder as they'd left the Night Owl and arrived at the large opulent building Charles Delamere owned. She punched the code into the box by the front door and heard the click as it unlocked. She'd seen it so many times the place didn't even register any more, but with Lucas standing there behind her she suddenly felt self-conscious as they made their way across the marble foyer.

"You've been here before, right?" She didn't want him to get the idea that she was rich or anything. But she'd never thought anything less of Isla for living here, so why would she think Lucas was any different?

Maybe because it mattered what he thought, and she wasn't quite sure why.

"I have. Isla liked to entertain, so I've been here several times."

Entertain. As in a group? Or just Lucas? "Oh, um…"

"We were never involved," he murmured, as if sensing her thoughts.

"Oh, I didn't think—"

"Didn't you? You thought I might be involved with a whole horde of females at one time."

She had. And when had she moved so far away from that initial opinion she'd held of him? Maybe when she'd met Cora and seen how much he cared about his niece. And maybe—when she put all those phone calls into context—they'd become sweet. Whatever it was, she no longer believed many of the things she'd once thought.

"People change," she murmured.

His hand tightened on hers for a second and his footsteps faltered.

Had she said something wrong?

"Yes, they do."

They stopped in front of the lift and Darcie punched the button to call it. Lucas leaned a shoulder against the wall next to her and studied her face, a slight frown between his brows. Right on cue, heat surged into her cheeks.

His mood seemed to clear and he smiled. "I don't think I've ever seen a woman blush as much as you do."

"I can't help it. It's just the way I'm made."

His eyes skimmed down the rest of her, pausing at the neckline of Isla's slinky dress. "I'm kind of partial to the way you're made."

Her face grew even hotter and he chuckled. Then the lift arrived, saving her from having to respond to his comment.

They both got on, and Darcie nodded at the camera tucked into the corner of the lift, hoping he'd understand her meaning.

He did, because he leaned down, his warm breath washing over her cheek. "Don't worry, gorgeous. I don't want an audience this time. Although later…"

When her eyes widened, his hand went to her lower back, fingertips skimming up her spine until he reached her nape. One finger made tiny circles there beneath the curtain of her hair. Pure need spiraled through her as he added a second finger, the pair trailing down and

around the back of her dress, which was scooped like
the front of it was. To the camera, it would appear as
if they were both just standing quietly, but inside her
chest her heart was jumping and things were heating up.

A fine layer of perspiration broke out on her upper
lip as she struggled not to close her eyes or utter the soft
sounds that were bubbling up in her throat. Was there
a microphone connected to that camera?

Up, up they went, racing toward the penthouse while
Darcie's legs turned to jelly, and the need to touch him
back began growing in her chest. In her belly. In her
hands.

She curled her fingers into her palms to keep them
from reaching for him.

"Do you like that?" he whispered.

Was he joking? Couldn't he tell? She glanced at their
reflection in the mirror across from them and noted
her nipples were puckered, showing even through the
fabric of her strapless bra and her dress, although both
were thin.

Ping.

The lift slowed, and Lucas stopped stroking her neck,
his warm hand wrapping around her nape instead. When
the doors opened, she practically fell out onto the dark
glossy floor of the entrance to the flat. Hands shaking,
she tried to hit the lock with her key and missed the first
time, only to have Lucas's fingers cover hers and guide
them to the keyhole, unlocking and opening the door in
one smooth movement.

They went inside. "D-do you want a tour?"

"Mmm...yes, but not of the flat." He took the keys

from her hand and the purse from her shoulder and put them both on the slate surface of the entry table.

Her teeth dug into her lower lip as Lucas came back and put his hands on her shoulders, thumbs edging just beneath the fabric covering them. This was a man who bungee-jumped and practically made love to her on an open beach. Who teased and tormented her senses on the dance floor and again in the lift. He didn't want a feeble tour or a half-hearted response from whatever woman he was with.

Robert's face as Tabitha had thrown herself into his arms was branded in her mind. That was what her ex-fiancé had wanted. Not a mild-mannered woman who was far too "safe."

Was Lucas going to find her wanting as well? Would he regret having put all this effort into getting her into bed?

That brought up another question. Was that why he'd done everything he had…the trip to the beach, the list, the nightclub? To sleep with her? Her insecurities grew.

She had no illusions that this was anything but a one-night stand. She'd made it clear that she didn't want anything more than that either. But maybe she should make it clear that she probably wasn't as wildly experienced as some of the women he'd been with.

"I—I'm not…" She licked her lips as Lucas went still. "I'm probably not very good at…" Her voice died away a second time, so she had to use her hand to made swirly motions in the air and hope he got the gist of her meaning.

He tightened his grip on her shoulders slightly. "Please, tell me you're not a virgin."

"No!" The denial came out as a squeak, so she cleared her throat. "My fiancé just found me a bit…dull in that respect."

Lucas didn't move for several seconds, but a muscle pulsing in his cheek made her squirm. Was he wondering how to get out of the flat without hurting her feelings?

"You don't have to stay if you don't want to." There. She'd given him a way to escape.

He shook his head. "I'm not planning on going anywhere, unless you decide to throw me out." He then gave a smile that could only be described as rueful. "My experience with you has been anything but dull."

She remembered his curse when he'd seen her name on that rotation list. Actually, she had been more outspoken with him than she was with most people. But only because he'd irritated her with his attitude and his tardiness. Okay, so maybe she wasn't dull at work. But here? "I'm not very adventurous."

He leaned down and gave her a slow kiss. One that started off soft and easy and gradually built…his hand sliding into her hair and gathering the strands in his fist. When he pulled back again she was breathless and right back to where she'd been in the lift—melting with desire and wanting nothing more than for him to drag her down those three steps to the living area and take her right there on the couch.

"Then you won't mind if I'm adventurous enough for both of us."

The pressure of being someone she wasn't lifted. She could do that. She could let Lucas call the shots and introduce her to things she'd never tried before—

just like he had standing on that high tower, and again after she'd landed in the pool.

This man lit her senses up like no one ever had. "No. I won't mind."

"Well, then." He began bunching her dress in his fists, gathering more and more material in them until the hemline was at the very tops of her thighs. "We won't need this." Up and over her head went the dress, which had no zipper, the stretchy material allowing him to strip it off her body with ease. He turned and carried the garment across the space, going lightly down the steps and placing it over one of the leather chairs in the living room.

When she started to follow him, he held up his hand to signal her to wait. He slowly made his way back up, his eyes on her the whole time. "You're beautiful, Darce. I don't know what your ex told you, but 'dull' is not a word I would ever use to describe you."

He reached for her hands as a warm flush crept up her body. It only increased when he carried her hands behind her back and moved in to kiss her again. This one slow and lingering, his lips brushing across hers, the friction driving her crazy. "Where's your bedroom, sweetheart?"

"Down the hall. First door to the right."

"Down the hall we go, then." Before she could move he released her hands and swept her into his arms as if she weighed nothing.

He arrived at her room and edged her through the door, stopping for a second as if to take in the space. Although she was sleeping in Isabel's old room, she'd boxed up the other woman's mementos and substituted a few things she'd brought with her. But other than that the space was devoid of a lot of personal items other than the bed and dresser. There were built-ins that were still almost empty.

Walking over to the queen-size bed that had her wondering if it would hold Lucas's frame, he glanced down at her, eyes unreadable. "You never planned on sticking around, did you?"

She was surprised by the question. Everyone at the hospital knew she was only here for a year. After that she'd be leaving. Had he expected her to fill the room with stuff, only to have to get rid of it all a few short months later? And that's what it was looking like at this point: a few short months. Her time in Australia had flown by. Much quicker than she'd thought it would. But it had done what she'd intended it to do—erased the pain of Robert and Tabitha's betrayal. "You knew I was only here for a year."

His muscles relaxed, as if she'd given the correct response. Except she didn't know what the real question was. That he didn't want her to stick around, because of the conflict that had flared between them periodically? Or that he was making sure she wasn't going to place any more importance on tonight than he planned to? He didn't have to worry on that account. She'd already bought her return ticket months ago, right after their first big blow-up.

She blinked up at him. "Are you sure you want to stay?"

"You keep asking me that as if you hope I'll change my mind." He dropped her on the bed and then followed her down. "I won't."

She wound her arms around his neck. "Well, okay, then. As long as we're both clear on what happens on the other side, we should be good."

"Let's worry about right now. And then we can deal with the other stuff tomorrow." With that, his mouth came down, blotting out everything except for the fact that this was exactly where Darcie wanted to be. In this man's arms.

CHAPTER SEVEN

HE WAS GOING to make this a night she would remember.

Not because he was that good but because her words had picked at a sore spot within him. No, he didn't want any permanent relationships, but he was stung by how easy she seemed to think it would be to walk away from him. An idiotic response, considering his own attitude, but he'd never been a rational man when it came to Darcie.

Her bra had no straps to peel down so he settled for following the course of an imaginary strap with his fingers, making sure his short nails kept light contact with her skin as they made their way across her shoulders.

Her reaction was to arch a few centimeters off the silk duvet cover. His flesh reacted in kind. Arching up and away from his body, only to be stopped by the fabric of his dress trousers. That would soon be remedied. But not quite yet.

He continued down her arms, going past the crook of her elbows and only stopping when he reached her wrists, which he caught up in both of his hands. He carried them over her head and rested them there, catching sight of bright green eyes as they stared at his face. He wanted her hands out of the way for what he did next.

Her lips were parted and glossy from his kisses, so he leaned in for another quick taste, glorying in the way they clung to his and followed him up an inch or two as he moved away. He gave a pained laugh.

Dull? Hell, her ex was an idiot. This woman was responsive, giving, and sexy as they came. She hadn't put any limits on their time together. When he'd said he was going to be adventurous enough for both of them, her glance had heated instantly.

Which brought him back to his point. He wanted to make this good. Wanted to leave her with no doubt that she was exciting and desirable. Not just to him but to plenty of other men. He'd caught Max's glances at her during the bungee jump. And the guy at the bar? Oh, he'd been interested all right. The thought made his blood pressure shoot up, just as it had at the Night Owl.

Hooking one of his legs between hers, he edged her thighs apart, keeping his foot just behind her ankle in case she was tempted to squeeze them shut again. She didn't even try. That in itself made Lucas's flesh surge, putting up some new demands. He was willing to oblige some of them...but others would have to wait.

He let his fingers slide over the sweet curves peeking just above her bra. Her skin was smooth and incredibly soft. He wanted more. Keeping his leg between hers, he reached beneath her body and searched for the clasp. Found it. Flicked it open.

He then dropped the garment over the side of the bed, and drank in the view before him.

Heavenly. In every way.

Her nipples were drawn up tight—pink and perfect.

Darcie's eyes were open now. She made no move to cover herself with her hands, although her breathing ratcheted up a notch.

That was as far as he got before he could stand it no longer. He leaned down and tasted her, drawing one peak into his mouth and letting his tongue wander over it.

She moaned and arched higher, pushing herself into his touch.

Yes. This was what he needed. He applied more pressure, using her response as a gauge for how much friction she wanted from him.

Hell if she didn't ask him to up the ante even more. When his teeth scraped over her, her hands came down on his head, but instead of pulling him away her fingers buried themselves in his hair and she pushed hard against him.

He came up panting, body raging, wanting to end it all right here, right now. Instead, he let his mouth cover hers, tongue plunging inside again and again, while she maintained her grip on his hair.

Pulling away in a rush, he ripped her undies down and found her hot and wet and ready. He kissed her once again, letting his index finger sink deep into her. Just like he was about to. He got off the bed.

"Do. Not. Move." He growled the words, stripping in record time, letting the sight of her flushed body drive him to action—to find the condom and rip into it, sheathing himself.

Then he was back with her, over her. Finding her. Sliding home to a place where pleasure and madness fought for supremacy.

He set up a slow, easy rhythm that was all for her, ignoring his own wants and needs.

"Lucas." His name was whispered. Shaky. A silent plea he couldn't ignore.

"I'm here, gorgeous." He edged out and then pushed deep.

Darcie responded with a long drawn-out moan, lifting her hips, her hands going to his shoulders and holding on.

Kissing and licking the length of her neck, he allowed her tight heat to wash over him in a wave, careful to hang onto whatever control he still had. He wanted this to last.

And that surprised him.

He usually saw to his partner's pleasure first and then concentrated on his own. He had it down to a science almost. But here he was, breaking his own rules. She hadn't climaxed. And he didn't want her to. Not yet. He wanted to lose himself when she did—wanted to watch the exact second she came apart. He could only do that if he knew when...

He rolled over, carrying her with him until she was on top, straddling his hips. Her eyes jerked open, and she looked at him uncertainly.

"You set the pace, Darcie. Do what feels good to you."

While I watch.

She hesitated for a second then her instincts seemed to take over. She braced her hands on his thighs, just behind her butt and lifted up and came back down as if seeing how it felt. Then her eyes fluttered shut, teeth digging into her bottom lip as she moved over him a second time. Then a third. Again and again, she lowered herself onto him and rose back up. His own personal angel, set on propelling them both toward paradise.

Until Lucas began to ache from holding back.

It was time.

Pressing his palm against her lower belly, he allowed his thumb to find that sensitive place between her thighs. Her head went back, little whimpers coming from her throat and spilling into the air around him. Sexy sounds. Earthy and full of need.

Her movements grew jerky, hands tightening on his thighs.

"Yes, sweetheart, that's it," he gritted. "Let it all go."

With that, Darcie's whole body stiffened, her insides flaring for a split second before clamping down hard on his erection and exploding into a series of spasms that rocked his world, that made him grab her hips and pump wildly, washing her orgasm down with his own. He poured every emotion he had into the act, until there was nothing left.

And yet he was still full. Full of Darcie. Full of those luscious aftershocks that had him pulling her down hard onto him, eyes closed as he absorbed all of it and more.

When he looked up again her eyes were open. Looking at him. A trembling question in those bright green depths.

She had doubts?

He drew her down until she was lying across his chest, her face nestled against his neck. "You okay?"

"Mmm-hmm." A hesitation. "You?"

"Perfect. Absolutely perfect." He leaned down and

kissed the top of her head. "And you're about to cross one thing off your list."

"The kiss?"

He should say yes. End it once and for all. It would be on a good note. One they could both smile about years from now. But he didn't want to. Not with his body already beginning to reset itself. So he said instead, "Not yet. I'll tell you when."

With that he rolled her back beneath him and pressed his mouth to hers.

Darcie had been walking around in a daze.

Beginning with the moment she'd woken up in an empty bed. For some reason, she'd thought Lucas would wake her to say goodbye if he decided to leave. He hadn't. But after the second lovemaking session she'd been exhausted. And replete. And something about going to sleep with his arm anchoring her close to his body had given her a sense of comfort she hadn't felt in a long time.

How long had he stayed once she'd drifted off? A few minutes? An hour?

The only thing that had made her smile—since she'd been squirming with embarrassment over some of her actions—had been that Lucas had ticked the "kiss a non-triangular Aussie" box and drawn an arrow out to a smiley face. *A smiley face*. She'd never known a man to use one before.

And the fact that he'd rolled out of her bed and actually felt like smiling made a lump come to her throat. She'd assumed with Robert it had been her problem... that he'd been rejecting her. Maybe he'd been rejecting them as a couple. Because although Lucas had used the word "uptight" when he'd grumbled about that roster, he hadn't given any indication last night that he still found her that way.

Instead, he'd smiled.

She kept twisting that fact round and round in her head. It had to have meant he was as satisfied as she was, right?

Grabbing the clipboard for her next patient, she glanced at the name. Margie Terrington, their redback bite patient. She glanced at her mobile phone, wondering if she should call Lucas in to join her for the consultation, but she was leery. She hadn't actually spoken to him yet today. Why ruin her mood before she had to?

She pushed through the door, only to stop short. Lucas was already in the room. But, then, why was the chart…?

He glanced at her with an undecipherable expression. "I thought you might eventually make it to work today."

Eventually make it? She'd been twenty minutes early, just like most days. Which meant he'd been…

Even earlier.

The very corners of his mouth went up, making her heart lift along with them, but she was careful not to let on to her patient that Lucas was teasing her. "I did indeed." She greeted Margie and flipped through her chart, asking a few questions.

Lucas sat and listened to the back and forth for a minute or two before asking his own question. "Any problems from the antivenin?"

"None." The expectant mum rubbed her belly. "I

can't thank you both enough for figuring out what was wrong."

"Thank Lucas, he was the one who realized you'd been bitten."

The young woman shuddered. "My husband tore the rest of the house apart to make sure there weren't any more of them."

They finished checking her over, letting her listen to the baby's heartbeat to reassure her that all was indeed well after the scare the previous week. "Did your mum come to Australia? With your husband working, I know it'll be a great help to have her here. We could all use a little support." As Darcie well knew from her parents' support after what Robert had done.

They'd been thrilled that she'd been able to go to Australia to get away from everything that had happened. She'd barely prevented her dad from punching her ex-fiancé right in the nose. But she'd grabbed his arm at the last moment. Everyone had parted semiamicably. And the only heart that had been broken that day had been hers. She'd been left in the wedding chapel all alone after everyone had left—her mum seeing to all the last-minute explanations and canceling the venue for the honeymoon.

"Yes, she arrived just a few days ago," Margie said. "She already loves it here. And, yes, we could all use the support of family. After our other…loss…I wondered if I would ever be happy again. I thought I'd never get over it."

Lucas stood with a suddenness that made both women look at him. He glanced at Darcie and then away, muttering that he needed to check on another patient.

She frowned.

That look wasn't anything that resembled a smiley face. And she had no idea who that "other patient" could be because there wasn't anyone listed on the schedule board for another hour. There were a couple of patients in rooms, and she'd noticed one poor woman was curled on her side, sucking down nitrous oxide with a rather desperate air, but they all had other midwives attending them. After saying goodbye to Margie, she went into the hallway and glanced down the corridor, but there was no sign of him. Darcie had hoped to talk to him about how they were going to treat last night.

Already one of the other nurses had cornered her and asked why she'd left the nightclub so early. She'd feigned a headache and said she'd caught the train back to her flat. Not a total lie. But she certainly wasn't going to tell anyone she'd dragged Lucas home with her. She couldn't even bring herself to admit all they'd done together, much less admit it to anyone else. It would be much better if they had some kind of joint cover story to hand out to anyone who asked. Present a united front, as it were.

Even if they weren't united.

Oh, well. Stepping outside the hospital to get a breath of fresh air, she heard her name being called. Not by Lucas but by a child. Darcie swung round in time to see Cora and her dad coming toward them on the footpath. Cora broke into a run and gave her a fierce hug as soon as she reached her, Felix trailing along behind. When he finally caught up he looked a bit shamefaced and maybe even a little shaken up. "Do you know where my brother is?"

"I don't. We just finished up with a patient, though, so he's here somewhere." Darcie didn't want to admit that she had no idea where he'd gone or why. Her stomach was beginning to do a slow dive to the bottom of her abdominal cavity, though.

"I can stay here with Darcie, Dad. She won't mind, will you?"

Felix scratched the back of his neck. "I don't know, Cora. I think we should just go home."

"But you can't! You promised me, and you promised Uncle Luke." Cora's voice came across shrill and upset.

If anything, her father looked even more unsure. "I know, but Chessa is sick and I'm not leaving you home alone."

Darcie didn't have any idea what was going on, but whatever it was sounded important, judging from Cora's overly bright eyes. Tears? Looking to defuse the situation, she said, "Why don't I try to reach his mobile and see where he is?"

But when she tried to do that, the phone went right to voicemail. Strange. Unless he had it off so he wouldn't have to talk to her. His behavior in Margie's room had set her alarm bells ringing earlier. And now this. Her stomach dropped even further. She settled for leaving a message. "Hello, Lucas, it's Darcie." Why she felt compelled to explain who she was when he would know from the caller ID was beyond her. She went on, "Felix and Cora are here at the south entrance. Would you mind stopping round if you get this within the next few minutes?"

She pressed the disconnect button, only to have Cora tell her, "We tried to ring him too, but he didn't answer."

That didn't sound like Lucas. He doted on his niece. "I could keep her here with me for a while. I have an office where she could hang out until Lucas turns up."

A look of profound gratitude went through Felix's eyes. "Are you sure it's no trouble? I have an appointment and our childminder is ill."

"It's fine. Leave it to me." She took Cora by the hand. "We'll get on famously until then."

Felix looked uncertain for all of five seconds then he nodded. "Okay, I appreciate it."

"Bye, Daddy," Cora said. "Maybe Uncle Luke can drive me home and get me an ice lolly on the way."

Darcie's heart twisted. So much for hoping he might want to come home with her. Again.

What? Are you insane?

Evidently, because her mind had, in fact, already traveled down that path and was trying to figure out a way to make it come true.

Giving Felix her mobile number and waving him off with what she hoped was a cheerful toss of her head, she made her way back inside the hospital, Cora following close behind.

Once in her office, the little girl found a pull-apart model of a baby in a pregnant belly that Darcie kept to show her patients. She'd forgotten it was on her desk when she'd offered to bring Cora here. "I'm not sure your dad would want you looking at that."

"Oh, I know all about how babies are born. Uncle Luke's a midwife. I have to know."

Darcie couldn't stop the smile. "You do, do you? And why is that?"

"Because I'm going to be a midwife too. Did you know that Uncle Luke helped my mum have me? She couldn't make it to a hospital."

No, she hadn't known, because Lucas hadn't talked about anything personal, she realized. In fact, he knew some pretty intimate stuff about her, while she knew almost nothing about him. Like whether or not his parents were still alive. Or why he'd gone into midwifery in the first place.

Because it was none of her business.

Careful not to pump the girl for information, she settled for a noncommittal response that she hoped would end the conversation.

It didn't. "Mummy died of cancer."

That she *did* know. "I'm sorry, Cora."

"I don't remember much about her. But I do remember she always smelled nice...like chocolate biscuits."

Darcie swallowed hard, forcing down the growing lump in her throat. What would it be like to lose your mother at such a tender age? Her own mum was still her very best friend and confidante. She decided to change the subject once and for all, since neither Felix nor Lucas would appreciate knowing her and Cora's chat had revealed old heartaches. "Speaking of biscuits, Cora, would you like to go down to the café and see if they have something good to eat? I'll just let the nurses know where I'll be."

"Yay!" Cora grabbed her hand and tugged her toward the door. "Does the coffee shop have espresso, do you think?"

She gave the little girl a sharp glance, not sure if she was joking or not. "How about we both stick with hot chocolate?"

"Even better. Daddy sometimes forgets to buy the chocolate powder."

"Then hot chocolate we shall have."

Fifteen minutes later they were in the cafeteria at a table, with Cora imitating the way Darcie drank her chocolate. It made Darcie smile. She could see why Lucas was so very fond of her. The girl was exuberant and full of life, despite the tragedy she'd suffered at such a young age. Then again, children were resilient, a characteristic she often wished was carried into adulthood.

The buzzer on her phone went off and when she looked at the screen her eyes widened. Lucas. He must have got her message. She answered, forcing herself to speak cheerfully, even though her heart was cranking out signals of panic. "Hi."

"May I ask where you are, and why my niece is with you? You're not in your office."

"I…uh…" Oh, God, it hadn't been her imagination in Margie's room. He *was* upset with her for some reason. Only she had no idea why or what she could have done. "We're in the cafeteria. Felix said he tried to ring you, but you didn't answer."

That was really the crux of the matter. Why Lucas had failed to answer anyone's calls.

"I forgot to charge my battery after…" He paused, then forged ahead, "I got home. I had to get the extra charger from my vehicle in the car park."

Oh, well, that answered the question about where he'd gone and why he hadn't picked up his mobile. It didn't answer why he was acting the way he was. "Okay. Well, Felix said the childminder is ill and he had an appointment to keep. He asked if I could watch Cora for a few minutes."

Had Felix not left him a message, like she had?

"I'll be right down to get her."

She tried to smooth things over. "Why don't you join us instead? We're drinking hot chocolate and eating biscuits."

He mumbled something under his breath that she couldn't hear before he came back with, "One of us should stay on the ward."

It was a slow morning and there were several other midwives on duty. Surely he didn't mind sharing her break time?

She simply said, though, "Whatever you think is best. I'll see you when you get here." Then she disconnected before he could say anything else. The last thing she wanted to do was get into an argument with him just when she thought they'd turned a corner.

Turned a corner? Sleeping with him was so much more than that.

Was that what this was all about? Did he suddenly regret what they'd done? Or was he just afraid she was going to become clingy and expect something from him he wasn't willing to give?

She suddenly felt like a fool. Played with and then discarded, like she would have expected him to do with other women. And why *not* her? She was no better than anyone else. Certainly not in Lucas's eyes.

"Darcie, are you okay?" Cora's worried voice broke into her thoughts.

She forced a smile, picking up her hot chocolate and taking a sip of the now-tepid liquid. "Fine. Your uncle is on his way down to have tea with you."

"Shall we order him something, do you think?"

"Oh, I think he can manage that on his own." Another quick smile that made her feel like a total fraud. "And once he gets here I need to get back to work. I have patients that need attending to."

"Can't you stay a little while longer? I know Uncle Luke would want you to."

No, actually he wouldn't. But there was no way she was going to say that to a little girl. "Sorry, love, I wish I could."

The second Lucas arrived Darcie popped up from the table. "See, here she is all safe and sound."

His eyes searched hers for a moment, and she thought she caught a hint of regret in their depths. "I had no doubt she was safe with you."

His hand came out as if to catch her wrist, but Darcie took a step back, going over to Cora and leaning down to kiss the top of her head. "I'm off. Have fun with your uncle."

Then, without a backward glance, she made her way

out of the café, wishing she could grind the last fort-
night of their rotation into dust and sweep it into the
nearest bin.

CHAPTER EIGHT

LUCAS FOUND HER just outside the Teen Mums-to-Be room.

Isla had the door to the tiny conference room open, and she and Darcie were discussing ways to promote the program and give it more visibility. When Isla's eyes settled on him, however, they widened slightly. "I think someone wants to talk to you."

Darcie glanced back, and then her chin popped up, eyes sparkling. "May I help you with something, Mr. Elliot?"

Her sudden formality struck him right between the eyes. He wasn't the only who noticed. Isla looked from one to the other then murmured that she would see Darcie later and left, quietly closing the door behind her.

He'd cursed himself up one side and down the other for the way he'd spoken to Darcie on the phone yesterday. Margie talking about her miscarriage and wondering if she'd ever be happy again had scrubbed at a raw spot inside him that just wouldn't go away. Because he'd wondered the same thing about his brother time and time again—whether he'd ever be happy again, or if he'd simply wander the same worn paths for the rest of his life or, worse, destroy himself and damage Cora in the process. Love and loss seemed to go hand in hand.

But that had been no reason to take it out on Darcie.

Better make this good, mate.

"I wanted to apologize for being short with you yesterday."

"No need. I should have simply asked your brother to take Cora home when he couldn't reach you, appointment or no appointment. I didn't realize you were so against me spending time with her." Her lips pressed together in a straight line.

She was angry.

And gorgeous. Especially now.

He'd settled Cora in his office yesterday while Felix had gone to his therapy session, and between him and the nurses they'd taken turns keeping her occupied. Every time he'd checked in on her she'd chattered nonstop about Darcie. She'd loaded the pictures from their time at Max's bungee-jumping tower onto his computer. One of those shots had taken his breath away. It had been taken just after he'd unhooked her carabiners, just after he'd kissed her. She'd broken through the surface of the water at the same time as he had, brown hair streaming down her back, fingers clutching his.

And their eyes had been locked on each other. He could only hope none of the nurses had seen the picture.

But in that moment he'd realized why he was so against Darcie and Cora spending time together. Because Darcie was too easy to love. Much like Melody had been.

Cora had already grown attached to the obstetrician. That fact made his chest ache. She'd lost her mother, and very possibly her father. This was one little girl who didn't deserve to experience any more hurt. And she would if he wasn't careful. Because Darcie would be leaving the country. Soon.

He'd tried to apologize to her yesterday, but by the time his brother had come to pick Cora up, Darcie had been flooded with patients and unable to stop and talk. At least, that's what she said. And when their shift had ended, she'd left immediately.

"No, you did the right thing," he said. "I was upset with myself for not getting those calls and leaving you to deal with the whole mess." A partial truth. But if his mobile phone had been charged, he could have avoided all of this.

"Mess?"

Damn, he wasn't explaining himself very well. "Things with my brother are complicated at the moment, and I was worried."

Darcie's brows puckered, but she didn't ask what the complications were. "It was no problem. Cora and I get on quite well."

"Yes, I've noticed."

If he were smart he'd have let things continue the way they had yesterday—with Darcie put out with him—until their rotation ended. But the note of hurt in her voice, when he'd demanded to know where Cora was, had punctured something deep inside. He'd found he just couldn't let her think the worst of him.

Which was why he was here.

She glanced at the door Isla had closed, probably planning her escape. So Lucas blurted out, "Which thing on your list were you thinking of tackling next?"

He'd made a promise. He couldn't very well renege on it, could he? Yes, he damn well could. He was just choosing not to.

"I hadn't given it much thought today."

He should have said goodbye when he'd woken up in her bed, but he'd been too damned shocked to do anything but throw his clothes on and get out of there. He rarely spent the night at a woman's flat, most of the time leaving soon after the physical act was completed. Because the aftermath always felt uncomfortable. Intimate. And holding a woman for hours after having sex with her? Well, that was something a husband or boyfriend did. Lucas didn't want either of those titles attached to his name.

But he didn't want to hurt anyone unnecessarily either. Especially one who'd already been treated badly by someone else. One he'd promised wouldn't have to accomplish her to-do-while-in-Australia list on her own.

Besides, he'd promised Isla as well.

"How about the pier? We could walk along it tonight, see the moon shining on the water." It had been on the tip of his tongue to suggest a trip to the dock where his sailboat was moored, but he had the same internal rule about that as he did about spending the whole night with a woman. He didn't do it.

"That wasn't on my list."

He offered her a smile. "Maybe lists were made to be changed—added to."

She stared up at him for a long second. "Maybe they were. Okay, Lucas. The pier. Tonight."

Relief swept over him, not only because he wasn't breaking his promise to show her the sights—and the pier at night was one of his favorites—but that she was back to calling him by his first name. He liked the sound of it on her lips.

Especially in that breathy little voice that—

Back to business, Lucas.

"Okay, then, do you want to meet after our shift?"

"Sounds perfect."

Just as Darcie reached for the door handle of the teen mums' room, Tristan Hamilton, MMU's neonatal cardiothoracic surgeon, came sprinting down the hallway. "Flick's in labor."

Isla pushed the door from the other side, making it known that the rooms were not soundproof. "Are you sure?"

Tristan dragged shaky fingers through his hair. "I'm sure. So is she. She knows the signs."

"It's still early." Lucas said what everyone was probably thinking. Heavily pregnant, Tristan's wife had already been through a lot. So had Tristan. The baby had inherited his father's heart defect—a defect that had required Tristan to undergo a heart transplant when he'd been younger. Thankfully, a specialized team had done surgery on the baby in utero a few weeks ago, repairing the faulty organ and inserting a stent, but the baby was still recovering. The fact that Flick had gone into labor wasn't a good sign. It could mean the baby was in distress. A complication from surgery?

He glanced at Darcie, who nodded. "We're on our way."

Isla, the worry evident on her face, said, "I'll come too."

"No." Darcie moved closer and squeezed the other

woman's hand. "You're needed here. We'll keep you up to date on what's happening."

"Promise?" Lucas noted Isla's hand had gone to the bulge of her own stomach in a protective gesture he recognized.

"I promise."

Then the trio was off, Tristan leading the pack, while Darcie and Lucas followed behind. Once back on the ward, it was obvious which room Flick was in by the bevy of nurses rushing in and out.

The second they entered the space, Flick—already in a hospital gown—cast a terrified glance their way. "They're coming faster, Tristan. Every two minutes now."

While her husband went to hold her hand, Lucas and Darcie hurriedly washed their hands and snapped on gloves. Lucas nodded at Darcie to do the initial exam while he hooked up the monitor.

Without a word being said, she moved into position. "Tell me if you start contracting, Flick, and I'll stop."

Lucas watched the woman's expression, even as he positioned the wide elastic band of the monitor around her waist. Once he switched it on the sound of the baby's heart filled the room, along with a palpable sense of relief. No arrhythmias. No dangerous slowing of the heart rate. Just a blessedly normal *chunga-chunga-chunga-chunga* that came from a healthy fetus.

Darcie's face was a study in concentration as she felt the cervix to judge its state. If Flick was still in the early stages of labor, it might be possible to halt it with medication.

Grim little lines appeared around her mouth as she straightened. "Have you noticed any leakage?"

"The baby's been pressing hard on my bladder so…" Her eyes went to her husband. "The amniotic sac?"

Darcie nodded. "It's trickling. And you're at five centimeters and almost fully effaced. There's no stopping it at this point, Flick. Your baby is coming."

"But his heart…"

Tristan, standing beside his wife, looked stunned. "You'd better get Alessandro down here."

The neonatal specialist was in charge of the hospital's NICU. Once the baby was born, Alessandro would make sure everything was working as it should and that the child's tiny heart was okay.

Darcie asked one of the nurses to put in a call, and then she moved up to stroke Flick's head. "It's going to be all right. You're only a few weeks early."

"Mmm…" Flick's blue eyes closed as she pulled air in through her nose and blew out through her mouth. Tristan leaned closer to help her, while Lucas glanced at the monitor. Contraction. Building.

The baby's heart rate slowed as the uterus clamped down further, squeezing the umbilical cord. Everyone held their breath, but the blips on the screen picked up the pace once the contraction crested and the pressure began to ease.

Lucas came over and said in a low voice, "She's going fast for her first."

A few seconds later Alessandro appeared in the room, along with a few more nurses. He studied Flick's chart and then watched the monitor beside the bed for a minute or two. "Let me know when she's getting close. I'll have everything ready."

He shook Tristan's hand. "Congratulations. It looks like you're going to be a daddy today. Have you got a name picked out for her?"

The baby's sex wasn't a secret any more. Tristan and Flick were having a girl.

"We're still having heated discussions about that," Flick said with a shaky smile. "I hoped we'd have a few more weeks to talk it over."

Her husband laid a hand on her cheek. "Let's go with Laura. I know how much you love that name."

"Are you sure?" Tears appeared in her eyes, but then another contraction hit and her thoughts turned to controlling the pain.

Alessandro's attention turned to the monitor to watch the progression. "Everything looks good so far. Call me when the baby crowns, or if you need me before that." He gave Flick's shoulder a gentle squeeze and then nodded at the rest of them and left the room.

Once labor was in full swing, the room grew crowded with healthcare workers. Flick refused the offer of nitrous oxide, afraid that anything she put into her body at this point would affect the baby, even though the gas was well tolerated and often used to manage labor pain.

"I need to push." Flick's announcement had Darcie at her side in a flash.

She checked the baby's position once again then nodded. "You're all set. Are you ready, Mum?"

"Yes."

They waited for a second as Flick found a comfortable position.

Tension gathered in the back of Lucas's head as he assisted Darcie, while Tristan remained closer to his wife's head, murmuring encouragement.

Lucas saw the climb begin on the monitor. "Okay, Flick, here it comes, take a deep breath and push."

The woman grabbed a lungful of air, closed her eyes and bore down, helping her contracting uterus do its job. Tristan counted to ten in a slow, steady voice and told her to take another breath and push again.

The pushing phase went as quickly as the rest of the labor had gone. Ten pushes, and Darcie signaled that the baby had crowned. "Someone ring Alessandro."

He must have been close by because he entered the room within a minute and stood at the far wall.

"Here we go, Flick."

Another group of pushes as Darcie guided the baby's shoulders. Then the baby was there, cradled in Darcie's hands. She passed the baby to Lucas, and then worked on suctioning the newborn's mouth and nose, the red scar from surgery still very evident on her tiny chest.

A sharp cry split the air, and Lucas smiled as bleary, irritated eyes blinked up at him. Laura cried again, waving clenched fists at him and probably everyone else in the room. "Welcome to the world, baby girl," he murmured.

Tristan cut the cord, and then Alessandro took over, carrying the baby over to a nearby table and belting out orders as he listened to the baby's heart and lungs for several long minutes. There was no time for Lucas to worry about that, because they still had the afterbirth to deliver.

A few minutes later baby Laura was placed on Flick's chest with a clean bill of health.

"I don't foresee any problems." Alessandro smiled down at the new parents. "Her heart sounds strong so the surgery was obviously a success."

Flick grabbed her husband's hand, her eyes on his. "See? Don't you start worrying, Tristan. She's fine."

Lucas knew the man had agonized over the baby's health the entire time, but the problem had been caught and corrected early enough to prevent any major damage to her heart. She would need additional surgery as she grew and her veins and arteries matured but, other than that, she had a great prognosis.

Isla stuck her head into the room. "How are they?"

Flick heard her and motioned her in. "See for yourself."

The head midwife crept closer to where Flick was rubbing her baby's back in slow, soothing circles.

"Good on you. She's beautiful, sweetheart. Congratulations."

Alessandro put his arm around his wife's waist, his hand resting on her pregnant belly. "And now we need to let them get to know one another."

As soon as the room had cleared of most of the nurses, and the baby had successfully latched onto Flick's breast, Tristan leaned down and whispered something in his wife's ear that made her smile, although her face bore evidence of her exhaustion.

Lucas's chest tightened. What if all hadn't gone well in here today? What if something had happened to Flick? It was obvious Tristan was deeply in love with her.

His brother's face swam before him. The times he'd drunk himself into a stupor or lain in bed, unwilling to get up and take care of himself or Cora. On days like that it had been left to Lucas to care for them both.

He glanced over at Darcie and found her looking back at him, although her eyes swung away almost immediately. What would it be like to love a woman and not fear she might one day disappear off the face of the planet?

It was better not to even entertain thoughts like that. *Haven't you already?*

No.

He and Darcie had been on a few outings. Spent one night together. That did not a relationship make. And if he kept telling himself that, he could make sure it stayed that way.

He glanced at his watch and realized the end of their shift had come and gone. They should have been off duty an hour ago. A deep tiredness lodged in his bones and suddenly all her wanted to do was sit on that pier with Darcie and stare out over the water.

Just for companionship. Just to have someone to share today's victory with.

He walked over to the happy couple. "Do you need anything else? Something to help you sleep?"

"I don't think any of us are going to have trouble in that area." She kissed the top of her baby's head. "Thank you so much for everything."

Tristan echoed that. "I'm going to stay here with them tonight to make sure everything is okay."

And that was their cue to leave. Darcie must have realized it too because she smiled then walked over and kissed Flick on the cheek. "Take care, young lady. Ring if you need anything. You have my mobile number?"

"Yes. Right now, though, all I want to do is watch her sleep."

Lucas followed Darcie out the door and to the nurses' station. "Are we still on for tonight?"

She pushed a lock of hair behind her ear, glancing at the clock. "Do you still want to? It's after nine."

"If you're not too tired. We can get something to eat on the way."

"I'm fine." She hesitated. "As long as you're sure."

Right now, Lucas had never been more sure of anything in his life.

The moon was huge.

Seated on the side of the pier with her legs dangling over the side, Darcie stared out at the light reflected over the water. "I've never seen anything quite like this."

"I know. It's why I enjoy coming out here from time to time."

She cocked her head in his direction. "I should have made time to do things like this right after I came to Australia. But I wasn't in the mood to do anything besides work."

"Your ex?"

"Yes." This was probably the last thing Lucas wanted to hear while he sat here: her tale of woe. But somehow she found the whole story pouring into the night air. And it felt good. Freeing to actually tell someone besides Isla.

Lucas was silent until she'd finished then said, "Your

ex was a bastard. And your maid of honor…well, she wasn't much of a friend, was she?"

She shrugged. Nine and half months had given her enough distance to see the situation more objectively. Yes, Tabitha and Robert could have handled things differently, but it had been better to learn the truth this side of the wedding vows than to have faced the possibility of cheating and a divorce further on down the line. "I think it was hard for both of them. And I don't think they meant to hurt me. That's probably why our engagement continued for as long as it did. But it would have been easier if they'd been honest with themselves… and with me."

"Being honest with yourself doesn't mean you have to act on your impulses."

She frowned. "So you think it would have been better for Robert to go ahead and marry me?"

"No. Maybe it would have been better for him not to become engaged in the first place."

Interesting. She was seeing a new side to Lucas. "Is that comment speaking to my situation? Or do you simply not believe in marriage?"

"It's not so much that I don't believe in it, I'm just apathetic about the whole institution." He leaned back on his hands and stared at the night sky before looking her way again. "But I didn't bring you here to talk about my philosophies on marriage or anything else. I came to enjoy the view."

"I am enjoying it." She took a deep breath, the salty tang that clung to the air filling her senses and rinsing away the stress of the last two days. "It's lovely. You're

a very lucky man to be able to come down here whenever you want and take it all in."

"I am a lucky man."

When she turned to glance at him, he was watching her.

"What?" She pulled her cardigan around herself, unsure whether it was because of the slight chill in the air
or because he was making her feel nervous.

His brows went up. "Nothing. I'm just taking it all in."

Her? He was taking her in?

A shot of courage appeared from nowhere. "The view's
quite good from where I'm sitting as well."

The breeze picked up a bit, and a gust of air flipped
her hair across her cheek and into her eyes. She went
to push it back, only to find he'd beaten her to it, his
hand teasing the errant locks behind her ear. The light
touch sent a shiver through her.

His fingers moved to her nape, threading through
the strands there and lifting them so the air currents
could pick them up.

Why did everything the man said or did make her
insides coil in anticipation? And how could he go from
cool and distant to so…here? Present. Insinuating himself into her life and heart in subtle ways that took down
all her defenses.

Her mind swept through the events of the day and
replayed them. How he'd deferred to her in the delivery room today, letting her take the lead in Flick's delivery while not losing that raw, masculine edge that
made him so attractive to her.

And to a thousand other women like her.

Just when she started to thump back to earth his fingers—which were still at the back of her neck—suddenly tangled in her hair, using his light grip to turn her head.

"Your fiancé missed out."

His brown eyes roved over her face, touching on her lips then coming back up. "You're the whole package, Darce. A beauty. Inside and out. And I…"

He let go of her so quickly she had to catch her balance even as he finished his thought, his tone darkening. "And I shouldn't have brought you here."

Where had that come from? One minute he was going on about her hair and how he found her beautiful. The next he was saying he regretted having brought her to the pier.

Hurt—a jagged spear of pain that slashed and tore at everything it came in contact with—caused her voice to wobble. "Then why did you?"

"Because I wanted you to see what I do when I come out to the bay. But all I see right now…is you. And I want to do more than just look."

Everything inside her went numb for a second. Then a swish of realization blew through her, soothing the hurt.

He wanted her. Wanted to touch her. Just like the other night at her flat.

"You can. You can do more."

Before she had time to think or breathe he moved. Fast. His mouth covered hers in a rush of need that was echoed in her. She wanted him. Now. Here. On this pier.

His hand went behind her head as his tongue sought entry. She gave it to him, opening her mouth and letting him sweep inside. He groaned, and the sound was like a balm and a stimulant all at once, although she didn't know how that was possible. Maybe just because of who he was.

Darcie's mouth wasn't the only thing that opened. Her heart did as well, letting him in. Just a crack at first, but then growing wider and wider until he filled her. Surrounded her. Inside and out.

She allowed herself to revel in it, at least for now. Soon she'd have to come back to the real world, but for the moment she would inhabit the land of wish lists and wishful thinking—a place where anything was possible. Where anything could happen.

And, God, she hoped it happened. Soon. Because the need inside her was already too big to be contained.

She pulled back, even though everything was screaming at her to keep going. "Lucas."

"I know." Both hands sank into her hair and he held her still as he ran a line of kisses down her cheekbone, over her jaw, until he reached her ear. "If I don't stop now, I won't."

What? Stop? That's not what she'd meant at all.

"I don't want you to."

A flash of teeth came, followed by, "I don't think you want me to rip your clothes off on a public pier, do you?" A brow lifted. "Unless you're into exhibitionism. Although the thought of having you pressed naked against that bank of windows at your flat—with me inside you—is pretty damned tempting."

Something in her belly went liquid with heat. Not at

the thought of exposing herself to thousands of people but at Lucas—inside her.

"My flat is too far away."

He paused for a moment and then stood and held out his hand. "I know the perfect place."

CHAPTER NINE

"I DIDN'T KNOW you had a boat."

No one did. This was the one place Lucas could come that was totally private. Totally his. Where he could get away from the stresses of the day or—when Felix had been in a particularly bad state—the horrors of his own thoughts. The small sailboat had cost him several months' salary, but it had been money well spent. He would live on it were it not for the fact that he needed to be close to the hospital…and to Cora and Felix.

And he'd never brought anyone here…especially not a woman.

So why Darcie?

He stood with her on the deck as the boat swayed at its mooring. Why was this the first place that had come to mind when he'd realized what she wanted?

It was close. And they both wanted sex. It was the obvious choice. Even as he thought it, he knew that wasn't the reason at all.

She was waiting for an answer, though, so he said, "I like the water, and it's nice to have a place where I can enjoy it."

She smiled, leaning against the railing on the far side of the vessel. "I thought that's what the pier was for."

"Sometimes I want a little more privacy." His lips curled, and knowing she'd probably take the words the wrong way he went on, "For myself. Not for any love triangles."

She eased over to him and ran her fingers from the waistband of his jeans up to his shoulders. "I thought we'd already established you don't do any angles at all."

He didn't do a lot of things. But he liked the feel of her hands on him.

Gripping her waist, he dragged her to him, making the boat rock slightly. "So…do you want to stay topside? Or go down below?"

Her brows went up and a choked laugh sounded. "I assume you're not referring to parts of the body."

"No. Because in that I'm definitely an all-inclusive kind of guy." He leaned down and brushed his cheek against hers. "I meant do you want to stay here on deck or go to the cabin?"

"Okay, that makes more sense."

More than once he'd slept beneath the stars on the boat, letting the sounds and movements of the water lull him to sleep. As cool as it was right now, there was no need for air-conditioning.

Darcie glanced at the dock. "Does anyone ever come out here?"

Rows of other boats surrounded them. The small marina was the place of weekend sailors. But in the middle of a workweek? It was always deserted.

"Just me." He smiled, playing on his earlier theme. "Sorry, no one to watch us but the seagulls."

Even in the dark her face flamed. "That's not what I meant."

"Wasn't it?" His hand slid up her side until it covered her breast. The nipple was already tight and ready. "How brave are you feeling, Darcie?"

He tweaked the bud, glorying in the gasp it drove from her throat.

"Right now? Braver than I was during that bungee jump."

"Let's stay out here, then, where we can see the moon."

His hands went to the hem of her cardigan and shirt and swept them over her head, letting the garments drop onto the plank deck. When he touched her arms they were covered in goose bumps, although her skin felt warm. "Are you cold?"

"No." As if in answer, she undid the buttons of his shirt and yanked it from his jeans, helping him tug free from the long sleeves. She tossed it on top of her clothes. The sight stopped him for a second. But just one. Then he was curving his hands behind her back and finding the clasp on her black silk bra. "Last chance to back out, Darcie."

She leaned up and nipped his shoulder. "Just take it off, will you?"

"My pleasure." He unsnapped the bra, and on impulse dangled it over the railing beside them.

Yes, he liked seeing it there, the inky color contrasting with the sleek chrome. It was his declaration to the universe that she was his for tonight. And he knew something else that would look perfect beside it.

He allowed his fingers to trail over the curves he'd exposed. Just for a second, then he released the snap on his jeans and pushed them down his legs, kicking them to the growing pile of clothes beside him. Then he did the same for her. Much slower, kneeling down, so he could savor every inch of her along the way.

Black silk met his eyes. The same color as her bra. He allowed his palms to trail over her hips as he stood, until the slick fabric met the perfect mounds of her ass. He squeezed, pulling her against him and allowing his stiff flesh to imagine that silk sliding over his bare skin.

He had to know. He pulled away, only to have her reach for him. "Just a second, gorgeous. I'm coming right back."

Reaching down to scoop up his jeans, he retrieved a packet from his wallet and set it on the rail next to her bra. Then off came his boxers. His flesh jerked as he drew her back to him.

He closed his eyes as his naked arousal met the silk of her undies. And it was everything he'd imagined. Slick. Arousing. His hands went to her behind and kneaded as he pumped himself against her, slowly, reveling at the contrast between the silky fabric and the warm skin of her belly.

When he felt hands on his own ass, his lids flew apart. "Hell."

He pushed beneath the elastic, and then, unable to wait any longer, he slid her last remaining item of clothing down her hips, waiting until she stepped free before draping it next to her bra.

Mmm…yes. Just like he'd thought. He liked seeing her displayed there. Liked having her on his boat.

Grabbing the condom, he swept a hand beneath her thighs and her shoulders and hauled her into his arms, where he kissed her for what seemed like forever. This time she gave a little shiver, and he noticed the breeze was a bit cooler than it had been on the pier. Still kissing her, he eased to his knees and then lowered her to the deck, her pale skin looking glorious against the shiny teak planks. The raised edges around the deck provided a windscreen, and, balling up their clothing, he lifted her head so she'd have something to cushion it. "Better?"

"It's all good, Lucas. Nothing could be better."

He grinned down at her. "Wanna bet?"

Kneeling between her legs, he sheathed himself, then let his hands move in light, brushing strokes up her inner thighs, until he reached the heart of her. She was already moist and his fingers wanted to linger and explore, but he knew once he let them he was there to stay. And there were other places he needed to visit.

He lowered himself onto her, supporting his weight with his elbows, then murmured against her lips, "Too heavy?"

"Mmm…no. Too perfect."

That made him smile. He didn't think he'd ever heard a woman refer to him that way before. He liked it.

He'd told her the truth earlier. She was gorgeous, inside and out, sporting an inner glow of health and life that made him wonder how he could have ever thought of her as cold.

She didn't feel cold. She felt warm and vital and he itched to lose himself in her all over again.

But first…

He nuzzled the underside of her breast, savoring the taste of her skin as he came up the rounded side and across until he found her nipple. Drawing it into his mouth, he let his tongue play over the peak, hoping to coax the first of those little sounds he knew she made.

And, yes, it was heady being out here in the open, even though he knew no one could see them unless they climbed aboard and walked to the port side of the boat. But the thought that someone could...and that Darcie was letting him love her beneath the stars...was testament to her trust. One he wasn't sure he deserved.

But he liked it.

He applied more suction, and there it was. A low moan that pulled at his flesh and slid along the surface of his mind like a lazy day in the sun. Or maybe it was more like being in the eye of a storm. A fleeting moment of calm, when you sensed chaos lingering nearby...knew you'd soon be swept up in an unstoppable deluge.

And when that happened, he knew right where he wanted to be. And it wasn't pinning her to the deck where he couldn't see or touch.

He pulled back and climbed to his feet, holding his hand out to her.

"Wh-what?"

"Trust me." He picked up his shirt and helped her slide her arms into it, leaving it open in the front and allowing his fingers to dance over her breasts and then move lower. Touching her and relishing the way her eyes closed when he hit that one certain spot.

Putting his forehead to hers, he stopped to catch his breath for a second. "I want you on the railing."

It was the perfect height. She'd be right on a level with that core part of him. And Darcie's silhouette on the water? There was nothing he'd rather see…experience.

She glanced behind her, where her bra and undies were still draped, and backed up until she was against the chrome, her hands resting on the gleaming surface. "Help me up, then."

Gripping her waist, he lifted her onto the rail, his blue shirttail hanging over the other side, giving them a modicum of privacy, although they didn't need it. Her arms twined around his neck and her legs parted in obvious invitation. He moved in, his chest pressing against the lush fullness of her breasts, his flesh aching to thrust home.

"Hang onto me, Darce." Letting go of her waist, he allowed a couple of inches of space to come between them so he could touch her. Her face. Her breasts. Her belly. And finally that warm, moist spot between her legs that was calling out to him.

"Ahhh…" The sound came when he slid a finger inside her, her feet hooking around the backs of his thighs as if she was afraid he was going to move away. Not damn likely. He was there to stay.

His mind skimmed over that last thought. Discarding it as he added another finger. Went deeper. Used his thumb to find that pleasure center just a few millimeters to the front.

Darcie leaned further back over the side of the boat, her hands going to his shoulders, her legs parting more. This time Lucas was the one who groaned. Splayed out like this, he could see every inch of her, watch the way her breasts moved in time to his fingers as he pressed home and then pulled back.

"Want you. Inside…" The words were separated by short, quick breaths. She was getting close. So very close.

And he didn't want her to go off without him.

There it was. The same sense of need he'd had the last time they'd been together. He moved into position and guided himself home. Paused. Then he thrust hard. Sank deep. His breath shuddered out then air flooded back into his lungs.

Tight. Wet. Hot.

All the things he knew she'd be.

And it was all for him.

He held himself still as she whimpered and strained against him. It wouldn't take much to send him over the edge. He counted. Prayed. Closed his eyes. Until he could take a mental step back.

Only then did he wrap his arms beneath the curve of her butt to hold her close. He eased back, pulling almost free. Remained there for an agonizing second or two before his hips lunged forward and absorbed the sensations all over again. Over and over he drove himself inside her and then retreated.

He leaned forward. Bit her lower lip. Made her squirm against him.

"Please, Lucas. Please, now."

He knew exactly what she was asking for. "Make it happen, gorgeous."

Changing the angle, he reconnected with her, then pushed deep and held firm as she ground her pelvis against him, letting her choose her own speed, her own pressure, all the while cursing in his head as his eyes reopened to watch her face—taking in the tiny, almost desperate bumping of her hips.

His hands tightened on her, barely aware that the vibrations from their movements had sent her undies over the rail and into the water, and that her bra wasn't far behind. He didn't care. Didn't want to stop for anything.

Legs wrapped tight around him, Darcie's movements became frantic, nails digging into his shoulders...for all of five seconds—he knew because he was busy counting—then her head tilted toward the sky, hair streaming down her back, and she cried out in the darkness.

That was it. All it took. Lucas pumped furiously as the tsunami he'd been holding at bay crashed down on top of him. He lost himself in her, legs barely supporting his weight as he rode out his climax, knowing a tidal wave of another kind was not far behind. Coming on him fast.

He stared straight ahead so he wouldn't have to see it, wouldn't have to acknowledge its existence, and found her watching him, her gaze soft and warm.

Accepting.

At that moment the second realization hit him, splashing over his head and making it impossible to breathe. To think.

He loved her.

In spite of everything he'd been through with his brother. In spite of the dangers of letting himself get too close—too emotionally involved—the unthinkable had just become reality. He'd fallen for a woman. And now that he had, there wasn't a damned thing he could do about it.

She could only avoid him for so long.

Two days had passed, and she was still reeling from

what they'd done on Lucas's boat. How he'd buttoned her into her cardigan and slacks—her undergarments nowhere to be found—probably resting on the bottom of the boat slip, waiting on some unsuspecting soul to find them when it was daytime. Mortified, she made Lucas promise he'd go back and see if he could locate them—hoping her argument against pollution had been convincing enough.

They'd been in her locker the next day—how he'd known the combination she had no idea, but she was thankful no one had to see him handing her the plastic bag that contained her errant underwear.

If anything, though, it made her feel even more embarrassed. How had he found them? A net? A gaff from his boat? Or had they just been floating on the surface of the water, trapped between his boat and the dock?

That thought made heat rush into her face. She picked up her pace as she went down the hallway toward the double glass doors of the waiting room, which swished open as soon as she got close. She was supposed to meet Isla for lunch.

But when she arrived she saw her friend deep in conversation with Sean Anderson. Oh, no. Surely he wasn't giving her a hard time again about Isabel. She sped up even more and arrived in time to hear her ask if he'd heard from her sister. The opposite of what Darcie had expected to hear.

"No. And I'm not sure I want to, at this point."

"Really?" her friend asked, giving Darcie a quick glance. "After all that, you're just giving up?"

"I don't know. But I do want some answers. And I don't think I'm going to get them here."

"I'm sorry, Sean. I wish I could help."

Darcie decided to speak up. "Maybe you should consider going to the source."

"Funny you should say that," Sean said. "I decided to take Isla's advice. My contract runs out at the end of the week. I'm flying out as soon as it does."

The two women looked at each other, and Darcie's heart began to thump. Maybe she couldn't fix her own growing problems with Lucas, but maybe Sean could solve his. "So you're going…"

Sean nodded. "To England."

Isla clasped her hands over her belly, knuckles white. "Don't hurt her. Please. You have no idea what she's been through."

"I have no intention of hurting anyone. All I want is the truth about why she left."

Her friend studied him then reached out and touched his arm. "Good luck, Sean. I really mean that."

"Thanks." And with a stiff frame and tight jaw he strode down the hallway toward an uncertain future.

Well, join the club. Who really knew what the future held. Certainly not Darcie, who was busy hiding out and praying that Lucas gave her some time to recover. She needed to figure out what it was she wanted from him before he suggested tackling the next thing on her list.

Because that list had begun to revolve around a common theme, one that was getting her in deeper with each item ticked: Sit on a beach and kiss an Aussie. Bungee jump from a tower and kiss an Aussie. Dance at a club, and make love to an Aussie. Climb on a boat…and open her heart to an Aussie.

Darcie didn't know how much more she could take.

Because her heart was now in real danger, and she was more afraid than she'd ever been in her life…even during that moment when she'd realized Robert didn't love her. He loved someone else.

Because if that happened with Lucas, she didn't want to stick around to see it. The result would be a gaping wound no amount of surgery or medical expertise could repair. It involved who she was at an elemental level. And in opening her heart she feared she'd set herself up for the biggest hurt of her life.

Isla said something, and Darcie swung her attention back to her friend. "I'm sorry. I missed that."

The midwife smiled. A quick curving of lips that looked all too knowing and crafty. "I said, don't look now, but trouble is headed your way."

That was the understatement of the year. Then she realized Isla's eyes were on something behind her.

Darcie turned to look, thinking one of her patients was coming to see her, only to catch sight of the same glass doors she'd just come through swishing open to let in the last person she wanted to see today.

Lucas.

He looked devastating in a dress shirt and black slacks. Her glance went back to the shirt. Blue button-down.

Oh, no. Surely that wasn't the shirt he'd draped around her while they'd…

Warmth splashed into her face and ran down her neck, spreading exponentially the closer he got.

"Hello, ladies."

Instead of sweeping past and continuing on his way, he stopped in front of them.

Isla's smile grew wider. "Darcie, I think I'm going to

have to back out of our lunch date. I need to see Alessi about…tires for his car."

Tires? For his car?

Before she could call her friend on the obvious fib, Isla had retreated back through the doors, leaving her with Lucas and a few folks in the waiting room, who seemed quite interested in the various dramas unfolding in the MMU.

As if he'd noticed as well, he pulled her over to the far wall, well out of earshot. "Felix and Cora are on their way to the park with a picnic lunch. It's not far from the hospital, so I thought you might like to tag along. It's something you should see before you leave the country."

Leave the country. Why did that have an ominous ring to it?

Lucas went on, "From what Isla said, I take it you haven't eaten yet."

Rats. That would have been her first excuse if he approached her. It was why she'd practically begged Isla to have lunch with her for the last two days. And now her friend had turned traitor and abandoned her.

Her eyes met Lucas's face. He seemed softer all of a sudden. As if the weight of the world had been lifted from his shoulders. But what weight? Maybe he was just happy to be having lunch with his niece and his brother. It was obvious he loved that little girl and that she adored him back.

As if sensing her hesitation, he added, "Cora would love to see you. She's been asking about you for days."

Well, that was a change. Before, he hadn't seemed keen on her spending time with his niece.

Her heart settled back in place. The comment about

leaving Australia hadn't meant anything. "I guess it would be all right."

"I'm glad." One finger came out and hooked around hers and the side of his mouth turned up in way that made her stomach flip. "Did you get my little package?"

He was definitely in a cheerful mood today. Did she dare hope it was because of the time they'd spent together over the last three weeks? How strange that something she'd dreaded with every fiber of her being could have turned around so completely.

She decided to add some playfulness of her own. "Little? I thought the package was a decent size. But, then again, I don't have much to compare it to."

"Witch," he murmured. "Maybe you need a refresher. It has been a couple of days after all."

A refresher? He wanted to be with her again?

Maybe she wouldn't wind up on the hurting side of the fence after all. As long as she was careful. And took things slowly. She'd been thinking about seeing if the Victoria had any permanent positions available, but she'd been putting it off because of Lucas. She didn't want to stick around if they were going to end up fighting each other further on down the line.

But right now she didn't see that happening.

"Maybe I've just forgotten." She threw him a saucy smile.

"Mmm...I need to work harder next time, then, to make sure that doesn't happen." The finger around hers gave a light squeeze. "Meet you in the car park in fifteen minutes? I have one more patient to schedule, and then I'll be free."

"Okay," she said. Her spirits soared to heights that were dizzyingly high. A fall from up here could...

She wasn't going to fall. For the first time in a long time she caught a glimpse of something she hadn't expected to feel.

Hope.

Pete the Geek was on a rampage.

Reclining on the blanket that Darcie had somehow scrounged up, Lucas lay on his back, hands behind his head as he watched his niece chasing the dog around their little area of the park. Pete never went far, but seemed intent on having his little bit of fun on this outing, since the cold packed lunch hadn't been on the menu for him.

Darcie sat next to Lucas's shoulder and laughed as Cora just touched Pete's collar, only to have him leap out of reach once again. "He has his timing down to a science, doesn't he?"

"He does at that." He couldn't resist taking one of his hands from behind his head and resting it just behind Darcie's bottom. No one could see. But he just needed to touch her. Not in a sexual sense, although that always hovered in the background where this woman was concerned. But he found he wanted that closeness in more areas. Just for now. In a very little while she would be gone, and while there might be pain in letting her go, at least she would be alive. It wouldn't be like losing someone to death. He could accept loving her within those parameters.

He'd warred with himself for the last two days but

had come up with a compromise he hoped he could live with. He would let himself go with the flow. For the next couple of months.

She sent him a smile in response.

Warm contentment washed through him. Maybe this was why Felix had gone so far off the rails after losing Melody. Lucas had never felt like this about a woman. He loved her. He no longer even tried to deny it. And after staying away from her for two days he'd found he was miserable—and he'd had to find her. Be with her.

For the next two months.

He found himself sending his subconscious little memos. Just so it wouldn't forget. This was a temporary arrangement.

Felix seemed better. His therapy was evidently kicking in. He was fully engaged in what Cora was doing with Pete, really laughing for the first time in years. "Maybe if you tempt him with the ball?"

Cora spun back toward them, while Darcie held out the ball that had landed near her hip a while ago. Leaning down, the little girl flung her arms around Darcie's neck and popped a kiss on her cheek. "I'm so glad you came!"

"I'm glad I did too."

Lucas tensed for a second then forced himself to relax. Darcie and Cora could still keep in contact, even after she flew back to England. There was email and all kinds of social networks. It wouldn't be a drastic break. Just one that would fade away with time.

His niece rushed off with the ball in hand and threw it hard toward Pete, who loped off after the offering with a bark of happiness, scooping it up in his jaws and trotting back toward the blanket.

Lucas smiled and shook his head, his attention going back to Felix.

Only his brother wasn't watching Cora any more. His gaze was on Lucas, his eyes seeming to follow the line of his arm to where it disappeared behind Darcie's back.

Swallowing, he returned his hand to behind his head, and then as an afterthought sat up completely. Darcie glanced at him, head tilted as if she was asking a question. Swamped by a weird premonition, he got to his feet and slapped his brother's shoulder, urging him to come with him to help Cora round up the dog and bring him back to the picnic area.

He watched Felix as they worked, but whatever he thought he'd seen in his brother's face was no longer there. Felix smiled and joked and was finally the one to grab hold of Pete the Geek's collar and snap the leash onto it. Once they were all back at the picnic area he saw that Darcie had packed everything up and was on her feet. "I probably need to get back to the hospital."

That uncertainty he'd caught in her expression from time to time was back.

Because of him.

This was ridiculous. He was imagining demons where none existed. Probably excuses created in the depths of his own mind. There was no reason history had to repeat itself. "I do too. I'll walk you." On impulse, he leaned down and kissed her cheek, watching as they turned that delicious shade of pink he loved so much.

He turned back to say goodbye to Cora, noting his

brother's eyes were on him again. He returned the look this time. "Everything okay?"

"Yep. I need to get Cora home so Chessa doesn't worry. Besides, I have some drawings I need to get to."

Felix had once been a respected architect. When he'd married Melody he kept on working, even though she'd been wealthy enough that he hadn't had to. He'd inherited a fortune after she'd died, but it had meant nothing to him. He'd withdrawn from work and every other area of his life, including Cora. It made Lucas's heart a little bit lighter to see him showing an interest in something he'd once been so passionate about.

"Anything interesting?"

"I don't know yet. I'll have to wait and see what it looks like before I decide."

Kind of like Lucas himself? Waiting to see what things with his brother looked like before going on with his life?

Maybe. He wasn't sure. He still hadn't sorted it all out in his head, but he knew he wanted to spend more time with Darcie. Both during their rotation and after it was over.

For how long? Until she left for England?

He slung an arm around her waist, no longer certain of that, despite his earlier lecture. That drawing hadn't been completed yet. Maybe, like Felix, he should wait to see how things shaped up before deciding things like that.

Felix's eyes were on them again, although a smile stretched his lips. "I'll see you tomorrow, then, right?"

"Definitely." He walked over and kissed the top of

Cora's head then ruffled the fur behind Pete's ears. "Be good, you guys."

"We will, won't we, Pete?"

Lucas gave his brother a half-hug. "You'll be okay taking them home?"

"Of course. I wouldn't have brought them otherwise." His brother's voice was just a little sharper than he'd expected, and Lucas took the time to really look at him. Felix's skin was drawn tight over his cheeks, but he still had that same smile on his face. Maybe he was just tired. He hadn't done outings like this in years. Lucas couldn't expect him to spring from point A to point B in the blink of an eye. It was better not to push for more until his brother was ready.

Just in case, he didn't put his arm back around Darcie's waist. That could wait until his brother and Cora were in the car and out of sight. Besides, he didn't want them to witness him kissing the living daylights out of her right there in the park. Which he intended on doing. Then they could go back to work and act like nothing had ever happened. And hopefully Darcie would be amenable to him driving her home afterward. Enough so that she'd ask him up for coffee?

His brother loaded everything in the car. Cora gave one last wave before she got in and they drove away.

Taking hold of Darcie's hips, he tugged her close.

She grinned up at him. "You know, I think *you* might be the one with exhibitionist tendencies, not me."

"Where you're concerned, anything's possible." With that, he proceeded to do what he'd said he was going to and slanted his mouth over hers, repeating the act until she was clinging to him, and until he was in danger of really showing the world what he felt for this woman. "Time to get back to work."

Her mouth was pink and moist, and her eyes held a delicious glazed sheen. He'd put that there. And he intended to keep it there for as long as possible all through the night.

And then he was going to invite her to come to dinner with him at Felix and Cora's house tomorrow evening. They wouldn't mind, especially since he was the one doing the grilling.

After that? He wrapped his arm around her waist and walked with her the rest of the way to the hospital.

He'd have to see what the drawing looked like further on down the road, but he could afford to give it a little more time to take shape. At least for now.

CHAPTER TEN

LUCAS WASN'T AT WORK.

Darcie did her rounds, trying not to think the worst. He'd been fine at the picnic yesterday. And he'd spent most of last night at her place, making love to her with an intensity and passion that had taken her breath away. After several different places and positions, he'd finally groaned and dragged himself from beneath her covers. "I need to get home so I can be at work on time tomorrow morning." He leaned over and rested his arms on either side of her shoulders, bracketing her in and swooping down for another long kiss. "My rotation partner is a slave driver. She gets all put out when I come in rumpled, wearing the same clothes I had on the day before."

"Maybe that's when she thought you were involved with all sorts of different women."

He'd laughed. "How disappointing it must be to find out what a square I actually am."

"Just the opposite. I was jealous of the way the patients in the MMU always seem to fawn over you. I just wouldn't admit it to myself."

With a laugh, he'd scooped her up and kissed her shoulder. "See you in the morning, gorgeous."

That had been the last she'd heard from him.

She'd walked on cloud nine as she'd got ready for work. Then, when she arrived, she eagerly waited for him to make an appearance and toss her one of those secretive smiles she was coming to love.

But there'd been nothing. No phone calls. No text messages. And nothing on the board to show his schedule had been changed.

Surely he'd made it home safely.

And even though he hadn't said the words, he had to care about her. The way he'd touched her at the park and put his arm around her in full view of his brother and niece had said he wasn't embarrassed to be seen with her.

She cringed at that thought. That was something the Darcie of old would have worried about. Her experience with Robert had shaken her confidence in herself as a woman to the very core. Lucas was slowly building it back up. Kiss by kiss. Touch by touch. He acted like he couldn't get enough of her.

Well, the feeling was mutual.

Today she was not going to let his tardiness get the better of her. She was going to simply enjoy what they'd done last night and not worry about anything else. He'd eventually turn up. He'd probably stopped in to see Cora or something. Or maybe he'd had to drive her to school, which he'd said he'd done on occasion.

He wasn't in bed with someone else. Of that she was sure. Because she was feeling the effects of his loving this morning. It was a delicious ache that reminded her that, no matter who fluttered their lashes at him, Lucas had chosen her.

She sighed and glanced at her watch again. An hour and no word. There was nothing to do but go on with her day and not worry about it. She was tempted to ring his mobile, but was afraid that might seem desperate or needy. So she let it go.

The morning continued to race by at a frenetic pace. Then one o'clock came with no time to break for lunch. She'd just completed one delivery and was heading for the next laboring patient when she saw Isla at the nurses' station. She hurried over.

"Have you heard from Lucas? Or do you know if he's arrived at work yet? I haven't seen him all day."

Her friend blinked at her for a second and then her eyes filled with something akin to horror. "Oh, sweetheart, you haven't heard?"

Only then did she see that Lucas's name had been crossed off today's rota and Isla's name was written in instead. That had to have been done after she'd looked at it this morning.

Darcie's vision went dark for a second or two. "Heard what?"

"Oh…I'm so sorry. I got a call around an hour ago, asking me to step in." She reached out and gripped her hand. "Lucas is in the emergency department…"

Isla's voice faded out in a rush of white noise but the words "alcohol poisoning" and "gastric lavage" came through, before a nurse came out of the room of her next patient. "Mrs. Brandon is feeling the urge to push, and she's panicking. She isn't listening to instruction, Dr. Green."

Somehow, Darcie managed to stumble into the room, and despite her clanging heart she was able to coax the nitrous mouthpiece from between the woman's clamped jaws and get her to focus on pushing at the appropriate times. The baby was a large one, and Darcie had to do some fancy maneuvering to get the baby's shoulders through the narrow space. Then he was out and wailing at the top of his lungs. Darcie wished she could drop onto the nearest chair and join him for a hearty cry. But she couldn't. And it was another hour of praying for a break before one finally came and she could make her way down to Emergency.

Her heart was in her throat. Lucas had alcohol poisoning? How could that be? She'd never seen him touch a drop of the stuff, except for the sips she'd talked him into taking of her drink. And he'd made the most god-awful face once he had. She'd convinced herself he was a teetotaler, that he just didn't like alcohol. But maybe she'd got it all wrong. Maybe he was a recovering alcoholic. Or, worse, one who binge-drank for seemingly no reason.

But alcohol poisoning was more than just a couple of drinks. It was a life-threatening toxic buildup that came from downing one drink after another without giving the liver time to filter the stuff out of the blood.

Why hadn't Isla come back to find her as soon as she'd heard the news?

Maybe because she'd been just as swamped as Darcie had been—and just as exhausted. She saw on the patient board that the letters "TMTB" had been scrawled beside two of the names, so her friend had to have been run ragged with those girls—and with all the aftercare that went along with teen pregnancies.

She paused just outside the doors to the emergency

department, unsure what she was going to find. Isla would have surely told her if Lucas was in danger of dying, wouldn't she? Maybe the stomach pumping had done its job and he was already on the road to recovery. Maybe he was simply too ashamed to face her.

As well he should be.

Anger crawled through her veins, pushing aside the worry and fear. If he were an alcoholic, shouldn't he have told her? Refused that offer of a drink she'd given him?

A thought spun through her brain. What if that sip had sent him over the edge? An alcoholic shouldn't drink *any* type of liquor. Ever.

All those late mornings…the rumpled clothes. The surly demeanor when he finally arrived.

God.

She squared her shoulders and stepped on the mat that would open the glass doors and went through. Noise and shouting hit her. The place was just as busy as the MMU had been. Making her way over to the desk and hoping to find a nurse or someone who could provide her with information, she searched the patient board for a familiar name.

Out of the corner of her eye she caught sight of him. Lucas.

He was on his feet, leaning against a wall. She'd recognize those broad shoulders and wavy hair anywhere. But he didn't look right. He was slumped, leaning against the flat surface as if he could barely hold himself up.

The waiting room was crowded, but surely he'd been seen already. Alcohol poisoning was normally run up to the top of the list. Could Isla have exaggerated or made a mistake?

At that moment his eyes met hers.

And what was in them tore apart any thought of exaggeration. There was torment and pain in that red, bleary gaze.

So much pain.

Hurrying over, she stopped next to him.

"Lucas, what's wrong? Are you ill?" she asked.

He didn't answer, just shook his head. His hair was tousled, and two of the bottom buttons of his shirt were undone, as if he'd thrown himself together in a rush.

"I don't understand. Isla said something about alcohol poisoning. She wasn't talking about you?"

"No." Lucas's hands fisted at his sides. "Did you think she was?"

"I didn't know what to think." Confusion swirled around her head. Why did he seem so angry?

"It's not me. It's my brother."

"Felix?" The sound of a siren drowned out his response as an ambulance pulled up to the front entrance. The sound of slamming doors came and then a gurney rushed in with a patient who was obviously in bad shape from the number of healthcare staff heading toward him. When she could finally be heard again she asked, "What happened?"

Two seats opened up as a couple with a child were called back to one of the exam rooms.

She took his hand to lead him over to the chairs so he could sit down before he fell down. He tugged free of her grip but followed her over to the seats. A chill went through her that had nothing to do with Felix's condition as they both sat.

"What happened to Felix?"

He propped his elbows on his knees and stared at the ground. Without looking at her, he said, "He drank himself into a stupor."

"Oh, no." So it was alcohol poisoning. Isla had been right about that. "What about Cora?"

He gave a mirthless laugh. "She's the one who rang me this morning. Felix was out all night, and when he finally made it home he collapsed in the foyer. Chessa had to spend the night at the house because she couldn't reach me. And so here I am."

Her heart squeezed tight. They hadn't been able to reach him because he'd been at her house until almost three that morning, his mobile and car keys deposited on her entry table. "I'm so sorry, Lucas. Will he be okay?"

"I don't know. He may be too far gone this time."

This time?

Things fell into place in the blink of an eye. This was why Felix had seemed off when she'd met him those weeks ago—why he and Lucas had argued. He was the alcoholic, not Lucas.

"He seemed fine at the park."

"He was." Lucas lifted his head long enough to glance in her direction. "At least I thought he was."

That explained something else. Lucas had seemed light and happy. Happier than she'd ever known him to be. She'd assumed it had been because of their budding relationship. But maybe that hadn't been the case at all. Maybe it had been because his brother had been doing so well. Maybe all those affectionate touches and looks had been spillover from what had been going on with Felix.

And last night? Had that simply been an overflow of happiness as well?

Her brain processed another fragment. He hadn't rung her to tell her where he was this morning. Or that his brother was in trouble. He—or someone—had notified Isla instead.

Maybe he hadn't wanted to worry her.

But surely he knew she'd be frantic when he didn't show up for work.

Her thoughts spiraled down from there. He hadn't bothered to tell her the truth about his brother's condition. Or what he'd been dealing with for who knew how long. He'd led her to believe things were fine. With Felix and Cora.

With her.

Just like Robert had done.

When trouble had come to visit, she'd been the last one to find out—and the result had been devastating.

You're jumping to conclusions, Darcie. Give the man a chance to explain.

Only he didn't. He just sat there. She'd had to drag every piece of information out of him the entire time she'd known him. Was this what she wanted? A lifetime full of secrets? Of wondering if things were okay between them?

No.

Something inside her wouldn't let her give up quite so easily, though. Not without trying one last time to reach him.

"He'll be okay." She knew the reassurance was empty.

She had no idea exactly how bad things were. Only Lucas and the doctors knew how much liquor he'd ingested or how much damage had been done to his liver and other organs.

"Will he?"

"What did the doctors say?" She had to keep pushing. To see if he was worth fighting for.

Because she loved him.

Oh, God, she loved him, and she didn't want to have to let him go, unless there was no other option.

"They pumped his stomach. Rehydrated him with fluids and electrolytes. I just have to wait for him to wake up."

She didn't understand. "Will they not let you back to see him?"

"I needed to think about some things. I'll go back in a little while."

"And Cora?"

"She's still with Chessa. We both thought it best not to have her here until we knew something definitive. She's already lost her mum. I don't want her to panic over what might happen to her dad. Unless it actually does."

"It might not come to that." She licked her lips and got up the nerve to slide her hand over his. This time he didn't shake her off. But he also didn't link his fingers through hers or make any effort to acknowledge the contact. "Is there anything I can do to help?"

"If he makes it, he'll have to go to rehab. A residential one this time. I can't trust him to care for Cora at this point."

Which was why he'd been late those other times. Another piece fell into place.

He'd had to take care of his niece when his brother had been too sick or too drunk. And what had she done? She'd yelled at him in front of a roomful of people on one of those days. Guilt washed over her, pummeling her again and again for assuming things that hadn't been true. For not asking him straight out if something was wrong. Maybe she could have helped somehow.

Maybe she still could.

"If you need me to watch Cora, I—"

"No." The word was firm. Resolute. "We'll be fine."

Another chill went through her, and the premonition she'd had earlier came roaring back to haunt her.

He was still going to pretend that things were okay—shutting her out without a moment's hesitation. She removed her hand from his and curled it in her lap.

Lucas sat up, his mouth forming a grim line. "I think I'm going to take some personal time. I have Cora to think about, and I'll need to deal with Felix. I can't do that and work at the same time."

Her heart stalled. "How will you live?"

"I have some savings. And Cora's care comes from a trust fund her mother left for her."

"I see." She licked her lips. "How much time are we talking?"

"A couple of months at the very least. Maybe more." He didn't skip a beat. He'd obviously already thought this through.

She did the calculations and a ball of pain lodged in her chest. He'd be out until after she left Australia and headed back to England. Surely he couldn't mean to drop out of her life as quickly as he'd come into it. Not after everything that had happened between them.

"I could come by after work, help with the cooking."

"I think it would be better if you didn't, Darcie. Please. For everyone's sake."

For everyone's sake. Whose, exactly? His?

"I don't understand."

"Felix is here because he can't get over the death of his wife, despite years of therapy. When he saw you and I together at the park…" He shrugged. "You knew there was never going to be anything permanent between us. At least I thought you did. And right now I have to think about what's best for my family."

His eyes were dull and lifeless. So much so that it made her wonder if he even knew how much he was hurting her with his words.

Then he looked at her, and she saw the truth. He knew. He just didn't care.

The ball grew into a boulder so big she could barely breathe past it. He was dumping her. His brother's illness provided the perfect excuse.

Only, like her ex-fiancé, he didn't have the decency to come to her and tell her until it was as obvious as the nose on her face.

Well, that was okay. She'd survived being jilted at the altar, so she could survive the breakup of something that amounted to a few nights of sex and adventure. He'd wanted to do some wild and outrageous stuff? Well, she'd done enough to last a lifetime. And she didn't have it in her to stick around and watch her world fall apart piece by piece.

One thing she *could* do was make this final break as

easy as possible for the both of them. "I'm truly sorry about Felix, and I hope everything works out with him. But if your decision to leave the MMU has anything to do with me or the time we spent together, this should put your mind at ease. I've decided to go back to England early."

He eyed her for several long seconds before saying, "When did you decide this?"

Right now. Right this second. When I realized I'm good enough to warm your bed at night but not good enough to take up permanent residence in your heart—to share your joys and heartaches.

But she couldn't say that. Not unless she wanted the remnants of her shattered pride to fall away completely and expose everything she'd hoped to hide.

Then the perfect response came to her in a flash, and she snatched at it, before taking a deep breath and looking him straight in the eye. "I decided last night."

CHAPTER ELEVEN

Isla slammed open the door to his office, green eyes flashing. "What did you do to Darcie?"

Lucas hadn't seen her for the last two days, so he'd assumed she'd already flown home. In fact, that was why he was still at work, tying up loose ends, albeit with shorter hours. Chessa was staying with Cora during the day, and at night he went and slept on the couch.

Felix was still in the hospital, but he was slowly regaining his strength. His brother had admitted what Lucas knew in his heart to be true. That seeing him and Darcie together had reopened wounds that had scabbed over but never fully healed.

And what about Darcie?

He'd hurt her, but he hadn't known what else to do. His brother's life was at stake—because of something he'd done. He couldn't let that happen again.

Besides, hadn't he seen time and time again how love brought you to the brink of disaster and sometimes tossed you over the edge? Everything he'd seen lately had reinforced that. Margie's miscarriage. Tristan and Flick almost losing their baby. His brother almost losing his life.

Isla crossed her arms over her chest, clearly waiting for him to answer her.

"Thank you for knocking before you burst in." When the jibe earned him nothing but a stony stare he planted both his hands on his desk. "I didn't do anything to her, Isla. She said she decided to go back to England earlier than planned."

"Why? Did you sleep with her?"

Hell, if the woman wasn't direct. "I don't see that that's any of your business."

"Maybe not. But I think she was right about you. You're nothing but an arrogant, self-righteous bastard who thinks he can sit above all of us and not dirty his hands with real life and real love. I know…because my husband was once just like you."

"She said that about me?" He tried to ignore the hit to his gut that assessment caused. "As for Alessandro, I bet he didn't have a drunken brother to contend with. Or a niece who needed him."

"And that justifies you hurting Darcie?"

No. Nothing justified that. And he would be damned every moment of his life for what he'd done. But she'd said she was going to leave anyway.

It was a lie, you idiot. You'd practically hung a do-not-disturb sign on your heart and dared anyone to knock. And then once she did, you slammed the door in her face.

Because of Felix.

Really?

Was it because his brother had relapsed—which he'd done on several other occasions without any help from him—or was it because he was too afraid to "dirty his hands", as Isla claimed.

He'd once sat on a beach and dared Darcie to do something wild and outrageous. And she'd risen to the challenge and beyond. And yet here he sat, too afraid to make a list of his own because "loving Darcie" would be at the top of it.

He was terrified of holding his hand out to her for fear of losing her. And the thought of becoming like his brother—a shell of a man…

But what about what Isla had asked? Did any of that excuse what he'd done to Darcie? Because of his own selfish fear?

"No," he said. "It didn't justify it."

Isla seemed to lose her steam. "I didn't expect you to agree with me quite so quickly."

"I know what I did. And I'm not proud of it." If he had it to do all over again, would he? He'd made an impulsive decision while his brother had been fighting for his life—a huge mistake, according to the experts. He should have given himself a day or two before deciding something that would affect both of their lives.

The memory of her laughter, those pink-cheeked smiles…that raw sincerity when she'd offered to help with Cora's care. He'd thrown it all away. He hadn't given a thought to how she might have felt, or how right it seemed to be with her. He'd only thought of himself. And in that process he'd done to her what he'd been so afraid might happen to him. He'd abandoned her. Left her standing all alone.

"Isla, you're a genius. And I'm a fool." He got up

and went around the desk and planted a kiss right on her forehead.

Her face cleared, and she laughed. "I won't tell Alessi you did that. He might knock your teeth right out of your head."

"He knows you're crazy about him…and the whole world knows how he feels about you."

"True. So what are you doing to do about all this other stuff?" She rolled her hand around in the air.

What *was* he going to do? He'd run Darcie off and it wasn't like he could do anything about it. He was here. Having to make sure his brother made it in to rehab as soon as he was released from the hospital. He couldn't just hop on the first flight to England and leave Cora by herself. He was stuck.

"I don't know, actually. I have responsibilities here."

Her mouth curved into a half-smile. "Isn't it lucky, then, that Alessi loves me as much as you say he does?"

Lucas had no idea what that had to do with anything. "Yes, I guess it's lucky for you."

"And for you too. Because he happens to know someone high up at the airline Darcie was scheduled to fly on."

He only caught one word of that whole spiel. "Was?"

"It seems her flight was overbooked, and she was booted to one that leaves tomorrow afternoon."

Hope speared through him, causing him to drop back into his chair. "She's still in Melbourne?"

"For another day. Yes."

"Why the hell didn't you say something before now?"

"Because I wasn't sure you loved her enough to fight for her. And if you don't, she deserves better."

He swallowed. She deserved better anyway. Better than that bastard ex of hers. Better than *him*. "You're right. I'm not good enough for her."

"I might have agreed with you a few minutes ago but I saw your face when the enormity of what you'd done hit you. You were frantically trying to figure out a way to make it right…to get to her. Well, Alessi and I have just given it to you. Don't waste it, Lucas. Because by tomorrow afternoon she'll be gone, and it'll be too late."

He got to his feet. "If she's gone, it'll be because she doesn't want me. Because as of right now I'm going to fight for her with everything I have in me and hope to God she'll forgive me."

Darcie wandered through the empty flat, which was in much the same state as when she'd arrived. There were suitcases sitting neatly side by side, and in her purse was a one-way ticket. She'd come here looking to escape a painful past, only to end up fleeing a new situation that was even worse.

Her feelings for Lucas were light years beyond the ones she'd had for Robert, which maybe explained why he'd found her lacking that certain spark. She had. It had taken Lucas to put a match to it and bring it to life.

Only he'd evidently felt even less for her than her ex had. Because he'd made no pretense of loving her or even wanting a long-term relationship with her. Hadn't he told her that in plain English at the very beginning, when he'd first suggested putting pen to paper and making that list?

She gave a pained laugh. "He did, but you just couldn't

accept that, could you? You had to fall in love with the man, didn't you?"

A knock sounded at the door and Darcie froze, wondering if someone had heard her. The doorman was supposed to ring the interphone if she had a visitor. Her heart thumped back to normal. It was probably just the taxi. She'd asked the airport to send someone if they found her an earlier flight. The sooner she was out of Melbourne the better.

She felt like such a fool and every second she stayed in this flat—in this country—was a horrid reminder of how she'd practically groveled at the man's feet, only to have him knock her offer aside and ask her to leave him alone.

Which was what she was trying to do.

She scrubbed her palms under her eyes, irritated that she had turned into the weepy female she'd vowed never to be again.

Hauling her suitcases to the front door, she went back for her purse and opened the door. "Do you mind getting those? I…"

It took three or four blinks before she realized the man standing at the door wasn't a taxi driver. Or the doorman.

It was Lucas.

Oh, God, why was he here? To make sure she really, really, *really* understood that he didn't want her?

Well, Lucas, I might have been a little slow on the uptake, but once the message sank in it was there to stay.

"I thought you were the taxi driver. How did you get past the doorman?"

"I didn't. He recognized me." He paused. "From before."

Said as if she might not remember their last encounter in this flat. Unfortunately it was burned into her brain with a flamethrower.

She strove for nonchalant. "How's your brother doing?"

"He's out of danger. Looking forward to getting the help he needs. I think being in hospital gave him the shock of a lifetime."

"I'm glad." She was. As hurt and angry as she was at Lucas, she hoped Cora would finally have her father back. "And Cora?"

"She misses you."

Pain sliced through her chest. "Don't. Please."

Lucas glanced to the side where her suitcases sat. "May I come in for a minute?"

"Why?" She didn't think she could take another blow. Not when she was struggling not to memorize every line and crag of that beloved face.

"Because Cora isn't the only one who misses you."

The words took a moment to penetrate her icy heart. Then she started to pick them apart. "You mean Isla and the rest of the staff?"

"Yes, but not just them."

She licked her lips. "Then who?"

Fear buzzed around in her stomach while she waited for him to say something. Anything.

His chest rose as he took a deep breath. "Me. *I* miss you. I don't want you to go."

"You practically offered to pack my bags."

"I was stupid. Scared. My brother is the way he is because he desperately loved his wife. When she died... well, he was never the same. I don't want to end up like that."

She worked through those words. "And you're afraid if you meet someone, you will."

He nodded.

A terrible, wonderful atom of hope split into two. Then three. "Come in."

She stepped aside as he moved into the room and glanced around. Waiting for him to finish and turn back toward her, her brain continued to analyze what it knew. Somehow he'd found out she hadn't left.

Isla.

Darcie had called to tell her that her flight had been delayed. But why would she tell Lucas?

"You say you miss me, that you don't want me to go, but I need something more than that." This time she wasn't willing to settle for less.

He came back and took her hands in his. "I know you do. Which is why I want you to come with me."

"Where?"

"It's a secret. But by the end of it I hope you'll have the answer you need."

The buzzing fear turned into a tornado that whipped through her system and made her doubt. Was he was going to lead her on a merry chase, only to get cold feet again and decide he was better off without her?

Maybe.

So why was that list they'd made a couple of weeks ago stuck in the front pocket of her purse...complete with the smiley face he'd drawn next to the kiss-a-non-triangular-Aussie entry? Because she didn't want to forget. But, like him, she was afraid.

He'd overcome his fear long enough to drive to the flat, though, without knowing what kind of reception he'd get. Didn't she owe it to herself to follow this through to the end? She could always catch that flight tomorrow if it didn't work out.

"Okay, I'll come."

He closed his eyes, the lines between his brows easing. When he opened them again, the brown irises seemed to have warmed to a hue she recognized and loved. A few more atoms split apart, some of them coalescing back together and forming a shape she could almost decipher. He glanced at her clothes. "Can you get those wet?"

"Wet?" Was he going to kill her and toss her lifeless body over the side of his boat? That made her smile. A few more particles merged together. "I think they'll survive."

Twenty minutes later they pulled up to a place she recognized. But it wasn't his boat. "Why are we here?"

"Trust me." He got out of the car and came around to her side and opened the door. She stood on the footpath, staring up at a familiar tower.

"We're going bungee jumping? Now?"

"You're not. I am."

She had no idea what was going on but he'd asked her to trust him. So she walked with him to meet Max, who stood waiting at the entrance. The man pushed his glasses higher on his nose, looking spectacularly pleased with himself for some reason. "Come in. Come in. Everything's ready." He disappeared through the wooden privacy gate.

Lucas murmured, "Remember when you jumped, I waited for you in the pool at the bottom?"

"Yes." She wasn't sure how she got the word out as her throat felt dry and parched.

"I want you to go to the side of the pool and wait for me this time." He gave a half-smile. "Don't ask me why until you've unhooked me."

They went through the gate, a million questions swirling through her mind. Max led her down to the pool, while Lucas climbed the steps to the tower.

She gasped. The water was crystal clear, just as before...but the surface was littered with rose petals. Thousands of them in every color imaginable—red, purple, yellow, white, pink.

Max didn't explain, he just asked her to wait there. "Lucas knows how to unhook himself, but he wants you to go into the water and do it for him this time."

"I don't know how."

The engineer gave her a knowing smile. "He says you do. Just do what your heart tells you."

If she did that, Lucas wouldn't be diving head-first into a pool. They'd be hashing this whole thing out on the couch in her flat. Or in bed, depending on how well the discussion went.

But then Max was gone, joining Lucas in this crazy game of who knew what.

He appeared at the top. His shirt was off. He must have worn swimming trunks underneath his jeans because his tanned legs were on display. He looked strong and powerful. But from the words he'd said back at the flat, he'd hinted he was anything but.

But, then, neither was she. She had her own fears to struggle through. And if they couldn't do it together, then they needed to work on them as separate individuals.

Except those atoms were still dividing. Still joining. She peered, trying to make out what it was becoming. Then, just as Lucas dived far out into the air, arms spread apart, she saw it. It was his face, and the expression on it was similar to the one he had when he looked at Cora. When he looked at his brother.

Love. And fear.

A mixture of two emotions that were intertwined so tightly it was impossible to completely separate them. She knew, because the two were battling it out within her heart as well.

Lucas hurtled toward the pool before being jerked back at the last second, just as he'd been the previous time. The air displaced by his fall made the petals sift over the surface of the water, like ice skaters twirling in colorful costumes. Then the winch began to whine as it slowly lowered Lucas closer to the water. Time for her to get in.

She slipped into the pool, surprised to find some kind of footing where they'd had to tread water before. It felt like wood, but it was high enough that she didn't have to swim, she could simply walk toward him in chest-high water. When she looked up at him, she found his eyes on her. In their depths was a question. She swallowed, emotion bubbling up in her throat and threatening to escape as a sob. She loved this man. Loved him with all her heart. And she was willing to take him as he was, fears and all, if that's what he wanted.

God, she hoped that was what he wanted.

He didn't say anything, but when he was close

enough to touch she gave him a quick kiss on the lips just before his head disappeared beneath the surface, followed by the rest of him. Soon he was hidden from view by the layer of flower petals. Momentary panic went through her. How was she supposed to unhook him? Max hadn't shown her, and Lucas hadn't said anything at all.

Just do what your heart tells you.

Darcie ducked beneath the surface and found him lying on the boards three feet below, the petals shading the area. He could just stand up if he wanted to... it was shallow. But he didn't. She pushed herself down and followed the cord that held his ankles. Unsnapped it. Then the one attached to the harness at his back. It stuck for a second and she wiggled it, suddenly scared he wouldn't come up if she couldn't get it off. There. The hook released.

He was free.

Lucas grabbed hold of her waist and hauled her to the surface, breaking through the layer of velvety petals.

The question he'd told her to ask once he'd completed the jump came out before she could stop it. "Why?"

He pushed damp strands of hair off her face. "Do you remember what it felt like to take that leap?"

She nodded.

"What did you feel?" he murmured, his arm now around her waist.

She thought for a moment, trying to gather her jumbled thoughts. "I was so scared. I didn't want to go through with it, and I felt like screaming the whole way down. But once I reached the pool, and you unhooked me, there was this sense of exhilaration… I can't even describe it."

He nodded. "I know. Because I felt the same things as I sat on the beach with you and started making that list. Terrified. Like I'd lost my stomach, my heart and my head all at once. I fell, and I haven't stopped falling. But I was too afraid to finish it. To let you come alongside me and undo those ropes."

Her eyes watered. She knew exactly what he was talking about. "I feel it too," she whispered. "The fear."

"I love you, Darcie. It took me a while to understand what I'd find once I reached the bottom of that jump— to get past my fear and open my eyes, to really look at what was waiting for me. It was you."

She threw herself into his arms and lifted her lips up for his kiss. It was long and slow and thorough. Once she could breathe again she laid her head on his shoulder. "I love you too, Lucas. You're right, it was scary and making the decision to go over the edge wasn't an easy one. But it was worth it. All of it."

"Yes, it was."

"Hey, Uncle Luke," a voice came from the top of the tower. "When is it my turn to jump?"

Cora stood peering over the edge at them, and even from this distance Darcie could see the little girl's infectious smile.

Laughing, she nipped the bottom of his jaw. "Good thing I didn't leave you there to drown. You were awfully sure of yourself."

"No. I wasn't sure at all. But I hoped."

She hugged him tight. "Aren't you going to answer her question? When can she jump?"

Lucas kissed her cheek, and then shouted back up, "Not for many, many years, sweetheart."

EPILOGUE

Welcome Home!

The words, scrawled in pink childish letters and flanked by a heart on either side, greeted them as they opened the door to Lucas's flat.

Three weeks on a beach, and Darcie was still as white as the paper banner. She didn't care. Besides, they hadn't actually spent all that much time sunbathing while in Tahiti. A fact that made her smile.

"Aw, I think I know who wrote that." Darcie twined her arms around her new husband's neck. "But at least we're all alone, because I have something I want to—"

The panicky sound of a throat clearing came from behind the black leather couch, followed by a yip. And then two. A child giggled.

"Oops." Darcie's face heated, as she whispered into his ear. "Not so alone after all."

Lucas made a face at her, just as people came pouring from seemingly every room of the place. The kitchen, the two bedrooms, the veranda. And finally, from behind the couch, appeared Cora, Pete the Geek, Chessa…and Felix.

Cora and Pete launched themselves at the newlyweds

and her poor husband *oomphed* as the dog—apparently forgetting everything he'd learned—careened into his side, nearly knocking him down. Darcie barely managed to keep from falling herself.

"Oh, my gosh!" Darcie knelt to hug Cora, peering at the mass of people around them. It looked like most of the MMU staff had turned up for their return—which begged the question: who was minding the maternity unit?

Isla came over and planted a kiss on her cheek as Darcie stood, keeping hold of Cora's hand.

"How was the honeymoon?" her friend asked.

She returned her friend's hug. "Spectacular. How's the baby?"

"Growing like a little weed." She motioned over at Alessandro, who was cradling their infant in his arms. "I barely get to hold him. Flick says Tristan is the same way."

It certainly appeared so, since Tristan had a baby carrier strapped to his chest with his daughter safely ensconced inside it. Flick waved at her.

Darcie gazed around at the people she'd come to know and love over the past year and her eyes threatened to well up, although she somehow forced back the tide. Lucas was still a little spooked by tears. He'd overcome a lot of his fears, but every once in a while he looked at her as if afraid she might disappear into the ether.

And she might. But that's not how she planned to live her life. And she certainly wasn't going to let her husband dwell on it either.

Then her eyes widened as her gaze skimmed the rest of the room.

There, still standing behind the couch, were Felix and Chessa. And the childminder had a certain pink tinge to her cheeks that looked familiar. And— Oh... *Oh!* Felix's arm was slung casually around the woman's waist. It looked like she and Lucas hadn't been the only ones who'd been busy over the past couple of months.

Felix had completed his rehab program a few weeks before the wedding and had been on the straight and narrow ever since, according to the texts they'd got from Chessa. But she hadn't mentioned anything about a budding romance.

As if noticing her attention was elsewhere, Lucas glanced up from the group of people he was chatting with and caught her eye. She nodded in Felix's direction. She saw the moment he digested what he was seeing. His Adam's apple dipped. And then he was moving, catching his brother up in a fierce hug that was full of happiness.

And hope.

It was the best gift anyone could have given him— seeing his brother on the cusp of a bright new future. And little did Lucas know that another surprise awaited him. One she'd postponed telling him until just the right moment.

That moment was now. He could handle it. They both could.

When the tears came this time she didn't stop them, feeling Isla's arm come around her waist and squeeze. "It's wonderful, isn't it?"

"Yes."

Before she could say anything else he was back, grabbing her to him, his breathing rough and unsteady.

"Lucas." Her fingers buried themselves in the hair at the back of his head, praying she was doing the right thing as she leaned up to whisper, "I know it's early, but our friends aren't the only ones having babies."

He leaned back and looked at her for a long second, a question in his eyes. She gave a single nod.

"I love you," was all he said, before he drew her back against him, burying his face in her neck.

And when she felt moisture against her skin, she knew it was going to be okay. Her big-hearted husband was finally ready to accept that the world could be a good place. It brought sadness at times, yes, but it was also full of kindness and laughter and contentment.

All because they'd dared to do something outrageous and wild and completely dangerous: they'd fallen in love.

* * * * *